The Iron Urn

Book Eleven of the Iron Soul Series

J.M. Briggs

J.M. Briggs

Contents

For childhood friends
remembered in dreams.

1

An Evening with Merlin

Magic was rare at Merlin's house. The very idea was strange. If you'd asked Alex as a child what she thought a Grand Mage's house would be like, her response would have included all sorts of magical things happening all the time. Spoons and bowls would be cooking for you, a magical mop would be cleaning the floors, and the books would arrange themselves on the shelves.

The reality was much more boring with the same reliance on electricity as most other people. Tonight was a rare exception as Merlin was actually using a little bit of magic. Alex chuckled as she put her dishes in the sink of Merlin's kitchen and watched the water wash over them. Faint green sparks shimmered at the surface of the soapless water, and when Alex pulled her plate out a moment later, it was glistening. Morgana had shaken her head when Merlin cast the spell, but he'd gone ahead with it anyway rather than deal with all the dishes. Alex thought that Merlin might have done it just to amuse them.

Placing her plate in the drying rack, Alex pulled out her fork and her glass. Both of them were sparkling clean as well. She made a note to try this spell herself. It would be nice to give Timothy a break from time to time. Then again, when they tried to do that, the Brownie seemed to take it as an insult.

She pulled back the curtain on the kitchen window and peered outside. The wind was picking up, and Merlin's back porch light was making the small snowflakes glitter. They weren't completely into winter yet, but it was close, no matter what the calendar said about the first day of winter. Shaking her head, Alex went to the cupboard and pulled out another glass. She poured herself some iced tea from the large container in Merlin's fridge and headed back into the living room.

The others were sitting in various chairs around Merlin's small living room. Nicki and Avani were sharing one armchair, with Avani almost sitting in Nicki's lap. Neither of them looked unhappy with the situation, and Alex smiled fondly at them. Aiden and Bran were with Merlin on the sofa. Morgana was seated in another armchair, sipping at a cup of tea, and Alex retook the last armchair. The only ones missing were Lance and Jenny, who were off at a movie, and Robin, who had been making herself scarce for the past week.

As she focused on Aiden and Bran's conversation about some new research project into something to do with magnets, Alex could almost believe that they didn't have anything to worry about. In truth, the last week had swung wildly between near celebration and fear. Arthur was dead. Nicki had run him through, but something else had taken hold of his body, and they had yet to get a good reading on just what it was.

The room was a bit small for all of them, and the armchair she was in was new. Alex didn't know why they even came to Merlin's house for this sort of thing. Morgana's house, or even their house, was better equipped for this many people. But Merlin seemed happy enough to have them here, and the massive buffet of food he'd fed them had been a great treat.

Still, Alex was waiting for the other shoe to drop. Merlin had to have a reason for gathering them all here away from their home. Maybe he wanted them off balance and wondering what he wanted. Arto hummed with disapproval at her thoughts. Thor was laughing and remarking on her development as a tactical warrior. She wasn't sure how much that really meant from Thor, who'd been more of an attack first and ask questions later sort, but it was close to a compliment. The others provided running commentary that washed over Alex.

She was able to pick out individual voices now much more easily. Sometimes they provided details that helped Alex research where they were from and their home era. Josfa was an African warrior, but his time period and culture were still a mystery to Alex. Temur hailed from the early days of the Mongol Empire and made frequent references to Genghis Khan that at least gave her some dates for when he fit in. Timur came from a village in the mountains, and that was all Alex knew for sure. His name's similarity to Temur's made her believe that he was Eurasian as well.

It was also getting easier to tune them out when she wanted to. Smiling, Alex put her head on her hand and listened to the boys' conversation. Parts of it were lost on her though, and she regretted not focusing a bit more on science. It would have been nice to better understand the things happening around her without relying on the explanation of magic.

Then Merlin cleared his throat, and the atmosphere of the room shifted. Morgana set her teacup down on the coffee table and folded her hands in her lap, ready for the discussion. But before Merlin could speak there was a knock on the door.

"Merlin?" Bran frowned and glanced towards the door, and then back at Merlin. "Are you expecting anyone else?"

"No, but please give me a moment."

Standing up, Merlin exchanged a look with Morgana. She nodded, and Alex listened carefully as Merlin walked to the front door. It opened with a high-pitched squeak that made Alex grimace. From her position, she couldn't see who was at the door but caught Aiden's expression. There was a hint of relief, but also nervousness, and worry. That told Alex a lot about who was at the door. She wasn't surprised when Merlin returned with Robin beside him.

"Sorry to intrude," Robin said. On her face was a small smug smile that made Alex certain that she wasn't all that sorry. Robin stepped further inside, her eyes jumping over to Aiden, who looked like a deer caught in headlights. "I've been meaning to speak with you."

Morgana rolled her eyes. She was not fooled by the innocent act. "Alright, Puck-"

"Robin, if you please." She smiled widely at Morgana. "I find I prefer it."

"Yes, given the amount of trouble you caused as Robin Goodfellow, I suppose you would," Morgana replied dryly.

"You wound me, Morgana," Robin protested, "but that's not the point. I've been reaching out to other Old Ones who are awake. Just to see if anyone knows anything about this Light."

Merlin's eyes sparked with interest. "And?" He settled back into his seat, leaving Robin to stand.

"Well, Sif is awake, as you probably know. Her father Odin was a bit off when he woke, so he's gone back to sleep." Morgana sighed at that. "Baldr is awake, but he doesn't know anything. He's going to try to do some research once he's caught up, but it was unfamiliar to him." Robin paused. "Uh... Sun Wukong is awake." Both Merlin and Morgana groaned loudly. "He's already contacted Shiva and has promised to help hunt down any hostile Demons outside of India."

Alex frowned in confusion while Bran's eyes widened. "He's real?" Bran asked.

"He's not as powerful as he is in the stories," Merlin answered, "but yes, he's an Old One."

"Is his staff real?" Bran asked. "And the ability to transform?"

"He has a staff, but it is an extension of himself," Merlin explained. "Morgana and I investigated it many years ago. We thought it might be an item gifted to an Old One like the Trishula to Shiva. It wasn't."

"Any Old One can change their form," Robin added. "It just takes a lot of focus and can be painful, so we tend not to do it lightly." She smiled a little, her dark eyes lighting up. "I'd only met him once before. He's a character."

Alex was missing something and made nothing of the name. Hopefully she'd be able to find something to give her context. "So he's on our side?"

"Sort of," Robin said. "He's not interested in a formal alliance, but he likes humanity well enough to keep an eye out for trouble."

"Where is he?" Alex asked. "Is he in India?"

"No, China," Robin answered. "The rest of the Hindu Old Ones are still asleep. Shiva is keeping things in check over there now that the portal has been closed."

Alex shifted in her chair. Robin had contacted a lot of beings and learned a lot of what had been going on in only a week. It was a little worrying if she was honest. Robin was an ally; her own memories were certain of that. She and Alex's past life Michel had been very close as young men, and even closer as adults. Alex pushed away some of the memories that tried to come forward. Those images wouldn't help her focus right now.

"One thing you should be aware of is that, according to Sif, Anansi is awake," Robin said. "He left Lake Victoria four months ago."

"Isn't he a Trickster God?" Bran asked.

"He is," Morgana agreed. "We've never had problems with him, but he is powerful, and the last time he woke up his mental state wasn't good. I didn't expect him to come out of the water for at least another century."

"Well, he's awake. So is my mother Brigid," Robin said. "I made a point of speaking with as many of the others as I could. So far, the one thing that everyone awake seems to agree on is that the feel of the Iron Realm has changed."

"Feel?" Merlin repeated.

Robin shrugged as if unconcerned, but the lines around her eyes revealed her uncertainty. "I don't know how to explain it. But something has caused many of us to wake up at once. It's something subtle. I didn't even think about it until Sif asked me if something felt different. I'm not sure if it is all the electricity or global warming or what, but it's like a... background hum, that's just a little different."

"We've noticed nothing," Merlin said.

"You two live in the Iron Realm all the time," Robin reminded them. "It's likely been a slow, gradual change that you wouldn't notice. Those of us who sleep would be more inclined to discover it. As I said, I suspect it might have to do with what woke us."

"We assumed it was the sudden increase in magic," Merlin explained.

Robin shrugged, slipping her hands into the pockets of the leather jacket she wore. "Maybe, but magic goes up and down all the time, and it doesn't always wake us up."

"You think there is something else," Morgana said carefully. A frown appeared on her face. "That's an unpleasant idea."

"Sorry to have to tell you then." Robin sighed. "It might be nothing, but once Sif brought it up, it became clear that all of us have felt something."

"Interesting," Merlin considered. "It may not be anything to worry about as you suggested, but thank you for bringing it to our attention. Did any of the Old Ones have thoughts about the Light?"

"We weren't all together, so there wasn't much brainstorming." Robin shook her head. "Nothing came to mind. I know that human myths have tales of possession, but that's never been real. At least not as far as any of us have ever encountered. Sif did have time to ask Odin before he went to sleep. He thought that the Light might come from the same branch, but was certain that it was a different species."

"Do you think it's possible that the stories of possession come from another Light?" Bran asked Merlin.

"I don't think so," Merlin stated. "Morgana and I have investigated possessions in the past. We've usually found mental illness at the source of such things. On the few occasions that it wasn't, it was an Old One toying with a human mind, but even then, it is always external."

"We have to remain in one solid form," Robin said. "Though, I suppose it is possible that someone at some time tried to form inside of a human." Disgust and unease filled her features. "But no, I'm certain that this thing is something else. It may be a being of energy like us, but there's nothing to say that my mother's homeworld is the only connected world where life isn't born of matter."

The way Robin said her mother's homeworld made Alex frown. A memory from Michel of Puck describing his creation sprang to mind. This was the home to Puck who had been born here, just like Sif. She didn't know about Anansi. It was the same for all the Fae who were descendants of the Sídhe who had invaded centuries ago.

"We'll have to keep our eyes open for any more Old Ones waking up," Morgana said. "I wish we knew for certain who is still around."

"I'm afraid that we don't keep good records." Robin raised an eyebrow and smirked.

Morgana glared at the Old One, but Alex thought the corner of her mouth turned up a little. Honestly, she thought that Morgana was holding onto her dislike of Puck out of sheer stubbornness at this point. After that first ugly interaction in Europe a few centuries ago, she was pretty sure that the trickster hadn't any major issues.

"Do you have any theories?" Merlin asked. He stood up and went to a small closet in the hallway. Alex watched him pull out a folding chair. "Please have a seat." He gestured to his armchair and Robin blinked in surprise.

"I'll take the folding chair," Robin said. She took it from Merlin with a soft smile. "Thanks, old man. Always did like you better."

"Puck," Morgana hissed.

Robin ignored her and set up the folding chair, bringing it closer to Alex's armchair. "My theory is pretty much the same. This creature is from a branch close to the world of my ancestors. Using Arthur, it jumped into our world. I didn't think anything like that was possible, but it happened. At this point, I'm more curious about its powers. After all, Arthur is dead. Is this thing still using his body? Can it keep the body functioning, can it change hosts or is it stuck in Arthur's body because it was the one it jumped into?"

"All good questions," Bran said. He frowned, his green eyes darkening with thought. "And worrying ones. Let's hope that this thing is tied to Arthur; otherwise, we may need to worry about possession."

"Great," Nicki muttered. "Killing Arthur was supposed to help things, not make them more complicated!"

"Hey, him being dead is good," Aiden said. Despite being on the sofa, he was leaning away from Nicki nervously. "I feel properly avenged."

"It's okay, honey." Avani squeezed Nicki's hand, making the redhead blush. "Arthur was a danger, and now he's gone."

"The problem," Alex interjected. Everyone turned to look at her. "Is that we don't know the extent to which Arthur was working with this Light. Was he aware of it? What is it after? Arthur was at least a known quantity. Mostly," she added.

"I think Puck, sorry, Robin, has the right idea," Merlin said. Standing up, he dusted off the sleeve of his button-down shirt absentmindedly. "We need to speak with others and find out if anyone knows anything. I know that given recent events you're all frustrated, but the death of Arthur is a good thing. The Fae are backing down." He headed for the kitchen. "Now, one moment and I'll be back with some dessert."

Robin glanced her way, and Alex shrugged. There wasn't much she could say in response to that. Arthur's death should have been a good thing. It was a good thing. The traitor was dead. Yet, Alex knew she wouldn't relax until they had some answers about this newcomer. Though, when Merlin came back into the room and put a large cheesecake on the coffee table, things did improve a little.

2

Message of the Light

Alex missed the large lecture halls that so many of her freshman courses had taken place in. There'd been more room to spread out. You could have a few seats between you and the next person, stretch out your legs and slump down in the seat. But those halls were usually used for the lower-level courses, the ones with fifty students that were designed to get the students through their core requirements — the ones where you were lucky if the professor learned your name... or unlucky.

Upper-level classes, on the other hand, were in the small rooms, stacking and racking students. No one dared miss too many of these classes in contrast to freshman year. Shifting in her seat, Alex kept her tablet balanced on the small surface that passed for a "desk" and tried not to knock into the person next to her. The chairs were too small. There just wasn't room. At least she lived in the tablet era rather than the time of the large laptops.

Contemporary American Fiction was usually more interesting than this, but Alex's mind kept going back to the other night. She'd seen Robin around campus today, but the woman seemed content to respect Aiden's need for space while he sorted it out. Alex sympathized with his need to process that the woman he'd liked and had been considering dating wasn't who or what he thought they were. It wasn't as drastic as having a sword stabbed into your gut, but Alex was still sympathetic.

Professor Granville was starting to talk about the modern shift into more strict understandings of 'genre', which made Alex perk up a little. The boy in front of her who was watching a cat video even paused it. But before Alex could really sink into the subject material, her phone vibrated in her bag. She got a glance from the girl next to her, but otherwise, no one seemed to notice.

In the past, Alex would have ignored it until after class, but being a mage meant needing to stay in contact. Pulling out her phone, Alex turned the screen so that she could check the message, and instantly froze.

She knew that number. She didn't have it on her phone anymore, but she knew it. That number was the only one she knew from memory. It was Arthur's phone number.

I need to speak with you and your fellow mages. It is very important that I can explain things to you.

She didn't answer. The message was there, in black and white on her screen, but she still didn't believe it. Alex shifted her thumb away from the tiny keyboard before she did anything rash. Re-reading the message, she focused on one of the first meditation techniques that Morgana had taught her to stay calm. The Light, the very being that they had so many questions about, had reached out to her. She had to be careful. Her phone buzzed again.

What I am is difficult to explain in words. You must have questions about what I am. Where I am from and what happened that night. I want to answer them.

Alex swallowed and, with a trembling left hand, went to the main message screen. Was there a way to forward a text? She thought she'd heard about that somewhere, but she couldn't remember. Typing in Morgana's name, Alex was starting a text to the professor when another notification popped up. Against her better judgment, Alex tapped the notification, and the new message took over the screen.

I have his memories. I know what he did, and I can only imagine how much it hurt you. I am deeply sorry for the pain you suffered at the hands of this body. Please contact me. I need to explain things. The Darkness is coming. You know that. We can still stop it.

Instinct screamed at her to respond. The voices were all talking at once. She couldn't understand anyone in the mess of noise. Keeping her fingers away from the keyboard, Alex reread all of the messages. The Light had told her a lot already. For an olive branch, it wasn't bad.

But could she trust something with Arthur's memories? Something that knew everything that had happened? Something that remembered ensuring the death of her parents, something that remembered trying to kill her? Surely those memories would have an influence. Even if they didn't, that still didn't mean it could be trusted.

The problem was that Alex didn't remember what had happened with the Light that took over her. She and her past selves had fought it on the landscape of her mind, and someday she was going to figure out what that meant, but she didn't remember what had happened after it took over. The others had been attacked, but the thing had created a beacon and been more interested in drawing attention. It must have wanted to alert the Light in Arthur that it had control.

Arthur had come and brought Fae with him. According to the others, there'd been a battle with the Fae while they also made sure that the Light didn't run off with her body. Arthur had come and tried to help it escape. But had it still been Arthur then, or had the Light have control of him too? She didn't know.

Alex put the phone down. Taking a deep breath, she returned her attention to the professor and tried to listen. It was no good. Too many different emotions and ideas churned through her head. Vivid memories not just of Arthur, but also of Arto's cousin Medraut pushed their way forward and replayed in her eyes. The classroom faded away, and she was back on that hillside fighting the Sídhe only to be stabbed by a family member.

He'd killed Arto's father. They'd assumed it was a Síd, but it had been Medraut in an attempt to make sure that Arto wasn't named the heir instead of him. Memories of Medraut's actions, words, and seeming support hit Alex like blows from a whip. They'd never seen it coming. Shock and despair had colored Arto's last moments, overpowering even his triumph with the last Iron Gate he ever made. He'd won the war but lost his life.

The world had changed, and Medraut had seen it. Looking back now with Arto's memories whispering to her, Alex could see it too. Arto's focus had been on the Sídhe, on stopping the raids and protecting the Iron Realm, but his introduction of iron had started the decline of the profitable piece of the bronze trade that the islands had with Europe. That trade brought wealth and power. That was what Medraut had cared about. That's why he'd made a deal with the Queen.

Queen Scáthbás had been a fool to forget that. Shaking her head, Alex held back a snort. Since the Queen's death, Alex hadn't given her much thought. If there was one thing she'd learned from Nicki's random history rants, it was that sometimes important figures fell in strangely simple ways. She'd expected a major battle with Queen Scáthbás one day, but instead, Arthur had slain his mother and then had died himself in a small battle. Nicki hadn't killed Arthur because he was a threat. Not really and they all knew it.

But all that and now this message left Alex at a loss. Who was the enemy or was there even an enemy now or just those still alive against the Darkness? The professor's words washed over her, the rhythm of their tone and energy oddly soothing. Thankfully, the phone didn't hum again, and Alex was slowly pulled back into the classroom. The lights were a bit too bright now, and Alex blinked slowly to dispel a growing headache.

She glanced at the phone, unsure of what to do. Nothing in her stories had prepared her for this. Her enemies were gone. Those that she'd been focused on were no more, and that big looming threat that had been growing in her awareness was much more tangible now. She started to reach for the phone before pulling her hand back. Careful, she reminded herself. What mattered now was thinking, not just reacting.

Suddenly the people around Alex started to move out of their chairs and pack up. Jumping a little, Alex raced into action and packed up her things so as not to be left behind. A few others were talking to each other, but most were checking their phones as the class poured out into the hallways. The professor paid her no mind, packing up his things while speaking with the doctoral students who were his teaching assistants.

Alex hung back and let most of the others push their way out first. She had another class in only a few minutes but knew she wasn't going to bother with Russian Literature today. Picking up her phone, she barely remembered to grab the coat that was now critical for life in Ravenslake. The professor glanced her way, so Alex hurried out into the hallway, not wanting to get a lecture about paying attention in class.

Walking down the hallway, Alex stared at her phone and waited for another text. None came. The Light had delivered its message. It was quite the claim. Arthur's memories and Arthur's body. Alex shuddered and put the phone into her pocket. Clearing her throat, she pulled her backpack on a bit tighter and headed for the front door. A guy leaning against the wall smiled and nodded at her, but Alex kept walking.

When she reached the door, the sudden blast of cold air made her stop and remember herself. Shrugging off her backpack, Alex pulled on her coat and shook her head before stepping outside. The morning frost was gone now, but dark clouds overhead teased that tonight snow could fall. Alex followed the flow of students down the long walkways away from the Carlson Building. The voices around her faded away, the figures of her fellow students becoming almost ghost-like as the voices in her head pushed forward.

"Don't answer," Arto cautioned. "Speak with Merlin and Morgana first."

"You can't wait on them," Lokpal insisted. "Allies can be found in surprising places. Shiva was a threat who is now a supporter."

"Don't forget the Darkness," Gofiben offered. "You can't ignore that threat."

"Talk to the others," Cuthbert said. Alex started at the sound of his voice. He almost never sought to give real advice. "This could be a trap. You need support."

"Be careful," Gottfried said. His voice was softer than the others. "Be careful."

There were others, less loud and less well known to her. Alex found herself searching for one in particular. A voice that she didn't even know the name of yet. The man with the iron jar who had spoken of the Darkness to her when she'd joined her other selves in confronting the Light. But his name and voice did not come to her. Alex kept walking.

Living off campus meant that she always had to drive. Their home, while comfortable and far enough away from the packed streets to grant them privacy, was far from the local bus routes. She'd come in with Nicki and Aiden that morning, her schedule similar enough to theirs that it was easy to share. They still had another class each. Aiden was probably in the library or in one of the small labs that engineering students could use for projects. Alex thought that Nicki was in one of her history classes, but she wasn't sure. In any case, she wasn't going to call them to head home early.

She needed to think. Alex adjusted her backpack and started walking. The others kept talking, whispering to her, and Alex focused her thoughts on trying to sort them out. Some of the voices were distinct, but others were difficult to place. Some memories that pushed forward were too similar to others for Alex to be sure if they were different lifetimes at all. Perhaps it should have been a comfort to know that a peaceful and quiet life was possible, but those memories were of no use to her current plight.

Alex was fairly certain at this point that if she focused on it, she would be able to use some of their skills, but their skills were of limited value in the modern world. Knowing when and how to plant crops in an age of tractors had some value, but she knew that there were other concerns such as soil chemistry that none of her other lives had any experience with. She hesitated to even give too much weight to her memories of other battles. Situations changed too much. Beings that had been enemies were now allies or at the very least weren't at war with her.

Through all the conflicts had been the Sídhe or the Fae. They had been the first enemy, and the most troublesome. The Demons had been vicious, but their reach was limited thanks to her alliance with Shiva. The Dvergrs had slipped underground and died out. The giant frost monsters had been killed off quickly by Thor, and the Dark Elves had not survived their mutation from Sídhe. No other people had ever been so dangerous, such a persistent threat, as the Sídhe. Even now, Alex had no doubt that the Sídhe princes were bickering and trying to find some way to break into the Iron Realm. If they hadn't proven time and time again to be so horrible, she might have been inclined to open negotiations with them, given the Darkness.

Alex passed over the river, barely glancing at the traffic zipping past. It was too cold for most people to be out walking. The whole of the sidewalk was hers, but she was starting to get uncomfortable. She tugged gently on her magic, feeling it pulse in her veins and rush up her chest and limbs on her command. She no longer had to try and visualize what she wanted magic to do for her. At this point, none of them had to use that method often. Merlin and Morgana had trained them well, and a soft push in the right direction with a firm idea of what the magic was to do was enough. It warmed Alex's limbs, especially her legs which were only protected by jeans, at the gentle command.

She kept walking. Up ahead, the road split into multiple directions, taking cars to the different roads where houses were tucked up in the trees. Ahead of her, the mountains that towered over the valley and its lake were obscured by clouds. Alex turned east on the far side of the river and followed the road along the riverbank back towards the lake.

Were there even any Old Ones still living in their own world? Alex couldn't remember its name. It had sounded like Avalon the first time she'd heard it, if memory served. What about the Dragons? Were Emrys and his white Dragon prisoner in Wales the last of their kind? Already they were locked underground for who knows how long. Surely someday even the mind of Emrys would collapse under the strain of his long watch, and he would become a danger. That would be a task for another of her incarnations to deal with.

Pulling out her phone, Alex reread the messages from the Light. Then again... If the Light was right, and the Darkness came quickly, maybe there wouldn't be any future incarnations.

3

Mountain Band

4 33 C.E. Bighorn Mountains

The wind was howling through the hills, making the trees bend and threatening to rip the wild grasses out of the earth. His buckskin breechcloth and vest did little to hold back the chill. His leggings were a bit heavy for the season, but they protected his legs from the bushes and long grasses. He stepped forward, mindful of the rocky outcroppings of the hills. Above him, the mountains loomed like fierce warriors with hats of white. Looking up, he studied them for a long moment. Their beauty was impossible to deny.

He knew these mountains well. The tribe had been coming into them during the spring his whole life every year to hunt and gather. It was still early, and the snow was only just melting. Still, the chill was preferable to the heat of the plains.

"Akule!"

The sound of his name made his jump, and he turned around quickly. A few feet away, the rest of the hunting party had finished dressing the elk, and Caphan was giving him an impatient look. Hurrying over, he glanced around more one time, mindful that he had been assigned to watch for predators.

"You are well named," Caphan remarked. The other man was taller and broader than Akule, but he was smiling despite his irritation. Shaking his head, he picked up the bundle of meat that was wrapped in a thin, woven mat. "Always looking up."

Akule nodded in agreement. There was little else he could do. He accepted his bundle without any complaint and watched as Sahal drew his bow. It was unlikely that anything vicious would find them, but they would take no chances while smelling of a fresh kill. The gutted remains of the elk were quickly packed up and hoisted by the strongest of them, a tall man named Hakan.

Their small band began walking in single file, all of them watching their surroundings. Caphan took the lead, holding his meat under his left arm and keeping a spear at the ready with his right. Sahal was behind him, his long black braid swinging wildly and distracting Akule. He was next, his bow and quiver still strapped to his back. He was the smallest of the band, but thankfully he was not a sickly man. The pounds of meat he carried were less a burden and more a promise of a good meal. Behind him he heard Hakan start humming, and quickly joined in. It was only a short time before three of them were singing. Caphan remained stoic at the front but didn't seek to scold them.

A game trail wound its way down the rocky hill. They weren't into the highest parts of the mountain yet and likely wouldn't need to go so high. The elk were moving into the mountains for the summer, the mountain sheep were in the area, and they'd already heard the cry of one moose. Game would not be an issue, and they would be able to stay for at least part of the season in one place. Something moved in the bushes, but a moment later a pheasant rushed away from them in a panic. Caphan chuckled, but no one risked going for the bird. With their elk meat weighing them down, it would only be a waste.

The tribe had camped in a flat section of the hills that was sheltered by a large jagged wall that burst from the ground. Each small round house had a framework of sticks and leaves, and in some places hides, stretched across them. Smoke curled out of three of the seven houses already. Dogs were running around and playing with a few of the children while a group of girls were diligently helping their mothers with weaving baskets away from the ruckus.

When they were spotted, a cheer went up, and Akule couldn't help but smile. Judging from the meat he could already see on drying racks and roasting over the large communal fire, the other groups had been blessed with good luck as well. Children were called out of their way, and he quickly presented their spoils.

Then the work began. Everyone knew what to do. Women rushed forward to take the meat and ensure that no one was injured. He glanced into the baskets that the gatherers had taken out that morning and smiled. They were almost full of the rich, dark mountain berries. Hakan handed the bones and hide of the elk over to one of the elder men, who nodded in approval. Nothing would be wasted, and when they moved on, old tools and worn-out clothing would be replaced.

He stepped away from the mess of noise and activity, taking a moment to center himself. His ears rang with the sounds of the others speaking. Akule checked the position of the sun. There was still plenty of light, and he started walking away from the people and the fire. His skin cooled down, and he exhaled gratefully. Turning back, he checked to make sure that all was well before he climbed atop the rocks that sheltered them from the wind.

From there he could see their small temporary village, the plains below them, and the rough rolling hills around them. He turned and looked back up at the mountains. Here, between the worlds of the steep peaks and the plains, they had access to game, plants, and fresh, melting snow-fall. The area and the view were familiar to him. This was a familiar journey. They'd stay here for a time before moving to another hillside to find more game. When the weather turned colder, they would move down into the plains.

Movement drew his attention. A woman was walking towards the outcropping, her buckskin dress swaying gently around her legs. He beamed down at her. Hakola had long black hair that she wore in two braids. They framed her face perfectly, and her keen eyes took him in quickly. A smile tugged at her lips, and she shook her head fondly. Akule smiled in return.

"A good hunt."

"We found a strong elk," he answered. "The mountain trails are full of them. It should be a good season. I see that the gathering went well."

"It did. Little Halo didn't want to stay with the group. He's as inclined to look around and explore as his father."

Akule took the teasing with a nod. She knew well enough that when it mattered, he could and would focus. Carefully, he climbed down and stepped closer to her, leaning his head towards her. She smiled and touched his forehead with her own. Akule enjoyed the soft moment of contact, breathing in the same air as his wife.

They started walking together towards the small hut that they shared with their two children. His youngest, Halo, came running the moment he caught sight of them. Akule bent down to sweep the small boy into his arms. His daughter was next to the hut, sewing a small dress for her doll with a look of intense concentration. She looked so much like her mother in such moments.

"Minal!" Hakola called.

The little girl looked up sharply, her brown eyes a touch dazed, and Akule laughed warmly. Then she recovered and smiled at her. She set her doll aside in a basket and scrambled to her feet. His daughter's hug was not as eager and clingy as her brother, but he enjoyed the warmth of the embrace all the same.

His fellow hunters were with their own families. Everyone would be back to work soon, but a hunt where everyone returned whole and healthy was always worth a few moments of celebration. There was work to do. They needed to build a few more huts so that all the families had their place to sleep. And judging from the pile of wood, more trees needed to be felled, as well as more water should be fetched for the evening.

Chapan was the first to go back to work, calling Hakan to join him in wood collection. He scanned the camp. The second hunting band had yet to return, and he enjoyed a moment of pride that his group had come back first. At least they were focusing on elk now rather than the bison of the plains. There was less risk involved.

Their band was small. Only two years ago, the larger band of seventy people had split when feeding everyone became a challenge. Now with the children, they were a community of thirty-two people. Akule found that he missed a few of the friends who had left with their families, but it had been for the best. At this size, an elk ensured that everyone ate, and the women and children could forage enough on a day-to-day basis to build up their food supply.

He needed to get to work. They had to finish with the elk and start tanning the hide. They needed to collect materials to build at least one more hut tonight. It was hard to pull himself away from his family. Minal did not have that problem. She gave his leg one more hug and then returned to her spot working on the dress for her doll. Hakola laughed while he sputtered.

Then out of the corner of his eye, he saw something. There was a painful flutter in his chest that made him gasp. He blinked. It was gone. He put Halo down, ignoring the boy's protests, and quickly moved away from the huts. The hillside curved around the mountain. There was something out there. He wasn't sure how he had even seen it, but the need to check pounded through him. Then he was in a new position and could see more of the area west of their camp. On the far hillside near some trees, there was a series of dark patches. Halo tugged at his hands, and he picked up his son once more without thinking about it.

"Akule?" Hakola called. She was hurrying after him, holding onto the hands of their other child. "What's wrong?"

"Look over there." He pointed towards where he thought he had seen the dark patches, but there was nothing on the hill.

"What is it?"

"I thought I saw dark spots on the hillside," he said softly. Confusion surged through him.

"Could be burn marks from a fire jumping through the area." Her voice quivered a little, and she put her hand on his arm. "We've only been here a few days. They might be old. It's alright." She squeezed his arm gently. "Don't worry about it."

"I don't know," he said carefully. "Something about them... they looked wrong."

"Akule, you worry too much." She shook her head and picked up her basket. "If you aren't lost in dreams and thoughts, you're worrying. I don't see anything on the hills."

"I just want to be sure that we're safe." He gently set Halo down close to his wife. Putting his hand on the boy's head, he rubbed the short hair gently before looking up once more. "I'm going to take a closer look."

"But the others-"

"I'll be fine," he assured her. He tapped the bow still held on his back. "I won't go far. I just want to take a look and be sure it isn't anything to worry about." Taking her hand, he squeezed it gently, hoping to reassure her. "If we camped in a bad spot, it is better to learn that quickly."

Hakola's frown didn't disappear. He didn't know how to explain it. Akule was sure that he'd seen something, and that odd sensation in his chest only added to his worry. His wife studied him for a long moment. Then she sighed in defeat and nodded. Akule ignored her words about seeing nothing. He'd always had better eyesight than his wife. There was something strange on the nearby hill. He just needed to check it out. Hakola grabbed Halo before the boy could run off again.

"Be careful and be home before dark," she ordered.

"I will," he promised.

"I'll tell Chapan. You don't need him mad at you again."

"He's your brother; he'll always find some reason to be annoyed with me."

Hakola's lips twitched with amusement, but she still didn't smile. Holding back his own sigh, Akule made himself start walking. He adjusted his course to go up the hill a little towards the mountain. It would let him see the dark patches more clearly. Behind him, the sound of his tribe was comforting, but he wasn't tempted to turn back.

He walked until he had a clear view of the hillside. Then he turned to look back towards the camp. He couldn't see it. How had he seen the dark patches before? Shivering, Akule told himself to remain calm, but nervous suspicions were beginning to whisper in his mind. Akule looked around himself carefully. There were no signs of danger. Behind him, the hill sloped up towards the mountains. Birds were chirping nearby, and the wind rustled the grasses. The world seemed as it should.

He peered out in confusion. The dark patches were stark against the greening grass, spots of black against an otherwise living landscape. Hakola wasn't wrong, they did look a bit like burned out patches, but there was something wrong with them. Something distorted his view of them. There was a thin veil of darkness that was like smoke, but wasn't. Frustration tore at him, and he checked the sun. There wasn't time for him to go and take a closer look.

Then just as that idea came and went, other ideas took hold. Was this the work of a spirit? Was the land cursed? That didn't seem right; he could hear the birds, and they'd had a good day of hunting. Nothing seemed wrong with the mountains. Yet... Akule didn't like it. He stayed and watched the patches. There were five that he could see, but there might be more.

The sun was creeping towards the horizon when he finally tore his eyes away. Something stirred in his gut. A hint of fear that Akule didn't understand. Instinct urged him to get away from the spots. Instead, he leaned forward a little more, trying to get a clearer look at the faint hints of darkness above the spots. Not smoke, but what else could it be.

Somehow he pulled himself away. Turning his back towards the dark patches was difficult. Every step he took brought a shiver down his spine, a sense that there was danger lurking behind him. He looked back over and over again. There was nothing following him that he could see. Perhaps the spirits were toying with him. Then the black spots were out of view, making him wonder once again how he had even seen them before.

It was a mystery. Akule's steps faltered. He wanted to go closer and get a better look. But there was work to do and no clear threat. He forced himself to keep going back to the village. If there was time, he'd slip over and get a better look tomorrow. The promise did little to calm down his heart as it raced in his chest and that odd fluttering returned.

4

Old Man

The wise old man: that was how he was remembered by humanity, in myth and legend, if not in the history books. It was a point of pride for Merlin. His youth had been a struggle as he held back Sídhe raiders and sought to understand the visions that the Iron Realm had gifted him with. It had aged him quickly, and even in his forties, he'd already seemed the wise old man even if he lacked the long white beard of the stories.

He'd been the guardian of the Iron Souls for three millennia, finding them, protecting them, and teaching them. With Arto and Michel, he'd served as a father figure for most of their childhoods. With others, he'd been the wise mentor who helped them find their place in this increasingly complicated world. Even when he didn't have the exact answer, he'd known enough to be able to offer counsel.

Now, after all these years, he was at a loss.

Alex was waiting for him to say something, shifting nervously in the center of his living room. He wished she'd brought it to him right away that afternoon in his office rather than stewing in her thoughts for so long. Merlin tried to summon up some reassuring words, but he wasn't sure what to say.

"This is all the messages?" he asked.

"Yes," Alex said. She started to pace. "I didn't delete anything, and I didn't respond. I thought about it, but I decided to wait." Glancing at the door, Alex stopped and then slumped onto the sofa. "When will Morgana get here?"

"Soon," Merlin assured her. "Did you tell the others?"

"Not yet," Alex admitted.

Satisfaction jolted through Merlin's chest. She brought this to his attention first. His relationship with Alex was not as close as he wished it was. She'd always gravitated more towards Morgana than himself. It was one of the oddities of this life, compared to most of her others. Usually, Merlin was the favorite, but in this life it was Morgana. Perhaps it was simply a matter of them being the same biological sex.

"I wasn't sure what to say. It feels like a big thing, but I'm not sure how to feel." She sighed again and closed her eyes, letting her feet hang off the far armrest. "I know that I'm emotionally involved when it comes to anything concerning Arthur. I don't think straight. Neither does Nicki."

"Indeed."

Merlin stared at the words again, reading them carefully. It seemed honest and sincere enough, but it was difficult to pull tone from texts. He longed for the days of face-to-face conversation or even written letters. You could draw a lot of information from a letter. The handwriting could give away a great deal about the writer's emotional state.

This Light was a mystery. Merlin hated it. Nothing in his past gave him clues on how to approach this problem. Instinct warned him to be cautious. After all, the other Light had taken control of Alex and used her body and her powers to attack them. He knew Alex well enough that he believed her descriptions of trying to communicate with the thing, trying to convince it that they could work together rather than fighting.

And the Light had ignored her.

Anger brewed in his chest, but he pushed it down. Alex had come to him for advice. She was seeking him out as the wise old man. He couldn't allow his emotions to cloud his judgment. Someone had to be objective, and it wasn't going to be Morgana.

"I think that we should hear it out."

"Really?" Alex didn't sound sure.

"This being... I can understand your worries. I share them, but we are dealing with issues and species that Morgana and I have never seen." He kept his voice as calm and even as he could. Alex needed him calm. "We don't have to trust it, but listening to what it has to say could reveal critical information. This being was able to enter the Iron Realm in a manner that I never imagined to be possible."

Alex nodded, blushing slightly at the memory, but her eyes remained hard. They were dark gray now, like a building storm, and it worried him. He handed her back the phone and caught her hand gently within his own.

"I will discuss the messages with Morgana, Alex. Try not to worry."

"I- I think you might be right," Alex said. "But it looks like Arthur. Morgana is going to want to rip it apart."

"You aren't wrong," Merlin admitted. She was right on that point. His anger and resentment didn't linger. He was too old for it, but Morgana had a brutal temper, and her rage could simmer like embers for centuries. "Let me speak with her. I'll try to calm her down and convince her to see reason." He squeezed her hand gently around the phone and then released her.

"Then what?" Alex asked. "This Darkness changes the status quo."

"So it seems." Merlin's stomach tightened. How could such a threat be real? Surely it wasn't at the scale that Alex seemed to believe. "We need more information before we can make plans."

"I suppose so." Alex shifted in her chair nervously, but then took a deep breath. "Maybe it is time for something different."

"Different? How so?"

"A summit," Alex answered. Her eyes brightened a little. He could see determination settling there and then in the young woman's shoulders. "We have allies, and I know Robin brought us some news, but this is big. This is much bigger than anything I can remember us ever facing."

"A summit? Alex, it is the duty of mages-"

"To protect the Iron Realm," Alex finished. She didn't roll her eyes, but he could tell it was a close thing. "But this is about more than just the Iron Realm. Besides, this Darkness could be the source of most of the threats. The Sídhe probably started the conquest because of their dying world. The latest Demon invasion was because of it. Can we really afford to wait and see what else tries to get into the Iron Realm because of the Darkness?"

There was more to it than that. Merlin could see it in her eyes. Compassion. Despite everything, Alex still worried about the other worlds. Merlin had long since dismissed them. His world needed his attention, but Alex might have a point. The notion that he and Morgana's focus on the Iron Realm had only put their world into greater danger sat uncomfortably in his gut. He wasn't sure what to make of this. Of any of it.

"Your idea is not without merit. Puck's messages were valuable, as you said, but there is no substitution for a chance to truly talk with others." He sighed, that sense of being far too old weighing on him once more.

He would endure it. He always had. "It might take some time to reach out, but I suspect you have it in mind to invite not only the Old Ones."

"Fae and Demons should be there too," Alex said. "I know that the Demons aren't as well known to us, but there are probably survivors from the army or local Demons who learned more about what was happening. The Fae don't know as much, not unless Arthur told them, but they should still be heard."

"It won't be easy. Many of them hate us," Merlin reminded her. "We'll need to hold it outside of the town so that the blood protection doesn't harm the Fae." His mind was running over details. He didn't like it. Too many things could go wrong. "I'll speak with Morgana."

A slight frown tugged at Alex's mouth, but she only nodded. He was relieved. Arguing with her would do no good. She was exhausted. It was written into every part of her face. She'd walked too much that day only to call him as soon as his classes were done.

"Okay," Alex said. "That's probably for the best."

"And you should go home and rest," Merlin said kindly. He stood up and gently put his hand on the top of her head. The familiar comforting behavior was soothing and not even greasy with this incarnation. Thanks to modern hair care products, Alex had the cleanest hair of the Iron Souls he'd known. "Please."

"Okay." Her exhaustion showed more plainly now, and Merlin ached for the girl he'd met when she'd first started school. A burden always fell on the Iron Soul, but it seemed to have crashed onto Alex. "I'll just relax tonight."

She stood up and gathered her things. Merlin stayed close, walking her to the door as she pulled on her coat. He considered driving her home, but his distraction wasn't much better than her exhaustion. Besides, he was certain that she'd be unhappy leaving her car here. He didn't shut the door behind her and instead watched Alex walk out to her car. Autumn leaves blew across his lawn. He hadn't bothered with them yet, and it was probably too late now.

Then she was gone, and he was alone with his thoughts. Merlin tidied up his entryway, packing away the excess coats and scarfs into the closet. He didn't want to sit still. He turned on the stereo, letting the classical music fill the sudden silence. Still, it didn't muffle his thoughts.

This Light worried him. Alex needed advice; she wanted advice, but he wasn't sure what to tell her. The idea of a summit had merit. It was new. They'd met with some Old Ones and regional creatures, but not on the scale that Alex suggested. Moving into the kitchen, Merlin put away all the dishes in the drying rack. There were times that he missed having Timothy live with him. Not having to worry about even the simplest chores had been pleasant.

Timothy would probably be asked by Alex to help speak with the Fae. If the Light had broken ties with Arthur's army, there was no telling what kind of a threat they were. A new leader may have taken hold or without Arthur's charisma it might have already fallen apart. Of course, that was if it had revealed that it wasn't their leader. Merlin's hands tightened around a glass, and he had to close his eyes for a moment.

Rage still burned in his chest at Arthur making a fool of him and hurting Alex. He'd been so blind. It wasn't that Arthur was like Arto, not exactly, though Arthur had certainly tried to act that way. He'd overlooked the possibility of a female Iron Soul. Just thinking about it made him recoil from his previous assumptions. He'd been surprised by the number of mages, both pleased and worried, but he'd ignored both Alex and Nicki as possibilities for the Iron Soul.

Arthur had stood out from Aiden and Bran. Merlin wondered if the boy had used some magic on him and Morgana without them noticing, some subtle mental suggestion. He preferred that theory to the idea that it hadn't even been necessary. It would take some time for the sting of that mistake to ease. If it hadn't been for Aiden, they would have lost Alex, and despite his conversation with Morgana at the start of the school year, he knew now that they did not have time to reincarnate the Iron Soul.

Besides, he was very fond of Alex. She was among his favorite incarnations of the Iron Soul. She wasn't Arto or Michel. He'd raised those boys, being both a father and teacher to them, but Alex was something special. She stood out among her fellow incarnations, and not just because she was a woman. There was a determination in her that made him proud. Despite everything she had faced, everything she had lost, Alex was still fighting for the good of the Iron Realm.

And yet, he had no idea how to help her. Shaking his head, Merlin sighed out loud and put some water on to boil. If he was lucky, talking with Morgana would spur on some useful realizations. He doubted it, but even an old man could hope. He wiped down the kitchen counters. Then he checked on the lines of iron in his window sills. When he returned to the kitchen, the water was ready, and he put in the tea to steep — no point in giving Morgana subpar tea. Her mood would be bad enough at the potential threat to Alex.

She didn't bother to knock on his door. He heard the keys in the lock and pulled two mugs out of the cabinets. Hurrying to the living room, he laid out the tea things and went to meet Morgana at the doorway. Her hair had come loose from her customary long braid, disrupting her usually neat appearance. Sharp green eyes alight with anger met his own, and she nodded in greeting.

"Alex forwarded me the messages." Morgana pulled off her long red scarf and hung it by his door. "What do you make of it?"

"I'm not sure," Merlin admitted. "Alex was here first, but I had little to offer her."

Morgana paused and just looked at him for a moment before passing him to enter the living room. "You hate not knowing what this is," Morgana observed. She sat down with all the grace and poise of a queen in her preferred armchair. "I can see it grating on you."

"This is not the time for you to be amused," Merlin said. He sat down in his chair, slumping more than he liked. "You don't know either."

"No, I don't." Morgana studied him for a long moment. "Long ago, we didn't always know all the threats. We were good at adapting and learning, then." She poured them each a cup of tea and put in just the right amount of sugar for him. "I hope that we have not lost that skill."

Merlin grimaced at the truth of her words. Yes, long ago, they'd had to confront the unknown and mysterious. But it had been a long time since any threat, any event, was anything other than a slight adjustment on known factors. The last time he'd been this confused had been regarding Oberon, desperate to find out how a Fae had possessed such power. In the end, it had just been Puck trying to play the hero — an Old One taking an unusual form.

"This is different," Merlin said. "The Darkness and a Light." He accepted his tea as Morgana gave him a knowing look. "We need a different name for it. I'm not sure what to make of all this."

"We should listen to Alex more." Morgana fixed him with an intense stare, her green eyes sharp and determined. "She's been right about the Darkness thus far. She tried to warn us, and you were dismissive of her worries." Morgana sighed. "We both were. Yet... I hate to say it, but such a threat does explain some things."

"Not everything. The Old Ones don't flee here; they exile here. At least... they used to."

"Hard to say now if that world even still exists."

"Let's hope they do; they are only one world over," Merlin replied. "I've always hoped that their government and culture finally changed to something more pleasant once they couldn't simply exile those who didn't fit in." He took a sip of his tea and studied Morgana. "What of the Sídhe? Does it change anything, knowing what they are running from?"

Morgana's eyes snapped to him, and he could see that suppressed rage boiling over. "No." The word was cold in the air. "Not at all. Running they may be, but they enslave and rape as they go. They've built a culture of monsters to make their flight possible. It changes nothing. They will get no sympathy and no quarter from me."

Merlin hadn't expected any other answer. The Sídhe were a danger; he knew that. His father's people were cruel and vicious, but now in light of everything else they no longer seemed as important. It didn't matter, he decided. They'd failed to mount a real invasion when the Iron Gate's power faded, and new defenses had been constructed. Without Arthur and the Queen trying to help them, they'd remain locked out of the Iron Realm. It was just a pity about all of their slaves.

Resting his chin on his hand, he found himself longing for the simpler days of long ago. Indoor plumbing was marvelous, but some things had been easier back then. Morgana raised an eyebrow and began to share her observations. He listened with one ear; his mind unable to focus on his partner's words. Even the sweetness of his tea didn't cheer him up. He just felt so very old.

5

Coffee Conversations

Their living room, while built to accommodate many people, was still full whenever the whole group assembled. Aiden had pulled out a couple of folding chairs from the closet so that everyone didn't have to pack in on the sofas and armchairs. Alex herself had taken one so that she could sit a little apart from the others and have space to think. Timothy had put together a platter of snacks sitting on the coffee table as if this was a social gathering. She still didn't really understand how the Brownie's mind worked, but something sweet was starting to sound very good. A glass of water sat on the floor by her foot, and Alex picked it up, running a finger around the rim thoughtfully.

"So that's the whole of the message," Merlin said. "Nothing new has come through?" He looked her way.

Alex shook her head. "No, nothing new. But I suspect if I don't respond soon that more messages will follow."

"We're not trusting this, are we?" Nicki asked. Her eyes scanned the room, taking in everyone's facial expressions. Not even Avani sitting next to her was spared. "We aren't trusting this thing."

"We don't know anything about it," Aiden said gently. "Of course, we aren't trusting it, but we should give it a chance to speak."

"I don't like it." Nicki shook her head and glared at the floor. "It admits that it has Arthur's memories."

"But it isn't Arthur." Avani touched Nicki's shoulder gently. "I know that I don't have the history with him that the rest of you had, but you need to try and keep that in mind."

"I thought it was over," Nicki snarled. "I killed him. I saw him collapse. I was sure he was dead."

"We all were," Merlin said gently. "Whatever this Light is, it didn't take over right away. That could be important."

Alex bit her lip and looked at her hands. That night was hazy, but thinking back on it, she thought that maybe something had sparked off her hands. She hadn't been trying to use magic, but now she had to wonder if she gave the Light a surge of magic. Nicki and Merlin were right; they'd been sure that he was dead. His body had been taken away only for him to suddenly wake when Alex touched him.

Her head started to hurt, and Alex leaned back in her chair, hoping to ease the growing tension in her shoulders. She'd managed a little sleep the past two nights, but exhaustion was starting to creep up on her. There'd been a moment. One glorious, flickering moment that she'd actually thought that maybe things would get easier. Instead, they only got more complicated.

"We can't trust anything it says!" Nicki insisted. "Look, I know it's the 'Light,' and we're worried about the Darkness, but let's not get lost in traditional symbolism. We have no promise that this thing isn't dangerous. The one that took over Alex-"

"That was a different one though," Lance pointed out. "It's not fair to put all the species together. We know that Arthur was looking at the Tree of Reality too. Maybe he tried to make a deal with this Light, and that's how it got here."

"Besides," Jenny added. "We do need information."

"I'm just worried that Arthur's memories could influence it." Nicki crossed her arms stubbornly. "Or maybe we're completely wrong, and this thing kept Arthur alive after all." She almost spat the words, her nose curling up in disgust. "We can't be careless."

"No one is going to be careless," Merlin interrupted. "Alex has proposed the idea of holding a summit, to discuss the Darkness and the threat it poses." Merlin's voice shifted lower, and Alex frowned. It almost sounded like he was pouting, but it was gone before she could be sure. "Any thoughts?"

"I think a summit is a good idea," Bran said. His voice was calm and low, signaling to the others just how loud they'd gotten. Nicki flushed a little, nodded, and focused on Bran. "I know that we had bad blood with a lot of the Fae, but in light of recent events, opening better lines of communication seems wise." He looked over to Merlin and Morgana. "I'm guessing nothing like this has been done before."

It was Morgana who answered, "On occasion, we have had small meetings. For example, Thor met with Odin, Sif, and Baldr with us, along with a representative of the local Fae community during the crisis in that region."

"When necessary, we have spoken with beings who had a stake in events," Merlin confirmed, "but nothing to this level. I'm assuming that Alex intends to invite all those we know are alive."

"We need to," Alex said. She didn't flinch as everyone looked at her. "Shiva, Sif, Odin, if he wakes up in time, and any other Old Ones who are awake and might have some knowledge of their homeworld. The Fae, the Faery creatures, and hopefully even a few Demons." She paused, and then sighed. "And The Light. If it wants to talk to us, then we should at least listen. It probably knows more about the Darkness than any of us."

A chill ran through her body. She knew it wasn't fair to already be judging this Light. It wasn't the same one that had ignored her pleading to stop, but those memories... Those moments of struggling for control as her body was wrestled from her would haunt her. Forever. Swallowing, Alex wished the others would look somewhere else. She was trying to be professional here, but there were limits.

"It's a valid plan," Morgana said. "While I dislike having so many beings from other worlds gathered in one place, it may be our best option. I'd hardly trust them to sort out an online meeting." Morgana almost smiled at the thought and Alex had a sudden vision of Odin trying to sort out a software update. "And in person gives more opportunities to build trust. If we take precautions and limit the time we spend in any one place, then we should be able to avoid causing too severe a spike in magic."

There was that too. Alex was a bit ashamed to admit that she hadn't even thought about that. It just didn't seem very important now. Then came the guilt for that thought. She had one job. One job that she was born and reborn for over and over again, and she was ignoring an aspect of it. Not to mention that the more magic there was the harder it was to hide. She didn't want to be the Iron Soul who blew the secret of magic to the whole world.

"Alex?" Merlin called.

"Huh?"

"Are you alright?" Bran asked.

"Sorry, my mind is just drifting," Alex replied. She shook herself and sat up a bit straighter. "So, we probably want to sort out a date for this."

"Merlin and I will worry about that," Morgana said. "That will be based largely on us finding a venue we're comfortable with." Morgana's tone did nothing to hide that she wasn't happy. "Until then, there is a limit to how much we can plan."

Nicki spoke up, "I'll see if I can find a way to get the book working again." Her jaw tightened. "Inconsiderate bastard, changing just enough that the magic doesn't know it's looking for him."

"I think that's enough for today," Morgana said. There was a small smile on her face as she watched Nicki. Alex had the dark sense that she approved of Nicki's anger. "We're only spinning our wheels. I have papers to grade."

Morgana cast a glance over the group, the sort of look that only a teacher could give that seemed to know exactly who among them had unfinished homework waiting. Alex almost started giggling. How could they balance all of this? She supposed that after three thousand years of threats, you learned to shut off the fear and worry so it didn't drive you insane.

Alex stood up when Morgana did. The older mage set her mug on the table and grabbed one more small shortbread cookie. Glancing Alex's way, she smiled, and Alex walked with her to the front door. Merlin was a few steps behind them, talking with Nicki about ways to alter the magic in the book. Alex retrieved Morgana's coat which was hanging next to her own and held it up for her former sister.

"Thank you, Alex." Morgana turned and pulled on the long coat. "Be careful if you go out today. I think we'll see more snow tonight."

"We do need it," Alex said mildly. She didn't care all that much. "We'll be careful on the roads."

Morgana hummed thoughtfully and then turned to kiss Alex's forehead. "Try to relax," she whispered. "We will sort this out." Alex didn't believe her and didn't think that Morgana believed it either, but she nodded anyway. "I'll see you tomorrow."

Merlin's goodbye was faster, though he stopped long enough to put a hand on her shoulder. He had started to reach for her head before hesitating and drawing his hand back. Alex was grateful. Her emotions were delicate as it was without invoking memories of Merlin being paternal. Then he headed out to his car. Alex kept the door open long enough to watch them drive away in their separate cars.

She lingered, tapping her fingers on the wall until the two Grand Mages were long gone. The voices were chatting about the idea of a summit. Thor and Michel were the loudest in favor while Arto was slightly hesitant. Nervous energy built up in her back and legs. Alex grabbed her coat and pulled it on just as Avani stepped into the entryway.

"Alex?"

Tossing her long hair, Alex smiled at Avani and shrugged. "Just going out for a bit."

"You're not shopping, are you?" Jenny asked. She seemed a touch suspicious. "Because if you are, please get something more interesting than just another t-shirt."

"Thanks for that, Jenny." Alex rolled her eyes. "Nah, not shopping."

Waving goodbye, Alex walked outside and kept her ears perked for the sounds of anyone following her. No one did. She climbed into her car, aware that she was being a touch rude, but she didn't want anyone offering to come along or the pressure of asking. Through the windshield, she caught a small smile and nod from Bran through the living room window. Relief washed over Alex, and she exhaled before slowly pulling away from the other cars and heading out.

Licking her lips, Alex debated what to do as she drove. The voices were murmuring in her head, not focusing on anything in particular. Maybe ice cream. She had to turn on the car heater and quickly dismissed that idea. Coffee, she decided. Something over the top and indulgent.

Alex couldn't remember the last time she'd gone to get coffee on her own. They had a good coffee maker in the kitchen, so she usually just made what she wanted. Or Timothy did. Timothy was a little angel who had coffee waiting every morning with eggs and sometimes ham or bacon. It was glorious, but right now Alex wanted just to get something with way too much sugar. The idea made her smile and she started to hum softly, an old song whose origin she couldn't remember.

For the sake of familiarity, she drove across the river and headed to Central. There were plenty of spaces to park. It was a quiet day downtown, with the rolling gray clouds overhead threatening more snow. Alex loved it. She fed the meter and walked across the street to Bookend Coffee, already smelling the beans and baked goods. Once inside, she ordered a large mocha and a chocolate chip cookie. If she had to be a mage, then she was going to make use of the improved metabolism.

"Alex?"

She jumped, nearly dropping her coffee, and spun around. Robin was behind her, looking a bit sheepish at having startled her. The Old One was dressed like a normal college student with a black winter coat, a long red scarf on, and jeans. Her curly black hair had been styled into tiny buns. Alex just stared at her blankly, trying to reconcile the knowledge that this was an Old One with how very modern and normal she looked.

"It's Robin."

"Yeah, I know." Alex shook her head. "Sorry, it's been a day. Uh, hi." She extended her hand to shake Robin's before dropping it back to her side and feeling like an idiot. "Good to see you."

"Good to see you too." Robin glanced around the coffee shop, no doubt looking for the others. "Are you alone?"

"Yes." Alex wasn't worried about admitting that. "Just needed something sweet." She held up her coffee and Robin nodded.

They didn't move for a moment. Then a group departing made them both step to the side so they could leave. It left a table free near the back and Robin gestured to it with a hesitant frown. Nodding, Alex slowly moved for the open table, very aware of Robin walking alongside her. There was a strange tingle across her skin, even under her coat, when the Old One brushed her arm. Alex took the seat that kept her back to the wall and double checked the front door and the back exit.

"Calm down," Robin said. "I'm not going to hurt you."

"I know." Alex blinked in surprise. "I didn't- sorry, I've been a bit on edge today."

"Any reason in particular, or just... life?"

"Life." Alex took a long sip of her mocha. A burst of chocolate hit her tongue and made the world a slightly better place.

"So how is mage central?" Robin asked. "Any news?"

"We're working on setting up a summit," Alex said. "Bring everyone together to talk about this Light and the Darkness." Robin nodded thoughtfully. "What do you think?"

"It sounds like a good idea," Robin agreed, but Alex could hear a hint of worry in her voice.

"But?"

"But a lot could go wrong," Robin replied. "It isn't like all of us have the best histories with each other. I can see someone using it as a chance to grind an old axe. Even with the threat of this Darkness. Not everyone will believe it."

Alex groaned. "I know. It took a while for Merlin and Morgana to accept it."

Robin snorted and sipped her coffee. "That doesn't surprise me. As brilliant as they are, they can be a bit set in their ways. Michel loved them dearly, but even he complained about them."

"They don't talk about him," Alex said softly. "They talk about Arto, but they've never really mentioned Michel."

Robin didn't say anything right away. Then she sighed and shook her head. "Alex, I haven't got the best track record for smart decisions. I just want to say that before I open my big mouth."

"Okay."

"There's a lot you don't know about Merlin and Morgana. A lot that they walk away from when it's over. They loved Michel, but by that point, I think they already had some barriers up. Arto was first. They didn't know that they were going to live a long time. It's harder to get attached to something, to someone, if you know you'd outlive them."

'She's right,' Thor whispered. 'Sif kept me at arm's length for a long time because of that.'

"That's not to say that they don't care," Robin added. "I know that they've both taken in children over the centuries. One rumor said that Morgana even got married at one point in the 17th century, though I'm not sure if that's true."

Alex swallowed. Michel and Arto were both reacting loudly to the idea. They weren't upset exactly, but there was a definite sense that they thought they should have known that. Alex tried to ignore them. It was difficult. She glanced around to make sure that no one was listening to them. No one was paying them any attention.

"Alex?"

"Right, sorry, I'm here!"

"Okay," Robin said slowly. "If you don't want to talk-"

"No, I'd like to talk. How are you, Robin?"

"I'm okay. Classes are interesting." Robin smiled a little. "I'm taking Merlin's Shakespeare class right now. Related credits. He keeps looking at me whenever he talks about Puck. It's probably funnier than it should be."

"I remember that class," Alex said. "I was taking it when I found out about magic."

"Really? That must have been helpful... or terrifying, if you had to do the worksheet on what the Fair Folk were actually like."

"Did the worksheet. I do think it helped me wrap my brain around everything. At least, it didn't hurt."

"Good. Anyway, I'm trying not to cause trouble. Merlin doesn't dislike me as much as Morgana, but I don't want to push it. I seem to be on thin ice." There was a sad note to her voice that made Alex grimace.

"Aiden still isn't talking to you, huh?"

"I understand," Robin said. "I get it. It's all a bit much. Finding out that the girl you're flirting with is only recently a girl."

"Knowing Aiden it probably isn't that, it's probably more that you're an Old One," Alex said. "I think he's just feeling a bit used."

Robin leaned forward, moving her hand, but stopping short of touching Alex. "I wasn't trying to use him. I didn't even set out to flirt. He was just nice, intelligent, and funny. After sleeping for a century and then spending a year studying as much about humanity as possible, it was nice to feel like a part of it."

"Then maybe you should tell him that."

"I keep trying!" Robin groaned, lowering her head in despair. "He just tenses up when I see him in person or ignores my calls." Then she shook her head and waved her right hand dismissively. "You know what, never mind. It doesn't matter! That's not the most important thing at the moment!"

"It matters to you though," Alex said. "And I'd like to see another mage have a bit of happiness."

Robin looked down for a moment as the tension in the air rose. Then Robin cleared her throat and rolled her shoulders. "Speaking of a happy mage, Nicki is dating that magician girl, right?" Alex nodded and a grin took over Robin's face. "How's her family taking that?"

"I'm not sure it's come up yet, but I'm sure it'll be fine. They are magicians after all, and Nicki is a mage. That'll count for something, even if they aren't thrilled by the whole lesbian thing."

"I hope it works out. They're cute together."

"So, you really do want to date Aiden?"

"I suppose so. It surprises me too, but I liked talking to him. Dating isn't necessary, but it isn't like I have a real peer group." Robin's dark eyes met Alex's. "That was, after all, a huge part of Michel and my friendship. Think about it: Puck isn't part of any pantheon or family in mythology. I'm young. A lot younger than most Old Ones. I'm not sure why, but after the first few centuries, no one wanted to create more children. My parents were rare in being willing to make me."

"That's... that's familiar," Alex reflected.

"Well, I've told you about that before, even if it was a few centuries ago."

Sometimes that was hard to remember. Alex took another sip of her coffee. It still tasted good. Robin studied her for a moment, picking up her drink and raising it in a silent toast. Then the Old One started talking about her classes and the things she liked about Ravenslake as if they were a pair of normal college students. It wasn't necessary, but Alex appreciated the temporary illusion.

6

Death Spots

33 C.E. Bighorn Mountains

4 Akule tried to put the odd, dark spots out of his mind. His worry had led to Hakola telling her brother about it. Caphan had at least sent someone else to look, but they'd just dismissed it as signs of a fire jumping. None of the others had mentioned the shimmer in the air around them, the distortion like smoke, and it worried him.

He did not know what to make of it. Nothing like that had ever been seen before in the memory of the tribe. Yet it was real. He was sure of that. No one was interested in investigating it though. It was easy to give the hillside distance, as none of the animals seemed to go there now. That more than anything gnawed at Akule. He respected their instincts too much for it not to make him uneasy. During the day he was busy enough to put it mostly out of his head, but every so often he caught sight of it out of the corner of his eye, even when it should have been impossible for him to see it, just like the first time.

At night he closed his eyes and saw it all over again. He just couldn't dismiss it. Something was wrong. It churned in his gut and rested heavily in his heart. Strange dreams played out in his mind each night, but he was left with only scraps and faint memories upon waking. He suffered this state of affairs for several days before he caved.

He did not tell Hakola where he was going. Guilt taunted him. He was scouting, that was true enough, but he knew that he was still hiding the full truth from his wife. There would be no animals in the area; he was certain of that. His stolen glances towards the hillside had told him that much at least.

Walking towards the hill, Akule listened to the wind rush through the grasses. He could hear no birds nearby, but there were still other natural sounds to soothe him. A nearby creek was bubbling along through a cut in the rocky slope. Snow was melting high above him, and Akule almost thought he could hear the soft cracks of the snow and ice collapsing echoing down. He was getting closer to the hillside, but it was different now.

Then the world shifted. Smells faded away as if he was suddenly struck very ill. Sounds were distant and muted. It was as if he was no longer in the world. Run! his instincts urged — every fiber of his being wanted to leave this place. It was wrong. And yet something else drove him forward — a strange kind of fear that was not for himself. It was greater than him, leaving his personal fear wailing to an unheeding master.

Akule walked forward. The smaller dark patches were gone. In their place was something much larger. It was at least twelve feet across now. There was a hole in the earth, but no displacement. No hole had been dug, and there was no mound of earth around it. All that should have been there was gone. He crept closer and frowned at the shape. It was a perfect circle like the moon, he concluded as he walked around it.

The color of the ground was not black. There was a hint of the rich brown color that the dirt should have been, but it was... tainted. He moved a little closer, not daring to step into the circle, but stopping right at the edge. Inside he spotted stones that provided a slight variation in color. Remarkably, they were smooth on the exposed side. Their natural roughness had been carved away by whatever had made the hole in the land.

As close as he was now, he could see how deep it really was. The shadows of the trees before had disguised it, but it was as deep as his foot to his groin. Like a bowl, he decided. But even with knowledge of the shape, Akule could not explain it. How could something have created this so perfectly?

It was not burned as he'd tried to convince himself in the past few days, and it was much larger. All the small patches had been consumed into this much larger hole. He regretted not inspecting the patches more closely. Had they been such perfect circles?

No explanation came to mind, and the odd sensations crawling over his skin continued. It was wrong. This was not the work of a friendly spirit. This was something else. Something bad. Above the circle, there remained a faint hint of something in the air: a darkness, a shadow that was unnatural. He dared not come closer or reach towards it.

Akule just stood there, staring and trying to understand what he was looking at. His mind whirled, but nothing came. Their band needed to leave. They'd planned to stay a few more days at least, but Akule wasn't sure that was safe any longer. This... thing, had already changed. There'd been small patches before; he was sure of that. At least, he thought he was. Moving slowly, he circled around it again, as close as he dared, and looked around. He didn't see anything else. There was only this one much larger spot.

Swallowing, he backed up and leaned against a nearby tree while he caught his breath. His head was fuzzy. The air still tasted off. Stale, yet he was in the middle of the fresh air. A mountain breeze was floating through and plants and flowers were beginning to grow. The air fresh and cool. He turned back to look at it once more. The shadow above it taunted him. That shimmer in the air was all wrong.

Akule glanced around and found a rock. He tossed it up and caught it, weighing it as he considered the hole. Then before he could think of some other horrible what if, he threw the rock forward. It sailed through the cloud and landed in the circle. Moving forward, he watched it and waited. He didn't have to wait long. The rock was already polished smooth, but now began to collapse slowly as if it were melting.

Stumbling back, Akule could neither breathe nor understand what he was seeing. The stone was falling away like snow with hot water poured upon it. Then his lungs expanded, and he gasped for air, his need for breath overcoming his shock. A cold tremble overtook his limbs. He didn't understand and didn't dare draw closer. Something ached in his chest. For a moment, he feared for his heart. When he felt strong enough, he stepped back and inhaled slowly. It seemed that he was safe enough where he was.

He looked above the hole once more, trying to see the source of the dangerous mist, but there was nothing. The sky looked the same as ever. The certainty that he was missing something fell over his shoulders like a buffalo robe. Picking up a stick, he tossed it forward. Like the stone, it was destroyed. This cloud did not just threaten the earth itself, but anything. It explained why there were no animals nearby.

Akule had no idea what to think of it. Frantically, he reviewed all the stories from his youth — nothing matched this. If dark spirits were behind this, then it was a completely new means of attack. The ache in his chest was still there, and he rubbed the space over his heart nervously through his shirt. It wasn't a pain, but a pressure. He moved further away, and the feeling eased a little more.

There was nothing he could do here. Akule knew that, and yet he was still slow to move away. Then he turned back and gathered up a few sticks before inching forward. When he was within an arm's length of the hole, he pushed the sticks into the ground. Laying out a perimeter, he watched the hole lest it expand all at once and swallow him. At least, he might have a chance of seeing how fast it reached the sticks. His small curved line was in place, and he felt as if he had accomplished something here.

He hurried home, eager to return to that which was familiar and warm rather than alien and cold. Yet Akule found himself stopping and looking back several times. He was too far to see the sticks, but the fog was distinct. Wisps like smoke rose out of the hole. Bile threatened to fill his mouth, and his throat constricted to keep it down. Weakness filled his limbs as the fear refused to ease its grip on him.

Despite his weakness, despite his fear, he was able to muster the strength to climb towards the camp. Already the sounds of the world had returned. There were birds chirping, animals moving in the underbrush, and the wind singing through the mountain peaks. He could smell the grass, the trees, and the living creatures that roamed the mountains.

The camp was right ahead of him. Relief threatened to knock him off of his feet. He could hear the children and the voices of the women as they worked. The ache in his chest eased a little more, but it lingered still. He paused and studied it. There was a warmth in there now. It was almost comforting. It flickered, and while it left him sore, his instinct wasn't to be afraid. Akule shook his head and kept moving. There was too much already today that he couldn't understand.

His wife caught sight of him almost at once. Her eyes widened and she handed Halo to one of the other mothers. Minal looked over and waved to him, but kept working on weaving the new basket in her lap. Hakola was in front of him in moments.

"Akule," Hakola said. Relief filled her eyes, and he grimaced at how long he'd been gone. "There you are."

"I am sorry," he apologized. Stepping forward, he caught her hand and sighed happily at the skin-to-skin contact. The lingering chill in his bones faded. "I went to check the black spots."

"Oh." She frowned at him, raising a hand to his cheek. "You seem distressed. Are you alright?"

"I'm fine," he assured her. "But they are not burn marks. And they are all now one large spot. Whatever touches it... melts." He struggled to explain and watched the emotions dance across his wife's face. "It's dangerous. I know it."

"Akule... is it spirits?"

"I don't know... I don't understand it, but there is something there. Some black fog is hanging over it. I don't know why you don't see it."

"Calm yourself," Hakola whispered. "We'll speak with Caphan tonight." Nervousness settled on her face. "He'll help you with the elder. It will be okay. We're already planning on leaving in a few more days. It'll be alright."

Right, he thought. Leaving. They were supposed to leave soon. The tribe had been successful with the game in the area, but they'd need to move on to fresh trails and areas where the forage hadn't been gathered yet. His heartbeat didn't slow. He didn't want to stay, but leaving almost sounded worse.

"Sit down and help with the rabbits," Hakola ordered. She nodded towards a nearby woven mat where a few of the animals killed by snares waited. "You need to calm down."

Sitting down, he obediently took the first of the rabbits and slit down its belly. He didn't have to think about how to skin the creature; it was almost instinctive at this point. His mind churned with thoughts and worries about that dead spot. It was not from a fire, but he had no explanation. The others somehow were not concerned about it. In truth, it was still small compared to the whole great world, but it was growing.

Distraction proved hard to come by throughout the afternoon. Every so often, one of his hands began to tremble, and his heart started to race. The small ache in his chest remained, leaving him always conscious of the strange happenings in his otherwise peaceful world. It was sometime later that his brother by marriage approached him with a sour expression. What Hakola had told him, Akule didn't know, but he was grateful that Caphan seemed to be taking things seriously. He set aside his tools and stood up, nodding away from the others. Caphan raised an eyebrow but nodded and followed.

"What happened?" Caphan asked when they reached the edge of the camp. "Hakola said that you went to the burn spots."

"They aren't a burn. Something is very wrong there." He shivered, remembering the rock and stick. Quickly, he told Caphan about what he had seen and watched the other man's expression shift between uncertainty and worry.

"I'm not sure I understand," Caphan said. He frowned at Akule, not doubtfully, but worried. "I've only noticed them once, and I was on the far side of camp."

"I can't explain that." Akule lowered his eyes for a moment. At least Caphan had seen them. He wasn't going mad. "But I kept seeing them, and there was this strange haze over them. I was worried, so I went to look at them, but now they are one large hole. Whatever the fog is, it destroys." Despite the stress of it all, he was happy to see that at least his brother was taking his words seriously. "It is dangerous."

"I will speak with the elder in the morning," Caphan promised. "He'll have questions for you."

"I have no answers."

"I don't like the thought that we are near evil spirits, but I cannot think of what else it could be." Caphan took a deep breath and calmed down, smiling a little. "But we can move on a bit sooner."

He was too at ease. Akule wanted to shake him, to shout that they were in far graver danger than his brother knew. Hakola touched his shoulder, grounding him in the present, and he breathed a little easier. He didn't know when she had joined them but was suddenly very grateful for her presence. Without a word, she guided him towards their small hut. The evening meal was waiting for him, and she gave him water. His throat was parched from talking, and he greedily gulped it down.

Laying down to sleep for the night was difficult. The bison fur blanket was warm in the cool mountain evening, but he knew that the dreams would come once more. They'd be worse now that he'd gotten close. Beside him, he felt Hakola relax and looked towards the smaller lumps in the hut that were his children. Not too far away, something was growing — something that destroyed the world around it slowly. The urge to grab his family and run rose in his chest, but he choked it back.

Soon, he'd speak with the elder, and the band would move on. They'd warn the other bands in the tribe as they came across them and be careful of the area. But that wouldn't last forever. It was growing. In just a phase of the moon it had grown into something large and deep. Surely it would continue to do so.

Closing his eyes, he counted his breaths and listened to the sounds of the world. There were the sounds of the night birds, and he thought he heard some bats. Up in the mountains and down on the plains, animals that preferred the night would be out living their lives. The horrible black fog hadn't changed that. Eventually, sleep sank its claws into him, and his head became foggy. Akule surrendered to it, and slowly, very slowly, he slipped off.

There was no peace for him. Akule found himself once more on the hillside, but it was transformed above the hole in the Earth. Gone was the clear blue sky or the stars. Instead, the sky had been torn open. It was a thin rip, but it shuddered, and he caught glimpses of something beyond it. Something dark and shimmering.

He was dreaming. Akule knew that, but it wasn't enough to wake him up. The wound in the sky pulsed and twisted, like the beating heart of a dying animal. Each pulse distorted the sky, but even worse, something was coming through. Small droplets fell from the rip like rain. But they were thicker. They pooled along the tear and then fell. He tracked a droplet to the ground. It hit softly, but instantly ate away at the ground.

The effect didn't last long, but it radiated out. Akule swallowed. He had his answer as to what had caused the dead spots. The pulsing shifted the wound and its droplets, creating small areas that sooner or later would join into one.

What if it grew bigger? He eyed the wound nervously. Was this real? It had to be. The spirits were showing him the truth, showing him what his mortal eyes could not see in the sky over the dead spot. But why? What could he do? Panic rose in his chest. His limbs trembled. What could he possibly do?

7

The Mountain Fog Hotel

Three weeks was all it took for Merlin and Morgana to organize what Alex was sure was going to be the most awkward day of her life. In all other things, life had been calm and almost normal. There were no Fae attacks, even the Redcaps hadn't caused any problems, and the Light remained silent. Alex managed the first truly good midterm of her college career since freshman year, and Aiden even started texting Robin a little. Nicki had made some progress on changing the book's magic just enough to track the Light, but it had stayed in the Seattle area with no sign that it was causing trouble.

They were all braced for the other shoe to fall.

Morgana drove her car faster on the snow and ice than Alex would have dared, but the car made smooth turns and Morgana didn't seem at all worried. She was beside Morgana in the passenger seat with Nicki and Avani in the back. Avani was humming softly, and every so often made soft sounds of appreciation at the snow-covered landscape outside the windows. Tall pines were covered with a layer of ice making them glisten in the rays of sun that managed to escape the gray clouds overhead. There was another click of Avani's camera, and Morgana chuckled.

"I'm glad you're enjoying the trip, Avani," Morgana said.

"It is very beautiful," Avani agreed. "Thank you for driving me."

"Well, you don't have a license, and it is better that we go together," Morgana replied.

"You should learn to drive; I could teach you," Nicki offered.

"Maybe in the spring," Avani answered. "It hasn't been necessary yet."

"No, but it might be one day," Morgana pointed out.

They turned off the highway, and Alex shifted in her seat. Cathanáil was strapped to her back, and while it wasn't too bad, the Sword ensured that she could not lean back in the chair. Her dagger was in a sheath on her belt, and Alex could feel the gentle magical hum of Mjǫllnir and the Chalice in the trunk.

"So, how did you choose the location?" Avani asked. Her tone was pleasant, and Alex was grateful for the calm presence.

"Merlin and I have attended weddings here." Morgana chuckled and tapped her fingers on the wheel. "I was surprised that we didn't immediately think of it. The rooms are nice enough. Everyone will have space to retreat to and relax. Hopefully, that will keep tensions from rising too much."

Alex couldn't help it. She turned in her seat to look at Nicki who was behind Morgana. The redhead shook her head with a dark frown. Apparently, she still thought this was a bad idea. With every rotation of the wheels and turn of her stomach, Alex was beginning to think the same thing. So many powerful beings in one place was bad enough, but their news could start a panic or a fight. That many powerful beings in one place spoiling for a fight was even worse.

"Hopefully this won't take long," Morgana continued. "Merlin and I are hoping that magic won't spike too much. If you start feeling light headed and excited, try to use your magic to prevent too much of a buildup. Trust me, too much magic at once can make a mage foolish."

There was a story there. Alex wondered if it related to any of her lives, or maybe another life when she was too young to remember it. Morgana didn't offer any details, and Alex looked out the window as a building came into view.

The hotel was nothing special, and the name wasn't at all familiar to Alex. As Morgana parked the car, she and the other mages looked out the windows and carefully studied it. The main building was three stories tall and a brilliant shade of white that matched the snow surrounding it. There were a few other cars in view, but the place seemed empty even if it was in good repair. A sign declared it the Mountain Fog Hotel.

"I'm getting a Steven King vibe," Nicki said softly.

"It's a nice enough place," Morgana said. Turning in her seat, she looked at all of them. "It wasn't easy to find a place nearby that was outside the blood protections and isolated. This is an old family hotel with a large room for meeting space. It should serve our purposes."

"I'd be happier if we didn't have to spend time with the Light," Nicki muttered.

"Open mind." Avani smiled gently at her girlfriend. "We agreed to hear it out and try to learn from the other representatives."

"Fine," Nicki grumbled, "but the only ones I'm happy to see are Timothy, Sif, and Shiva."

"It will be nice to see Timothy again," Alex agreed.

"Sorry that I denied you your house Brownie." Morgana raised an eyebrow and gave Alex a knowing look. "But he's our best contact with the Fae." Then she opened her door. "Time to get a move on girls."

"Are we sure this is private enough?" Avani climbed out of the car and looked up at the massive house.

"This hotel mostly serves as a wedding venue," Morgana explained. "Especially in the spring and summer. The staff is small and shouldn't bother us. Merlin and I will put some protections against spying in place before the meetings start." Morgana closed the driver's door and looked at all of them in turn. "Keep your wits about you, but remember that this is a diplomatic event."

"Yeah," Alex agreed. She exhaled and watched her breath dance in the air. "There's a bigger threat now."

"I know," Nicki said. "I know. Still... I don't like meeting with the Light. It just feels wrong."

"I'm not looking forward to it either." Alex shivered and moved towards the trunk, eager to get her overnight bag. "But how we feel isn't important right now."

Nicki sighed, but nodded and leaned her shoulder against Alex's arm. She accepted the silent apology with a nod. Fighting with her friends, even arguing that was driven just by their nervousness over this meeting, was the last thing that Alex wanted. Morgana caught her eye and Alex gave her a soft smile. Alex was nervous, but not frightened. They'd keep each other safe through this.

The path to the front door was shoveled and dry. Nearby on the lawn was a frozen over bird bath and on a nearby oak tree hung two bird feeders. A couple of birdhouses were secured to the upper branches, and Alex felt herself smile in response. It was a simple thing, but pleasant to see. The heavy wooden front door had a pretty glass window and an empty planter stood beside the door. Perhaps they should look at adding some new features to their yard come spring.

Inside, the main foyer was warm. There was an open living room to their left with a collection of sofas and armchairs. A fire was burning merrily in an old stone fireplace, with small photos and knickknacks covering the mantle. Warm wooden walls accented with landscape paintings surrounded them and added to the charm of the locale. It wasn't a polished chain hotel. It was out of the way and private. Alex started to relax a little bit.

"Good afternoon!"

Ahead of them was a wooden counter with a middle-aged woman behind it. They could just see the top of a computer screen. Behind her was a grid of mailboxes and a wall of small hooks with keys on them. It looked like the reception desk of small hotels that Alex had seen on television or in movies, but had never actually been to. Yet, it had a charm about it, and it wasn't in the middle of a city.

"Good afternoon," Morgana replied. She set her purse on the counter. "I am Morgana Cornwall. We spoke this morning. Is everything still in place?"

"Yes, ma'am, there haven't been any changes. We haven't received any calls from your guests…"

"That's to be expected." Morgana smiled charmingly. "Our group is all already in transit. There shouldn't be any problems."

Alex hoped that was the truth. Robin and Sif had learned about the modern world, but what if the other Old Ones were confused? What if Shiva didn't make himself look human? Magic could alter memories, but she loathed the idea of picking through the woman's brain. Thankfully the woman didn't seem too worried yet. Alex supposed that as a wedding venue, they were used to a bit of crazy. Morgana handed over a card and signed a few pieces of paper while Alex and the others moved closer to the fire. It was a real one with red, hot flames licking over a black log. Tension flowed out of Nicki's body as she held her hands closer to the heat. Avani slipped up next to her and whispered something that made Nicki nod. Then they made disgustingly happy, soft eyes at each other.

"This way," Morgana called a moment later. Gesturing them to follow, she added, "I want you to see the meeting space."

Her unsaid words about familiarizing themselves with the exits and layout weren't needed. Alex adjusted her backpack and followed quickly, with Nicki and Avani behind her. The hallways were half wood on the bottom with a tasteful floral wallpaper on the upper half. More paintings and photos lined the wall and, Alex was grateful that the hotel was as small as it was because so far there was a distinct lack of anything to help her navigate.

The conference room was larger than the average classroom but smaller than most lecture halls. Alex glanced at the capacity sign and noted that it held fifty. That was probably all that they would need. Merlin and Morgana hadn't shared the full list of those who had agreed to come, but Alex knew that at least six Old Ones were going to attend and a group of Fae. Shiva had agreed to approach some of the Demons. Alex had no idea how that meeting had gone.

"This feels ridiculous." Nicki wrinkled her nose and looked into the room.

Large windows looked over a snow-covered back garden. There was a small dais set up and doors into the back stairs that went to the kitchen. Right now, it was simply arranged with three tables in a horseshoe pattern, but Alex imagined that with the right decorations it was a very nice place to hold a celebration.

"This will do," Morgana said. She stepped into the room and nodded as she studied the layout. A large white screen was set up opposite the tables, and Alex prayed that Merlin didn't have a PowerPoint presentation to show them. "This will fit everyone comfortably, and we can control the entrances." She reached into her purse and pulled out a drawstring bag. "Iron shavings," Morgana said. "Just in case."

"I'm not sure if that makes me feel better or worse." Nicki started pacing out the walls thoughtfully. "There's not much we can do to make this safe, is there?"

"The point is a peaceful conversation," Avani reminded them. Pulling out her phone, she started sending a text. "I'll let Lance and Jenny know we made it here safe."

"I still don't like this," Nicki said. A scowl had taken over her features. "Arthur was more than happy to use a bomb."

"Please don't say things like that," Aiden said.

They all turned to find Merlin, Aiden, and Bran walking into the room. Aiden's bag was over one shoulder, and he walked like a calm and relaxed man. His eyes gave away his worry though, and Nicki nodded to him. Bran smiled at her and moved to one of the tables. He dropped his bag in a chair and pulled something out of the front pocket. It took Alex a moment to recognize it as his deck of tarot cards.

"No problems on the drive?" Morgana asked Merlin.

"No, everything went well enough." Merlin walked further into the room and studied it. "This will do. Neutral territory and breathing room. Better than some places we've had such meetings."

"What about the Old Ones?" Bran asked. "We aren't that close to the river? Are they walking up?"

"Robin agreed to oversee their arrival." Morgana's nose curled slightly at the words and Alex had to choke back a laugh. At least she was using Puck's chosen modern name. There was some respect there, despite what Morgana might claim. "I believe they have scheduled their arrivals and will be driving the rest of the way."

Nicki froze and blinked. Then she blinked again. Then she started to laugh. "Members of the Norse Pantheon, the Hindu Pantheon, and the

Trickster Puck all in the same car. Sounds like the start of a joke or a weird story."

Aiden snorted in response, and Bran pointedly worked with his cards. Resisting the urge to creep closer, Alex decided trying to read the future was best left to Bran rather than her trying to analyze the meaning of the artwork on the cards. Watching his face, Alex waited for anything, even horror and fear. Instead, he just frowned slightly and narrowed his eyes.

"Anything?" Aiden asked.

"No." Bran shrugged and gathered up the cards. "No visions, and nothing clear here." He held up the world card for them to see. "This keeps coming up, but I'm not sure what to make of it."

"Let's hope that is a good sign," Avani offered. Her cheerfulness was forced, but Alex was oddly reassured by it.

"That's enough of that," Merlin said. "Why don't you children find your rooms and relax for a little bit. Morgana and I will see to the rest of the setup."

Alex chafed under the dismissal. Several of the voices gave their protests, but she quickly recognized that lingering here wasn't going to do any good. Meditating in her room might help her get through this. Morgana quickly handed out keys that had the numbers marked on them while Merlin tried to convince Nicki once again that everything was fine. Even Avani was struggling to calm her girlfriend. Alex paused at that thought. Was it too soon to call Avani Nicki's girlfriend? She was pretty sure that they were actually dating when they went out for lunch together, but she was rusty on the whole dating thing.

Pushing the thought and the memories that followed away, Alex grabbed her stuff and headed down the hallway. While the halls all looked very similar, there were small golden plates fixed to the walls with numbers and arrows on them. Already Alex was discovering that this place was larger than it seemed from the outside. Behind her, she heard the others talking and glanced back. Bran had his bag and gave her a small wave and smile.

"Hey."

"Hi," Alex said. "Plans?"

"I'm going to try and meditate again." Bran shrugged. "It just feels like I should be able to get something."

"I know what you mean."

They walked a short distance together before finding Bran's door. He hesitated after slipping the key into the lock. Then he seemed to decide against what he'd been going to say.

"See you later," Alex offered.

"Yeah, don't get into any trouble."

Bran held her gaze for a moment before slipping into room number seven. Alex glanced down at her key. Room thirteen. That wasn't a bad omen at all. She headed further down the hall only to hit a staircase with a sign directing her up. Alex only grumbled briefly before heading upstairs and finding herself in another hallway. But the other person in the hall made her freeze.

Arthur stood at the far end of the hallway. Sunlight poured in through the window behind him, making his blond hair almost gold. His blue eyes were wide with surprise at seeing her. His hair was cut short again and neatly combed. He wore a blue button-down shirt that made his eyes pop. For a moment Alex forgot. Her heart jumped, and she reached for Cathanáil. Then he raised his hands in a gesture of peace.

"Please, wait," he said. His voice was a little deeper than she remembered. "I mean you no harm, Iron Soul. I did not mean to startle you."

Slowly, without taking her eyes off of him, Alex lowered her hand away from the hilt of her Sword. The voices were deafening, everyone was shouting at once, and she couldn't understand anything. It was a mess, and her own emotions were no help as they churned in her chest like the sea in a hurricane.

"I'm sorry," the Light said once again. His voice shifted just enough that it was believable. "I didn't mean to startle you." It shook its head and slowly walked towards her. "There's so much that I want to tell you, that I need to explain, but I want- I need you to understand that I'm sorry about what happened."

"Arthur wasn't your fault." The words were bitter on her tongue, but they felt true.

"No, not about the boy." The Light shook his head. "When you were taken over. I'm sorry. That was a mistake. It was driven by fear and nothing more."

"What do you know about that?" Alex took a step back, narrowing her eyes and resisting the urge to draw her weapon.

"It's... complicated." The Light lowered its eyes and sighed. It was so human. "I will explain, but my kind are different than anything you're used to. At least in higher life forms." A dry chuckle escaped the being. "Different universes, different rules."

His behavior, his unease, and his guilt were almost human. Alex was left staring at him, unsure of what to say or do. Around them, the hallway was silent and still. Arthur- the Light, lowered its hands and took a step back.

"There's so much..." He trailed off, seeming lost for a moment.

"Yes, well, you'll have a chance to speak later," Alex said. "To everyone," she added.

Walking down the hallway, Alex was hyper-aware that he was behind her and her heart raced painfully. She wanted to go home. This territory had no protections, no defenses. Suddenly, she was all too conscious that there was a staff here. Those people might be harmed if this went badly. Maybe the mages should agree on casting a spell to set off the fire alarm if something went wrong.

Or maybe she just needed to accept that this was going to suck. She found room thirteen, opened the door, and locked it behind her.

8

The Unusual Assemblage

Everything was proceeding smoothly. Pu-Robin had arrived with the other Old Ones in tow, though it took her two trips in her small sedan. The mages had all refreshed themselves in their rooms, and Timothy's group of Fae had slipped in quietly while he had muddled the mind of the hotel manager. Merlin felt a touch bad that it was necessary, but if they didn't then there would have been no rooms for the Fae and that would have started everything off on a sour note. Shiva had even escorted three Demons who represented three of the main families that lived in India. Merlin had been a bit surprised. He and Morgana had little experience with the Demons, thanks to Shiva largely overseeing India.

Maybe in his next identity, he should give event planning a go. He'd never worked in that industry before. It might be a nice change. Then again, he'd heard that it was stressful, and if things didn't quiet down then juggling the schedule would be difficult. Already it was proving a challenge to make all of his classes, attend department meetings, and tend to his duties as a mage. Merlin longed for the days when being a mage was in itself a job, and the community made sure that you had food and necessities. It was just one more way that the world had grown more complex.

The meeting room and their guests were ready. Each faction had been given its own area to ensure no one felt caged in. The Old Ones were a bit more complicated as their loyalties varied greatly, but Merlin was optimistic. This idea of Alex's might prove to be very useful, even if Morgana was still hesitant.

The problem was Alex. She'd retreated into herself and frequently sported the glassy-eyed expression that he'd come to understand was her listening to the voices of her past selves. It was uncomfortable to realize that she could speak with Arto, that dear boy who had lived so long ago, while Merlin could not. There was so much that he would have said to Arto if he had the chance. And to Michel, that boy that he and Morgana raised together, but who never really escaped Arto's shadow. He would have liked to apologize if he ever made Michel feel that he didn't matter.

He couldn't though. Alex was more than a conduit for him, but that didn't stop his occasional fantasies. Right now, Alex was sitting in her spot, and while her eyes were clear, she was slumped over. Nervous and glancing at the door frequently, she looked ready to run, like an animal trapped where it knew there was danger. Morgana was watching her as their guests filed into the room, so Merlin did his best to put his worries away. He was a Grand Mage; the best thing he could do for Alex now was take the attention off of her until she recovered her footing.

Sif entered the room first. She looked completely human at the moment and had charmed the hotel receptionist with her slight accent. Her long golden hair was done up in an elegant crown braid that looked too formal for the jeans and sweater that she wore. Baldr was escorting his sister, dressed in a simple button-down shirt and slacks that were very nondescript. His blond hair was still long but tied back in a simple leather band. Robin was behind them, wearing a purple dress with a collection of bracelets on her right arm. If there was significance to them, it was lost on Merlin.

It took him a little time to properly recognize the other Old Ones. Anansi had thankfully taken on a much more human appearance and looked like a tall black man with the slightest hint of white in his short dark hair. He wore a brightly colored robe that would certainly stand out in the memories of the human hotel staff. To Merlin's amusement, in one of the broad stripes of the robe was a line of small spiders that looked to be weaving the rest of the fabric. He didn't know where or how Anansi had gotten the garment, but it suited him.

Stepping forward, he extended his hand to Baldr who quickly shook it. The Old One smiled slightly at him as Merlin turned and took Sif's hand to kiss.

"Greetings to you both," Merlin said. "Thank you for coming."

"Thank you for the invitation," Sif replied. "I think that this gathering is very wise in light of what seems to be happening."

"I fear that Father has already returned to the waters," Baldr added. "We considered waking him, but his temper was short when he woke earlier. He deemed it necessary to continue resting."

"While we shall miss your father's insight, I am grateful as always that Odin remains so concerned about his state and the safety of the Iron Realm."

The two Old Ones nodded and moved to allow Robin to step forward. Given that he had seen her recently, she settled on a quick nod and wink before making a beeline for Aiden. Merlin barely kept himself from frowning. He hoped for everyone's sake that Robin understood what she was doing attempting to court a mage. Her relationship with Michel had been bad enough, but Nicki was very protective of Aiden, and the last thing they needed was for Robin to do something stupid. Then again,

Robin paused and said something to Alex that made the young woman relax a little. Maybe the old trickster wasn't completely hopeless.

"Merlin," Anansi greeted. His deep voice rolled over Merlin, and he found himself calming down. "Thank you for the invitation. Puck's report was worrying."

"Hopefully we will find a solution quickly," Merlin said. He shook Anansi's hand. "Thank you for coming. I know it is a great distance."

"It was easier for me than most." Anansi chuckled. "Lake Victoria provides an easy means of water travel."

They shared a smile, and Merlin relaxed a little. Anansi had never been a problem. He'd been a friend of Cyrridven and had taken her warning about resting in the waters very seriously. Suffering a pang of grief, Merlin found himself wishing that he'd made a better point in keeping in touch with Cyrridven over the years. He missed her more than he'd ever imagined possible. At this juncture, her wisdom and insight would have been greatly valued. He found himself glancing towards Alex. Cyrridven had seen fit to give her life protecting one incarnation of the Iron Soul, a being that she knew would return. Merlin had never thought about what that might mean, but now he found himself wondering if his mentor had seen something before she came to pass on Cathanáil. Anansi moved to join Robin, who introduced him to the younger mages. Nicki was clearly fascinated by him, and Merlin returned his attention to the other arrivals.

Sun Wukong was an Old One that Merlin had only ever met on three occasions. The first had been organized by Shiva so that the Grand Mages knew the Old One who had chosen to watch over what was now China. The second had been a random encounter in the Middle East during the 14th century. Merlin had been living there, and Sun Wukong had been hunting a particularly stubborn and violent demon that had fled the east.

The third had been when a Demon army rallied during the Opium War and tried to use the chaos to carve out a kingdom for themselves. He and Morgana had arrived only to find the army already broken and scattered, thanks to the region's Old Ones.

Today, Sun Wukong appeared as a tall, broad shouldered Chinese man. He walked with a slight swagger and possessed an easy-going smile. Dressed in simple red linen clothing, he lacked the bright reddish facial hair and monkey-like features that he usually adopted. Merlin only knew who he was for certain thanks to the red staff that he carried. He'd long wondered about that staff, and how many of the legends surrounding it were true. Morgana believed that it was an extension of his true self rather than a separate item, but Merlin was uncertain.

"Greetings, Merlin," Sun Wukong said. "Thank you for the invitation."

"Thank you for coming," Merlin replied eagerly. "I'm very grateful to have your knowledge and outlook to call upon."

Sun Wukong raised an eyebrow. His face was that of a man in his late thirties and reflected his amusement, but his dark brown eyes were sharp and thoughtful.

"Then I am glad to be of service."

He said nothing more and slipped past Merlin, stopping to greet Morgana. He'd always been an odd one, shifting from warlike to wise as needed. At least Demons and other dangers to humanity had always been his only targets. Merlin heard Bran greet Sun Wukong and held back a chuckle of amusement at Bran's excitement.

Shiva had also opted for a human appearance, though his skin still retained a slightly blue tint. Even after centuries, the Old One had yet to escape the mark of his prior tainting. Yet, Shiva seemed unbothered by it and had even worn blue clothing, which only highlighted the quirk of his appearance. In his right hand he carried the Iron Trishula, which glowed gently with power. Behind him were three humanoid figures that were a bit larger than average. They all looked human, but there was something off about their facial features that instantly confirmed for Merlin that they were demons under their guises.

It was odd to Merlin. The Sídhe were a race that had gained mastery over the magic they generated when they entered the Iron Realm. He remembered their magic users and the damage they were capable of. When the Iron Gates had cut off their empire from the Iron Realm they had lost their magic, but the Demons still retained the ability to alter their appearance. Until recent years, he'd had no answer, but now he was fairly certain that it was just an aspect of their biology and not magical at all. Sadly, there never seemed to be a good time to ask. The relationship was too strained.

This was the time to change that. Merlin did his best to appear friendly and unconcerned as Shiva introduced the Demons in rapid succession. The tall older woman was Rushita, the small thin woman was Jisha, and the short, stout man with the boxy jaw was Prajval.

They sounded like human names. Merlin was strangely pleased by the reminder that this was the only home they'd ever known. He'd heard from the young mages of course that the Demon King had been forcing the longtime residents to give him information, but this little reminder soothed one of his many worries. He greeted all of them politely and with a more real smile than he'd originally intended.

"Thank you for coming, Shiva." He shook the Old One's hand. "And thank you for helping the young ones while they were in India."

"I had never seen Cathanáil with my own eyes," Shiva replied. "But I can understand why it's recovery was a victory. I am pleased to say that those Demons who came with violence in their hearts have either hidden or are dead."

"I never doubted that would be the result." Then Merlin turned back to the Demons. "You are most welcome here. Thank you for being willing to come and offer your thoughts."

They moved on, and Merlin smiled as Timothy came bouncing out of a bag carried by one of the Fae. There were two Sídhe descendants, two Pixies, and Timothy. It was far from a good mix of representation, but it was a start. The Sídhe descendants lowered their hoods, revealing their pale skin. Violet eyes met his own and Merlin couldn't help but notice the fear in them. It shouldn't please him, but it did.

"Greetings to you," Merlin said. Then just to be welcoming, he added. "You are safe here. Our history is unimportant in the face of the issue before us."

Timothy grinned, but the others were not as reassured. It was a pity. He had hoped that Timothy's residence with the younger mages would help calm some of the tensions, but he supposed not everyone was so willing to let go of old hurts. Watching them move on, he noted that only Timothy and one Pixie stopped to greet Morgana.

Then came the Light. It had hung back to allow the Fae to enter without him being too close. Merlin inwardly approved of the move, given what Arthur's actions had cost the Fae. He and Morgana didn't have a real estimate of the population of the Fae, but he was certain that Arthur's attempts at war had cut them down considerably.

The Light nodded. His-its posture was straight and formal in a way that even Arthur's most poised moments had never managed. Arthur's hair had been cut back and was neatly combed. While not in a suit, the creature was in a button-down shirt and dress pants. The visual difference to the Arthur they had thought they'd known was appreciated.

"Greetings, Grand Mage Merlin." The Light inclined its head. Arthur had never been so formal. "I thank you for hosting this meeting. It is an opportunity for all sapient species to discuss our plights in peace. You have my gratitude."

"You are welcome here." The Light began to step forward, but Merlin caught its arm. Lowering his voice, he added, "But try nothing. You wear the face of an enemy, and any hint of a threat towards one of my students is enough for me to end you."

Confusion flashed across the Light's face, but then it was gone quickly. "Understood."

Merlin released the Light's arm. The body was cooler than it should have been, and he frowned as he watched it move. Was Arthur's body even alive any longer? What was this creature's power over the physical form? There were too many questions, and they grated on his nerves, stinging like salt in an open wound.

As he closed and sealed the door, Merlin took a breath to center himself. This was new. So many different species all in one place... The only one missing was the dragon Emrys, and there was simply no way to manage that in person, even though Alex had the Iron Chalice ready to attempt contact. It was almost enough to make him laugh, but he took his seat with Morgana. Suddenly, as he looked around, he regretted not adding a fourth table. Maybe everyone would have felt better if they'd all had their own distinct table.

"Thank you all for attending this meeting." Morgana folded her hands neatly in front of her, and her Triskelion necklace gleamed in the artificial light. "Now, many of you have heard already that we are concerned about a corrosive force that has taken hold in the Tree of Reality. It is only known as the Darkness, but it has now reached the Demon homeworld and triggered an invasion of the Iron Realm." Morgana paused and her face twisted for a moment with disgust. "It is also theorized that this Darkness is what drove the Sídhe into their long series of invasions. Our goal at this conference is to share information and find a way to stop this threat before it causes any more damage."

The Light raised its hand, drawing everyone's attention to him. Merlin grit his teeth. It wasn't ideal for him to start, but they couldn't ignore him. Morgana tensed but gestured for him to start. Alex flinched, her face paling slightly. He saw Bran's arm move, but his hands were below the line of the table.

"I do not believe that there are any here who are not aware of the fact that this world is only one of many. There is no clear information as to how the Tree of Reality came to be, but it links worlds with sapient life throughout multiple universes together." The Light paused, licking Arthur's lips thoughtfully. "These worlds were not meant to meet, and seek to repel each other. And yet, the Iron Realm is now home to creatures from many different worlds and several different branches. Why? The answer is that many have been fleeing the death of their worlds for centuries if not longer. The memories I have from the half Sídhe, half human Arthur indicate that his creator spoke of leading her people away from the Darkness. It was a closely guarded secret. The rulers before her hid the problem, and she sought to take the Iron Realm as the next stage, as a way to ensure survival."

Merlin looked around the table. The others were watching the Light with cautious interest. Nothing he was saying was news to Merlin, but the Fae were listening carefully, as was Shiva. He realized with a grimace that they'd neglected to brief some of the others on the situation properly. Then again, far more people were involved now than had ever been before.

"Many of us do know this," Sif said. Her sweet voice had an undertone of warning. "What is it that you truly wish to say?"

"The Iron Realm cannot keep being a haven for all that come here," The Light answered. He folded his hands on the table and looked around. "Those here except for myself have been here a long time. Some born," he nodded to Sif and the Fae. "And others displaced here, but it all affects this world. The mages have put up defenses in the form of their Iron Gates, but I am proof that there are ways around even those defenses."

Merlin glanced towards Alex. So far, she was staying calmly in her seat. Her face was a blank mask, and her eyes were almost distant. Worry percolated in his chest. It was difficult to imagine that she didn't care about this gathering.

"And what matter of being are you?" Shiva asked. "You are not Arthur. When I look at you, I see a twisting mass inside a corpse."

Grimacing, Merlin tried not to let his shock show. He'd had no idea that the Old Ones could see such things.

"I am a being of light," it replied. "My kind is very different, from all that I have gathered of you. I slipped out of my world when the Darkness came and into this one through the Mage that I now wear." It paused and seemed to consider for a moment. "My physiology is very different from yours, but I mean no harm to any here."

There were thoughtful looks exchanged around the table. Merlin wasn't sure if he felt that the creature had sidestepped the question or not.

"Very well, we will hear your suggestions," Shiva said. "But you are unknown to us." In his hand, the Trishula glowed softly.

"Shiva," Sif whispered.

The Trishula stopped glowing, and the Light nodded to Sif. "Allow me to speak, Lord Shiva," the Light began again. "I will answer any questions that any of you might have. I am only trying to set the stage, I believe it is called, for my proposal. It is... radical, to say the least, but I firmly believe it is our best chance. While Arthur sought power, recognition, and purpose, I only seek to save what can still be saved in the Tree of Reality."

Alex spoke up, her gray eyes fixed on the Light. "So, what is your proposal?"

"Break the links between the Iron Realm and the Tree of Reality," the Light answered.

The floor seemed to give out beneath Merlin. Somehow the words were not real. He blinked and replayed them, trying to understand what the Light was saying. Leaning forward, he heard a collective intake of breath and saw numerous expressions of confusion. It was not just him then.

"I'm sorry," he said, "can you repeat that?"

"The Iron Soul used the magical Iron Hammer to break the magical links between the Iron Chain and the Fae," the Light said. "Similar, though stronger, links bind the Iron Realm with the rest of the Tree of Reality. I propose that it is the purpose, the true purpose, of the Iron Soul, to break those links and free the Iron Realm from the threat of Darkness." While Merlin was staring at the Light in stunned silence, the being leaned forward. "Arthur knew how strange a female incarnation was. This form can take the magic of others and put it to use, and there are more mages now than ever. Surely these changes mean something."

"No," Alex said. She shook her head, drawing the attention of everyone at the table. "We have no idea what the side effects would be." The Light narrowed its eyes slightly at her, but Alex didn't flinch. "You're not wrong about the connections between The Iron Realm and the rest of the Tree of Reality. We're the trunk; we connect to all of the branches at their roots. But there are..." Alex struggled for a moment. "Lights, beneath our world. We don't know if they are other worlds, but I don't think so. I'm not even sure how many there are, but they seem to be the source of the energy that travels through our world into the others. If the link is cut, we don't know what all that power will do to Earth. We might escape the Darkness only to cook ourselves. We don't know enough about the nature of the Tree of Reality."

"But the Darkness is coming," the Fae said. "Isn't that worth the risk?"

Watching Alex carefully, Merlin could see that she was struggling with something. He prayed that she didn't bring up the poison. That was the last thing they needed. Even their allies around the table would be horrified to learn that they had such a thing, that Merlin had kept such a thing secret for so long. Then Alex shook her head.

"We aren't in any position to make that decision," Alex said. "The Darkness is still moving, but it is slow. There may be hundreds of years before it reaches us. And at that point, with some dedicated research, we might have a better idea of what we're dealing with."

Merlin frowned in disappointment. Radical, yes, but perhaps the idea had some merit.

9

The Purple Spark

33 C.E. Bighorn Mountains

4 The Elder didn't know what to make of it. The old man had listened carefully, and for that Akule was grateful. He explained everything that he knew, talked about his first glimpse of the dark spots, and his growing worry. The Elder nodded from time to time, looking thoughtful. There was no inference that he was mad, and he could see the consideration in the old man's brown eyes. Tapichi had always been fair. Their band was lucky to have him. He knew how to bind wounds and the oldest of their stories. Yet, he had no explanation for this. Akule could see the man's confusion and worry before he ever spoke.

"I shall consult with the spirits, Akule," the Elder promised. "This sounds like the work of dark spirits, but what their goal is...that is a mystery."

"We should leave," Caphan said. He shifted nervously behind Akule, just out of his line of sight. "That's the best way forward, isn't it?"

"We can leave," Tapichi agreed. "And we will soon follow our game." The Elder looked into the small fire and frowned. "But I do not know if we can run from this."

"It's growing," Akule reminded Caphan. He finally turned to look at the brother of his wife. His features were pinched and his dark eyes kept jumping between Akule and Tapichi. "I don't think it's that simple."

"Yes." Tapichi nodded, using a stick to stoke the fire up. "Your brother has found something very dangerous. I do not have the answers you seek."

"Then what should we do?" Caphan asked.

"We must be wary of acting too quickly," Tapichi answered. "Haste could lead us to ruin. For now, make sure that everyone stays away from it."

"What about that cloud that only Akule could see?" Caphan demanded. "I don't see a haze."

"It's there," Akule insisted. "And it's dangerous!"

"Yes," Tapichi said. He held up a hand. "No one should go near it. We'll leave soon, and I'll send out messengers to the other Elders. We will meet and discuss what to do to appease the spirits."

That wasn't right. The words almost jumped from Akule's mouth. That wasn't enough. That wasn't the solution. Certainty burned in his chest beneath that dull ache he'd been carrying for the last few days. Worry, fear and desperation all fought for dominance, but only cold silence won. He couldn't explain it. He'd tried, but clearly, something wasn't translating.

"Elder, I fear that's not enough." His mouth was almost too dry to speak.

"Akule, you have done well, but this matter is in the hands of the spirits." Tapichi's voice was warm, thoughtful, and considerate, but Akule still wanted to lash out. "Go and rest. This burden is not yours to carry."

Wrong. That was wrong. Even now, he could see the dark spot. It pulsed in the corner of his eye, despite being out of his line of sight. The

Elder was worried too but trying to stay calm. Panic wouldn't help. He met Akule's eyes with a stern gaze that demanded obedience. Akule was sure that Tapichi knew how worried he was. It was probably clear in his eyes, but he nodded in spite of it.

Caphan had to help him to his feet. The world was quaking. There was something here, but it slipped just beyond his reach. Nonetheless, he nodded to the Elder and quickly took his leave from the small hut they'd been talking in. Suddenly he was very grateful that the Elder had demanded privacy. Panic amongst the band wouldn't help at all.

Stepping outside into the light, he took in a deep breath and willed himself to relax. Caphan was still beside him, and Akule could feel the weight of the other man's gaze.

"Sorry," Akule said. "I didn't mean to find trouble."

"I know." Caphan paused and squeezed his shoulder. "Just be careful. Please, and if not for your sake then for your family. I would hate to see my sister without her husband."

The underlying fondness shined through, and Akule nodded gratefully. Someday, he and his family would have to shift away from the same band as Caphan so their children could interact with others, but he was grateful that they were together for now. He promised himself to enjoy it while it lasted. However, even those warm thoughts weren't enough to distract him completely.

The sun was shining in the sky, still high above the horizon as the summer solstice approached them. It was warm, even this far up, and the world should have been pleasant. The high heats of summer had not yet begun, and yet Akule was filled with dread. With each moment, he felt compelled to return to the dark spots, but the Elder's confusion left him fearful.

Dark spirits. It was possible of course, but Akule was doubtful. This wasn't directed. He sensed no guiding hand when he thought of the dark patch. When he'd been near it, there had been no malice. Maybe he was arrogant for assuming that he'd even notice such a thing, but the thought was there. He couldn't help but wonder. Was this truly a dark spirit, or just some raw force of nature? The line had always been blurry to him. In the past he'd been able to count on the words of the Elders, to take comfort from his mother's stories and believe that the friendly spirits would protect him, but now he wasn't sure. If the Elder was wrong and they ignored it, then who knew what would happen. That strange spot would only grow larger and larger.

Doubt. It sank into his flesh. It curled around his heart, and that odd ache that had been plaguing him suddenly eased. Akule frowned and closed his eyes, inhaling deeply. It was true, it was suddenly better as if reacting to his doubt. That made no sense; surely his doubts should make him weaker. Yet, the pain had eased. There was a strange flutter, like a butterfly brushing against his heart. It tickled and alarmed him. But somehow, it felt safe. The more that ache eased, the more it fluttered like it was a living thing.

Why did his doubt matter? Why did it release this flutter? Was it the dark spot, or something else? More questions that he didn't think the Elders would have the answers to. Caphan moved off, leaving him with his thoughts. Some hunters had returned with a new elk that was being skinned by a group of women. Children were playing or helping with small chores nearby.

His feet moved before he fully considered it. Without a word to anyone, he walked to the edge of camp and followed a small trail that he'd cut through the grasses up the hillside. Standing next to the rocky outcropping, he could see the dark spot in the distance. It mocked him. It mocked the Elder and their stories.

"Akule?"

He turned to find Hakola carrying a basket with roots. She was studying him with a guarded expression that he hated. Opening his mouth, he tried to find some words, but nothing came forth. How could he explain these odd feelings churning in his chest? How could he voice the dread creeping over him? Akule didn't know how he didn't even know where to start.

Hakola touched his arm gently. "Don't go back there, Akule. Please. You've told the Elder, and we'll be leaving soon. Caphan told me that he believed you, that he listened. Isn't that enough?"

"It was growing." Shaking his head, he dropped his eyes to his hands and watched as he clenched them into fists. "I saw it. I see it all the time-"

"We'll be leaving-"

"No, Hakola," he interrupted. "You don't understand. I'm sorry, but I see it all the time. At night I dream of it and... horrible visions." Shuddering, he met his wife's eyes. "It haunts me and calls to me, all at once. There is danger there. It cannot be ignored."

"Akule..."

Watching her doubt and worry dance across her face ached like an antler slicing through the flesh of a leg. The scar on his left leg throbbed at the memory, but somehow this hurt worse. He wished he could know what she was thinking. Then again, that knowledge may be what finally broke him down into tears.

"I'm worried," she finally said. "I know you dream of it. You haven't had a quiet night since the first day you saw it. The things you say..."

"What do I say?"

"You whisper about a dead world." A dark, violet sky and a plain of ash flashed to the front of his memory. "You cry out in fear, and I don't know what to do." Then she touched his face gently, her soft calluses brushing across his jaw. "I believe you, I do, but is it so wrong for me to not want my husband and the father of my children to approach a place plagued by dark spirits?"

"I know." And he did. Akule didn't want to go back there, but it was calling to him. Some instinct was urging him to fight through his fear and confusion and learn what was happening. "I don't want to go back, but I feel that I must."

"Why?"

"There is something I need to learn."

The words filled up the empty space between them, but Akule still wished that he could take them back. Hakola's eyes dimmed. She was afraid. He didn't blame her. Even now, with her by his side, there was still an urge, a need to go and check on the dead patch. He didn't know what he could learn there that he hadn't already, but there was something more.

"I want to stop you." Hakola's eyes gleamed with tears that she held back. "This worries me. I want to stop you, but you won't thank me for that."

"I might," Akule whispered.

"No, you won't." She touched his face again and nodded. "Please be careful." Her voice was so soft that the wind almost carried her plea away. "I love you. Don't let this..." She trailed off and shook her head. "Come home tonight."

"I will," he promised. That was an easy promise. He had no desire to remain in that area after night fell. "I love you."

Then he turned back to the dark patch before the urge to stay could overwhelm the persistent itch to go and check the hillside. It was strange, he reflected as he walked; as a child he'd never envisioned himself as brave. He was a decent hunter, but it was Caphan who had the talent. He'd been fascinated by the stories as a child but had never been the most in tune with the spirits. Something was changing. Akule didn't know where the change was coming from, but the trigger, the reason for it was clear. The flutter in his chest that seemed to respond to his thoughts and determination.

He kept walking. The flutter grew stronger with each step. Feeling it pulse in his chest, through his heart, and down his arms was an alien sensation, but somehow that wasn't what frightened him. Akule almost remembered it, as if it was a memory from a dream. It was so strong that he was certain he could have reached out and touched it.

Then he saw it again. His trembling legs threatened to give out under his weight. Even at this distance, he was certain that it was larger than before. Akule took a deep breath and walked forward. The quiet stretched out around him. There were few birds. Out of the corner of his eye he noticed a bush now heavy with berries, and yet nothing had approached it. Whatever this place was, the animals shared his fear.

Stopping near the edge, Akule studied the circle. It HAD grown. Not a huge amount, but it had. The depth thankfully wasn't much worse, but the haze above the hole was thicker. He longed to fill the gap in but knew that it would do no good. He couldn't hide it or bury it. That hideous fog, that poisonous slow drip that he saw in his dreams, would destroy anything he put in its path. It was no wonder that the animals were afraid.

Sniffing at the air, Akule searched it for any scent that would give him a clue. There was nothing. It wasn't even that there were only familiar smells; everything was suppressed. Terror flashed through him, and the ache threatened to overtake the flutter. Akule swallowed and closed his eyes. There was nothing to hear. He was lost in the dark, with nothing around him. Had he not felt the ground beneath his feet then he might have screamed in fear. This was unnatural. The world was not meant to be so still and silent.

He exhaled, relishing the small sound it made. His huff lingered in the thick air. None of this made sense to him, but Akule kept his eyes closed. The flutter was shifting, and the ache was fading quickly. His unease, fear, and doubts remained, but it was a little easier now. He inhaled slowly, concentrating on the sound of his heartbeat and trying to clear his mind. There had to be something he could learn here.

If it was spirits, maybe they would speak to him if he didn't show fear. He inhaled and exhaled slowly, urging himself to relax and pay attention. Then he heard it: a strange, soft sound that seemed to come from the haze itself. It was faint, but there was a soft crunching sound, like dried out leaves being walked on. Was that the sound of dark spirits, or was it something else?

Then beneath his feet, he felt a pulse — a gentle beat like that of a heart. In his chest, the flutter transformed, blooming like a flower into a small spark. In his mind's eye, Akule could see the purple spark pulsing in time with the beat beneath him. Slowly, he knelt and touched the ground. The purple spark grew, and Akule was aware of the last of the lingering ache vanishing completely.

10

A Light Against the Dark

The Light's words crashed over Alex's shoulders like a cold splash of water, seeping into her bones, and running down her back. She waited a heartbeat for the punchline, but it didn't come. Alex stared at him, at the strange creature, unsure of what to even think. Bran's grip on her hand beneath the table tightened, and he helped ground her back in reality. Her mouth was dry, and she was shocked that she'd managed her initial reply at all.

"We should discuss this in full," Merlin said.

Eyes widening, Alex almost yelled at the older mage. How could he possibly entertain such a notion? Breaking the branches off the Tree of Reality; the very idea made her cold and scared.

"We need more information," Alex said once again. She tried to inject more authority into her voice. "There could be side effects."

"Worlds are dying!" The Light hissed. For an instant its calm was gone and it leaned forward, fixing Arthur's bright blue eyes on her. "There isn't time to wait!"

"I know that worlds are dying," Alex said. "I was aware of the Darkness first and have been investigating it, but we can't risk breaking reality in our fear."

For a heartbeat the room stilled. Alex's magic flared in response to so many creatures from other worlds. She blinked, and the world dimmed. Her magic stretched out and swept over all the beings, outlining them in colors that reflected their alien nature. Beside her, Bran glowed yellow. Nicki glowed blue, and Aiden red. It was familiar, but there were so many others.

The Light was a fluid swirl of dark blue, twisting around as if confined. Trapped in Arthur's shape. It wasn't like the Old Ones, who were their own shapes at least. She swallowed and let the magic dissipate. All the creatures were still looking thoughtful, and Sif was studying the Light with cold eyes. Shiva's skin was growing bluer by the moment, and he gently spun the Trishula, making the gleaming iron catch the light of the ceiling lamps.

"I understand your concerns," the Light said slowly. It was judging its words carefully. Alex tried not to let that bother her, but it did. "I do, but I have just watched a world be consumed in a tidal wave of the Darkness. I can't watch it happen again." Its voice caught on the last sentence and Alex had to suppress a shudder.

"A passionate plea," Morgana observed, coldly. "And we will listen, but perhaps it is best to start with information about what you are and provide us with context."

Everyone at the tables shifted at the cool tone. The Fae looked ready to run for the door, but Timothy said something too soft for her to hear. They stayed. The Demons exchanged nervous glances, but stayed in their seats. Alex felt a bit sorry for them. The recent invasion had put them in danger, and this likely wasn't helping them feel more secure. Thankfully, the Old Ones at least seemed calm. Sif's body language was tense even as she kept her hands folded on the table. Baldr was relaxed in his chair, but he was watching the Light intently. Shiva's grip on the

Trishula hadn't loosened, and Alex wondered if they should have made him leave it behind. Then again, the only reason she hadn't left the room to get away from the Light was that she had Cathanáil on her back.

"Your proposal is radical indeed," Baldr said. Alex glanced at the Demons and the Fae; they were still silent. "But surely you can understand our worries. The reason why the Tree of Reality even exists is a mystery to this day. If it serves a purpose, then breaking the connection could lead to disaster."

"Not breaking it will certainly lead to disaster."

"And what of the other worlds?" Sif asked. "We might destroy them."

"They are already doomed," the Light insisted. "I'm sorry, but that is the truth at the heart of this matter." It gestured towards the Demons. "Their kind staged an invasion the instant they found a way through. Even though the portal led to water, they were willing to try. Does that not tell you the danger they are in? The Demon's world isn't that far from this one." Then he folded his hands once again. "And the Sídhe are a long-standing danger in this world. The Queen was seeking a way to destroy the Iron Gates and let her people through. If the Darkness has reached the Demon world, then it may already be in the nearest Sídhe world."

Muttering broke out amongst the Fae delegation. Timothy nodded at one whisper, more serious than Alex had ever seen him before. Her stomach tightened and her throat constricted as bile tried to push its way up. She needed to speak up again. Needed to say something, but all she had to go on was a sense of dread. Merlin caught her gaze.

'Do not tell them about the poison.'

His command came through loud and clear without Alex needing to use any magic. She briefly wondered if it was possible to read the thoughts of the Light. Alex hadn't tried that form of magic in months, too distressed by the idea of someone doing it to her. But Merlin's attention was back on the Light, and Alex knew that if it was possible, he would probably try it.

"My kind are not like any of you," the Light said. Alex forced herself to look at it again. She couldn't afford to miss critical information, not now. "We are beings that are energy, tied together by will."

"That's not dissimilar to us." Baldr was frowning and didn't seem impressed.

"Similar, yes," the Light agreed. "I believe we come from the same branch of the Tree of Reality, but there are more differences than similarities." Then the Light paused, scanning the room to make sure that everyone was looking at him. "We separate, similar to your single-celled organisms on Earth. When we are large enough, we just split apart. But if we are hurt, we can also merge together. Rejoin in order to regain enough energy to keep ourselves together."

Chatter broke out around the room. Alex glanced at Bran, who was frowning and studying the Light with great concentration. She looked at Nicki and found her glaring at the Light. Alex wondered if it was the Light or Arthur's body that she was glaring so fiercely at.

"Merge," Bran repeated. "What does that entail?"

"Well, our essences combine, the memories blend together, and all knowledge becomes shared." The Light was looking at Bran oddly. Alex didn't like it. "I fear that it is a touch difficult to explain." Gesturing to its head, it almost seemed frustrated. "There aren't words that properly describe it. They and I become me. When times are peaceful and we can absorb energy, there are millions of us, but when things become dangerous and difficult our numbers drop as we join together to pool our knowledge." The Light swept his eyes around the horseshoe. "The

Darkness caused such a time. I am the result of thousands of us joining together in a short span of time. It swallowed everything."

"Was that how you survived when Arthur didn't?" Bran asked. "Energy from the Sword, or..." Alex saw him tense, and he glanced her way. "Or merging with the remains of another one of your kind?"

She understood what he was asking — that spark from her fingertips when she'd touched Arthur's body. They'd beaten the Light controlling her, but maybe there'd been something left. Just enough to transfer and restore the Light in Arthur. Maybe they'd combined into this Light.

The Light looked right at her, locking their gazes, and then he nodded. "You are correct. Two escaped into this world, but now there is only one. The crossing was difficult. Adjusting to your world, even more so."

Merlin at least frowned at this, picking up on the truth hinted at by Bran. At least he hadn't completely lost his temper. Fighting to stay still, Alex refused to show weakness. Did that thing have the memories of her life that the other Light had gone rooting through? It must. It had to. Then the Light looked away from her, smiling at the others in the room.

"My nature is changeable compared to yours. I find you creatures fascinating. You are born yourself alone and grow on one path throughout your existence." It shook its head with a soft, almost whimsical smile. "Such a thing is unknown to my kind."

"So, you produce asexually?" Aiden asked. He tapped his fingers on the table. "If you grow strong enough, you'll split apart in our world." That made the others shift and glance at each other. "Is there a limit to how much you can split? Have you already done so?"

"I have not," the Light assured him. Alex wasn't sure if he was to be believed. "As it stands... I dare not leave this body. I believe the flesh is helping to keep me safe from this realm pushing back against me. The resistance was incredible."

"Yes," Morgana said. "But you and your other half did enter our world by possessing people. You bypassed the Iron Gates and their defenses. I'm certain that the Iron Realm isn't sure what to make of you." Morgana's lips were pressed tightly together, and there was tension clearly evident in her body. She reminded Alex of a wolf ready to strike at that moment. "And now you propose something potentially dangerous to our world."

"I mean you no harm," the Light insisted. It bowed its head submissively. "What I saw... When the Darkness came, it was slow at first. We quarantined the area and tried to study it, but it just kept coming. Slowly at first, but with each droplet, it ripped further into our world. I remember... one part of me was watching the area, and it kept spreading. My world had limited matter, but it ate through all of it that it touched."

Alex tightened her hold on Bran's arm. A new memory pushed its way forward; a strange dark circle that was stark against yellow and green natural grasses. The air above it shimmered strangely as a drop of black liquid with a purplish shine gathered in an unseen crack. Merlin was frowning when she blinked her eyes and pushed the memory away. The poison: it was just like the poison that they had made. But why? She knew that was true, but how was such a thing even possible?

"What of your people?" Sif's tone was more sympathetic and gentle now.

"A single drop destroyed us. It distorted us, and they were gone in mere moments. Matter was slower, but our energy just..." The Light shuddered, gripping the table so tightly that Arthur's fingers warped. "We didn't believe that energy could be destroyed. We didn't cease to be; we just shifted in the shape of our consciousness. Ever since the beginning, we knew that. But now we were dying. The survivors gathered together, and we frantically sought a way to escape. One of us opened a new hole in our reality, using a bit of the Darkness in fact. It destroyed them, but two of us slipped out before the Darkness was upon us."

"So, you are the last," Shiva said.

"I believe so. I suppose some may still live, but they will not for long." The Light raised its face once more. "I do not seek to save my world. It is lost. My kind is lost. I will grieve as long as I can survive in this world, and I fear that is not long, but it must be stopped. Do not give it the chance to come into your world. It corrodes. It does not think; it cannot be bargained with; it is just destruction. It brought death to a world without death."

Swallowing, Alex held back a shiver, but the chill remained in her spine. The words were good. They struck to the heart of the matter. They conjured terrifying memories of the visions of the Sídhe homeworld, and made her once again wonder how many dead worlds were at the outer edges of the Tree of Reality. But the words didn't make her trust the Light.

"We need more information," Alex repeated. She raised her chin. "The Tree of Reality binds our worlds together. Having visited it personally, I can tell you that energy flows out of the roots, through the Iron Realm and into other worlds. That connects us, but for all we know Earth might burn up if the connection is broken and all that energy stays here in our world." Bran was watching her carefully. Alex considered reading his mind; she wasn't sure what he was thinking.

"That's a good point," one of the Fae said. It was the small, more effeminate one. Their voice wavered slightly. "There may be other means to turn this Darkness back. The Iron Gates have protected the world for centuries, perhaps they will hold it back."

'No, they won't,' a voice whispered. It was the voice of the man who had that strange iron jar in her visions of the Light. 'They won't hold it back, but it can be stopped.'

"We won't make a decision today," Morgana declared loudly. "This is too great an issue to take drastic action." She nodded imperiously to the Light. "Tell us what you know of the Darkness. How long did it take? Were there any patterns noticed? You mentioned that it consumed matter more slowly."

"Yes," the Light nodded. "Much more slowly." It tapped its fingers against the table. "I cannot say for certain how many worlds away I am from. I believe that I was two out. In fleeing, I know that we..." It frowned and shook its head. "I am sorry, that is blurry, but there was another world closer to your world. We bypassed it by accident and fell into the void." It shuddered, and Alex wondered what it was like to float in that dark, glittering nothing around the Tree of Reality. "I cannot even say how long ago it was. It might have been only a day, or it might have been centuries ago. Perhaps the Darkness has already eaten the closer world."

"Perhaps," Nicki said. "But we need to know that first. The more information we gather, the better a decision we can make."

"But wait too long, and the Darkness will be upon us!" The Light was trying to stare Nicki down.

Shiva and Sif exchanged irritated looks. Baldr seemed more uncomfortable, but Robin merely raised an eyebrow. Only Shiva was actually from the homeworld; the other three had only heard of it from their parents. Did it affect them to hear about it possibly being destroyed? But it raised a good question. They needed to check on the Darkness. Alex tried to remember how far spread it had been, but they needed to know for sure.

A few others spoke up. At least so far, people were listening to their concerns about the Light's proposal. But Alex was also aware of the curious and hopeful looks being shared. The Light stared at her, and Alex conceded mentally that this wasn't a suggestion that was going to go away. When Morgana called for a break, Alex leapt up from her chair and made a show of stretching her arms as she hurried from the room, and away from the Light.

11

Empty Memories

At first, Alex didn't think anyone followed her. Nicki had caught her eye on her way out, but none of the mages had tried to stop her or walk with her. The Fae and Demons had drawn back as if a storm surrounded her. If she'd been calmer, Alex might have felt worse about inspiring fear in them. Right now, she didn't care at all.

She could hear people moving in the hallway and kept up the show of stretching her arms. Leaning against the wall, she stretched out her legs and listened. She didn't hear anyone and started to relax. Up ahead, a pair of double doors with foggy glass windows opened onto a back porch. Alex didn't have her coat, but magic was flaring in her chest.

Exhaling, Alex pulled on her magic and ordered it to keep her warm. It washed over her skin, leaving a warm tingle in its wake. Opening the door, Alex stepped out onto the porch, listening to her feet crunch against the snow. The wind had died down, and everything was still. In the back garden were several trees with a layer of ice coating their branches and a few bird feeders swaying in the breeze. Up the hill were pine trees coated with silver. Had she been in a better mood it would have been beautiful. As it was, it was calm and quiet, which was enough for her.

Leaned up against the back railing, Alex ignored the snow as her magic kept her warm, and inhaled slowly. She needed to calm down and stay rational. The Light's suggestion had certainly put an uncomfortable slant on all future conversations here. It had been a mistake to let it talk first, but it did have the most experience with the Darkness. Not for the first time, Alex wished that she'd had more of an opportunity to talk with one of the invading Demons, but their fear of both their King and the Darkness had made them dangerous.

"Stupid." Alex shook her head. "Stupid."

A bird chirped, the sound muffled in the snow. Alex vaguely remembered Nicki telling her once that snow absorbed sound. It sounded like the sort of random tidbit that Nicki would know. Alex sighed. She should go inside and talk with the others. The deep worry in her stomach kept turning, and she closed her eyes, trying to draw up the memory once again.

It fought back. Alex frowned. Normally she couldn't stop the memories. What was wrong with this one? Trying to remember the face of her prior self, Alex couldn't be sure if she was really seeing his face or just putting together something. She was pretty sure that he'd been a Native American, but that was all she was certain of. The others were loud, and she could remember huge chunks of their lives, so why was this one such a mystery? It didn't make sense, and given the information she needed, it was dangerous.

Frustration welled up in her; Alex kicked the wooden railing, sending snow falling off the porch. It helped a little, and she slumped against the railing once again. The memories teased her. Tall mountains with snow and a sweeping vista of rolling hills and golden plains below. Flashes of faces framed with long shining black hair. But none of it settled. No names came forth. No details settled into her mind. Amongst all of the hauntings of her former lives, this one was truly a ghost.

Then the door opened once again. Alex tensed, waiting for one of her friends to greet her or for Merlin to try and talk her into being more open to the Light's suggestion. No one greeted her. They didn't move for a few moments. Then the door closed and someone walked forward. Alex started to raise her hand for the hilt of her Sword and turned.

It was the Light. "I'm sorry," it said. The thing shifted like it was nervous, shrugging helplessly. The very human motion caught Alex off guard. "That wasn't how I imagined things going." It gestured towards the door with an almost sheepish smile.

It looked too much like one of Arthur's acts. Maybe it was. Maybe this was just some sort of repeat as the Light used Arthur's memories to try and manipulate her. It wouldn't work; she wasn't going to fall for that again.

"What, were we all supposed to listen to your suggestion without any concerns?" Alex raised an eyebrow, letting venom fill her voice. "Not likely."

"No, you bring up some valid worries." The Light groaned and rubbed its eyes. "I'm just very worried. Arthur was too. When he started looking into the Tree of Reality, he was searching for potential allies or the source of the Iron Soul's power."

"What?"

"Your power," the Light repeated. "Arthur had some theories about where your soul came from. He wanted to know if an intelligence made it or if it simply developed. Arthur was... almost obsessed with it. He was scared of you, and the Queen reminded him frequently that even if he killed you, it wouldn't be the end. So he wanted to learn what made your soul."

"And he looked out into the tree for that?"

"Arthur might have been Scáthbás' weapon and tool, but he was not without a good mind, at least in some regards. He thought that there might be a clue in the trunk of the tree, that maybe there was some sort of Underworld."

Alex almost asked if he had found anything. Below their world in the Tree was a light, or maybe two, Alex wasn't sure. That's where the energy came from, but she didn't know what it did. But she didn't ask; she stayed silent and on guard.

"Arthur was curious and ambitious, but not always to good effect. He... Arthur was damaged," the Light sighed. His voice was barely above a whisper. It implored her to look at him, but Alex didn't budge. Watching the clouds move, she battled her instinct to fight. "By the time he and I met... when we connected in the void between worlds, amongst the branches... I was dying, and he was lost. We didn't make a deal or anything like that. The boy was a mess. He'd destroyed his mother but found himself at a loss. He wasn't as much the unfeeling villain as he wanted to be."

"He killed me." Alex shivered, remembering Arto's death and Medraut's gloating.

"Arthur didn't remember any of that. He was told about it. Told so often that his mind tried to create memories, but they weren't real. His mother wanted to shape him into something she could use. She was willing to bend his soul to her will, alien flesh, and the magic of the Iron Realm to get what she wanted."

Alex didn't want to listen. Glimpses that she'd seen of Arthur's life had always told her that his life hadn't been happy. He'd been molded, but she didn't have the luxury of pity. If he'd come to the mages rather than playing the Queen's game, then maybe things could have been different.

"He still made choices," Alex said. "And he hurt people when he didn't have to."

"You're not wrong," the Light agreed. "But through him... through his memories, I learned a great deal about you and your world." He extended his fingers and watched them thoughtfully as he curled them into a fist. Alex remembered those hands, and quickly shoved the memory aside. "He did love things about this world. He simply lacked the conviction to fight for them. He couldn't even fight for himself, not without doubts and fears."

"Why are you telling me this? He's dead."

'Stay calm,' Cuthbert ordered. 'Don't give him the upper hand. Never let an enemy see weakness.'

'Breathe, Alex,' Leugio whispered.

"Yes, he is, but I still feel... pity, I suppose. He wanted power, but even more than that, he wanted to matter. I don't want to be the only being that feels anything other than anger towards him. Even the Fae who followed him have been quick to label him evil and move on."

"He was my enemy," Alex stated. Then she turned to face the Light. Looking into Arthur's face was difficult, but she raised her chin and kept herself from pulling her Sword or bolting. "Maybe he had reasons, and maybe he didn't. I've seen enough of his life to understand it wasn't easy, but that doesn't change what he did. It doesn't change the consequences. He struggled, fine, but he still killed my parents. I lost the family that I loved because of him. I buried my parents because of him."

"I'm sorry."

"You're not the one who should apologize, and no matter what you might like to think about Arthur, he never apologized for the harm he did." Feeling bolder, Alex straightened her shoulders and gave the being a tight, unfriendly smile. "Thank you though, for confirming that you aren't him. I suppose we'll have to see what the consequences of your choices are."

She met its eyes, daring it to speak about when it possessed her — daring it to apologize for taking over her body after ripping her mind apart. Even now, there were wounds that ached. The Light's jaw tightened. It looked like it might be ill, and that filled Alex with satisfaction. She wasn't going to run. She wasn't going to cry or flinch back.

"About what the other part-"

"Convenient that it's the other part of you," Alex interrupted. "You're happy to speak in the first person in regards to Arthur, but not about what you did to me."

"It's complicated."

"Always is."

"I mean it." The Light stepped closer, blue eyes flashing with real anger. Despite herself, Alex stepped back. Pulling on her magic, she let dark gray sparks swirl around her fingertips and brought up her right hand in a silent warning. "It is complicated. Sometimes one personality, one set of memories comes out dominant. What I absorbed, what became part of me, was weak. It had been badly battered by its fight with you and the other mages."

"My sympathies," Alex sneered.

"That's fair." The Light held up its hands and stepped back. "That's fair. I'm sorry. I'm not trying to upset you, but I would have thought that you'd understand why having different memories can be complicated."

She didn't have a response to that. The Light smiled a little, relaxing and slipping its hands into its pockets. They just stared at each other as Alex tried to process. It wasn't the same. For her it wasn't natural, it was distinct to her, but for the Light that was just part of its kind. It wasn't a fair comparison.

"I'm not one of you," Alex managed. The words sounded petulant to her own ears. She'd had the upper hand for a moment, why hadn't she left then? "And I do feel guilty for the sins of my other selves."

"You're right, you're right, it's not a valid comparison. I just-" The Light shook its head. "I just need you to listen to me. Alex, the Darkness is coming. It's dangerous. I don't want to watch your world fall like I did mine. We couldn't do anything, but you can. Mjǫllnir can smash the connections; it can block the way before the Darkness comes."

The Light's eyes were earnest, and it had tilted its head, almost shyly. It was pulling on all of Arthur's old tricks, and the spark of anger that stoked helped Alex stay strong. It was tempting. If it was right and they could just hide away, then that would have been great, but she needed more than fear right now.

"I'm not going to decide something that will impact the whole of the Tree of Reality right now because you ask!" She was fidgeting. Despite her magic, the cold was starting to sink into her flesh. "We asked people to come and share what they knew for a reason. I will hear everyone out in turn."

"They don't know the Darkness as I do." The Light took a step forward again. It started to reach for her before pulling its hand back. "Failing now because you're scared is a mistake."

Images flashed across Alex's vision. The view from the mountain, the plains dotted with wildflowers stretched out below, and a dark mass building ahead of her. There was something in her hands, solid and heavy.

"Killing ourselves out of fear is also a mistake." Alex's voice was suddenly calm and clear. "You've made your case, and it will be evaluated as we gather more information. I promise you that I will not let the Darkness gain a foothold in the Iron Realm."

The Light frowned and blinked, tilting its head to study her at her surprise shift. Alex didn't understand it either, but she let her magic dissipate and gave the Light a polite smile. Then she nodded and walked for the door.

"I'll see you inside after break. There's a lot to talk about."

She didn't look back. Alex quickly walked down the hallway and glanced at all the doors. It didn't take long to find what she needed. Pushing open the bathroom door, she smiled in relief when she found it empty. It was a small, one person at a time bathroom which thankfully had a lock on the door. She secured it with trembling hands. Leaning against the sink, Alex studied her reflection. Her eyes were their normal shade of gray.

"Okay," she said softly. "What do I need to see?" Nothing came to her and Alex bit her lower lip. "Come on. Something happened, I know it. What aren't you telling me?"

No one answered her. Arto provided only a soft apology that he didn't know what she wanted. There was no sign of the voice of her former self who had confronted the Darkness. She took her right hand off the rim of the sink and flexed it. In that last vision, she'd been holding something. There'd been a jar. That had to be important. She'd seen it and felt it too many times.

What was it? How did it connect to stopping the Darkness? Had they trapped part of the Darkness in the jar? No, she remembered the crack in the sky and shivered; that couldn't be it. That wouldn't have closed the crack and actually stopped the Darkness. She was missing something. More than one thing.

Alex met her gaze in the mirror, pulling on her magic and willing the memories to come forth. Summoning the images of the mountains, that cracked sky, and the memory of the metal jar at the side of the indigenous man, she ordered them to come forward.

There was nothing. Even the others had fallen silent to let her focus. There was only her, but still, there was nothing. Fear crept up her chest, curling around her lungs and heart. All the cold from the outside that she'd blocked with magic crashed into her limbs. Alex tightened her fingers around the rim of the sink to keep herself upright.

What had happened to her when she'd been that man? What did it mean that she couldn't remember?

12

Darkest Dreams

4 33 C.E. Bighorn Mountains

Darkness swirled around him. It was thick and churned slowly, too thick for water or even blood. Every so often, it pulled itself up as if to crash down on him. Already it stood as a wall over eight feet tall, blocking his view of wherever they were. Akule could only whimper as the shadows threatened to swallow him whole. The mass was only an arm's length away from him, trapping him in place. There was nowhere to go. He couldn't run. He didn't dare go any closer.

A soft light surrounded him, keeping the strange liquid at bay, but Akule didn't know how long it would last. His chest burned. That strange spark was bright with life, but it was draining him. A soft groan escaped him. His legs threatened to buckle. Beneath his feet was nothing, just more darkness that he was sure would give out at any moment. Then he'd be falling into more nothing. Maybe that would be better than this fear.

His cries were the only sound. The Darkness moved, but not even a hint of a scrape or bubbling escaped it. Not water; something else. Something far more dangerous. There were no smells, and each time he moved he barely felt any air moving over his skin. Null and void. Every so often, he caught a glint of light beyond the Darkness or a shine of dark purple on the surface of the dark liquid circling him.

"What do you want?" he called. No answer came. He hadn't been expecting one. "What are you?"

Still no answer. It never answered him. Akule doubted that it could. For all the talk of evil spirits amongst the band, he didn't believe it. This was something else. There were no words for how much that frightened him. Each day he tried to ignore it, but now he couldn't. Now it surrounded him, ready to swallow him up and destroy him. It would leave nothing; no bones, no flesh, no clothing for his family to find.

His chest hummed. That strange spark beckoned to him, but he didn't know what to do with it. All sorts of thoughts and emotions stormed in his chest, clashing and colliding in ways that he couldn't interpret. He felt that he was supposed to know something, but he didn't. There were whispers of knowledge that wouldn't settle. Maybe if he'd been a different sort of man, he'd understand, but it was too late for that now.

The spark flickered at the edge of his awareness. It wasn't really there, and yet he was constantly aware of it. One more thing that Akule didn't understand. Fidgeting, he glanced behind him. The Darkness was all around him, but it was keeping its distance. Akule wished he knew what that meant. Was something holding it back, or was it waiting? Could it think? What was it? Was it the spark in his chest?

Why was this Darkness haunting him? They were leaving. That strange purple spark in his chest flared at the idea, like a living thing angry at the very thought. He didn't understand. Desperation and fear filled him with no release, and no relief. Closing his eyes, Akule forced back the tears trying to gather. It wouldn't help.

This was another dream. Another nightmare. He remembered being home. They'd been packing their supplies into rolls for easy hiking in the morning. The children had been playing with the band's three dogs. Caphan had been eying the dark hill with a deep frown. It was visible from camp now. Just barely, but it had proven his fears about it growing true.

He'd gone to sleep with his family, confident that the effects were still far enough away that they were safe. So this had to be a dream. Akule's heart slowed a little, though it was still beating too quickly for a calm night of rest. He reopened his eyes. The Darkness was still churning around him, giving him just enough space to breathe.

Licking his lips, he studied the dark mass and tried to find something that gave him a clue. He didn't see anything. There were no arms or legs, no eyes, no nose or mouth. It was formless like water but moved like tree sap; thick and slow. The comparison did not settle him. What was the point of this dream, then? Were the spirits trying to tell him something or was it just his fears taunting him?

Suddenly the ground beneath him collapsed. It didn't fall apart like dried out earth, but instead ripped open like a torn hide. He jumped back, eyes wide and startled. Through the opening, he saw a blue sky and a patch of green. The Darkness twisted and began flowing towards him like water. That spark in his chest flared, sending strange sensations across his chest and down his limbs.

There was nowhere to go. The Darkness was coming. As the wall of liquid suddenly dropped, he saw more beyond it. There were lines of light in the sky, stretching out for things he could see all around him. They seemed to lead back towards him, but he wasn't certain.

He had no time to ponder it. The Darkness was sweeping towards him. All he could remember was how the rock had dissolved, how the land had been eaten away, and how the animals had all fled. Without waiting, he leapt for the tear and jumped down through it. Ice brushed his sides, but nothing stopped him. A scream escaped him. There was nothing below his feet, and he fell through.

Falling, he just kept falling — the green rushing towards him. Now there were blue mountains with purple shadows. Lines of blue curved across the green. There wasn't time to study anything too closely. The air rippled around him, twisting and distorting. He thought he heard something, birds maybe, but the roaring in his ears from his heart and frantic gasps drowned it out almost completely.

Still, he kept his eyes open as the green land approached him. Then with a huff of exhaustion, he twisted his body around to look behind him. Above him was the wound in the sky, and dripping forth was the Darkness. Then he hit the ground, a droplet chasing after him.

He opened his eyes and released a shuddering breath. He was in his hut, not that strange place or falling. Just a dream, as he'd thought. Just another nightmare to add to the tally since he'd first caught sight of those dark spots. In his chest, the spark danced and flared in response to his wild emotions. Akule's eyes searched the overlapping sticks and leaves overhead for any sign of light. No, it was dark. Probably early morning. He inhaled slowly, mostly picking up the smell of their dog, and the hide blankets, but there was a hint of the night air.

It took him too long to realize that he was still shaking. Then someone was moving beside him. He almost flinched away before remembering that it would be his wife. Stilling his body, he grit his teeth to hold in a whimper. The nightmare was over.

"Akule." A soft hand touched his face. Closing his eyes once again, he breathed slowly and focused on the sensation of the touch. It was comforting. The skin was warm and real. "Are you alright? You're shaking."

Hakola's voice was barely a whisper in the dark, but it settled him. Her worry sank into him, reassuring him that he wasn't alone with the Darkness. Swallowing, he struggled to find his voice. His terror was fading slowly, but the grief wasn't fading so easily. The fingers kept moving over his skin, letting him feel the small calluses on her fingertips. She seemed content to offer him the soft comfort as he recovered.

"Yes." His voice cracked, and he swallowed again. "I'm sorry I woke you."

In his chest, his heartbeat was beginning to slow. The ache had spread down his limbs, leaving them weak. Shifting his right hand, he touched the ground beside their bed. Though packed down, the earth was cool to the touch and he instantly felt stronger. He wished that there was still grass that he could have run his fingers through. Why couldn't he have woken in the morning when there was light outside? When he could crawl outside and have the sun shine down on his clammy skin.

"Akule, you're scaring me."

"What did I say?"

"You kept talking about Darkness." Hakola shifted his chin, turning his face toward hers. It was too dark for him to see her clearly. It didn't frighten him. This was natural; this was the nighttime, not the strange mass that didn't belong. "Akule... what is going on?"

"I don't know." Closing his eyes again, he inhaled slowly and focused on that new purple spark in his chest. "Something is happening to me. I'm changing." Shaking his head, he tried to pull the erratic thought together, to give voice to the instincts whispering to him. "Being near the dark spots is changing me. Something is growing inside in response to the threat."

"Akule, please don't say things like that."

"That dark spot is Darkness. Pure Darkness is coming, and nothing that touches it will survive."

"Maybe we can convince the spirits-"

"It isn't spirits. It doesn't have a mind. It just is." The words spilled from his lips. They were madness, and yet he was certain of them. "I keep seeing it."

"We're leaving tomorrow," Hakola reminded him. "Soon this will be behind us."

"I can't leave."

There. He'd said it. The phrase, the statement, the words that voiced that horrible growing worry he'd had in the back of his mind for days. Deep in his gut, he knew that he needed to stay. Akule didn't know why, but the dreams weren't happening to anyone else. He was connected to this strange event. Maybe it was for bad, and if that was the case, then it was better for him to remain than be a danger to his family and his band.

"What?" Hakola asked. "Akule?"

"I can't leave."

His wife moved swiftly, swinging her leg over his hips so she could loom over him. It was still too dark to see her. Across the hut, the dog whimpered at the movement but stayed near the children who were still asleep.

"Akule, please don't talk like that," Hakola whispered. He was grateful that he couldn't see her face; the confusion and grief in her voice hurt as it was. "You have to stay with the band."

"I have to stay here. I'm sorry, but I must."

"Why?"

He wanted to see her face. The spark flared to life, filling him with warmth, sinking into his flesh and bones. An idea, or maybe a memory, danced at the edge of his awareness, and he brought up his left hand. He needed to see Hakola's face so much it hurt.

Purplish light rippled forth from the fingertips of his left hand. A startled gasp escaped Hakola. She nearly kicked him as she scurried back, but she didn't scream. Sitting up, Akule stared at the sparks as they spun together to form a perfect glowing orb in his hand. It was the full moon, gleaming with light, but not so bright that he couldn't look at it. Raising his eyes, he found his wife gaping in shock at the light. They stayed like that for a long time, the soft light illuminating the small hut.

Hakola's dog shifted again, sniffed at the air, but put its head back down and stayed with the children. It didn't seem alarmed, and Hakola looked between the dog and the light. Then a soft sound like a cry escaped her. She covered her mouth and shook her head. The light began to dim. Akule slowly closed his fist, urging the orb to grow smaller and smaller until it was barely a speck of light in the dark hut.

Hakola shivered, leaning forward towards him. Reaching out with his right hand, Akule touched her arm. She settled over his hips once more. They rested their foreheads together and breathed the same air. Slowly, her hands moved over his shoulders and bare chest, comforting him and chasing the last of the nightmare away.

Focusing on the touch of Hakola and the sounds of their children's breathing, Akule finally started to relax. In his chest, the spark smoldered like an ember that was ready to burst into flame, but for the moment it left him in peace. He was making the right decision, but it hurt. His fingers tightened on Hakola's hips. She didn't object, and he closed his eyes, memorizing her scent and the touch of her fingertips.

This wasn't what he wanted. He'd never aspired to stand out. His brother did that enough for the whole family. Hakola had accepted him despite that. Yet here he was now, holding her in preparation for saying goodbye.

"I'm sorry," he whispered. "But I have to stay. Take the children and go with the band."

"Jar will stay with you."

"He's your dog."

"He's staying." Hakola reached to his right hand, gently opening it to reveal the speck of light, still glowing. "I can't- I don't know how to help you, but I won't leave you alone."

"Alright."

"Talk to the elder in the morning."

"I will," Akule promised.

Then the speck of light was gone. The tingling in his chest stopped, and he sighed. Hakola rested her head against his shoulder. Suddenly exhausted, he laid back on the blankets, letting Hakola drape over him. Around them, the night settled once more, and the world was quiet.

Hakola didn't fall back to sleep for a long time. She shifted against him, clutching at him as if to keep him with her, and started to speak several times. Nothing came out. Akule was certain she didn't know what to say. He was just grateful she hadn't argued. For the first time, he was able to relax even as grief filled him. Something inside him, that strange purple spark, finally seemed at peace now that the choice had been made. He was staying. Akule didn't know what he hoped to learn. He didn't know what he thought he could do, but he was staying.

There were many things to worry about. He'd have to explain it to Caphan and Tapichi, though he doubted that Tapichi would argue. Saying goodbye to the children would be difficult. He could keep sleeping in the hut for the time being. With luck, this would be resolved before the snows came. There wasn't a lot of game, but he should be able to manage foraging for just himself.

Still, it scared him. He'd been born into his tribe and into this band. It was rare that any of them were ever alone. There was a rush of fear at the thought. Maybe Hakola leaving the dog was a good idea. Then a soft snore escaped his wife, and he smiled. Worrying now would do no good. There'd be time enough for it in the morning. Closing his eyes, he listened to his wife's breathing and slipped into the first dreamless sleep he'd had since the first time he'd seen those cursed dark spots on the hillside.

13

Still Hated

The Fae were talking about nothing. It was a disturbing thought, but it was all Alex could think. Sitting in her chair, she tried her best to keep her eyes on the male Fae named Jordon as he spoke. He moved his hands a lot and his eyes were wide with passion as he spoke. Safe in this room, he'd pulled back his hood, letting Alex see his pointed ears and long white hair that was braided. She was paying more attention to the pattern of the braid than his words, to be honest.

Thankfully, Bran was taking notes and nodding every so often next to her. Merlin was frowning and looked like he wanted to protest. Morgana's face was indifferent, but her hands were grasped so tightly together that her knuckles were white. Blinking rapidly, Alex smothered a yawn and forced herself to pay attention. Shiva had dropped his illusion and was leaning on one hand while another took notes and a third doodled.

"Given the long history of the Sídhe breaking into the Iron Realm, it seems only natural that they will try again," Jordon was saying. "According to the stories, the last time they pushed through the defenses it drove them mad." Jordon looked to Morgana. "Can you confirm that, Grand Mage Morgana?"

"You're not wrong," Morgana agreed. She didn't look happy about it. "The locals called them Dark Elves; that's where that particular aspect of Norse Mythology came from."

"Yes, but what is stopping them from doing so again?"

"We were able to break down that tunnel," Merlin said. "And, bluntly, the Dark Elves attempted to invade their own home. They were a danger to the Sídhe as well. I doubt they'll risk that again."

"But if the Darkness comes, they will," another Fae said.

"Exactly," Jordon said. "Thank you, Cameron." He nodded and swept his gaze around the room. "When the Darkness comes to the other worlds, surely they will try to escape. They could rip apart the defenses with enough power and desperation. Surely the Light's proposal is sound. It stops not only the Darkness but any further invasions."

"Given your roots," Morgana said. "One might think you're being cruel."

"You're not going to save them," Jordon snapped. He glared at Morgana while she just watched him impassively. "You hate them. Don't pretend that you care!"

"I might care," Alex said. Everyone looked at her, and she wished she'd stayed quiet, but it was too late. Licking her lips, she swallowed quickly and pushed on. "I won't pretend that there isn't bad blood between the Iron Realm and the Sídhe, but using that anger to justify breaking a connection that might let us help is going a bit far. For all we know, there are ways to fight the Darkness." Shaking her head, Alex ignored those opening their mouths to speak. "At this point, we are just arguing from an emotional point of view. Some don't want the Connections broken while others do. The Light has been able to provide us with some information, but not enough to make a decision."

"There's no safe way to learn more!" Cameron protested.

"You underestimate the Iron Soul," Shiva replied calmly. Then he looked at Alex. "You have been unsurprised throughout these conversations. May I ask how?"

Merlin and Morgana both tried to catch her eye. There was a buzz of magic across Alex's skin, and she was pretty sure that Merlin was trying to talk to her again. She ignored them.

"My magic showed me the dead Sídhe homeworld," she explained. "And I was able to see the Tree of Reality. While my magic is tied to the Iron Realm, it does seem to be able to reach out beyond that. I intend to try and learn more; perhaps see more about what exactly the Darkness is doing." She paused and swallowed. "If I can find no other way to stop it, then you're right, we'll have to risk breaking the connections between our world and the other worlds."

Glances were exchanged. Merlin pressed his lips together, but nodded. Morgana relaxed a little. Alex wanted to look to Bran next to her and see his reaction. She almost laughed. This was a horrible system, this Iron Soul thing. Why wasn't Arto just immortal like Merlin and Morgana? Fine, maybe he'd been struck down, but Thor had died of old age. Why did the world keep putting a baby like her in charge? This was a bad system.

Nicki had creativity that put her to shame. Bran was calm and collected. Even Avani had the background and training for dealing with magic. A smart system would have made her both a mage and the Iron Soul.

"Do you have a timeline?" the Light asked. Its lips were twisted into a frown. Alex guessed it didn't like her putting an end to the emotional speeches about the dangers of waiting. "A deadline seems like a good idea."

"That's difficult," Aiden cut in. "You've been unable to provide a timeline for the Darkness' advancement. We could rush and miss something critical when there isn't much danger."

"We can't wait forever either," Jordon said. He was leaning forward in his seat and glanced at the Light for support.

Given everything that Arthur had put the Fae through, it seemed impossible that they'd still support him, but Alex couldn't dismiss the possibility. Alex just hoped that their loyalty hadn't transferred. She'd never understood it. His mother had enslaved them, and yet many of them had kept helping him, letting him use them as cannon fodder against her and the other mages.

"Let's schedule another meeting then," Avani said. She smiled pleasantly at everyone and pulled out her phone. "We don't even have to meet in person if everyone can arrange a phone call. That would let us update you on what we've learned and review any information that you've gathered. We could do a conference call monthly until something changes."

It was a reasonable suggestion, and Alex saw the Light's frown deepen. If she hadn't been so concerned about appearing calm, she might have grinned and cheered. Sif, Shiva, and Baldr all nodded in agreement without any hint of hesitation. Robin gave a thumbs up, looking more than a little pleased. The Demons and the Fae weren't as excited.

"Are you certain?" Jordon asked. "That seems..."

"We need to start talking to each other," Alex said. Guarding her voice, she did her best to let her honest hope show. "We all came from different places, but we live here now. This is overdue. Sitting here debating isn't going to give us an answer, but going out and trying to learn what is happening and sharing that information might."

Avani nodded in approval, a small smile on her face as she surveyed their guests. That made Alex feel better. Avani might not be a mage, but she was a capable ally. Jordon looked at the other Fae while Timothy nodded eagerly in agreement. His loyalty still astounded Alex, but she was grateful for it.

Morgana took charge, laying out potential communication options. Avani pulled out her phone and started texting one of her cousins for help setting something up for the Demons. Merlin and Nicki were both taking notes. It seemed like it was coming together. Alex should have been relaxing. This was good, but still there was an odd itch at the back of her brain.

She was just about to release some magic and check the perimeter when she heard scratching sounds against wood. Frowning, Alex sat up in her chair and looked around the room. The Light frowned at her, narrowing its eyes, but then the Fae seemed to take notice and started searching the walls.

"What is that?" Shiva asked. He stood from his chair and extended his extra arms.

Then came a giggle. Alex jumped out of her chair. The other mages followed, all of them moving away from the table. Another giggle was heard, and more little scraping sounds. Shiva shifted the Trishula, bringing it up as he readied himself to fight. Nicki grabbed Avani's hand and stood protectively in front of her girlfriend.

"Red Caps!" Timothy shouted.

"What?" the Light asked. "Why?"

There was no time for an answer. One of the ceiling panels was knocked out. It hit the ground with a heavy smack, and a dozen Red Caps came pouring out of the ceiling. A few landed on tables while the rest hit the ground running. They were all dressed in tattered clothes that had been altered to fit, most of them a shade of gray similar to their skin, and all wore bright red hats of differing styles. A few carried small knives while others had their long sharp teeth and talons bared. Another round of small high-pitched cries and giggles escaped the mass of attackers, sending a shiver down Alex's spine.

Alex didn't wait for a signal. Drawing Cathanáil forth, she swung at the nearest Red Cap as it clamored across the table, knocking over a glass of water. The blade sliced through the small creature with ease, cutting the clothing as the body rapidly turned to dust. She saw silver magic blast another Red Cap against the wall. Bran rushed to the doors, and a wall of yellow magic appeared around them. She hoped that it was a sound muting spell to keep the staff from running in.

Another Red Cap tried to jump onto her. Yelping, Alex hit it with Cathanáil's broad side and smacked it back to the ground. A bolt of red magic struck it, and the thing died with a sharp shriek. More were moving behind her, and Alex spun around to face them, trusting the others to watch her back. Three Red Caps had the decency to run along the actual floor rather than on the tables. Now that they'd been spotted, one rushed forward with a knife, trying to slice at Alex's ankles.

Instinct took over. Alex lashed a foot forward and kicked the creature as hard as she could. Light flashed off the small knife, and she shivered. It was impossible not to worry, not be scared by the idea of what they'd tried to do. The Red Cap hit the wall with a heavy thump. The other two attacked, but a wave of blue magic knocked them back. Alex didn't wait for them to recover. She thrust Cathanáil forward into the chest of the first Red Cap. Even the tip of the blade dwarfed the creature, but Alex didn't care. Red Caps were simple compared to everything else. The little bloodthirsty psychos were easy to hate and easy to fight. Quickly, she killed off the other two and spun back to check on the others.

Out of the corner of her eye, she saw a Red Cap slice into the Light's arm with a long knife. The Light twisted away as the creature lunged for its chest. Another snarled and leapt at Alex. More of the attackers were moving towards the Light than her and the other mages. Jordon and the Fae had retreated into a corner. In a strange twist, Shiva was in front of the Demons, protecting them.

A Red Cap attacked Sif, grabbing her braid and trying to stab her neck. Baldr grabbed it with his bare hand and threw it against the wall. Thor's anger took over and Alex extended her left hand, releasing a bolt of lightning across the room. It struck the Red Cap, which spasmed under the attack before collapsing into dust.

She turned to check the room. Shiva had just finished killing one, and a wave of green magic pulled the last two attacking the Light away from it. Blue bolts from Nicki finished them off even as she eyed the Light thoughtfully. Thankfully, Nicki lowered her hands and didn't attack.

Listening, Alex waited for any sound that indicated more Red Caps. There was only heavy breathing and people shifting uneasily. Then her eyes went back to the Light, who was staring down at its arm. A long rip had been sliced in its shirt, and blood was dripping out of the wound. It didn't seem to know what to do. Blood was dripping off the flesh and onto the floor. The only thought in Alex's mind was that they'd need to clean all of this up.

Then the Light shook itself, turned and rushed for the doorway. Bran jumped to the side and waved his hand. The yellow barrier vanished. Jordon rushed to join the Light, and Alex frowned. That could end up being a problem if the Fae decided to follow the Light. Given her memories of Michel and the series of events surrounding Oberon, she was beginning to suspect that the Fae were a little too happy to fall in line with anyone stronger than them, even to an extent worse than humans.

"Nicki, what are you doing?" Aiden hissed.

Turning quickly, Alex's eyes widened when she found Nicki, holding one of the small glasses provided by the hotel in her left hand, walking up to the Light's chair. The other Fae were talking to the Demons while the Old Ones gathered together with Merlin and Morgana. Nicki smiled a little, noticing that the group's attention was elsewhere.

"Nicki?" Aiden whispered again.

She didn't say anything to him and waved her right hand, still holding the empty glass. Her eyes were focused on the patch of blood on the floor and chair. Blue sparks swirled forward, sinking into the fabric, and for a moment, Alex figured that Nicki was simply cleaning up the mess.

But then droplets of red blood were pulled into the air and sailed towards Nicki. They formed a stream of red liquid that flowed into the glass that she was holding. Aiden shifted, standing up straight between the Demons who were still talking and the chair, blocking their view. Bran moved between Nicki and the doorway while Alex just stared in confusion.

Then all the blood was gone, and Nicki put her hand over the top of the glass. She closed her eyes for a moment, intense concentration showing on her face. When she pulled her hand back, there was a thin shimmering layer of magic over the top of the glass. Alex wasn't sure if it was ice, but it looked very similar. She said nothing when Nicki went over to her chair, keeping the glass with about an inch of blood in it, out of view. When she tucked it into her messenger bag, Alex finally realized that Nicki had plans.

She and the others gathered around Nicki, Avani taking the seat next to her girlfriend. Bran waved his hand, sending a pulse of yellow magic across the table, which dried up the messes that the Red Caps had made. She glanced towards Morgana to find the other mage using her magic to fix the ceiling tile and put it back into place. No one was paying attention to them.

"What was that about?" Alex asked. She turned and checked the wall to make sure that there wasn't any damage from the Red Caps.

"I never had Arthur's blood," Nicki said. "And when he died, I assumed he was dead, so I just cleaned off the Sword without saving the blood. He wasn't bleeding by the time we got him into the SUV, so I couldn't collect any there."

"But what's the plan with the blood?" Aiden whispered. "Please tell me you aren't doing anything too creepy."

"That Light is still using Arthur's body," Nicki reminded him. "And apparently keeping it at least a little alive, since it still bleeds." A nasty little smile appeared on her face, and Alex was momentarily scared of the other mage. "I bet that with his blood; I can link the book to the Light. Maybe improve it enough actually to keep tabs on it and learn what it is up to."

Aiden grinned, and Bran nodded in approval. Nicki relaxed under their acceptance and smiled a bit more nicely now. Alex's brain spun, and she found herself smiling a little. Maybe it was an ally of the Iron Realm, maybe it wasn't, but she had to admit that the idea of being able to keep an eye on what it was up to, was a very attractive one.

The door opened and the Light returned, paper towels wrapped around its arm and Jordon keeping his distance. The Light's face was a touch pale, and it still seemed alarmed. Then again, judging from how it described its real form, physical pain was probably largely unknown to it. She watched as the Light sat down and kept the pressure on its arm. It had healed Arthur's body. At least, she assumed that there wasn't still a hole in its gut from Nicki's attack, so why the delay? When the Light pulled away the wet paper towels, Alex grimaced as she saw the injury. It was already closing up. It was just slow, and the Light covered the injury again.

Nicki shifted in her seat and touched her bag protectively. A hint of guilt hit Alex, but she snuffed it out as quickly as she could. Under the circumstances, stealing some blood wasn't that bad. The Light might not be Arthur, but it wasn't a proven ally. They had to be careful, for the sake of the whole Tree of Reality.

14

Tainted Memories

They had to take a break after the attack. The Fae were disturbed by the Red Cap attack, and Alex had a disgusting sense of satisfaction that they now understood what that was like. All of them except for Timothy had gone to their rooms for an hour. Avani had excused herself to speak with the Demons and Shiva, and much to Alex's surprise, chuckles were coming from the group as they headed towards the back porch with plans to admire the snow. Merlin and Morgana were giving each other the silent treatment as they finished cleaning the room of any signs of the fight. Alex had no idea what had happened there but suspected Morgana might share her worries about breaking the Connections between worlds and was frustrated with Merlin.

Nicki had gone to her room, no doubt to stash the blood. Aiden had gone with her, looking a touch pale at the way that Nicki was clutching her bag with eager eyes. Anansi was speaking with Sif and kept glancing Alex's way curiously. Nothing stirred in Alex's memory when she looked at him and Sun Wukong. She hoped that was a good sign. Sun Wukong was pacing and kept looking out the windows and up at the ceiling. He was ready for another attack. Alex wished that she'd had a chance to watch him in action.

Then the Old Ones moved off, and the room cleared. A staff member came in to clean things up a little and didn't say anything about loud noises or any mess. Down the hall by the main desk a clock chimed, and Alex's stomach grumbled a little. At least dinner wasn't far off. They could eat, maybe talk a little more about when to speak next and outline who would do what before resting. If that went well, then they could leave in the morning — a quick, mostly painless conference.

This had been a horrible idea. Fatigue swept through Alex's body, and she quickly excused herself. The walk to her room took a long time. Every sound made her flinch. If the Red Caps had been smart, they would have waited until they'd all split up, but the little psychos were usually pretty stupid. That was a good thing, all things considered. There was no sign of the Light, and as Alex stepped into her room, she finally felt her lungs fully expand.

The room was nice and clean, but it was just like every other hotel room, with a bed, nightstand, desk with chair, dresser, and television. Its scent was very neutral, reinforcing that it wasn't home, but for now it would do. Alex made sure to lock the door and put the chain in place. It wouldn't stop the most dedicated attackers, but it would slow them down if they came that way. She eyed the window and frowned thoughtfully.

Her magic was sparking in her chest, reacting to the high number of beings from other universes all in one place. It was uncomfortable, and Alex wondered if it was affecting the others as much. She crossed the room and pulled gently on her magic. A tingling rushed up her left arm, feeling almost like an electric shock, and leaving her muscles sore and warm. Pressing her hand against the cool glass, Alex closed her eyes and focused on creating a barrier to keep anything that meant harm out. The glass warmed beneath her hand, and the pressure from the excess magic eased. It wasn't as good as home. There was no warning system, no protections that would keep things out, and she and her fellow mages were spread out throughout the hotel. Still, it would have to do.

Laying down on the bed, Alex held up her phone and set the alarm for herself. Then she dropped the phone next to her and crossed her ankles. She stared up at the ceiling of the room and studied it. Unlike the molding downstairs, this was much more modern and boring with the usual rough, white texture. Had she been in a better mood, Alex might have been interested in the history of the hotel, but she had no energy.

Emotionally, she was wrung out. Having the Light so close had put her on a knife's edge, and while the fight had let her work out a little aggression, it wasn't nearly enough. It just brought up more questions as to what the Red Caps were after. Attacking a room full of powerful beings just seemed like suicide.

Closing her eyes, Alex focused on her breathing and the steady beat of her heart. The attack had passed. There'd be plenty of time to pore over it with the others and try to figure out if the Red Caps had had a plan or if they were just lashing out. Right now, she had other concerns. Alex did her best to clear her mind, but the struggle with her memories kept returning to the forefront of her thoughts.

She wished that she could organize her mind. Books and movies always made it look easy, but the mess of interconnecting ideas, emotional responses, and vivid images that crowded her brain was anything but easy. Events that she was sure didn't connect tried to run into each other because of a random common thread. If it hadn't been for the emotional reactions of the voices, she'd probably never be able to keep anything straight.

Alex frowned despite her efforts to calm down. That Iron Jar was eluding her. It was important, and yet buried somewhere in her memories. She brought up her hands and flexed her fingers, trying to recall the weight and texture of the jar. It helped, and for a moment, a memory tried to ghost over Alex's mind, but it wouldn't settle. It couldn't settle. Alex pulled on her magic and tried to imagine reaching a glowing hand towards the memory to coax it back. A sharp pain radiated around her heart, leaving Alex groaning and gasping for air.

Lifting her head, Alex ran a hand over her chest, checking for injuries. There weren't any. Of course, there weren't any. She dropped her head back onto the bed and inhaled slowly. The pain didn't fade. Tears pricked at her eyes, and her left hand searched around for her phone. She gripped the plastic cover tightly, but the pain was starting to fade now.

Blinking back the tears, Alex closed her eyes again and turned her attention to the magic. It was difficult to shift her senses while fighting back the lingering pain, but she managed it. Her magic spun in a tight dark gray coil with a soft glow. Nothing seemed wrong, and yet there was a wall of some kind. Something was blocking her from viewing the memories. Twice now, she'd failed, and this time it had hurt, truly hurt.

She sat up slowly, mindful of the pain still sitting over her lungs. It was passing, but she'd need to be careful. Alex's mind frantically tried to sort out what was happening. Instinct told her one thing, but it didn't seem possible that her memories were blocked. After all, ever since the release of the soul fragment or whatever had still been in Arto's body, the issue had been oversharing, not lack of information.

Her phone beeped, and Alex stared at it in shock. There'd been over an hour before dinner when she came to her room. Picking up the phone, she checked the time and frowned. It wasn't a mistake. She'd either been trying to get to the memory for that long, or been in pain far longer than she'd been aware of. Alex hoped that it was the former rather than the later.

Alex stood up slowly, but thankfully her legs held her weight. Her tight grip on her phone hadn't lessened, but she decided against alerting Morgana to what had happened just yet. It could wait. She went to the bathroom, splashed some water on her face, and brushed her tangled hair into a fresh ponytail. Once Alex was confident that she didn't look like someone who'd just suffered magical backlash, she headed downstairs.

There was no opportunity to talk with her fellow mages. She was one of the last people back to the conference room, and the staff was bringing in plates with roasted chicken and side dishes. The Old Ones, Demons and Fae all looked uncomfortable as they avoided attention by altering their appearance or keeping their hoods up. Timothy was sitting on the edge of a chair, hidden under the table cloth with the mages passing bits of their dinners down to him. If the waiter and chef thought there was something off about them, they didn't say.

By unspoken agreement, no one tried to talk about the Darkness over dinner. They were still in their small groups for the most part, though Sif left her brother to come and sit beside Alex. Thor's pleasure radiated through Alex, and it was all she could do to keep calm through the meal. Nicki kept most of Sif's attention with questions about life in the Norselands while Thor was alive.

"Did Thor really have red hair?" Aiden asked Sif. "Or was he blond like they always show Vikings as being."

It was Alex who answered, "Red hair naturally, bleached blond."

Sif blinked in surprise at the answer, but then she smiled and nodded. "Yes, as Alex said, Thor had naturally red hair, at least until it went white." A wistful smile appeared on her face. "He was always very vain about his hair. Sometimes I wonder what he would have thought about being remembered with red hair."

Thor grumbled, but said nothing clearly enough for Alex to relay to Sif. Based on the small smile on Sif's face, Alex had a feeling that the Old One had expected that. Robin looked their way a few times, never looking very happy with the situation. However, Aiden glanced her way a few times as well. All the while, Michel kept muttering about stubborn Old Ones and humans. His memories of Puck bubbled up, and Alex did her best to ignore them. She didn't need memories of what they'd gotten up to over the years.

After the plates had been cleared away, there was little energy in the room. The Fae had retreated into themselves and were whispering to each other. Alex noted with a frown that Timothy was largely excluded even after he returned to join them. The Light had been silent throughout the meal, speaking with no one. Its gaze had settled on Alex multiple times, but she'd ignored it and the lingering ache in her heart.

Merlin made an effort at getting everyone's attention even after Morgana shook her head. Alex caught his eyes and let her exhaustion show. Her mind was still spinning, and her chest still hurt. She wasn't interested in playing diplomat anymore today; it had already been a very long day.

"I thank everyone for coming once again," Merlin said. He smiled at the assembled representatives. "But looking around the room, I can see that everyone is ready for a rest. Shall we plan on resuming at eight tomorrow morning? The staff will be preparing a breakfast buffet for us in this room so we'll have more privacy."

"Thank you, Merlin." The Light stood up, nodded sharply, and headed straight to the door.

Chatter broke out as he left, and Alex knew that she wasn't the only one confused. Until now, the Light had been polite and charming. Maybe it was tired, or just discouraged. Shiva rose next and hurried to the door, nodding her direction, but not stopping to speak with her. Alex had the feeling that he planned to catch up with the Light.

Staying in her seat, Alex watched the other groups slowly make their way out. None of them had the frantic stride of the Light, and all looked thoughtful. Watching the Demons, Alex tried to see the transition of their black skin and bright natural markings back to their human appearance, but all she saw was a blur.

The Fae hurried out, one of them taking Timothy with a reluctant expression. Anger flashed through Alex, and it was a welcome distraction, but when Timothy waved cheerfully, she found herself unwilling to make a scene. Instead, she raised her hand and waved back. The remaining Old Ones departed, Anansi and Baldr having a conversation about a book that Alex had never heard of.

"What are you thinking?" Avani asked. Walking up behind Alex's chair, she put her hand on Alex's shoulder. "You look worried."

"I'm not sure," Alex admitted. Morgana made a noise as she walked over, but said nothing. Merlin was saying goodnight to Anansi at the doors and smiling in a way that no one else was. "They're all... invested, but that could be dangerous. Jordon seemed very eager to listen to the Light."

"I noticed that as well," Morgana said. "It could be a problem. But the Light didn't seem eager to talk to anyone this evening."

"Yes," Alex agreed. "But we could end up right back where we started. At least the Demons were calm about the Darkness and willing to listen."

"They suffered recently because of it," Avani said. She dropped her hand off of Alex's shoulder and leaned against the table. "Most of the population is very peaceful. Sometimes even friendly with Shiva and his fellow Old Ones. They aren't going to risk it by doing something foolish."

"That's good at least." Alex sighed. "I wish I knew more about the other Old Ones."

"They're trustworthy," Morgana said. "Like the others, they won't want to see this Darkness advance, but I don't imagine we'll get much help from there." She studied Alex for a long moment with her dark green eyes. "Are you alright?"

"I..." Alex looked around once more to be sure they were alone. "I tried to look into my memories. One of my lives fought the Darkness. I'm sure of it, I've seen flashes of his memory, and when I was fighting the Light in my head, I saw him. He was Indigenous American, I think, and somewhere in the west based on the mountains. There was this jar made of iron-"

"That's not possible," Nicki interrupted. "Native Americans didn't have iron. Metallurgy was limited to soft metals like gold, except for a tribe on the coast that used remains from shipwrecks."

"Nicki," Morgana scolded. "Not now. Go on, Alex."

"I'm not sure. He might not have been Indigenous, that was just my instinct. It's why I didn't bring it up at the conference. I don't know enough yet, but something important happened!" She shrugged and dismissed it. "Anyway, when I tried to access the memories, there was pushback, and I felt pain."

"What?" Bran asked. He was at her side in an instant. "Are you sure?"

"Pretty sure," Alex said dryly. He grimaced in response.

"That's never happened before?" Morgana asked. "Nothing like that?"

"No," Alex said. "Never like that. My memories are difficult to navigate, but they've never been closed off to me."

Morgana's frown deepened. Alex almost reached out with her magic to try and read the older mage's mind but thought better of it. Morgana squeezed her shoulder. "The conference will wrap up in the morning. Once we have the schedule for communication, we'll get back home and see if we can help unlock this memory."

The knowledge that Morgana believed her made Alex relax. She licked her lips and exhaled, suddenly able to breathe properly again. "It's not a complete block," Alex said. "I heard him earlier. The man with the jar. He told me that the Iron Gates have failed to stop it before. And when the Light was talking, I saw flashes of when the Darkness reached us before."

"But you don't know how it was stopped?" Avani asked.

"I'm not sure, but the Iron Jar has something to do with it," Alex said. Then she looked back at Morgana. "It is like the poison, Morgana. It really is. I swear."

"I believe you," Morgana assured her. "I just don't know what that means, Alex."

"I thought about telling them that it's been turned back before," Alex admitted.

"I'm glad you didn't," Morgana said. "You're right; we need more information. When we get home, you and Bran need to try to scry together. We'll give you magic to strengthen you against the pushback."

"Morgana?" Nicki hesitated, glancing nervously at Alex. "What if the block is because of exposure to the Darkness? What if it did something to that incarnation of the Iron Soul? Or what if the Light did something to the memory so Alex couldn't use the information as a counter argument? Poking at it might be dangerous."

The words horrified Alex. Her heart sputtered as the others all voiced their concerns. She strained herself, trying to hear that man with the jar again. There was no sign of him. That might be the reason. What if part of her had been damaged? The memory of the fight in her head against the Light certainly didn't disprove the possibility. Morgana's grip on her shoulder tightened.

"I don't know, Nicki," Morgana said. "But Alex has knowledge locked away somewhere that might let us save not only this world, but others as well. If it was the Light then showing our hand and revealing you've discovered part of that information could be dangerous."

Swallowing, Alex nodded. "We need to try. Let's focus on wrapping this conference up and planning our next step." She smiled a little at Nicki, knowing that the redhead would see her worry. "Any thoughts you have on spells that could help would be appreciated. You too, Avani."

"We'll all help," Aiden promised. He glanced at the door. "But tomorrow. Alex, you rest tonight."

She nodded. That was not something she was going to argue about. Merlin walked over to join them, suddenly rather worried.

"Is everything alright?"

"That remains to be seen," Morgana replied. He blinked at her, and she sighed. "Come with me; I'll catch you up."

Taking his arm, Morgana pulled Merlin towards the doorway. Morgana looked over her shoulder and gave Nicki a look. The redhead nodded, and Alex was very certain that she'd been assigned her babysitter for the evening.

15

Magic Meets Darkness

4 33 C.E. Bighorn Mountains

The dog was barking, the sound far too loud in the quiet morning. Groaning, Akule sat up and blinked his eyes. The dog kept barking, and he thought that he heard a hint of panic. That ripped the last vestiges of slumber from his body, and Akule rolled over. He stumbled over to the entrance of the hut, barely remembering to grab his spear and hurried outside.

There were only two huts in what had once been a good-sized camp now. The others had been torn down to reinforce his own in the past few days. He slept in one while the other had been filled with the sticks and leaves from the other huts to be used as fuel, just in case. When the others had departed, they'd left what they could for him. He had some weapons, some tools, and some cooking supplies. What he didn't have was human company, and already it was beginning to make him uneasy.

He gripped his spear and surveyed the small camp. Akule found the dog near the rock outcropping, barking into the distance. As he approached, he relaxed as he found that the dog was barking towards the hill. The black circle had grown in size again. There was no mistaking the hole for anything natural now. It looked as if a giant being had dug into the ground with a smooth bowl. Even worse, he still had no idea what to do about it. Sighing, he lowered the spear.

Hakola's dog moved closer to him and whimpered. He lowered a hand and stroked the long fur without much thought. The poor beast missed his mistress and the children, but Akule was grateful that his wife had insisted that the dog remain.

"I know, I know," he said gently. "I don't like it either." Then he chuckled softly. "I'm sorry that you got stuck staying."

Talking to the dog was strange. His wife had always talked to it, so had his children, but he'd never been fond enough of the dog to treat it in such a human manner. Now though... he was finding that loneliness was making him treat the dog more as a person than he had in the past. The dog nuzzled his leg, seeming to draw comfort from him as well.

"Well... we should gather some food and go and take a look," he said.

Akule stretched his arms and legs, taking in the soft sounds of the world around him. In the absence of human voices, he was finding that the birds were much louder than he'd noticed before. Maybe the lack of people was encouraging them to come closer. He ate a stick of dried elk meat and emptied most of his waterskin. The dog got two sticks of the dried meat and then proceeded to lick his fingertips clean.

Grabbing a leather pouch and a small woven basket, Akule started walking toward the hill. It was a bit much to carry, but he wasn't willing to leave the spear behind. The dog whimpered once again but followed along after a moment. It didn't seem to like being alone any more than he did. Akule felt sorry for the poor thing. It was a companion, but in the event of famine... he pushed that thought aside, even if he was sure that had been another reason why Hakola had left the poor thing with him. He had no desire to be stuck up here in the mountains until winter, but at the moment he wasn't sure what was going to happen.

His first stop was the small stream that was running high thanks to the melting snow on the peaks above him. Kneeling beside the creek, he used the cold water to rinse his hands and face before filling his waterskin. That done, he scanned the area and quickly found the patch of trees that gave shade to some blackberry bushes.

One positive of the black mark was that it drove off the animals. They didn't like coming near it, leaving the berry bushes to grow without any competition for them as a food supply. Akule's skin cooled as they came closer. The dog drew back and found a place to sit where it could watch him without getting any closer.

Akule quickly picked the ripest of the dark berries, putting a handful straight into his mouth. They were sweet and pleasant, brightening the day, and Akule was grateful for them. Nonetheless, he'd need to get a deer or at least some rabbits today to restock his meat supply if he was to feed the dog. He worked quickly, moving from bush to bush in the shade of the trees, gathering as much as he could. There wasn't a lot, but he'd managed to fill about half of the basket. It was still a bit early in spring for the best of the berries to be ready for picking. In late summer the bushes and trees would be thick with many more varieties, but the blackberries were enough for now.

Listening to the wind, he tried to pick out the sounds of any animals nearby. He could hear some distant birds, but the thickness of the grasses and the silence confirmed that the animals had been avoiding this area. He frowned and looked down into the basket once more. That wasn't good. He'd have to walk further to find game, and without other hunters to bring it down, it would prove more difficult. With the rocky terrain he couldn't hope for many rabbits, but he promised himself to set up some snares on the far side of his camp, just in case. He'd wanted to stay, and now he needed to make do.

But first, he needed to check on the dead spot. Akule braced himself before turning and walking towards it. The instinct to run returned and grew stronger with each step towards it. The circle remained even on all sides, which continued to amaze Akule. If it hadn't scared him so, it would have been remarkable.

Setting down the basket, Akule crept towards the dark circle and studied it. In his chest, the purple flare sparked to life, sending small shocks down his arms and legs. It made his heart jump and his vision sharpen. His dreams at night had begun to include lines of purple and strange flashes of light from his hands. He had the feeling that he was supposed to understand, but it was all still a mystery.

The dog whined behind him, but he sat down on the ground and inhaled slowly. He had to stay calm. The strange flare in his chest was stronger when he was calm. Things were clearer now, and he needed all the clarity that he could muster. Closing his eyes for a moment, Akule did his best to ignore the subtle itch telling him to get up and run away. Then he opened his eyes and studied what he could see of the slow drip of the black liquid and the wound. No one else had been able to see it, but it was there. A thin line in the sky that didn't belong, surrounded by a dark, churning fog that even the strongest winds couldn't clear away. Flexing his right hand, Akule remembered the glow that his hand had produced the night he'd told his wife that he needed to stay. He'd wanted to see her, and it had let him.

"Is it really that simple?" He asked out loud. No one answered. No spirits were rushing to help him. "I doubt it."

The spark in the chest twinged at his doubt, and he huffed. It was like a living thing that had burrowed into him. Sometimes he thought that he might understand it, but at other times it had its own goal. A hysterical laugh almost escaped him. Maybe his mind was going; maybe he was going crazy, thinking that this thing in his chest was alive and aware. Then again, he had something with power in his chest. Maybe it was a spirit that was working through him. He had no other explanation for what was happening to him.

"Stop it," he told himself. "Stop thinking."

It was a tall order, but the thought didn't seem to make anything happen. This seemed to be one of those times when you couldn't think your way through but had to feel your way. Controlling himself, Akule counted his breaths and listened to the sound of the wind. Every so often, he thought he heard a droplet hitting the ground, but he didn't want to think about that.

His hands began to glow with a soft purplish light that was almost lost in the rays of the sun. Moving his hands, Akule inspected the light, trying to understand it. The wind blew across the hill, shaking the grasses around him for a moment before the glow shifted. It collected into small sparks that jumped off his skin and hung in the air. Gaping at the small sparks, Akule heard the dog make a noise of surprise, and grinned. This was it. This was something important.

"Light," he said. At first, nothing happened, and he narrowed his eyes on the sparks. "Light," he tried again, thinking of that night. They started to shift, but it wasn't enough yet. Inhaling slowly, he focused on what he wanted, what he needed the magic to do. "Light," he said softly.

The sparks spun together, forming a small glowing orb in his hand. It floated just above his palm, warming the skin around it. A laugh escaped Akule, and he grinned. Then he looked at the edge of the black. He considered it carefully and then looked back at the magical orb in his hand. It was so perfect; it was like a small moon was grasped in his hand. Another laugh erupted from his chest, and Akule shook his head.

He'd almost thought it was a dream. The spark in his chest had been so quiet, so muted when he watched the band leave without him. Even when they looked back sadly, he'd been unable to feel anything under the crushing grief. Akule pushed the sad memory aside and turned his attention back to the orb. He needed to learn how to use this power that he now possessed. If he didn't, then staying here would be for nothing.

The orb was unlike anything he'd ever seen. With a bit of hesitation, he raised his left hand and poked at it with one finger before drawing his hand back quickly. It was warm, but it didn't burn like a flame would. He shifted his right hand a little, but the orb didn't move. It stayed in the air, and he slowly lowered his right hand. The orb hung in the air, and he laughed again.

"Wow." Akule shook his head. "Now what?"

He sat there as the sun moved across the sky and experimented with the orb and the strange purple sparks. Slowly, he was figuring out what made them work and what didn't. Saying what he wanted wasn't enough; he had to focus on it and give the thought form. The dog inched closer to him throughout the morning, and he worried that he'd need to move the berries if it came any further. Yet, it never came all the way over. The dog, like the other animals, seemed to want to avoid the black edge of the circle.

With a small smile, Akule made the orb move through the air. It gave off no sparks, remaining a solid mass as it spun at his command. He found it was easier if he moved his right hand as he thought about it moving, but it wasn't necessary. Speech and movement weren't needed at all, just his will. He was becoming heady and laughed again. Somehow this was his life now.

Then his stomach rumbled, forcing him to look up at the sun, and frown. The day was moving on without him, and he still had hopes of gathering more food. There was new fatigue in his muscles. He'd been sitting for some time, but his legs were sore as if he'd been walking for hours over uneven terrain.

His eyes were drawn back to the orb. Of course. Akule sighed and nodded to himself. It made sense, he supposed, that power would come in exchange for something else. All of his playing around, while helpful, would have to have a trade-off. He plucked the orb out of the air, once more admiring the soft, gentle heat coming from it, and looked back at the black circle.

Already the grass on the edges was dying. The sun gave him more than enough light to see the smooth dark soil that had been dug down to. There were more signs of stone that had been destroyed now that it was going deeper. How deep it could go was a mystery, but Akule knew that it would only get worse. For now, the droplets of Darkness were carving away at the world, but what would happen if the wound grew larger? What would happen if it got into the water? Would it just destroy it, or be carried away even further? He didn't want to know the answer.

Akule kept hold of the orb. The pain was still there, but it wasn't growing worse. So, once he released the magic, if he left it alone it didn't drain him much. That was a relief at least. The dog whimpered, reminding him that he needed to worry about getting some meat today. Unsure of what to do with the orb, Akule eyed the dark edge of the circle and started to wonder.

This strange power had developed in response to this Darkness that was dripping into the world. That much he could be certain of. So, what would happen if he used this power on the dead spot? He climbed to his feet, stretching out the sore muscles. His stomach grumbled, and he rolled his shoulders. In his hand, the orb pulsed gently in time with his heartbeat. Taking a few steps back, he almost tripped over the basket and took a deep breath. For a moment, he hesitated, suddenly very unsure and worried. Akule took two more steps back and then threw the orb as hard as he could at the patch of black.

It hit the faint black mist. The orb instantly shrank in size, but small flashes of light like lightning burst through the cloud. It hit the ground, the purple color spreading across the dead surface. There was a strange crackling sound, and more small arcs of lightning across the bottom of the bowl. The smell of earth filled his nose, surprising Akule after smelling nothing here before.

But then it was over. The orb's power vanished and the black cloud thickened. Another droplet of black slipped from the wound and hit the earth, causing the ground itself to shrink back. Akule swallowed, fear tightening around his heart. This power had some effect on the Darkness, but it wasn't much. The thing, whatever it was, ate away at everything it touched. Even magic.

16

Seeking and Seeing

Alex groaned happily as Jenny's thumbs dug into her shoulder blades. Her head fell forward, and she pointedly ignored the soft chuckles and smiles from the others. They didn't matter. The tension she'd been carrying that whole damn conference was finally easing a little. Jenny's hands were warm on her skin through the thin material of the well broken-in Ravenslake t-shirt. Alex tried to make a mental note to go clothes shopping and replace some of her stuff, but knew that she wasn't going to remember it.

They were gathered around their dining room table with textbooks, notebooks, and pencils scattered around their laptops and tablets. The goal had been to do homework, but Alex wasn't the only one lacking energy. Jenny shifted behind her and put a bit more force into the impromptu massage.

"Jenny, marry me," Alex sighed.

Her friend laughed softly but leaned forward to kiss her cheek quickly.

"Hey," Lance protested. Alex didn't take him seriously, given he had an affectionate smile on his face. "I thought we weren't doing that in this life."

"Get a move on then," Alex huffed. "Or I just might have to marry her again. She can sleep with you, but give me back rubs."

"How about I just give you back rubs?" Jenny turned her hands slightly, digging the heels of her palms into Alex's flesh. "I'd rather avoid the drama. Besides, I'm already a member of the ex-wives club."

"You and Sif are hardly a club."

"I don't know," Nicki offered. "There is Robin to consider."

"Puck and I were never married." Alex pouted a little when Jenny pulled her hands away. "That was a different sort of relationship."

"Speaking of which," Jenny said, "being the Iron Soul doesn't mean you can't date. That guy Michael from your Russian culture class seemed pretty into you."

Alex had to think about who Michael was again. He'd introduced himself to Jenny and Alex when Jenny had met her outside the classroom for lunch. That had been maybe a week ago, Alex wasn't sure at this point. Michael hadn't said anything, and Alex hadn't noticed an interest, but then again, her mind wasn't exactly in that kind of a place right now.

"I don't know," Alex sighed. Her happy little cloud was evaporating quickly. "Honestly... I can't remember the last time I was physically attracted to someone. It's like all the wires have started getting crossed. My dreams..." she could feel herself turning red. "Well, I've got a lot of memories from married men, and so-"

"Oh god." Nicki smacked a hand over her mouth. Alex glared but was grateful that the redhead hadn't just started laughing.

"Anyway, nothing seems to inspire desire anymore. Maybe it's all the memories messing with me or just...." She trailed off, not wanting to admit that Arthur's betrayal might still be affecting her that much.

Jenny leaned forward and kissed the top of her head. The gesture was more comforting than Alex had been expecting, and she released a shuddering breath. She caught Lance's eye, suddenly a bit worried that he might be concerned by Jenny's affection, but he was smiling gently at her. Alex felt silly for the thought and relaxed, letting Jenny hug her. It was nice to be held, even if it was only platonic. In fact, maybe that was nicer.

"It's okay," Bran said. "Don't let it bother you. There isn't a right answer when it comes to attraction or how you feel about others."

"Sorry," Alex said. "I didn't mean to insult you."

"You didn't," Bran assured her. "I'm fine, Alex. I went through my worrying if there was "something wrong with me" phase early in high school. Give it time, and try not to worry." His expression turned serious. "You've been through a lot, and there's still so much to worry about, so don't be hard on yourself."

"He's right," Jenny agreed. "What can we do to help?"

"I don't know yet," Alex said. Lowering her head into her right hand, she groaned and toyed with some soft short strands of hair. "I need to get my brain working again, but right now I'm just drained."

"It's been a long two days," Nicki said. "But the conference was a solid plan. We were able to get some information and-"

"And you got some blood." Aiden wrinkled up his nose.

"Don't start." Nicki rolled her eyes and huffed. "If I can get that book working again then maybe all the effort I put into it the first time will be worth it."

Alex refrained from commenting on Nicki's dedication to her tracking book. It had been impressive to be sure, but Arthur's death had made the thing largely useless. She still hadn't made her mind up about the blood gathering, and Nicki had asked them not to tell Merlin until she'd had some time to try and use it. While Alex had agreed, it did feel odd keeping such a secret from Merlin. Then again, he seemed willing to consider the Light's idea of breaking the link, and just thinking about it made Alex's stomach roll.

"I'm sorry it wasn't more useful," Jenny said gently. "I know that you were hopeful."

"We learned a few things." Aiden shrugged. "But it's hard to say what will be useful in the long term."

"Honestly, the biggest concern is Alex's memories," Avani said. "This Jar you mentioned seems very important, but there's no mythology surrounding it."

Lance shook his head and said, "There can't always be myths around the Objects. As it stands, it sounds like even Merlin and Morgana have never heard of this incarnation, so they wouldn't know what he made."

"I'm not sure that he made it," Alex said. Her fingers tapped nervously against the table. "The one who fought the Darkness. I can't even find his name in my memories. I'm terrified about what that means. Was he hurt by the Darkness? Did it erase part of my soul?"

"Let's not panic," Bran said gently. Reaching over, he put his left hand over her right one and gave her a gentle smile. "Could you have memories from someone without memories?"

"What?"

"Amnesia," Bran suggested. "We don't know what the Darkness is." Everyone was watching him now, and he lowered his eyes a touch self-consciously. "Aiden and I have been discussing a theory."

"More of a hypothesis," Aiden corrected quickly. Now they looked at him, and he stumbled for a moment. "Electrical fields," he said quickly. "Uh, electrical fields are what keep atoms together. Now, if the Darkness disrupts those fields, then that could be what causes the destruction. Matter can't hold itself together. If the disruption is strong enough and comes into contact with a being that is living energy, then it could overwhelm that being. That would explain how it killed all the Lights.”

“And I told you about memories being based on electrical signals,” Bran reminded her. He squeezed Alex’s hand. “If he was exposed to the Darkness, killing him or not, then it still might have disrupted his electric field first. We don’t know how you got all these memories. Maybe you’re reaching through time, or they’re transmitted on naturally, but his pattern just might have been lost — just his pattern. There’s nothing wrong with your soul. You’re just missing one set of memories.”

Jenny’s hands dug into a particularly hard knot, and Bran’s words were oddly reassuring. She wasn’t sure if that was possible, but Bran’s science jargon made it sound plausible enough that the small bubble of worry in her chest finally shrank a little. It wasn’t all gone. The lack of memory was still an issue. Out of all her different lives, this set of memories was probably the most important. Well, this man and Gottfried, who’d hid Mjǫllnir in Paris.

“How?” Avani asked, breaking into Alex’s thoughts. “Do you have new ideas to try?”

“I think Morgana’s right,” Bran said. “We’re all going to need to give Alex energy. If we can’t link to him easily, then Alex is going to need to search for him.”

“I want to try again,” Alex announced.

“When?” Nicki pulled out her phone. “We can schedule a time with Merlin and Morgana-”

“Us first.” Alex tried to smile. “Let’s face it; while the idea of adding Morgana and Merlin’s magic sounds good, I haven’t used their magic much in the past. It’s you guy’s magic that I know. You’re my friends.” She really did smile now, fondness for them rising in her chest. “I think we have the best chance of making this work.”

Everyone's expressions softened. Jenny stopped her back rub and instead leaned forward to hug Alex, humming softly while Lance grinned. Even though they weren't mages, Alex knew that they'd picked up on her inclusion. Heat flooded her cheeks, and she fought back her smile a little, suddenly feeling exposed. It was silly. These were her friends, but still... It was a bit raw.

"We're here," Bran promised. "And you're not wrong; you tend to share magic with us the most."

"Okay," Nicki said. "But only one more attempt. Those Red Caps seemed to be after the Light, but we can't risk total exhaustion in case they attack us here."

"At least without Arthur there won't be more of those amulets," Lance said. "And Jenny and I are armed, just in case."

Avani nodded in agreement. "Still, it is wise to be careful. We don't want to risk anyone suffering from exhaustion." She looked at Alex. "I have something that might help. I'm not sure how much of an impact it will have, but it might be worth a try."

"We'll take all the help you can give," Alex replied.

"What if you're right?" Nicki asked Bran. "What if the memories are gone? What are we scrying for?"

"The Jar," Alex said firmly. She shifted her hands, trying to remember the shape and size of it. That was something that still bothered her. If it was as simple as she didn't remember it, then why did she feel pain? "It was magical. It had to be."

"I don't know," Aiden mused. "The jars that Merlin used to hold the poison weren't magical."

Furrowing her brow, Alex tried to sort that out. There must have been something special without Merlin knowing, or it was just that the poison from the potions had a grace period at first. "I don't know," she admitted.

Shrugging, Alex tried to hide her unease. "But the Jar's all I can think of that might still be around."

"Given what happened with the Light, are you sure you're up to this?" Bran put his hand on her shoulder. "You haven't talked about it much, but-"

"I think so." Alex took a breath and told herself to calm down. These were her friends, her allies, and at this point her only family. "The voices have returned, and honestly, I never heard this life before, so I don't think this issue is new." Alex tilted her head and focused on the voices. "Arto agrees. This person that we were isn't familiar to him."

"They... do they talk to each other?" Bran asked. His eyes widened, and everyone suddenly looked much more interested.

"I do not know," Alex admitted. Her mind twisted in on itself at the idea. "And I wish you hadn't asked that question. Now I can't help but wonder if they're all sitting on that field of grass watching my life like a drive-in movie."

Everyone managed to contain their laughs, though Nicki looked pained at the effort. Alex inwardly groaned. There were times that her mouth got her into trouble, and now that mental image was never going to leave.

"I hope they at least have popcorn." Lance's tone was dry, and he wasn't even smiling. Nicki cackled, Aiden snorted, and Bran shook his head fondly.

"I wonder what genre it is," Jenny added. "Do you think it counts as fantasy, slice of life, horror, or-"

"Stop," Alex groaned. "Just- no, stop it now. We were trying to be productive and complete a task."

"I suppose so." Lance gave her a small smile. His eyes were entirely too bright and amused. "Sorry."

"I'm sure." Shaking her head, Alex stood up and waved Jenny off. "Come on. Let's give this a try. If it doesn't work, then we order pizza for dinner and recover by watching a stupid movie."

Bran perked up, and Alex rolled her eyes. If this went badly, then their seer was going to ask to watch a kaiju movie and they'd all agree. Before college, she hadn't even known the term for the eastern monster movies. This was her life now: using magic, hunting for lost treasures, fighting some world-destroying force, and learning geeky references and genres. Although the monster fights were kind of fun, she wasn't going to admit that out loud.

Everyone split up to prepare for another attempt at scrying. Lance easily moved the furniture in the living room back while Avani fetched something from her room. Bran collected the Iron Chalice and filled it almost to the top with water in the kitchen sink. That did make Alex break into nervous giggles. Bran gave her a knowing look as the right side of his mouth curled up.

It didn't take long to get what they needed. Jenny was holding Cathanáil just in case it was needed, and Lance's dagger holster was on his right hip rather than hidden in the small of his back. Alex hoped they wouldn't have any untimely visitors, but she was grateful that they were worried.

Sitting down, Alex crossed her legs and stretched out the muscles, trying to sink into a more comfortable position. Maybe it was time to consider yoga. Her morning runs helped clear her mind, but something else to calm her down certainly wouldn't hurt. The others sat down beside her, forming a circle, and Alex smiled in amusement. The living room was a bit small for this, even with the furniture pushed back.

She glanced over at Lance, Jenny, and Avani, who were lingering in the doorway. Alex looked around the small circle. It wasn't even fair to call it that. Nicki was to her right, Aiden her left, and Bran was across from her. It was more like four cardinal points. The Iron Chalice sat between them on a brightly colored large paper mandala that Avani claimed helped open the senses. It was a form of magic that Alex had no experience with, but even she was aware of the mythology surrounding symbols of power. She'd take all the help she could get.

Aiden and Nicki took her hands, and Bran gave her a soft smile as he completed their little circle. She ignored the glow of their hands as the others summoned their magic and instead focused on the steady pulse of the energy. This was familiar, and her body relaxed, tight muscles uncoiling a little. As she gently collected the power, she felt a bit better about the world. Alex closed her eyes and imagined the different colors of red, blue, and yellow collecting together.

This got easier every time. Like some sort of muscle memory, her magic knew theirs and swirled around it gently to take control. Pressure built in Alex's chest. The spark was dancing, zinging around like an overexcited toddler confined to their room. It built and built, curling up inside of her until breathing became a chore. Alex released Nicki and Aiden's hands, shifting them to touch her knees. The magic fluttered, but the connection didn't break.

Leaning forward, Alex gently touched her hands to the side of the Iron Chalice. The water inside shuddered at the contact, but it didn't spill. Below it, the colors of the mandala were suddenly sharper and brighter. Allowing her eyes to trace the design, Alex focused her thoughts on finding the Jar and learning how the Darkness had been defeated.

Her magic danced across the surface of the Iron Chalice. While it was mostly her dark gray now, Alex thought she saw sparks of blue, red, and yellow as the magic sank into the metal. The Chalice began to glow, and the water rippled softly. Alex stopped breathing, nervously watching and waiting for anything. The hand on her right squeezed her knee, and Alex let herself exhale. She took in a fresh breath of air and watched.

The surface of the water shimmered. Lines of color appeared, spreading from the iron sides of the cup and swirling around each other to form a pattern. Narrowing her eyes, Alex's chest tightened, and there was a hum from the voices in her head. A new whisper tried to push itself forward, and she heard Arto quieting the others. Even Cuthbert listened as she strained to hear the new voice. The voice was too soft. She couldn't make anything out.

A small plain of grass with lots of rocks appeared in the Chalice. There was a circle made of pale stone that stood out against the greens and yellows of the ground. Long lines stretched between opposite points on the circle, forming a wheel and spoke-like pattern. Small piles of stones stood at different points along the edge. It shifted slightly, letting her see hillsides of trees below and the sun rising across from her vantage point. But the dark blue sky was interrupted by a strange mass of black along a dark line.

That was familiar. It was all familiar, but it was trying to slip through her grasp. Swallowing, Alex frantically tried to think. There had to be something she could do. The image pulled back, sweeping above the strange circle so that she could see all of it at once. There was no sign of the Jar, but this had to be important. Her magic flared, and a frightened and exhausted male face with deeply tanned skin and deep brown eyes appeared in the water. It looked up at her before swirling Darkness took his place. With a gasp, Alex broke the magical connection and pulled her hands away from the Iron Chalice.

17

Breathing Room

Electricity was still zinging through Alex's veins, and she had to consider that maybe she'd gathered up too much magic. As much as her earlier attempts had been like hitting a wall, this time it had been smooth and painless. The contrast was nice, but very surprising. Her muscles were a little sore from channeling so much energy, but that horrible heart attack level pain hadn't shown itself.

Still, her legs didn't want to work when she tried to stand up. Bran took the Chalice from her hands, and Lance very gently came up behind her and helped Alex to her feet. She made a point of not thinking about how strong Lance's arms were. They'd escaped one love triangle; she wasn't going there even if Lance's biceps were pretty impressive. The thought made her giggle, even if his muscles don't actually do anything for her. Lance gave her an odd look, but he kept supporting her.

Alex wiggled her toes as he eased her down onto the sofa. For good measure, he got Aiden and Bran to help him push it back into place. For a strange moment, Alex was back at her family's home as a child with her father pushing around the sofa while she and her brothers bounced around on the cushions so their mother could vacuum behind it. The memory was gone as quickly as it came, leaving wistfulness and homesickness in its wake.

Then she noticed that the others were watching her as they sat down. She needed to focus. Closing her eyes, Alex inhaled and smiled when she easily recalled the images that the Chalice had shown her. She gave herself a moment, letting the magic finish dissipating and her body adjust back to normal. Alex was still sore, but it was nothing that she couldn't handle.

"It worked." Smiling, she nodded to the others. "Thank you, that was so much easier. I didn't see what happened, but I saw a location. It looked really special. I think that it's where he fought the Darkness or where the Jar is hidden."

"Great!" Nicki was grinning with relief. "What did you see? Any landmarks?"

"Oh yeah." Alex couldn't help but smile back. She had something real to work with, and not just vague mountain ranges to try and identify. "There was this stone circle."

"Like standing stones?" Lance asked. "Stonehenge?"

"No, not like that," Alex said. She shook her head. "It was like a wheel with spokes. They weren't standing stones. They were pale and on the ground, which formed the design." Frustration began to grow in her chest. "There were a lot of mountains around it. Tall and jagged mountains, so that rules out some areas." Turning her attention to Nicki, she looked hopefully at the redhead. "Is this ringing any bells?"

"I don't know much about Native American culture," Nicki reflected, already going for her tablet on the end table, "but it does sound familiar. I think I've seen pictures." Ignoring them, Nicki sat on the sofa, pulling her feet up under her and starting to type something in. "I've heard of stone circles, and I'm pretty sure they're called Medicine Wheels." There was a pause, and Nicki grinned in triumph. "My obscure knowledge wins again. Lots of results on the symbolism...."

Impatiently, Alex darted around the back of the sofa and leaned over Nicki's shoulder to peer down at the screen. Her legs threatened to give out, but she was fine once she leaned against the back of the sofa. She ignored the fact that Bran had gotten up and hovered behind her. Nicki clicked on the second result, bringing up the Wikipedia page for Medicine Wheels.

"That's it!" Alex pointed excitedly to the picture. "That's the one!"

"Hold on," Aiden cautioned. "They might all look-"

"No, that's the place," Alex insisted. "The mountains are the same. I'm sure of it."

"Bighorn Medicine Wheel," Nicki said. Alex drummed her hands on the back of the sofa as she waited for Nicki to click the link to the new page. The images that popped up made Alex's chest ease. "You think this is it?"

"Yes." Alex nodded, and backed away from the sofa. "That's it. I know it is."

"Well, that was easy then," Nicki said. She didn't seem to know what to think but shrugged and smiled. "Hurray, internet."

Bran took the tablet from Nicki, ignoring her squawk of protest. "Apparently it has an astronomical alignment system just like Stonehenge. It aligns on the summer solstice."

Alex couldn't help it; she grinned and slumped into an armchair. "That's it," she said softly. "I know it is."

"There are other circles," Bran said carefully.

"No, the Bighorn mountains are right," Alex said firmly. "I don't remember much, but it was high and-" The memory was already slipping away. "We can try to verify if you want. Maybe a map as a focus."

"We can try," Aiden agreed. "But you really do sound certain. You're probably right. You usually are about this kind of thing."

"Question," Lance said. He held up his hand. "What is your plan here? Do you think that this Jar will be able to stop the Darkness? It just seems... I don't know, a bit crazy."

"I don't know if it can," Alex admitted. "Maybe not all of it, but if I can find the Jar and we can figure out how it was made, then maybe it'll give us some clues. Or hell, maybe I can shove the rest of the Darkness in it."

They all exchanged doubtful looks. Alex sighed. She didn't think it would be that easy either, but this past life had figured out how to stop the Darkness from destroying Earth without any help from Merlin or Morgana. That took some serious brains, creativity, and insight. She wanted to know how they'd done it because she lacked those things.

"It'll be okay, Alex," Jenny said gently. She came up behind Alex and started gently rubbing her shoulders. "We'll figure it out. I have faith in all of you."

Unsure of how to respond, Alex cleared her throat and told herself to focus on a plan. "We need to go to the Medicine Wheel as soon as possible. Maybe being there will help my memories or we can use our tracking spell to find the jar. It has to be intact somewhere in the area."

At least, she hoped it was. It had to be. Alex's gut said that there was still Darkness in there, and if the jar had ever cracked then the Darkness would have been released. Then again, based on what Merlin had said, the poison didn't last long after it was released. A dull pain was developing behind her eyes. Alex became aware that she was pushing at her own memories, instinctively trying to seek out the information. She wasn't sure when she'd started doing that. The voices were chattering, but none of them had any useful information. This Medicine Wheel was new to all of them.

"We do have a slight problem," Bran said. He looked up from his phone with furrows forming between his eyes. "Alex, the Medicine Wheel is at a very high elevation. You can't get there in the winter."

"We'll use magic," Alex replied. Jumping up, she started to pace. "That's probably for the best anyway. We won't have to worry about tourists seeing us."

"There isn't a river nearby like at Stonehenge, Alex," Bran protested. "If we go in winter then it is going to be a real pain."

"I get that," Alex said. "I do, but the solstice could be important."

"I'm not sure," Nicki called. She was still staring at the screen of her tablet. "I'm finding references to the summer solstice, but not the winter. Its alignment might only be valid in the summer, which makes sense if the weather made it impossible to get up there in the winter."

"Even if it isn't in alignment that doesn't make the trip useless," Alex retorted. "The solstices are powerful days for us. That boost might give me the help I need to find the memories. Remember what Bran did? He didn't really remember his past life, but had visions that guided us in Wales."

"That's true." Bran nodded slowly. He wasn't convinced, but her argument had at least made him thoughtful. "I suppose that being in the same place and reaching out on a solstice might help you look back. But we still don't really understand what happened in Wales."

"There's a lot we don't understand." Aiden shrugged a little when the others looked at him. "But it's a lead. We'll need to research the Wheel and make a plan. If the roads are closed and there isn't a body of water nearby, we might have to resort to using magic to help us scale the mountain. I don't know about you, but I don't want to get arrested for trespassing."

"We'll sort out the details," Nicki said. She was frowning a little now. "I can't find much online. This is going to take some in-depth research. No one really knows the origin of the Medicine Wheel from what I'm seeing. There are a couple of legends, but the Crow tribe which lives in the area acknowledges that they didn't build it and it predates them. Granted that information is only a few centuries old, but it does open the possibility that it was created at least in part with magic."

"I don't know," Alex said. "It's possible. I don't know if I- if he built it alone or if other people helped him; either is possible. Stonehenge wasn't built with magic after all. It predates Merlin."

"Pity Merlin and Morgana didn't know anything about this life," Nicki sighed. "It would have been interesting to pick their brains."

"We'll manage," Alex encouraged. Inhaling slowly, she debated her next words. "Did anyone else get the feeling that Merlin agreed with the Light?"

"Yes," Bran replied. When she looked at him, he sighed but nodded. "Merlin and Morgana are both focused on the Iron Realm. They aren't going to worry about the other worlds. To be fair, we are mostly the same way. From a certain point of view, the Light's plan makes sense." He held up his hand to keep the others from talking. "I don't agree with it. Something connected our worlds, some force, either directed or natural, and breaking that connection is sure to have side effects."

"On the other hand," Aiden added, "It is right that we can't just wait around forever. If this trip to the Medicine Wheel doesn't help, then we may need to take a serious look at the proposal." Nicki grumbled but didn't argue with Aiden. "We have to do something. Period."

"I know," Alex said. She licked her lips. Her fingers itched for her own phone so she could look up information on the Medicine Wheel. "I'd prefer to wait until the summer solstice, but you're right. We don't have much time."

"Plus side, that's only six weeks away," Nicki said. "That gives us time to plan our trip. Winter break will overlap nicely. If we're lucky, we can get the information on the solstice and still be home for Christmas." Then Nicki froze, and her expression fell. "Uh..."

It took Alex a moment to understand what had upset Nicki. Then she realized that everyone was looking at her, and Alex remembered. This would be the first Christmas without her family. She swallowed, surprised by the sudden rush of sorrow that brought. The temptation to curl her magic around the pain was sharp and strong, but Alex resisted. She couldn't go down that road again.

Still... time seemed to have slowed. They'd been so busy lately. She'd stayed busy since the death of her parents and saying goodbye to her brothers. Alex exhaled and closed her eyes, trying to dispel the sudden grief and tension.

"You can come with me for the holiday," Jenny offered gently. She touched Alex's shoulder. "Lance is coming with me for Christmas."

"Really?" Alex grabbed onto that topic and looked up at the pair of them. Lance had his arm wrapped around Jenny's waist. "Christmas together, that's a big step!"

"Yeah." Lance seemed a touch embarrassed but pleased. "Jenny's agreed to go home with me for Thanksgiving. It feels like it's time to meet the family."

"I wouldn't want to intrude," Alex protested softly.

"I'd love to have a buffer," Lance replied. "Her father can't kill me if there's a witness."

"Think about it," Jenny said. "We have to see what happens obviously, but you'd be welcome."

"You could hang with me and my Gran too," Nicki offered. Smiling at Alex, she seemed mostly recovered. "As Jenny said, we'll see what happens, but think about it. We aren't going to leave you alone."

Lowering her eyes, Alex swallowed the lump forming in her throat and breathed around the knot in her chest. Gratitude, affection, grief, and hope was a strange mixture that clashed together like a storm around her heart. It hurt, but almost in a good way. Jenny's hand had yet to move, and Alex was in no hurry to push away the gentle affection.

"One more thing," Bran said. His voice was cautious, but Alex was grateful for the distraction from all of the feelings. "Just a warning. The Medicine Wheel is sacred ground. I know that we've already desecrated a tomb and crawled over bones, but I'd like to see us at least try to be respectful here." He held up his tablet, showing them a picture of people gathered around a rope fence. "The site is still actively used for ceremonies by tribal members."

"We will be," Alex promised. Straightening up, she felt a bit stronger now. "But it's the best place to get the vision I need to solve this mystery."

"That's convenient." Bran smiled a little. "That's exactly what the site is used for. Apparently, vision quests were done up there."

"That is convenient," Alex agreed. "And I wonder... if that tradition is tied to what happened there, or if it was created later..."

"Question." Avani held up her hand looking a touch nervous. "When did you desecrate a tomb?"

"That was when we recovered Arto's skull and gave him his long overdue cremation," Nicki replied far too quickly. "I'll tell you about it later. Well, what I can remember." She shivered a little. "There was a lot of magic during that event. The whole thing is a bit hazy."

Alex sucked in a sharp breath as the memory of Arto's burial rites came to the forefront of her mind. She'd seen a series of faces, all of them turning to look at her, but their faces were blurring in her flawed human memory. Had this Iron Soul been among them, or had he been completely forgotten? No: he was still part of her. She'd seen him in her mind. He was there, buried beneath whatever had happened. She just needed to find it.

The image of the Medicine Wheel stayed with Alex. It was clear in her mind's eye, and she tried to understand it. Why was it like a wheel? She was pretty sure that Native Americans didn't have the wheel, or was that too much of a generalization? She really only knew of a small section of tribes from the Washington area. Nicki had mentioned the Crow, but even that meant almost nothing to her. She knew that they were a plains tribe and thought that they might be teepee dwellers.

"We need to learn more," Nicki said. She held her tablet against her chest and shifted forward to sit on the edge of the sofa. "I have a proposal, and it might be a little crazy."

"Careful, you sound like the Light," Aiden teased.

Nicki scowled at him, but it made Alex smile a little. "I suggest that we experiment with the poison from the potion." Everyone paused, but no one panicked. Alex tilted her head and listened intently. "From what Merlin said, it loses its power quickly so there shouldn't be much danger, but if Alex is right and it is like the Darkness then maybe we can figure out if there is a way to stop it. For all we know bleach might destroy it. Right now, all that poison isn't good for anything, but maybe we can make it do some good."

There were nods around the room, but Avani frowned. Then with a sigh, she raised her hand. "Another question; what poison?"

Alex chuckled and slumped back against the cushion. Jenny moved her hand and gently ran a hand over Alex's head, comforting her as Nicki started to catch Avani up. The last aches of using her magic were fading, and Alex could feel her body growing heavy, but she didn't even try to fight the urge to sleep. At least for right now, surrounded by her friends, she was safe.

Bringing a Spark to Life

433 C.E. Bighorn Mountains

Akule flinched as the mountain goat hit the ground. All traces of the purple bolt he'd thrown at the creature were gone, but the effect was apparent. Looking down at his right hand, Akule almost yelped in fear and cheered in victory. If he could manage this every few days, then food wouldn't be an issue. He expected smoke to be rising from his fingertips, but even the small purple sparks that had circled his hand were gone.

For a moment, he didn't move. His mind raced over the events of the day, trying to determine what had just occurred. He'd woken to a brilliant sunrise and checked his dwindling food stores. As the dead circle expanded, the area's game moved off. It made him grateful that his family was gone. He and the dog had headed away from the dark spot, and he'd spotted a mountain goat above him on a steep slope of rocks. Sadly, he'd known that he wasn't a skilled enough archer to hit the quickly moving thing.

A strange, strained laugh did escape him now. It had been a stray thought when he'd resigned himself that he couldn't hit the goat. He'd only been thinking how good some fresh meat would taste after yesterday's failed hunt. He'd thought about what a shame it was that his strange power could make light, but couldn't keep him fed. Then the flame in his chest had spurred to life, and the sparks had formed. He hadn't known what he was doing when he'd thrown out his hand, but the power had held onto his idea of killing the mountain goat.

Creeping forward, Akule observed the goat in case it suddenly woke. Its long, curled horns were a dangerous thing to be near if it did wake. But as he approached, he gasped softly and took in the hole in the creature's chest. It went all the way through the beast, no larger than his pointer finger. It was no wonder that the thing had dropped dead.

"I'm sorry," he said. "But thank you."

The dog trailed after him and sniffed eagerly at the beast. Akule smiled a little, his relief taking hold. This would keep him and his companion fed for a few days. He could focus on the issue of the Darkness. Flexing his fingers, Akule wondered if this was a one-time thing or if he could replicate that strange purple beam. If he could, then hunting alone would no longer be an issue.

Pulling out his knife, Akule put the matter out of his mind and focused on dressing the beast. Carefully slicing from the groin to the throat, he gently peeled back the fur and skin, leaving the layer of muscle whole underneath. The beast was warm beneath his hands, and he pulled the skin away from the muscles with little resistance. When he was satisfied with the space he had to work with, Akule cut through the muscles and began to remove the entrails. Nothing seemed out of place or damaged by the purple arrow.

Then again, he was a few miles away from his small camp, and there was too much for him to carry himself. Usually there would be a group of hunters to help cut the beast into more manageable pieces to bear home. Tossing some of the innards to the dog, Akule began to slice off one of the powerful hind legs and planning how to transport as much as he could home. It wasn't ideal without a chance to drain the blood, but he lacked options. Then an odd idea occurred to him. His power, that strange purple flare, had killed the beast at his wish, but maybe it could do more.

The sun shined down on his back, warming him against the crisp mountain wind. It grew warmer every day, but Akule knew he couldn't become complacent. Sitting on the balls of his feet, he studied the carcass thoughtfully. In his chest, he was aware of the purple flare pulsing in time with the beat of his heart. He still didn't understand it, but at least the initial fear was gone.

Sparks appeared around his fingertips, glittering in the sunlight and humming with power. Akule licked his lips nervously and awkwardly waved his hand towards the carcass. Some of the sparks went, but they did nothing. He struggled to understand what he needed to do. Earlier it had almost been an accident. He'd been thinking about an arrow though; maybe that was important.

It took some focus and more imagination that Akule was usually forced to call upon, but after some intense staring and waving, the sparks surrounded the carcass. A hint of worry churned in his stomach again. Was this safe? Was he going to ruin the meat doing this? But he moved his left hand and raised it into the air.

"Lift," he whispered. "Lift."

Slowly, the small sparks encircled the carcass, and it began to rise into the air. A sound of surprise left the dog, and Akule grinned. It was floating at his command! Excitement bloomed in his chest, almost overwhelming the power of the purple flare. Another laugh escaped Akule, this one surprised and pleased. He moved slowly. He didn't know the limits of this power the spirits had granted him yet. Even the dog wasn't able to jump up high enough to reach the goat's leg. He regretted that he'd even started dressing it. With this strange power, he could have gotten it home first. Blood began to drip out of the hole the bolt had ripped in the flesh, and Akule smiled. That would make things even easier. He bundled up the organs in a basket before the dog could pounce and headed out with a spring in his step.

By the time he made his way back to his hut, a strange hot ache was radiating through his chest and arms. The blood had stopped about half a mile back, to his relief. A few times the carcass almost dropped as he lost concentration. The sensation was similar to when he ran too long or too hard and his muscles burned. Akule could only assume that the spark was tired. He wasn't sure how that worked, but it had been enough to get the food home. Still, he'd need to remember that. Using too much of the power made him tired. He couldn't afford to faint or become weak if he was in a dangerous place.

His fingers trembled a little, but his grip was still firm enough to finish removing the goat's organs and begin the process of skinning. The dog kept sniffing around him, and he tossed it scraps as he worked. At least the beast had been well trained by Hakola and wasn't trying to steal the meat. Removing the legs proved to be a bit difficult on his own and Akule lamented having no one to help him, but he eventually finished his task.

His band had left him with two standing smoking racks that Akule quickly loaded up with long, thin portions of meat. He lit a fire and coughed lightly as a wave of smoke rolled into his face, but he was able to position everything properly. A slight breeze carried the smoke across the meat. A spasm in his hand made him hiss, but Akule pushed on and let his mind wander.

The power could do many things, it seemed. He'd only had to imagine what he wanted, and it made it so. No, that wasn't it, he realized quickly. If it was then his family would be back with him. It was more directed than that. He had to think about how the magic could achieve what he wanted. He wanted the meat, so the power had struck down the mountain goat. He'd wanted to carry it home, and the sparks had cradled the carcass. That had been more complex, and he'd needed to imagine the beast floating.

Akule wished there was someone he could ask. Surely he wasn't the first person to have such power. There had to have been others. Then again, maybe not. Walking to the edge of his small camp, he looked out towards the dead spot. It was growing slowly, but it was still a little larger each day. Half of the hillside had been eaten away, and the vegetation was long gone. Animals fled from it, and his dreams were haunted by it. Maybe this power could only appear in a time of great need, such as this.

There was too much to think about. Today had been enlightening, but it hadn't answered any of his more pressing questions. Akule stoked the fire and skewered a few choice pieces of meat for roasting. There was a limit to how much he could do with the skin tonight with his hands so weak. Still, he kept working at a slow pace. At least the Darkness nearby would scare off the wild animals from trying to come into his camp.

He kept busy for some time, enjoying the familiar task of dressing a carcass and deciding how to get the most out of it. Despite himself, he kept feeding the dog scraps. This was at least familiar. Only the smell of cooked meat drew his attention away from his prize.

Sinking his teeth into the rich, warm cooked meat, Akule sighed and chewed the bite happily. The dog collapsed with a grunt, too full to even beg for more scraps. It gave him a moment to relax and plan. He could smoke the rest of the meat and have food for several days. Akule was still struggling with exactly how long it would last for a single person. All of his life, he'd been in a band with many mouths to feed.

He took his next bite with less gusto. A pang ached in his chest, overtaking the slight burning sensation. It was already difficult to picture the faces of his family. It was all fading so quickly. He took another bite and reached over to stroke the dog's fur. With each passing moment, the burn from using so much power was fading. Beneath him, Akule could feel the gentle pulse of the world making him stronger. It was a dizzying feeling.

Why him? He couldn't help but wonder as he took another bite of his dinner. He was nothing special. If some great spirit was directing this and had given him these powers, then why not bestow them on more of the band? Surely more of them together would have been stronger, would have been a better match for this strange disease taking hold of the land.

The sun was beginning to set now. Animals made noises from up in the mountains, and the wind sang softly through the peaks. It was too quiet. The dark patch had already driven off so much of the wildlife that their natural melody was muted. He looked down at the carcass and sighed in relief. His hands were aching, but the skin and most of the meat had been removed. With the blood pouring out earlier there wasn't too much of a scent around camp.

Still, he cut the last meat off the bones and gave it to the dog. His hands were cramping, but he'd have plenty to eat. More meat was hung on the racks, and he set some to cook over the fire. Without anyone but the dog to help him, he was actually at risk of the meat going bad. Akule added more wood to the fire to build up the smoke.

Exhaustion weighed his shoulders down, and yet Akule had no interest in going to sleep. He resumed petting the dog and taking comfort in the beast's soft breathing and happy sighs. If only he was so easily satisfied by a full belly. Akule waited for a desire to sleep to take hold, but it didn't. Instead, he watched the flames of the fire lick at the sky and glanced up to find more and more stars appearing overhead. Stretching out beside the fire, he smiled as the dog laid out next to him to share its body heat, and stared up into the sky.

Above him, the deep blue faded to full black, and the stars filled it with tiny points of light. They stretched out forever. The fire was dying down, and Akule wasn't inclined to build it back up. Not just yet. He inhaled slowly as the weight of the night sky pressed down on him. The size of it all overwhelmed him, but he kept his eyes open. His breathing softened, and he swallowed.

"Hakola, I miss you." Only the night heard him, but maybe she was still awake wherever his band was. He could only hope that she and the children were safe and healthy. "I miss our children."

The wind brushed across his skin and sparked the fire back to life. A sigh escaped him. In the renewed brightness some of the stars faded from his view. He sat up slowly and reached for more wood. Putting another large branch from a downed tree into the coals, he pushed and prodded the fire a bit to make sure that the smoke was blowing towards the racks.

Then he stretched out again. He watched the stars, trying to find familiar shapes from the stories of his people. There were animals and warriors, and signs from the spirits that comforted him. It was something he shared with his family despite the distance between them. But the weight did not leave him. The world stretched out, but to what he did not know. In his chest, the spark fluttered as if suddenly renewed.

Akule closed his eyes and inhaled slowly. He could smell the smoke and the earth beneath him, and there was a hint of blood in the air. His heart rate slowed. He kept his eyes shut and turned inward. Flaring at his attention, the purple spark danced, and he could see it clearly. It burned brightly behind his eyelids, twisting and reaching up towards the heavens.

Before he could open his eyes and dismiss the twisting spark, he saw a face staring back at him. It was a man with pale skin and brown hair staring back at him. He wore strange clothing and carried a strange long stick that was smooth and gleamed in the sunlight. Behind him was a strange landscape. He smiled and reached towards Akule, but the touch never came.

The first man vanished, and more faces appeared, each showing itself only briefly before a new one took its place. They were all differently colored, skin, hair and eyes. A couple were dressed similarly to him, but they were all unknown to him. Then another face appeared and this time didn't just rush by like a running deer. It was a woman with sorrowful gray eyes. Long gold hair hung around her shoulders. She met his gaze, her eyes widening as though she was surprised.

A strange banging sound reached him. The spark brightened, flooding his chest with warmth. The woman vanished. Another bang. It wasn't the sound of rocks striking each other. Similar, but the tone of the ringing was wrong. There was an echo to this that he didn't understand. There was just darkness before him. He could see nothing. Akule struggled against it and tried to open his eyes, but something held him.

Without opening his eyes, he was looking up at the stars once more. A soft voice whispered to him. The words rolled over him and sank into his mind without him truly hearing them. His heart rate sped up — a warning. The long day was coming. He'd be stronger then, the voice promised.

There was another crash with that strange echo. The stars were gone again. The voice was silent. A glowing body appeared, shining as if on fire. Something clanged once more, striking the body and adding more definition to its shape. The head turned toward him. He saw the woman's face, her gray eyes meeting his own again. Another clang, and the face was gone.

Gasping for air, Akule opened his eyes, shocked that he could even move them. Beside him, the dog whined, and the fire flickered. His arms ached. The burning sensation was back in his chest and limbs. Gulping in breaths, Akule didn't dare close his eyes. Overhead, the stars twinkled, almost mockingly. There was more out there. More to see. Rolling onto his side, he shook himself and stared into the fire. The dog stood and whimpered at his distress. Then the darned thing proceeded to start licking his face.

Akule pulled his face back. A rough laugh escaped him when the creature proceeded to crawl on top of him. Shaking his head, Akule pushed the dog off. Before he could get up, something caught Akule's eye and drew his gaze up into the sky. A bright streak was moving across the horizon, a stream of light against the darkening blue. He'd seen such things before, but this was larger and brighter than any he'd ever seen in the past. It grew brighter and brighter, illuminating the mountains as it raced closer. Then it hit the ground. The earth rumbled beneath his body and he stopped breathing, fearing the worst.

But the world settled in seconds, and Akule inhaled slowly. There was a line of white in his eyes that he had to blink away. Slowly, he climbed to his feet. The dog had bolted, but he heard it whining in the hut. He didn't blame it. The lights had never hit before, or at least, not with that much of a shudder. It had to be close. He stood slowly. A glowing line remained against the dark sky, slowly fading and pointing the way to whatever had fallen. In his chest, the spark hummed with excitement.

19

Well Met in The Arboretum

It was far too cold to be outside. Merlin rubbed his hands together and pulled on his magic. Perhaps it was a touch wasteful to use his magic thusly, but even his thick woolen coat didn't seem to be doing much against the wind. Looking around the park, Merlin noted that he was still completely alone. The arboretum trees were all bare except for the evergreens, and the lake was still frozen over. A fresh inch of snow was on the ground, and everyone else was intelligent enough to be indoors.

He walked over to a nearby bench and quickly brushed the snow off of it. A jogger ran past on the shoveled sidewalk with their dog. They didn't even glance Merlin's way. That was for the best. He sat down on the bench with a slight groan, feeling the cold sink into his joints. The sun was sinking towards the horizon, and Merlin was beginning to think that it was best to leave now when a figure came into view, walking towards him. It didn't take long for Merlin to get a good look at the man, and he exhaled in both relief and nervousness.

The Light was moving slowly and deliberately. It was probably trying to reassure him, but all it did was put Merlin on edge. Warriors moved that way as they took in their surroundings and watched for the best moment to attack. He wasn't sure about the Light. Merlin knew that they couldn't confirm the truth of anything the Light said, and yet here he was. Dressed in a dark gray long coat with his hair neatly combed, the Light looked little like Arthur now. He was grateful for that, and he suspected that it was intentional on the part of the Light.

"Thank you for meeting with me," the Light said. He came to a stop in front of Merlin and made no move to sit on the bench. "I know that we are not scheduled to meet for a few weeks, so I appreciate you taking the time."

"You said it was important," Merlin said. Struggling not to fidget, he suddenly wished that he'd brought a mug of tea or coffee just to keep his hands occupied.

"Yes. As the conference decided, I've been trying to outline my knowledge of the Darkness and see if I can track any indicators that it is in your world."

"Do you think it is here?" Merlin leaned forward slightly as his heart rate jumped.

"I'm unsure." The Light looked down at his right hand and flexed his pale fingers. "I am still adjusting to your human form. Yet... I do believe that I can sense some flickers of the Darkness here. It just doesn't make sense to me."

"Oh?"

Merlin allowed himself to tense. That was natural, but his mind spun with worry. Could the Light really sense the Darkness? What if he learned of the poison? Merlin was still uncertain as to Alex's insistence that the poison and the Darkness were connected, but each passing day convinced him a little more. If the Light was sensing that, then it would answer some questions, but create many more. Then the Light drew a folded-up piece of paper from its pocket and held it out.

"I fear my notes may not make much sense. What I observed in my world doesn't translate perfectly to yours."

"That's to be expected." Merlin took the offered paper and unfolded it. Small drawings and scribbled notes described the basics of the Darkness. "No idea what it is? Point of origin?"

"No idea," the Light admitted. Then he began to pace, dragging his feet through the snow and seeming completely unbothered by the cold. Merlin filed that away. It might shed more light on the situation in regards to Arthur's body. "We didn't have any warning. I know nothing of where it came from."

"I suppose that was too much to hope for." Merlin tapped his cold fingers against the page as he stared at it. There was nothing new, nothing that the Light hadn't already spoken of. "I'll admit I had hoped for more when you said it was important."

"You need to convince Alex to use the Iron Hammer." Aggravation filled the Light's normally impassive face. "This can't be allowed to go on. I understand her worry, I do, but we cannot wait to address the danger. It is pressing. It is coming! Thousands if not millions are dying, and other worlds are choking as we speak!"

"I am willing to consider your suggestions about the connections between the worlds," Merlin said. Sitting down, he folded his hands in his lap and inhaled the fresh air. "But I'm sure you can understand our hesitation. You may not like it-"

"I do understand, but there is no time for doubt."

"Why did the Red Caps attack you?"

"I assume they suffer a sense of betrayal. Arthur was leading the Fae, at least some of them, and talked of grand plans for them. Most, I must admit, were lies, but the Red Caps are exiles even amongst the Fae. Their viciousness sets them apart, and Fae communities don't want them nearby. Arthur's army provided them with a structure. I believe that they enjoyed that. When I claimed this body, I made no secret of it. They know that I am not him."

"Simple revenge then." Merlin hummed thoughtfully. "Perhaps."

"I do not seek violence, Merlin," The Light assured him. Merlin wished he could accept that at face value. "I have seen too much death as it is. While many of my kind joined together, many more were swallowed and lost to us. I'm worried." The Light leaned forward, almost looming over him. "Your Iron Soul seems resistant to what must be done."

Irritation flared in Merlin's chest. He disliked the Light's dismissal of Alex. She might not be his favorite incarnation of the Iron Soul, but she'd had far more to contend with than any of the others.

"Alex has learned better than to let fear control her actions." He met the Light's eyes, puffing up his chest. "I do not understand what is happening right now, but the young mages are creative and insightful."

"Yes, but this is new territory, Merlin. You are a Grand Mage! You are here to guide the Iron Soul. She needs guidance." The Light exhaled and took a step back. "Arthur believed that the Iron Soul being born female was a sign. He believed that it was meant as a warning of a great change."

"Warning?" Merlin repeated. "Arthur was violent and cruel towards the mages."

"Arthur was damaged." The Light waved his hand dismissively. "Alex and I have spoken about him. He wanted power, needed to feel important, but was all too aware of the scale of the world he was a part of. Probably even more than you."

Merlin frowned at the very idea that Arthur was more aware than himself, but the Light just kept talking. "His mother talked about it; the worlds she had seen as she rose through the ranks of the court. She knew of the Darkness. She hid it to avoid panic in the court, but it was always there, driving her forward. Arthur heard of it and knew how important it was to her that the way be opened." The Light shook his head and sighed regretfully. "He was a boy that was afraid."

"I don't believe that," Merlin growled. "He was manipulative and cruel. He didn't need to date Alex; he chose to do that."

"He knew she was the Iron Soul. She interested him. For a time, he hoped that she might work with him, but he came to understand that wouldn't happen."

Merlin snorted and shook his head. "It doesn't matter. You seem determined to see a scared little boy in Arthur, but I don't. He was my enemy, and unless he knew something about Alex that is helpful now then don't speak of him."

"As you wish." The Light nodded and glanced towards the lake. He took a few steps away, giving Merlin space to breathe. "I do have a question."

"Yes?"

"The Iron Hammer? Mjǫllnir I believe it's called, is it bound to the Iron Soul, or can anyone use it?"

"That's a dangerous question."

"I only ask because if something happens to Alex, then what?" The Light turned back, spinning his right heel in the snow. "If things go badly and she's lost, then what? Surely you understand my concern."

"Nothing is going to happen to Alex."

Merlin gave the Light a stern look just in case any terrible ideas were brewing in his mind. With a slight tug of his magic, he tried to reach into the creature's mind, but there was only static. He pulled back before the Light could notice. There had been a time when he'd disliked invading another being in such a way, but after Arthur's betrayal it was impossible to feel guilty. If he'd only looked then, perhaps he would have seen the truth, or at least seen that Arthur's mind was too well defended for him to be a simple college student.

"As I said, I mean her no harm. But losing the world for want of the Iron Soul would be foolish."

"I don't know," Merlin admitted. "Sif took the Hammer after Thor's death and sealed it away. Morgana and I did not argue with her. It was found centuries later by a Nazi expedition and stolen by an officer who was the current incarnation of the Iron Soul. He hid it away where Alex found it. No one else has ever tried to use it, to my knowledge."

The honesty was bitter on his tongue. It was a valid point that the Light had made, and Merlin hated that. Loathing rolled in his chest, and he sternly reminded himself that not all of these feelings were actually about the Light. Arthur was dead, at long last, but once again he had failed to protect the Iron Soul from the traitor's soul. He swallowed and relaxed back against the cold metal of the bench.

"I see," the Light said. "Thank you for answering honestly. May I ask what plans you have in the event of Alex Adams' death? I wish to know that the world will be safe. From speaking with the other beings, it has become clear that this is the most dangerous period that the Iron Realm has ever faced."

"I will not argue with that." Merlin stayed still as the Light turned back to him. "Many old enemies have tried to return, and old issues have been stirred up, but this generation of mages is strong. There are more of them, for one, and they work well together. Additionally, with the power of the Iron Chalice, we are not at high risk of losing any of them."

"Humans die." The Light shivered, but Merlin was sure that it wasn't from the cold. "I'm sorry, you are fond of her. I can see that. This must be a difficult topic for you."

"If she falls, then she will be reborn. Morgana and I will find whoever she is reborn as. If need be, we can even push the process to make the rebirth immediate."

That brought back memories. Merlin wasn't ashamed of what he and Morgana had done with Nikolas and Michel. It had been necessary, but it wasn't the sort of thing that he wanted a potential enemy to know.

"I see." The Light smiled and nodded. "Thank you. I understand that this is a difficult conversation. You have given me some much-needed reassurance."

That was what he said at least, but Merlin saw something more in the eyes. He frowned and studied the Light's face. But the face was more like a mask than anything else. The Light was just wearing a body, a disguise. Merlin had to remember that. He couldn't trust the reactions he saw.

"I hope to hear from Alex soon," the Light added. "As soon as she is ready to use the Iron Hammer, please let me know."

Then he turned and walked back to the path, leaving Merlin frowning after him. The thing was assuming that Alex would break the connections between worlds. Foolish, he thought as he stood up. Very foolish to assume he knew what would happen. Merlin folded up the piece of paper the Light had given him and slipped it into his pocket. It lacked anything too useful at first glance, but perhaps Morgana or Nicki would find something in the mess of notes and drawings.

Rolling his shoulders and attempting to shrug off the cold, Merlin began to scale the hill himself, though he was sure to give the Light plenty of distance. His thoughts were a jangling mess that he once again found himself unable to sort properly. Too much was going on. Too many things that he had no guidance for. All of his experience, all of his knowledge was failing him, and all he had to rely on was instinct. And his instinct was warning him to be careful of the Light despite the helpful appearance.

He found his way to his SUV without running into anyone. Which was convenient, as Merlin wasn't in the mood for conversation. Quickly unlocking and starting the SUV, he sighed and leaned back in his chair to give the vehicle a few minutes to warm up.

"I'm missing something," Merlin said. He shook his head at himself. "There's something that I'm not seeing."

Another sigh escaped him, and Merlin finally pulled out of the parking lot. There were students out on the sidewalks despite the snow and plenty of cars on the road, but he barely noticed any of them. His mind raced, trying to come up with a solution. Alex said that the Iron Gates wouldn't be enough, and if Alex was right about the Darkness being similar to the poison then she was likely correct.

How could he have missed it? On the one hand, he'd had the poison tucked away for centuries, and had always been too afraid to use it or even look at it, so maybe it was understandable. When Alex had suggested it, he'd dismissed her conclusion, but now it seemed more and more that Alex was right. But how was it all possible?

Without even meaning to, Merlin found himself driving past the turn to his house and instead heading for Morgana's home. He quickly reviewed her schedule. She had nothing right now and would likely be grading papers or researching in vain trying to find some myth or legend that had even a fragment of information.

As it seemed that he wished to speak with Morgana subconsciously, Merlin did not fight it and pulled into her driveway. The roof of her Victorian house had a thick layer of snow on it that mostly hid the Christmas lights that she'd put up this year. Normally she did not bother, but Merlin was certain she was preparing her home in case Alex wished to spend Christmas in town. The thought filled him with sorrow. So very young and only a mage for a couple of years, but already Alex had paid dearly for it.

He knocked on the door and waited. Around him, the world was growing colder as sunset approached. If he focused, Merlin could almost feel the magic of the world building as the Winter Solstice approached. The door opened a moment later, and Merlin relaxed his features into a neutral expression.

"Ambrose." Morgana nodded in greeting, her green eyes sweeping over him and likely seeing far more than he wanted her to. She stepped to the side, giving him room to enter her house and smiled knowingly. "How are you?"

"I am as well as can be expected," Merlin answered. He pulled off his scarf and shrugged out of his coat, hanging both on the hooks by the door. "Yourself?"

"Nothing of interest to report." Morgana locked the house with a metallic click, and he heard her putting the chain across the door. "Warm up. I'll get you some tea."

He nodded, not bothering to argue. Outside, the wind was picking up as if reacting to his own stormy emotions. Walking into the living room, he checked the large windows first to be sure that the iron lines were still in place. They were, of course; they had been built into the house itself, but he couldn't shake the sense of dread hanging over him.

"Sit down, Merlin," Morgana ordered. She set a large mug with a tea bag in it on the table before sitting down herself. "And tell me what has you so on edge."

"The Light came to speak with me," Merlin said. He sat down with a groan. "Once again, I am left feeling very old."

"You have white hair and are over 3,000 years old," Morgana replied dryly. "You are old."

"Morgana."

"I understand." Morgana held her mug in both hands. "I've tried scrying. I've tried looking up strange and little-known stories and myths, but nothing seems to match what is happening. After centuries of being able to either know or find out, I hate being in the dark."

"I wish you'd had some luck. The Light knows very little, and I fear that he might become desperate."

"Desperate enough to be a danger to us?"

"Potentially. He is… fixated, on Alex. I am unsure if that is due to his experiences with her or Arthur's influence." Merlin allowed himself to shudder at the knowledge of what that thing had done to Alex.

"You should not have met it alone," Morgana said firmly. She leaned forward and met his gaze sternly. "You need to trust me, Merlin."

"It was not a lack of trust. He called this morning and asked to talk." He pulled out the piece of paper the Light had given him. "I did not consider it dangerous."

"Do not see it again while alone." Morgana's tone left no room for argument. "If it does become desperate then none of us are safe."

Merlin swallowed his next words and nodded. Morgana's worry was reassuring, even if a bit unnecessary. While their difference in age was so small relative to their true ages, he was still older than her. He'd been a man and an active warrior against the Sídhe when she'd been just a tiny girl. Still, he kept such thoughts to himself and sipped his tea. Leaning back in the chair, Merlin asked Morgana to review what myths she'd looked at with him. Maybe, just maybe, something would help them determine the origin of this Iron Soul that had fought the Darkness.

20

Impatience and Determination

Cold air nipped at Alex's exposed nose as she hurried across Hartung Avenue. Overhead the sun was valiantly trying to warm up the world, and there were reports that they could expect some warm winds later in the week. As far as Alex was concerned, they'd be welcome. She hummed a little as she walked, in a better mood than she'd been in for some time.

Merlin and Morgana had been shocked but thrilled when they'd called to report that they'd narrowed down the area of the Iron Soul who made the Iron Jar. Alex wished that they knew his name, but it was a massive leap forward. To her surprise, the pair had been together at Morgana's house when she called, which made things easier. Morgana had sounded incredibly smug, so she suspected that her call had interrupted some kind of argument.

'Don't worry,' Arto whispered. 'They will sort it out.'

'They always do,' Michel added.

They were more worried than Alex was. Of course they'd work out whatever concerns they had. At this point that wasn't even a real concern. She exhaled a long breath and watched it mist in the air. Even that made her oddly happy; she was relieved that some things were still working as they should. Though she still couldn't hear this particular former self, the knowledge that she and her friends had at least been able to track him to an extent helped immensely.

Alex still didn't know what to expect. It was strange having so little to go on. Historically, they had Merlin and Morgana's knowledge, or at least some visions, guiding them. In Wales, Bran had been able to guide them to the Chalice, and local legends had narrowed their search area down a great deal. Alex's dreams and memories had been enough to tell her that the Iron Hammer was in Paris when she'd needed it.

Now, however, she wasn't even sure what they were looking for. There was a metal jar which didn't seem to fit in the context of a plains Native American culture, but she'd seen it. What powers it had were a mystery, and what that incarnation had used it for was still unknown. At least the electrical theory about her memory had helped a little. Still, she wondered what had happened to that life. Had he lived past whatever he did? Did he have a family, or had he been alone?

The Student Commons was slowly being rebuilt, and Alex paused for a moment to look at the structure. As no one had died in the explosion, the school had mostly managed to move on. Those who had been shaken by it were long gone, having transferred to other schools, and enrollment was down a little, but life went on. Somehow, life always did, no matter what happened. She watched a construction worker come out of the small mobile unit that parked away from the sidewalk. Another man followed him, and they started talking and pointing to different parts of the large metal structure that was already taking form. She shook her head and shivered as the cold reminded her that she was outside in December.

Hurrying up the sidewalk, Alex noted that most of the other students out on campus were vanishing into buildings as another set of classes started. Out of the corner of her eye, she saw a figure move out of the shadows of the Carlson Building and head for her. She kept walking but pulled on her magic. It sprang to life, and Alex almost smiled. It was so much easier now, and she rolled her shoulders, stretching out her muscles as best she could under the weight of her backpack. As the figure approached, Alex sighed and stopped, turning to face it.

The Fae was a slight, young creature, and its features were so effeminate that Alex couldn't determine its sex. A few strands of their pale hair were falling out from under the hood, and thick sunglasses hid its purple eyes. It wore an undersized Ravenslake hoodie and looked like it belonged on campus.

Then Alex noticed another five figures with hidden faces closing in around her. She tensed and flexed the fingers of her right hand. The Fae glanced down at her hand and then pointedly looked around at the other students who were hurrying past.

"Careful," it said. "Don't want to expose yourself."

"You be careful. A group of people circling a young woman isn't going to go unnoticed," Alex countered.

She smiled but was eying the figures approaching. They were trying to walk normally as if they belonged there, but there was an edge to their strides. It was guarded and careful. Good, Alex thought; they should be afraid of her, given that they were trying to trap her.

'Stay calm,' Thor whispered. 'Don't let them get the upper hand.'

'Don't let them behind you,' Josfa said.

That wasn't helpful at all. Alex took a step back from the Fae and casually looked around, doing her best to appear unworried. She raised her right hand and allowed a few stray sparks to twirl around her fingers. Their warmth even managed to penetrate her gloves. It wasn't enough for the passers-by to see, but the Fae swallowed.

'The Khan never showed fear,' Temur huffed.

That was even less helpful. Alex managed not to roll her eyes at Temur's lingering awe for Genghis Khan. She already knew more about the Mongolian leader than she ever needed to. She watched the first of the Fae reach its ally. The second one stood shoulder to shoulder with the first Fae but was shifting nervously. This one didn't have sunglasses on, and its violet eyes were staring at the dark gray sparks around Alex's hand.

"I'm not breaking the connections until I know that it's safe," Alex said firmly. "It won't help us if we all die within a year due to a side effect."

"Everything that happened to our ancestors is the fault of the Darkness," the first Fae insisted. "It must be stopped."

"You didn't know about it until recently." Alex raised an eyebrow, doing her best to channel Morgana. "I hardly think you can blame every bad decision that your ancestors made on it. I understand your fear, but I'm not going to do something stupid about it. The other mages and I are closing in on information that might help us."

"There isn't time." The second Fae shifted, and Alex noted the protection amulet under its clothing. The amulet wasn't a surprise given the blood protection, but she was pretty sure it was one of the first-generation amulets that didn't stop her magic. "We can't just wait for the Sídhe to come and enslave this world! They hate us!"

"How do you know that?" Alex asked. She watched the other Fae come over and noted that she could see more amulets. Arthur must have left behind a stockpile when he was killed. "Did Arthur tell you that? Surely you know to be careful taking what he said as truth. I'm pretty sure when they broke through a few years back, they were more concerned with grabbing humans than you." Just the memory of the kidnapping made Alex want to shiver, but somehow, she kept herself thinking straight and calm. "Besides, the Iron Gates are still holding." Alex made a mental note to have Merlin recheck them. "I hear you. Your concerns aren't being ignored." She gestured towards the library. "Now, please excuse me. I have work to do."

The Fae closed in tighter around Alex. The first one, their leader, held their chin up, and Alex was pretty sure they were glaring at her behind the sunglasses. Tilting her head, she glanced around at the circle. Her mind spun as the voices all gave different advice, and she tried to figure out the best way out of this. She didn't see any weapons, but-

"Alex!" A voice called. Someone came running up, and several of the Fae retreated from her. The leader flinched. "Hey, Alex? What's going on?" The voice was extra loud now, and Alex leaned to the side to look around the Fae leader.

Robin was jogging up, her brown eyes sharp and cold even as she kept her voice friendly. Three of the Fae outright turned and walked away, heading for the street to the north. Alex almost smiled. They were fine as long as no one drew attention to them. Robin came to a stop beside the Fae leader and smiled at the three remaining Fae.

"You spook easily, don't you." Robin glanced at Alex and nodded in greeting. "Now, I speak for the other Old Ones when I say that we are just as concerned as you over the Darkness, but threatening the champion of the realm you live in is not a productive means of addressing it."

"She's not-" the Fae leader started to say.

"Not listening? Oh, she's listening. She's working on a real solution." Robin looked around suspiciously, letting her smile fall away. "Now leave her be and don't try anything. Especially not cornering her. It would have served you right if she blasted all of you to dust." The Fae was about to say something when Robin shook her head and glared. "Do not. Now go. We have phones. You can call us if the situation changes."

The other two scurried off, but the leader took a step towards Alex, reaching for her arm. Robin snarled and slapped the Fae across the face. The sunglasses were knocked off and hit the sidewalk with a soft crack. Violet eyes glared at Alex, but she could see real fear in them. Pulling back her magic, she touched Robin's extended arm.

"Don't threaten me again," Alex said firmly. "It won't do any good."

Maybe that was a step too far. Alex wasn't sure, but she wasn't interested in having to look over her shoulder every time she left the defenses of the house. Arthur's plan to give the Fae protection against their magic seemed to have been based on wearing them down. He'd been more successful than Alex would ever admit out loud. She held the Fae's gaze until it finally lowered its eyes and scurried away to join those that had already run.

"You okay?" Robin asked. The Old One gave her plenty of space, but the worry on her face was clear. "Alex?"

"I'm fine." Alex sighed and rubbed the right side of her temple. "Just lost my good mood."

"That's a crime." Robin's lips quirked into a smile. "Good moods can be hard to come by. It's a real shame that you lost yours."

Something in Robin's voice was lighter than before. Now that she thought of it, Aiden had been oddly chipper at breakfast. She'd thought it was the blueberry pancakes that Nicki and Timothy had made, but now Robin was happy too.

"Did something put you in a good mood?"

"Aiden and I are having coffee tomorrow," Robin replied. Then she shrugged. "I'm not sure if it'll go anywhere, but it's a nice change."

"He was cheerful this morning too." Alex paused and felt her cheeks heat up. "Sorry, it's rude to pry."

"A bit, but I figure between Michel's influence and you being protective of Aiden, you're being very nice about this whole thing." Robin smiled a bit and glanced around. "Did you need to get somewhere?"

"Uh, I was heading to the library," Alex said. "I have a break, so I wanted to look up something."

"About the Darkness?"

"Not directly. Merlin and Morgana have been trying to see if they can find a mythological link anywhere, but no luck so far."

"The only thing it reminds me of is the old stories about eclipses." Robin turned and nodded towards the library. "Come on; it'll be warmer inside. I've got a break too."

They resumed walking, and Alex realized that Robin was scanning all around them. "Are you worried there's more?"

"Maybe," Robin said. "It's stupid to try and attack you, but fear does strange things to sentient beings. That and Red Caps are crazy little psychos who like to kill. With all the changes, I have no idea what they might be up to."

"That's not reassuring," Alex said. She hesitated, but decided that honesty was the smartest move here. "They had protection amulets which means that they were loyal to Arthur at some point." Alex sighed and groaned. "Or that the Fae are trading around the remaining amulets that Arthur made."

"You're worried about revenge?"

"Maybe. His hold over them was... I don't know. Maybe he was using magic, but he was very charismatic. Sometimes I think he was just crazy, but he always seemed to know what strings to pull. Or maybe it was his mother." Alex shook her head. "I don't know."

Robin pulled open the door without a word and they moved into the warmth of the library. The front desk was busy with books being checked in and what sounded like one very stressed grad student who couldn't find the book they needed. Alex looked around quickly, checking the shadows for any Fae or other dangers. Finals were close enough now that students were sitting at study tables. Saying nothing to Robin, she went to the stairs and climbed up to the top floor where they'd likely have the greatest privacy.

It was warmer upstairs than downstairs, but mostly empty of people. Alex spotted an empty study room and headed straight for it. Around them the tall bookcases created too many hiding places, and Alex released a pulse of magic to check it out. The magic flowed around the large space, and Alex closed her eyes for a moment. Robin glowed brilliantly to her magical sight, but the three normal humans who were scattered around the floor at study tables were the only other beings here.

Robin followed her into the study room. If she was curious or simply being protective, Alex didn't know. She took off her bag and coat before slumping into one of the plastic chairs with a soft groan.

"Thanks for helping outside," Alex said. "I didn't want to make a scene. We do have a lead." Alex inhaled and nodded. "We're going to find a way to stop this."

The Old One held her gaze, those century-old eyes searching hers. Then Robin smiled and nodded. "I believe that, Alex. I do. Just hurry and take care of yourself in the meantime. I know you don't want a fight on your hands, but if Fae try to close in on you like that again, you need to defend yourself."

"I know." Alex opened her bag and dug out her tablet. "I know."

"You're tired," Robin said. She walked around the table to get closer to Alex. Her voice was soft and cautious. Robin's right hand started to move, but then she pulled it back. "Very tired."

"It's never-ending." Alex exhaled, listening to the mess of voices in her head. "The others had only one problem, but I've... god, it feels like we've had everything hit us." Lowering her head, Alex rolled her shoulders and rubbed the sides of her scalp. "It never ends. So, yeah I'm tired."

"I'm sorry." Robin touched her arm softly, a barely-there touch as if she wasn't sure if it was safe to touch Alex at all. "I'm sorry, you've lost so much and haven't been able to rest."

"Yeah." Swallowing, Alex dropped her hands and straightened up in her chair. Forcing a small smile, she shrugged. "Merlin and Morgana have kept going for thousands of years. I can manage a little longer."

"I don't have a class for another hour. Can I help?"

Alex looked up at the Old One, blinked, and then nodded. Pulling up the list they'd made of books in the library that had any possible relation to the Medicine Wheel or pre-Crow American Indian tribes, Alex held it out to Robin.

"I'm looking for these books."

The Old One looked at the list with a frown and nodded. "Right, I'll track these down." She paused for a moment and shook her head. "Sorry, I'm European in origin so I don't know most of the Old Ones who set up in the Americas personally."

"Can you connect us with Coyote?"

Robin smirked a little and shook her head. "Sorry, Alex, I'm afraid that he's been asleep for centuries, which your ancestors should be thankful for. He would have wrecked them."

A laugh escaped Alex and Robin grinned. She had no idea if that was true, or if Coyote was even real. Nodding, the Old One turned and headed out of the study room. Alex pulled out a notebook, took a breath, and pulled out her phone to get started with planning their trip to Wyoming. They had to keep going.

21

Fallen Star and Rising Sun

33 C.E. Bighorn Mountains

Akule wasn't sure what he was going to do the next morning, but he found himself packing up some supplies after feeding the dog and himself. He made sure to roll up a small hide for warmth against the cold of the mountains. The burning trail in the sky was long gone, and the sun was shining as it climbed above the horizon. His dreams haunted him, the strange visions he'd seen had lingered long after he'd entered his hut for the night. The memories of the images taunted him.

He almost laughed. Dreams and a spark were enough to send him out into the hills to find where a star had fallen. Akule shook his head and collected the smoked meats from the rack. He would have liked more time to prepare, but a sense of urgency had taken hold of him. Looking up at the mountains, his stomach tightened, and he looked down at the dog. It wagged its tail and looked up at him.

"You're staying here."

The dog whined a little, but Akule knew that Hakola had trained the damn thing to stay when it was told. Putting down his supplies, he left out food and water for the dog that should last a couple of days. It was a strange feeling, leaving the beast behind, but he couldn't risk being distracted while climbing. The dog whined again but stayed put when Akule ordered it to. Walking away, he did his best to ignore the beast's soft cries. He understood. He didn't like being alone either, but he was chasing after a fallen star in the mountains. The thought almost made him laugh.

Before he could talk himself out of this, Akule started walking south in the direction that he'd seen the burning trail point towards. The memory of the crash last night was vivid. He wondered if his family was still close enough to have witnessed it. What had they thought of it? He hoped that it was a good sign for all of them. He needed that.

Akule's mind wandered as he walked, and he found himself humming. The climb up the hills was slow, but the sun was warm, and he paused whenever he found berries to forage. There were more signs of animals further from the dark spot, which reassured him that the rest of the world was still out there.

"I miss my family," he said out loud. "I knew that being alone would be difficult, but I didn't understand the weight of silence. It surrounds you. It holds me down. I'm finally learning to sleep without the sounds of others nearby, but it's difficult."

The sound of his voice was harsh amongst the noise of the wind in the leaves. It was like it didn't belong, and so he fell silent. If he needed to talk, Akule decided he'd save it for when he returned to camp and the dog. At least talking to a living thing seemed more natural.

His leg muscles were starting to burn as he climbed a much steeper hill. Akule's hand ached from grappling with the rocks, but he didn't stop moving. The spark was shifting, twisting like a storm in his chest. It was reacting to something. That gave him hope. A tiny flicker of hope. Perhaps this was some sort of sign or deliverance from the spirits. Maybe the world was finally fighting back against the disease trying to overcome it. So, he climbed on.

There was no trail to follow, but the spark in his chest seemed drawn towards whatever had fallen. As strange as it was, Akule allowed that gentle pull to guide him. However, it was pulling him in a direction without a path. Instead, he did his best to navigate in the correct direction on the melted patches of snow and what animal trails he could find. His moccasins provided him with enough protection that Akule was able to climb over the rough and jagged rocks without injury, though the thick and treated hide didn't prevent him from feeling the sharp edges.

But then the spark led him to a cliff face. He eyed the cliff and huffed in disgust. The spark just kept pulling him. There were plenty of handholds due to the rock crumbling away, but Akule hesitated. He looked around, trying to find a safer route, but there were no game trails. Now he was in the domain of the mountain goats and wind. The spark flared in his chest, and he inhaled slowly. It calmed a little, but the need to find the falling star hadn't faded. He eyed the height of the cliff critically. The surrounding terrain was steep slopes covered in rocks from the crumbling mountain. If he lost his footing there, he wouldn't be much safer.

With a sigh, he made sure that his supplies were secure on his back and stretched out his arms and legs. Then, Akule began to climb. He went slowly, scoping out every hand and foothold as he went. The sun beat down on his back, and about half way up he longed for another drink of water but dared not let go to get it. He kept going, pushing himself towards the top until it was almost in reach.

Rock gave way beneath his right hand. His feet slipped out of place. Akule panicked, his heart racing so loudly that it echoed in his ears. He pulled on the spark, ordering it to come forth, begging it for help. It warmed his whole body and purple sparks flashed around his hands, but it didn't help. He felt his fingers slipping. His weight was pulling him down. Slamming his eyes shut, he tried his best to imagine something solid beneath him. Something hard and firm, not empty air. He looked down.

The purple sparks had formed a flat and solid surface beneath him. It was small, only just filling the space beneath his feet, but he was secure. He was safe. Exhaling, Akule almost crumbled in relief, but he didn't dare. He used the moment of safety to grab onto the rocks once more and began pulling himself up. The strange surface traveled with him, staying beneath his feet. He had just enough time to wonder if he could use it for the rest of the climb when he reached the top of the rock face. Crawling over the edge, he collapsed against the dirt as the terror caught up with him.

"That was foolish," he said to no one. "I'll take another path next time."

A nervous laugh escaped him. Turning around, he blinked as he found that the disk was gone. Then again, it had completed its task. He flexed his fingers and smiled. As strange as this power was, as much as he didn't understand it, it was certainly handy. His arms ached, but he slowly climbed to his feet. There was a rough trail following the edge of the cliff, and he quickly followed it around. The steepness of the mountain thankfully began to ease, and he swallowed in relief.

From there it was easier, which was a relief. Akule's legs were quivering with lingering fear and exhaustion from the full day of hiking. He stopped and refilled his waterskin when he came across a snowmelt creek. Upon spotting some berries, he ate as many as he could find to rebuild his strength before the spark drew him towards a small valley.

The valley had a creek cutting through it, and tall trees that provided shade and some relief from the wind. Around him the mountains loomed, and he could hear animals in the trees. But there was one feature that was not at all normal. A round hole had been formed in the earth, roughly ten paces from the west bank of the creek. It was a strange reflection to the one made by the dead spot growing on the other side of the mountain. It was about thirty paces across and as deep as a man was tall, with a ridge of earth all around the edge. Plants had been thrown to the side, and there were signs of charred earth, but nearby trees were still growing. Akule approached it slowly, watching for any sign of danger. The air was clear, and animals were moving in the bushes. The small valley had been disturbed by the crash, but not destroyed.

He took in the bent trees and the broken branches. It stunned him that such damage had been wrought by something so small, but he didn't turn back. As he came closer to the edge, he could see down into the crater. There was a mound in the middle, a thick layer of earth covering something. In his chest, the spark's hum grew.

Akule lifted his right hand and closed his eyes. Inhaling slowly, he whispered a prayer to the spirits and his ancestors for their protection. Purple sparks appeared around his hand when he opened his eyes. Walking forward, he marveled at the perfect circle, thinking back to how pebbles left marks in the dirt when dropped, but not at this scale.

He crossed the edge of the circle safely and sighed in relief. Dirt was being blown by the wind, and there were clumps of plants here and there, unlike the unnaturally open circle near his camp. When he reached the center, Akule found a rock and began to dig down. Something had fallen. He'd come here to find it, and find it he would.

A large strange rock came into view after only a few minutes. As his hand moved over the surface, he noted that the outer layer felt strange.

He gripped it only to flinch when it cracked beneath his hand like the shell of an egg. The black material coated his fingertips like ash. It was like sculpted charcoal. Akule began to break it off, needing to use more force in some places. Beneath was a much harder material, unlike that of most rocks he'd seen before.

Akule noted a strange shine to it. He quickly finished digging it out and set it down where he could see it all at once. Part of it had been smoothed down and had strange markings that radiated outward. Further back were strange, shallow depressions and deep cavities. It was like clay that had been molded by a child. The shine was similar to certain minerals that he'd seen before, but had a darker and richer color. The whole of the rock seemed to be made of the same material, rather than containing bits and pieces of many different types.

Picking it up, Akule decided that it wasn't too heavy. It weighed less than his young son, though he thought it heavier than most rocks of the same size would be. Fascinated by the material, he ran his hands over it, cleaning off the remaining lines of dirt. It had fallen through the sky. He touched the strange lines. It had left a trail of fire in the night sky and glowed like a star. Yet now it was dark and heavy.

How could this help him? Releasing the rock, Akule slumped back onto the ground, not caring about the dirt now covering his clothing. He'd been sure. Well, not sure, but hopeful when he left his camp this morning. Now after a day of exhaustive walking and using his power to help him, he had a rock. A large and strange rock.

Akule knew he wasn't going to make it back to camp tonight. Tomorrow might be easier, but he'd have the extra weight to be worried about. As the sun sank in the sky, Akule shivered and forced himself to his feet. There was plenty of fallen wood to pick up thanks to the fallen star, and he gathered the driest sections. Further into the trees, he found a long-fallen tree that had been dried out by the sun and tore off the branches that he could.

He worked hard and fast, ignoring his sore body. The night was coming, and he was higher up in the mountains so it would be colder. He built a small fire pit off to the side of the crash site and started a fire to warm his aching hands. Setting the strange rock beside the fire, Akule noted the way it glittered in the light, but the lines of shine were far longer and smoother than anything he'd seen before. The spark was humming in his chest whenever he was close to it.

Still, Akule had work to do. Pulling down branches and dragging over trees, he made himself a small shelter. There wasn't much room, but he could sleep inside sheltered from the wind. Satisfied, Akule scouted the area in the last rays of the sun that reached into the valley and harvested the berries he could find. When night finally enveloped the valley, he sat by his fire and enjoyed a meal of smoked meat and fresh berries. Akule stretched out his legs and arms, mindful not to hurt himself, and studied the rock.

What this rock was made of was a mystery to him, but Akule knew that he'd been pulled towards it for a reason. His power, his magic, wanted it. How it could help stop the dark spot, he didn't know, but his hope was renewed. Now he'd just have to get it back down the mountain, which sounded much easier than it was. At least he would have plenty of daylight thanks to the long days. Overhead, the stars were coming out. Akule laid out his hide and stretched out upon it. Already the temperature was dropping, but next to the fire, he was warm enough.

Staring into the night sky, Akule was aware of that weight falling over him again. The scale of all that was out there stole his breath away. Beside him, the fire was dying down, but heat was rolling off the coals. So he stayed put, breathing in and out slowly as the soft sounds of the night echoed through the small valley. The beating of his heart was in time with the gentle pulsing of the spark and the earth beneath him. Shifting his right hand, Akule touched the cool ground. Something gently rolled up his arm. It was warm and soothing, despite the strangeness. It fed the spark and Akule smiled. The world was truly aiding him. Even without his family and the dog, he wasn't alone.

Eventually, he crawled into his shelter and curled up to stay warm, but the calm he'd built remained with him. The spark's hum increased, but Akule wasn't worried. A soft fog wrapped around him, cradling Akule and keeping him safe as he drifted off. In his chest, the spark began to pull him towards something, but his eyes still fell shut.

He was dreaming. Akule knew that as soon as he turned around in confusion. He was high on the mountain, standing inside a massive medicine circle. Pale stones outlined the circle, but it had more than the four sections that he'd grown up seeing in ceremonies. There were twenty-eight lines of rocks going from a circle in the center of the ring to the outer edges. It was an unknown symbol, but he was certain that it was supposed to invoke the same powers as the medicine circle. Counting the lines, he smiled a little, realizing that there was a line for each of the days of the moon cycle.

Akule carefully stepped over the lines and studied the strange mounds of stone at different points on the outer circle. What they meant, he wasn't sure, but he walked to the center and watched the sunrise. He was here for a reason. This was the work of the spirits. A ray of light from the sun hit the edge of the circle, aligning with the first pile of stones, and Akule gasped in glee and shock.

"Who are you?"

It was a human voice. He spun around. As he did so, the spark in his chest burned hot, and he gasped. The world went hazy as a fog rolled in, obscuring his vision. When it cleared there was a thick layer of snow on the ground outside the stone ring, and people were standing nearby. They were all dressed strangely, and none of them seemed to notice him.

But one of them was inside the circle with him and looking right at him. They were dressed in a strange puffy shirt of some sort and wearing strange leggings. The person pulled back a hood off of their head, revealing their face. It was a woman, younger than him, with pale skin, long gold hair, and stormy grey eyes. She took a step closer to him; her eyes wide with shock and a flicker of hope.

"Who are you?" she asked. The spark burned and a strange tingling sensation spread across his skin. "Please," she called. "What did you do? How did you stop it?"

"I am Akule," he answered. His mind spun, trying to understand what was happening. Who was this spirit? "Stop what?"

"The Darkness." She took another step towards him. "Where is the Jar?"

"The jar?"

"The one made of iron," she said. "The Darkness is coming back. I need help."

"Jar," Akule repeated. "A jar?" He frowned as he thought of that strange rock and the clay jars that were used to store food from time to time. "What is this place?"

Now it was her turn to be confused. She shook her head and looked around them at the stone circle. "You built this. I'm sure you did. You built this to help you stop the Darkness on the summer solstice."

"Summer Solstice?"

"The longest day of the year," she said. "I came here, trying to learn what you did. To find the vessel you used to contain the Darkness."

The burning grew worse, and Akule flinched as the air was forced out of his lungs. He stumbled back and clutched at his chest. The woman came forward, reaching out for him. The fog was rolling in again. He couldn't see the other people anymore, just her. Reaching out his hand, he tried to speak. There were more questions at the tip of his tongue, but their hands passed through each other like mist, and she was gone. He was standing alone in the stone circle on a warm summer's day, with the sun rising behind him.

22

Calm in the Storm

The house was quiet. Other than Alex, the only person here was Bran, who was studying in the basement for his last final. Nicki was celebrating the end of her finals with her Gran and Avani, Aiden was helping at his family bookshop for the evening, and Lance and Jenny were out on a date. Alex had turned in her last paper that morning. It should have been a relief, but the start of winter break only reminded her that the winter solstice was fast approaching.

Alex walked into the living room and noted the stack of books on their coffee table. Most were general guides to Wyoming, and a couple were about the plains tribes. They'd thus far failed to find any books on the Medicine Wheel itself, even with the help of a university lending system. What they had found was based on stories and histories from the 18th to 20th Century, which while interesting to read didn't provide any information on the construction of the site. It worried her more than she wanted to admit. The only bright point was that the site was reputed to help with vision quests, which Alex desperately needed.

She wandered through the room, tidying up the discarded shoes and coats from the previous evening. Running her fingers along the bookshelf, Alex chuckled softly. There wasn't even a speck of dust. The low power magic that Timothy and other Brownies possessed was awe-inspiring in its context. It made her wonder what would even happen to magic if they cut the connections between worlds. Theoretically it would lessen, but Timothy had magic due to his own system pushing back against the Iron Realm. So, would it leave only a couple of Fae species with magic and humans without? She didn't know. It was one of many things that she didn't know and probably never would.

"I'll take care of that."

Alex almost jumped at Timothy's voice. She was at the closet now, hanging up one of Nicki's spare coats, and had to look around to find the Brownie. He was standing on the staircase banister with a soft smile.

"I've got it," Alex said. She finished hanging up the coat. "You take such good care of us. We really should be able to handle hanging up our coats."

"If you wish." Timothy swayed a little and looked around the room. "I didn't want to disturb personal items."

"Oh, feel free. If we leave them in the common space then totally feel free," Alex said. She shut the door with a soft click. There was a faint sound of music in the basement, but otherwise the house was quiet. "Timothy, can I ask you something?" She extended her hand and Timothy climbed into her palm, letting Alex carry him into the living room.

"Course!"

"Timothy, what do you think about all of this?" Alex asked. Sitting down in the armchair, she leaned forward and met the small dark eyes of the Brownie. "You live here with us, hell you take care of us, but you haven't talked about what you think. Do you think I'm being irresponsible?"

"No, no!" Timothy shook his head. "Alex is not irresponsible. Cautious and worried about others. That is good. That is needed now." The Brownie tugged on the hem of his small doll coat. "You inherited this danger. Ancestors did not warn mages. Leaders did not tell their own people. They just invaded and enslaved. You try to talk."

"I'm not sure that's enough at this point," Alex admitted. "Doesn't feel like it. What if I can't stop the Darkness and the Iron Realm falls too? That's it. Even if it isn't in all the branches, it will be after reaching us."

"You'll stop it," Timothy said. He sounded so certain. "I watch mages. You all try so hard. Work well together. When I lived with Merlin, he worked alone mostly. Talked with Morgana sometimes, but not like you and friends. You trust each other. You support each other. You share magic! Good people with good ideas. I know you'll stop the Darkness." Timothy smiled at her, and Alex wasn't bothered by the Brownie's sharp little teeth. "I believe in you."

"Thanks." Her throat was oddly tight, and Alex swallowed. "Thanks. And thank you for all you do. You're amazing at helping us. I'm sorry if we take it for granted."

Timothy laughed, his eyes gleeful. "Don't be sorry. Best house ever! Mages know I'm here, get groceries I ask for, talk to me and thank me. Best home Timothy ever had."

"Don't you miss being with other Brownies?"

Timothy smiled now, his expression a bit smug. "Other Brownies are nearby. When Timothy told others that blood protection only harms bad Fae, others moved in. House three doors down has two nice Brownies. One moved in with Nicki's grandmother, though she doesn't know she is there. Dora keeps away from art studio."

"Really?" Alex grinned. "You haven't told Nicki?"

"Not my house," Timothy whispered. "Most Brownies don't want humans to know they are there. Only a few humans ever notice that little things get done." He shook his head. "Two roads over almost revealed himself when he fixed the siding on his house, but humans just confused, so it'll be okay. He likes his humans."

Thinking back, Alex tried to remember if odd things had happened in her childhood home. She couldn't remember anything, but it was oddly pleasant to think that maybe a Brownie had been looking out for them. Still, it was a bit strange to realize that Brownies thought of the people they helped as theirs. Not wrong exactly, just strange. She had to wonder if Brownies had always been this way or if the Sídhe had done something to them while they were slaves. That was a dark thought, but given Morgana's history, Alex knew that the Sídhe would be very willing to experiment on their slaves until they had the perfect slave race.

"I do more than most Brownies," Timothy admitted. "Since I don't have to hide. I cook and clean more. Always busy! That's good!"

"That's... I'm glad you're happy here." Alex still wasn't sure what she was feeling. "We're happy to have you here, and you're a huge help in contacting the Fae."

"Glad to help." Timothy bounced off the table and onto Alex's knee. He patted her hand gently. "You on right track. I feel in my ears." Timothy flexed his small pointed ears. "Work with friends, and you'll be okay."

His optimism made Alex smile, but another idea nagged at her now that she'd thought about the Sídhe and their slavery. It was unlikely that Timothy would know anything, but she braced herself to ask. Timothy must have known there was something more, because he stayed.

"Alex?"

"Do you think- were there ever stories about resistance in the Sídhe Empire?" Alex asked. "Sídhe who didn't like the fighting and slavery?"

"Probably." Timothy shrugged. "Sídhe Empire is vast. You think of tunnels, but there are whole worlds — planets like Earth with Sídhe cities. There are schools, entertainment, poverty, and conflict just like with humans. My ancestors escaped the tunnels into your world. They served with the military forces, not in society. Very different, I assume." He shifted a little. "Probably not all evil."

"Yeah," Alex said. She slumped back in the chair, jostling Timothy a little though the Brownie was able to stay on her knee. "It's all so complicated."

"Work with friends. Do what you can," Timothy said firmly. "Won't be able to do everything, but do what you can."

Nodding, Alex tried to dismiss her thoughts. Timothy was right; there were limits to what they could do. She did think of the tunnels as the Sídhe world, but that was silly. They had conquered several worlds and taken over the surface. There were whole cities and societies that had been going on for centuries. Surely in all of that, there were those who disagreed with the leadership. Especially if it was as fragmented as Morgana seemed to hope. Still, Alex knew next to nothing about the Sídhe. She'd only been in the tunnels where the military worked, and they kept human slaves. They couldn't all be bad.

Then again, she couldn't save them. She knew that the Sídhe Empire had started with running from the Darkness in their branch. Earth had blocked their way, so now it seemed that she was helping to hold the line and trap them with their doom. It was almost poetic. All their violence, and it still wouldn't save them. They'd bought themselves time, but turned into monsters. Poetic, indeed, in a dark sort of way. Still... not even trying to help them; what did that make her?

Timothy watched her. Some of her thoughts and feelings must have played out on her face because the Brownie moved up her leg to pat her arm. Alex looked down at him and smiled. Dear little Timothy had been enslaved by magic and freed. She'd built the protections of Ravenslake so that they didn't hurt him and other peaceful Fae. Maybe she wasn't as good as she wished she could be, but she wasn't a monster.

"I need to do something," Alex said. "Can I help with something?"

"Well..." Timothy hesitated, but then nodded. "House could use a good scrub down."

Cleaning. Yeah, that sounded like a plan. That was productive and would give her a tangible result. It sounded perfect. Alex nodded in agreement and smiled. Timothy smiled in return and told her to start dusting the living room, and then admitted that he couldn't handle the vacuum himself without a lot of magic. Alex went upstairs to change into an old t-shirt and got busy.

It was easy to lose herself in the work. Sweat built up on the back of Alex's neck after she finished dusting the wood furniture throughout the house and scrubbing down the bathroom counters. Timothy was cleaning the kitchen with gusto, and as the floors were washed down by a mop that was moving on its own, Alex was amazed at how dirty they'd let the house get. They really did need to pitch in and help Timothy more. The poor Brownie was on his own.

Bran came up when she started vacuuming and took the task of shoveling the driveway from Timothy without complaint. When Jenny and Lance got home, they gathered up the old towels and rugs in the house to put in the laundry. Jenny turned on some music and tackled scrubbing the shower after giving Alex a quick hug. Lance moved furniture for Alex as she vacuumed.

By the time everyone was home, the house was cleaner than it had been since before they moved in. Aiden had slipped in at some point and built a lasagna with Timothy that was in the oven. Alex hadn't even known they had the ingredients for something like that. Still, all the cleaning had achieved three things: it had distracted Alex, gotten the house clean, and gotten everyone to collapse in the living room together.

"Well, that was productive," Nicki groaned. She slumped into the sofa beside Avani. "And exhausting."

"You came in at the last minute," Jenny teased. She and Lance were curled up together on the loveseat. "You literally organized the movies."

"We have a lot of movies! And they needed to be put away."

"Of course, honey," Avani said. She patted her girlfriend's shoulder.

Nicki blushed, and Jenny laughed. "Really, Nicki? Being embarrassed now? After drooling over Avani in Mumbai?"

"Yeah," Aiden teased. "You even called dibs."

"Dibs?" Avani repeated. She blinked and looked at Nicki, who was somehow even redder. "Really, dibs?"

"Sorry. I was trying to play it cool," Nicki said.

"Oh honey," Avani said. "Your crush was anything but subtle." She kissed the blushing Nicki's cheek and tossed her long braid back over her shoulder. "I knew that Nicki liked me before you even left India. Still, she's smart, funny, and knows about magic, so I decided to ask her out." Avani smiled and shrugged one shoulder with a teasing glint in her eyes. "I'm not much for drama."

"Yeah," Nicki said. Her strength seemed renewed, though the blush remained. "What about you, Aiden? I ran into Robin the other day, and she seemed very very happy."

"Nicki," Aiden yelped. "Don't!"

"And I do believe that-"

"Nicki!"

Lance laughed, his face lighting up as Jenny shook her head and snuggled closer to him. Aiden looked like he wanted the ground to open up and swallow him, but thankfully his magic didn't make that happen.

"Okay, okay," Bran said. "Enough. Stop torturing the poor man. If he and Robin want to give it a try, then that's great." He turned his attention to Avani. "So your family is okay with your relationship?" Bran asked. "Have you told them?"

"Father wouldn't have been," Avani admitted. "But he's not in the picture anymore. Grandfather is fine with it. Mother is already trying to make plans for the wedding and wants grandchildren."

Nicki's blush only got worse. Alex knew that she should have some sympathy, but honestly, it was just funny to tease her. It was nice to know that their family's supported them. Avani took pity on her girlfriend and took her hand, squeezing it with a soft smile. Alex's chest tightened for a moment with something like jealousy, but sadder. She pushed it away, not wanting to let go of this happy moment.

"Speaking of marriage, what about you and Lance?" Nicki looked over at Jenny with sharp eyes. "Lance is doing Christmas with your family, that's a big step."

"We've started talking about it," Lance said.

The whole room stopped. Alex blinked as Arto cheered in her head. Other voices chimed in with a mixture of happiness, sadness, and wistfulness. Nicki's mouth fell open a little, and Alex understood her surprise. It had been a ploy to take attention off of her that had exploded into something else.

"You have?" Bran asked. "That's nice to hear."

"We're not planning on it right away," Jenny explained. She seemed a touch nervous, but her eyes glowed with pleasure. "But Lance and I know that we're it for each other. We've had the kids talk and things like that. We're not in a hurry though. We want to be sure that the Iron Realm is safe."

Alex could hear the unsaid, 'and Alex is okay' part of the sentence. It warmed her and made guilt grow in her chest all at once. Poor Lance and Jenny were so determined to be loyal and there for her in this life. She just hoped that they wouldn't have to give up a happy life together to pull that off. But if they could stop the Darkness, maybe that would be a powerful enough show of strength that everything would back off. If that could be stopped then maybe some of the invasions would stop, and things could find a new equilibrium. That was the goal at least.

"I'm glad," Alex said. She smiled as she looked around the room. "Our lives are crazy, dangerous and difficult. I'm so glad that you've been able to find happiness amongst that chaos."

"Hey, Robin and I have gone on one official date," Aiden protested. "Let's not rush things."

"Oh, but I like the idea of having Puck as a sister-in-law," Nicki whined.

"I know that I've told my parents about magic, but I have no plans to tell them all of Robin's history," Aiden pleaded. "So please don't call her that around them."

"I won't." Nicki mimed locking her lips and tossing the key away.

"How is your family?" Alex asked. "I've seen Nicki's Gran recently, but not your folks."

"They're good. It's amazing how much day-to-day life distracts them from knowing that magic is real. Dad still occasionally asks questions, but..." Aiden shook his head. "I don't know. It's surprising, I guess. Aisling is doing well." He looked at Avani. "I did tell them a little about you. I didn't want to reveal too much without your consent. They think you're an advisor of sorts."

"Given that I know more of the history of magic than you do, that does make some sense," Avani agreed.

"It's scary how true that is," Nicki muttered.

"Well, there is a long history of mages and magicians," Avani said. She smiled a little. "I remember loving the stories about Lokpal and the Mage Brothers when I was growing up."

"Mage brothers?" Nicki asked before Alex could.

"They were members of my family. I'm descended from one of them. While there are no mages in my family right now, there have been in the past." Avani tilted her head thoughtfully. "A couple of centuries after Lokpal, a group of Demons allied with an Old One and several mages were called. A couple were from my family."

"You know, I think Merlin and Morgana have mentioned that." Nicki frowned, concentration filling her face. "Something about India having the largest number of mages at one time. More than us."

"That does sound familiar," Bran agreed. "Don't remember them giving any details."

"That's because they don't!" Nicki groaned and slumped back into the sofa. "Honestly, the knowledge that those two have and don't record or share, it's painful. It causes me actual physical pain!"

Avani patted her overly dramatic girlfriend's shoulder. Nicki turned her head and smiled softly, seemingly unable to even pretend to be mad. It was all a bit too sweet for Alex, who could also still see Lance and Jenny snuggling on the sofa.

"I'm not sure I remember that period," Alex said. She frowned and tried to poke at the different memories that she'd sorted. "I have memories, but some of them are hard to understand." She shrugged and frowned in concentration. "That period you were talking about in India.... I don't even know if I had an incarnation there. If I do, those memories are jumbled with Lokpal's because nothing stands out."

"I believe that there was an incarnation of the Iron Soul there," Avani said. "But I do know that he wasn't a descendant of Lokpal." Her fingers twitched, and she frowned. "I could ask Grandfather. He'll likely remember more of the details."

"It's not important." Alex waved her hand dismissively. "Sounds like they were on Demon roundup."

"Largely," Avani said. She pressed her lips together thoughtfully. "I think that Shiva was asleep in that era, so when the Demon population got a bit out of control, mages were called. The situation with the other Hindu Old Ones hadn't been sorted out yet."

"Sounds like an interesting story," Nicki said.

"Not really," Avani replied. "Not compared to your stories." She smiled at her girlfriend once again.

In the kitchen, a timer beeped, and the smell of lasagna rolled through the living room. Aiden perked up, and Alex's stomach grumbled. Lance chuckled at the sound only to receive a slight swat on the chest from Nicki. Everyone was safe and happy. They'd be off on another adventure soon enough, but for now they were together. This was the calm in the center of the storm that they needed.

23

Meal at Morgana's

Morgana's house was warm and filled with the blended smells of fresh baking and a roasting turkey. Thanksgiving had passed, but she'd insisted on a menu that seemed very much in line with the holiday. Once again, he wondered if she was trying to make things better for Alex. Merlin wasn't sure if Morgana's mothering would help. He did have to admit that the pair had an unusually strong bond. While Morgana had deeply loved Arto, she'd been professional and only mildly affectionate with most Iron Souls.

He was the last to arrive despite being a few minutes early. Sounds were coming from the kitchen, and he could hear Morgana giving instructions. It made him smile fondly as he hung up his coat and pulled off his scarf. Stepping into the living room, he found Lance and Jenny sitting together and talking with Avani.

Standing in the doorway, he watched the three for a surreal moment. Strange; it was so strange to have them here as if they belonged. He and Morgana made an effort to be kind to the reincarnated traitors for Alex's sake. Deep down, he knew that it hadn't been their fault. Not really. Still, it was odd to see them sitting there and discussing the finer points of a spell that Avani used to grant temporary telekinesis.

His mother had used such methods to gain control over a little bit of magic. She'd been a priestess, and his grandfather before him had been a mage. These two... it chaffed slightly to know that they were using magic. Unfair perhaps, but it was there. Still, he would stay silent about it for Alex's sake. She'd lost so much and cared about the pair. Besides, if she was correct and their wrongs had been righted, then he'd never have to worry about them being reborn again.

Then Alex came out of the kitchen. She jumped a little at the sight of him but quickly recovered. "Hello, Merlin. We were wondering."

"I believe that I am on time," he answered. "It's all of you that were early."

"Guilty as charged," Alex agreed.

She was smiling. The dark shadows that had been hanging beneath her eyes were lighter now. Not gone; he was starting to suspect that they'd be lingering for a long time. Alex cared so much, had such a big heart and a desire to help. Merlin wished that he knew how to ease her burdens. Alex headed into the living room and joined Lance and Jenny, completely at ease with their romantic looks.

It had never been this difficult with Arto, and he'd taken the young boy away from his parents. Arto had grown up on the move, learning magic, lore, and history as they visited different areas. And somehow, his dear boy had grown into a confident and powerful young man who had created the Iron Gates to guard the world. Alex had been born into a loving and supportive family and had the chance to grow up more slowly. Arto had never known anything else. Alex had known peace.

Shaking his head, Merlin firmly told himself not to worry about such things. It couldn't be changed. He and Morgana had not and were not going to get into the habit of taking each newly born Iron Soul, even if they could find it, to raise in their world. Michel had been an easy child, but Merlin was under no delusion that they had been ideal parents.

Besides, Alex growing up in the "real world" gave her a different perspective. There was value in that, and she had figured out the truth about the poison long before him. The question of how still haunted Merlin. He desperately wished that he remembered how to make the potion, but his memory failed him, and there were parts that Cyrridven had done alone.

"You're wool gathering."

He turned to find Morgana watching him. Her expression was carefully neutral, but those sharp green eyes were fixed on him. Despite the difficulty in meeting her gaze, Merlin held the look. He would not spread his discomfort and confusion to Morgana. Not now that she suddenly seemed to be becoming the optimistic one. That was a strange thought. One more thing that he didn't know what to make of.

"Dinner is almost ready," Morgana said. "I've poured us some wine."

"And the children?" he asked.

"If they'd like. They have enough control that I'm not worried about one glass of wine." A small, pleased smile appeared on her face, highlighting the small lines around her eyes, but also making her look younger. "Why don't you take a seat in the dining room."

Merlin nodded and did as she suggested. The children were all already crowding in. Alex set a large bowl of homemade mashed potatoes down on the table before taking her seat. Aiden was right behind her with a large crystal bowl of salad. Merlin took the seat at the end of the table, knowing that Morgana would sit opposite of him. Alex smiled at him once again. In a rush, the last of the food was set out, and everyone took their seats.

Morgana's dining room was a touch small for the number of people they had present, but no one seemed to mind. Nicki and Avani pushed their chairs close together to give Alex and Bran some room. Lance, Jenny, and Aiden sat on the other side with himself and Morgana at the two ends. Lit candles added a touch of elegance to the table, which should have been groaning under the weight of the food. Morgana seemed very pleased with herself as the children began dishing up their meals and passing the bowls around. Merlin caught her watching how much Alex took and smiling when she filled her plate. That was a good sign.

"Thank you for hosting us for this meal," Merlin told Morgana. "It is remarkable how I always manage to forget how strange finals can be. The atmosphere of the school shifts as the freshmen finally take things seriously and silence takes over."

The children chuckled and exchanged looks. Alex was the only one connected with his department, and he had confidence that she had done well. He hoped the others could claim the same. Someday this would be over, and they would go on to get normal jobs and build their lives. At least he hoped so. That was how things had always worked in the past.

"To be honest, after so many days of reading poorly written essays, a day in the kitchen was a relief. I'm almost ready to submit final grades. I should be finished after a few hours of work tomorrow." Morgana was smiling, but there was still something cautious in her eyes when she met his gaze. "Hopefully you've been taking time to relax as well, Merlin."

"I've been busy in the forge," Merlin admitted. "Alex requested that I check the Iron Gates, and while I'm happy to say that all is well, I thought it wise to build up a supply of enchanted iron, just in case."

The statement dimmed the cheer in the room, and Merlin instantly regretted it. Nothing had been said about tonight being a distraction, but it seemed it was needed. He gulped his water, ignoring the solitary glass of wine for the moment.

"I hope that everyone feels good about their finals," Merlin said kindly. "While I am still working on grading, I am pleased to say that most of my classes seemed to have performed admirably."

"Mine were a bit more mixed, I'm afraid," Morgana said. She sipped her glass of wine with a smile, savoring the treat. It was a pity that being a mage made things like drinking so dangerous. "I had very few students take advantage of my office hours for guidance."

"I believe they avoid you out of fear, my dear Morgana." Merlin couldn't help but tease her. "After all, you do make a point of terrifying them in your first class."

"I have no interest in those who think that history is not worthy of respect."

A soft laugh escaped one of the children. One of the girls, he thought, but Alex, Nicki, Jenny, and Avani were all smiling so he couldn't know which one. Morgana just smiled indulgently at them, almost radiating fondness. Even for Jenny it seemed, which surprised him. Then again, Alex meant a great deal to her, and she would hate to hurt the poor girl by not at least acting politely toward Jenny.

"I can't complain," Aiden said. "I don't have many tests anymore at my level of classes and the two projects I was working on went really well. It's odd, but homework is almost a treat after hours of researching magical topics."

"Agreed," Lance said. "When I get tired of one topic, I switch to the other."

"Doesn't work like that for me," Nicki said. "My major relates so closely to history and mythology that it doesn't feel like a change." She didn't look distressed. Merlin rather suspected that Nicki enjoyed it.

Seeing what she would do in the future would be fascinating. Of course, part of her future may very well be guided by her relationship with Avani.

Morgana cleared her throat, her eyes jumping over to Alex. "I'm just glad that you have the opportunity to continue your educations. I know it hasn't been easy on any of you, having to juggle the different responsibilities, but you've been doing a good job. We are very proud of you." Alex looked up at the praise, her features somehow brightening and turning sad all at once.

"Yes," Merlin added. "We are. You've remained calm and steadfast even under the pressure of recent events. It's no secret that the last couple of years have been challenging, even for Morgana and myself. You children should be proud of yourselves. It hasn't been an easy road."

They nodded, and the atmosphere turned thoughtful. Alex's expression was difficult to read, and Merlin almost regretted the words. Thankfully, they had full plates to distract themselves with, and someone turned the conversation to more general school topics. Bran shared some highlights from a recent article he'd read on DNA research which Alex found interesting. Nicki told a story about her and Aiden as children despite his half-hearted protests and lamented their utter failure to keep up with the fencing club. The words and calm tones washed over Merlin. Morgana's turkey cooking skills had certainly improved since six years ago when he'd last eaten a turkey dinner at her home. She'd had a tendency to try and rush things, cooking the meat at too high a temperature and then for too long.

"I want to use the poison," Nicki announced. She set her fork down against the plate with a loud clink.

Merlin blinked, not believing what he'd just heard. Her voice was so matter of fact and calm. The other young mages didn't seem at all surprised. Alex seemed braced for an argument. They'd been discussing this. Once again, the young ones were working things out by themselves. If he hadn't been so shocked, he would have been both proud and sad.

"The poison is dangerous," Merlin said flatly.

"I know that, but Alex is right about it and the Darkness," Nicki replied. "I don't know how, but it seems to be the case. That means that we can learn from the poison."

The urge to argue rose in his chest and the words danced on the tip of his tongue, but Merlin stilled the instinct. Thus far, the children had proven themselves both creative and strong in the face of so many dangers. Across the table, Morgana gave him a stern look that warned him to give them a chance.

"What are your thoughts?" Morgana asked. "What are you looking for?"

"There are many questions," Nicki explained, "but one of them is how long it lasts? It's possible the Darkness is so dangerous because there is so much of it. If it could be siphoned off, then maybe it could be more easily destroyed." Her eyes were bright with curiosity, and Merlin felt another twinge of worry. "Or it's possible that it does have a weakness and we don't know it."

"The poison destroys everything."

"Not everything," Alex said. "The jars held it, at first. We don't know why that is. There has to be some kind of magical interaction there that holds it at bay."

Merlin doubted that. The poison had eaten away at the earth when it escaped the jars. Yes, it had stopped after a short time, but trying to deal with the Darkness drop by drop would still eventually consume the world. Still, they were all looking at him expectantly, and Morgana's sharp gaze made her support very clear.

"Please understand my worry," Merlin said. "I kept the poison locked away and hidden for centuries because I feared it so." He swallowed and shifted in his seat. "But... but I am out of ideas, and you children seem to have some." Nicki started to smile, but he didn't want her getting too excited. "Caution is critical," he warned. "Your plan to travel to Wyoming and attempt to see more of the past is valid. Don't put that aside."

"We won't," Alex said firmly. "But we need to try different things if we're going to find a way to protect the Iron Realm. Nicki pointed out that for all we know, the poison could be destroyed by bleach or some other manufactured compound."

Aiden made a thoughtful sound. No doubt the son of a chemistry professor was already thinking of insane things to try. Merlin's gut warned him not to. He'd been warned of the danger of the poison. Only his desperation to stop Arthur and the Queen had forced him to pull the jars out of his hiding place.

Alex's insight into the nature of the Darkness and the poison worried Merlin. It hinted at a coincidence or a potential design of events that he didn't like. Even after all these years, the true nature of magic eluded him. There was an intelligence to the Iron Realm, but it showed itself so rarely. Now the very fact that they potentially had Darkness to study made him rethink everything that had happened with Cyrridven and her potion. Merlin didn't like doubt. He didn't like having to rethink the events that had unfolded throughout his life. Most of all, he disliked the sense of helplessness that clung to his thoughts.

"I will give you the poison I have," Merlin said carefully. It was hard to force the words out. "But all experiments should be carefully planned and recorded! I don't want you endangering yourselves!"

"We won't," Aiden said. The boy's face was serious, and he nodded his understanding. "We'll design the experiments, double check them for safety measures, and record them so we can review them after the fact. We don't want to die because we do something stupid."

Morgana cleared her throat. "Thank you, Aiden. I am sure that you and Bran's science backgrounds will prove useful. Keep Merlin and I appraised of what you are doing." She turned her gaze to Merlin now. "We know very little and are stumbling in the dark, I fear. Merlin and I had the benefit of knowledge from family and Cyrridven. I am only sorry that Merlin and I cannot provide you with more guidance."

The words struck like blows — nostalgia flooded Merlin. As bad as things had been at times in the past, he missed how much simpler things had been. Alex nodded her understanding. She seemed sad and resigned, but accepting. That chafed. Merlin picked up his glass of wine and took another long gulp. He didn't enjoy it as much as he would have hoped to.

24

Time of Creation

4 33 C.E. Bighorn Mountains

Akule somehow made it back to his camp the next day. Judging from the ache in his chest, he'd used some of his magic without even realizing it, which was frightening and exciting all at once. His mind was swimming with strange images and emotions that he had no context for, but the dream of the circle and that strange woman was clear. Summer solstice, she'd called it, and he knew what she was talking about. The problem was that he wasn't completely sure when it was. Soon, that much he knew, but fear that he'd miss it had been growing in his chest the whole way back to camp.

There was too much to do. Akule stumbled as the dog rushed over to greet him, happy to no longer be alone. He needed to make the jar the woman was talking about which was supposed to trap the Darkness. Raising his eyes, Akule looked out towards the black patch. The dead area was so obvious now, a wound on the landscape, but now he had some hope.

Then there was the medicine circle. He wasn't a wise man, but he supposed that it made sense to build a medicine circle given that he wanted to heal the land. But he'd have to find the right spot to make it.

Hopefully, his power would be able to help him with that. But then he'd have to form that stone circle, or at least most of it, and he didn't have much time.

Panic welled up in Akule. His hands trembled and his chest tightened. Then the dog pranced back over and nuzzled his leg. The contact was brief, but it pulled him back. Dropping his hand, he rubbed the top of the dog's head and exhaled slowly.

"Thanks, dog."

It barked in response, clearly happy with itself. Akule went into his hut and was pleased to find that the dog hadn't gotten into the packet of smoked meat that he'd hung from the roof of the hut. He took a piece and started eating it thoughtfully. There was enough food that if he foraged a little he wouldn't need to hunt. That was good; he'd need all the energy he could muster for the daunting task ahead of him.

First thing was the jar. The spirit woman had mentioned it too many times for it not to be important. If he couldn't manage that, then nothing else mattered. Going back outside, Akule studied the heavy mass once more. The last of the strange black crust had come off during his hike down the mountain. His magic had been enough to carry the thing, but he was drained as a result. Sitting down, Akule embraced the pulse of power beneath him and smiled as the world itself rose up to help dull the ache in his chest.

A hum was coming from the strange rock, and he reached out to touch it. The material felt odd beneath his hands with an unfamiliar texture. It was smooth like a rock worn down by a river, but there was something else about it. A warmth that he didn't fully understand. The spirit woman had called it iron. It was as good a name as any. The pulse of the earth grew even stronger as he touched it. He didn't understand everything that was happening, but that sense of power, that connection to the natural world, mattered. Akule slowly placed his left hand on the stone as well. His strange power reacted like an ember fed dried grass and flared to life, spreading a pleasant heat up his arms. The ache dulled and the warmth in his chest grew stronger.

"Whatever this iron is, dog, the power of the spirits likes it," he said out loud. "It makes it stronger... easier."

Akule licked his dry lips. He was beginning to understand why the spirit woman was insistent that he needed a jar. This material was taking in the power of the world and helping feed it to him. If he could shift that power's purpose into stopping the Darkness, then maybe he really would have a chance.

Clinging to that thought, Akule studied the strange stone and planned his next move. There were strange images in his head thanks to the dreams of material like this being worked, but he possessed none of the tools he'd seen. And he lacked time to worry about making them. His energy had to be committed to making the jar.

He still couldn't believe what had happened. That spirit woman had looked like no one he'd ever seen before, and her unusual clothing... Akule couldn't understand it. He just had to take her words on faith and make sure that the jar and the circle were made. There were a few things from the dreams that he understood, and Akule moved away from the strange stone to gather more wood.

Combing the hillside, Akule collected everything he could find and used his hand axe to cut apart a fallen tree. The images of fire heating stone were sharp and vivid in his mind. There'd been a smell that was similar to coals but had an unfamiliar tang to it. He focused on what he knew and expanded his fire pit, building up the wood around the stone, and lighting it using some flint. The wood caught slowly.

He watched and waited. Akule's body hummed with tension and energy. It was difficult to hold onto any one thought as he tried to plan out his next course of action. His eyes drifted up to the mountains as he tried to estimate where he needed to build the medicine circle. He wasn't sure, but hoped that the spirits would help him find the right spot.

The magic would be necessary. He didn't remember all the lines of the medicine wheel, but it was more than he could make easily. There was too much stone to be lifted into the air for him to do it alone in such a short span of time. Still, he had faith. So far his magic had helped him when he'd needed it, and he'd been slowly learning how to control it. He just had to keep moving forward, and he'd find the answers he needed.

But when he looked back at the stone in the fire, he frowned. The fire wasn't doing much, to Akule's frustration. It wasn't hot enough, and he didn't know how to make it hotter. In the dreams, he'd seen flashes of red-hot metal and heard strange banging noises. He knew that the shape needed to change. It had to change. A jar, the woman had said, so that it could hold the dead spot. He didn't understand how that was to work, but it was necessary. So how could he change the shape?

Frustration built in his chest. Purple sparks flashed around his fingertips, reacting to his need without clear instruction. Akule shook himself. He couldn't lose heart or control. There wasn't much time. The longest day was soon. Maybe two or three days away, and he couldn't risk missing it. He watched the flames lick over the metal and felt the heat rolling over his face.

That was the problem. Too much heat was escaping into the world. He grit his teeth and hummed thoughtfully. He could dig a hole, but that would starve the fire of air. The memories of his dream were too vague to provide enough direction for him. He needed more than what he had, but there was no time to experiment.

Anger rose through his chest again, followed by guilt and fear. Stumbling to his feet, he walked to the edge of his small camp and looked out at the Darkness. That was what the strange woman had called it. The name fit. It ate at the world, draining the light and life from everything it touched.

Looking out over the landscape, Akule couldn't help but slump his shoulders despite the green hills and warm sun. He was getting nowhere. He was alone, his family was gone, and he had failed. Every day the circle of decay and death grew a little larger. It might never overtake him. There might be years, even generations before there was nowhere left to hide from it, but he'd hoped to stop it.

Why had he ever thought he could? Failure weighed down his shoulders. From here, he could see much of the plains that stretched on below. They'd be hot now, so hot that tribes like his own moved into the mountains, but someday they'd be black. The bison herds would be gone. There wouldn't even be dust or ash left.

Walking to the large outcropping, Akule leaned against the rocks for support and inhaled slowly, trying to slow his frantic heartbeat. His hands trembled. This couldn't be it, he told himself firmly. There had to be a way. Maybe he wouldn't be able to manage it before this summer's longest day, but that was no reason to give up. Too much had gone in his favor for him to give into fear now. That rock had fallen from the stars, and it was just what he needed to make the jar that the woman said he was to make.

Taking a deep breath, Akule closed his eyes and breathed. In his chest, the spark flared to life with a comforting warmth, and Akule's mind sprang into action. The power had let him move objects and even rescue himself from falling. Maybe it was exactly what he needed to do this. Maybe he already had everything that he needed.

Nodding to himself, Akule went back to the fire and sat down beside it. The stone was still not melting, and Akule gave up on that idea. He lacked the tools and skills. It was time to use what he did have. Crossing his legs, he rolled his shoulders and pulled on the power in his chest. Immediately, tiny purple sparks appeared around his fingers. He focused his attention on the stone and remembered the goat carcass. Waving his hand, he envisioned the stone being lifted out of the fire and brought to him.

His purple magic flowed around the stone and pulled it out of the fire. There was a shine to the fallen star, and the light of the fire caught on the strange grooves that the fall had left in it. It was too hot to touch, but Akule was determined to get to work. Leaning forward, he ignored the discomfort that the heat caused on his skin and studied the way his magic rolled across the iron. Sparks sank into the stone, and a soft glow was beginning to appear, almost as if it was buried deep inside the stone itself.

Pulling back, Akule crossed his legs and moved a little closer to the stone. He glanced over at the dog but was pleased to find it taking a nap. That was good; the last thing he needed was to be knocked into the scalding rock. Akule flexed his fingers and pulled on the spark in his chest, asking for its help and drawing the power forward. He looked long and hard at the rock, trying to imagine it as a jar. The spark hummed and Akule almost sighed. Of course, it couldn't be that easy.

He'd have to guide it, Akule realized. The same way he would have needed to guide it if the stone became hot and moveable like in the visions. Scowling at himself, Akule felt foolish for even trying with the fire. He didn't have the tools for shaping it anyway. It was always going to come back to his magic.

At first, it was too hot for him to risk touching directly. Staring at it, Akule pushed his magic against the top and watched in amazement as the stone very slowly expanded on the side and shrank on the top. His hands trembled, and a nearly hysterical laugh escaped Akule. He did it again, working in short bursts to start molding the stone as it cooled down.

Under his hands, the smooth stone slowly shifted. It wasn't like liquid, it wasn't hot and melted like he'd seen in the dreams, but more like some sort of clay. Purple sparks sank into the stone and allowed him to pull and push it into shape. There was resistance, but it was giving way under the pressure of his magic and will.

A shocked laugh escaped him, but his lungs ached too much for it to go on for long. Akule struggled to breathe. Already his chest was burning, and the spark was dimming. Beneath his hand, there was the start of an opening at the top. He was dizzy but kept going. It took work and more strength than he'd thought he possessed to start wrestling the stone into the shape he wanted. Akule was beginning to understand what had made it look like it did now. That trail of fire in the sky had done something similar to it, heating it up and crushing it together. It was one more hint that the spirits had given him. He didn't have the heat, but he could replace it with his power.

Slowly, it took shape. He had to keep stopping and resting, stretched out on the ground so he could take in as much of the energy of the world as possible, but it was slowly changing form. Akule had managed to make an empty space in the middle and was in the process of smoothing out the sides. It was rough, like a jar made by his children, but with every attempt he could feel more magic sinking into the jar. Soon, it would be all but glowing with power.

Stopping to eat, Akule was short of breath. He crawled across his camp as his legs cramped and throbbed. Weakness competed with pride as he looked at his work. It was rough, but it was standing on a solid base. He turned his attention to his camp fire and fed the embers with sticks. Akule collapsed with a groan as the flames began to grow strong once again.

Turning his head, Akule studied the odd jar which shimmered in the light cast by his fire. It well over a hand high, having been built up as he pulled the material from the inside, but Akule knew it wasn't finished yet. There needed to be more room inside. He had to be able to hold the Darkness inside. That's what the spirit woman had said.

He panted for air and stared up into the night sky. Everything hurt, even as the small spark inside him started flickering back to life. The edges of his vision were dark, and Akule could only twitch his fingers weakly. They had their own bone-deep ache that wasn't from lack of power, but from clawing at the stone until it shifted. He'd badly misused them in place of the tools he'd dreamt of. It was no matter. He'd recover. All that mattered was somehow finishing this creation of his.

Turning his head, he ignored the stars for a moment and stared at the strange jar. Something about it was familiar, like a memory of a dream. It still needed a lid, he reminded himself. Once he'd recovered a little, he could pull more of the stone from the center and make a lid. The very thought made him giggle. He was molding rock as if it were clay. Stubborn and half dry clay, but malleable nonetheless.

Another giggle escaped Akule. His head pounded in response, and the dog whimpered, coming closer and licking his face. He sighed and raised a still trembling hand to pet the dog's neck. The creature settled down next to him, stretching out to warm his side that wasn't next to the fire. Akule sighed again, this time in relief, and looked back into the night sky once more, counting the breaths until he was strong enough to drag himself back to the jar and resume his work.

25

Experiments in Poison

Alex was woken up by the sounds of people moving around in the hallway. Something in the footsteps must have been familiar, because she had no desire to reach for the Sword and Hammer hanging beside her bed. Instead, Alex shoved her face into the pillow and groaned. It was winter break, but there was a lot to do. She sighed and shifted her face enough so that she could breathe.

She waited in her bed and listened. Jenny was talking to Avani in a voice that was too soft for Alex to understand more than a few words, but both sounded relaxed. A door opened and then shut, and she heard the shower turn on. These were familiar sounds, and she slowly stretched out her legs and back in bed. Her room was beginning to brighten as the sun started to rise, and Alex debated getting up to go jogging. It usually helped her think, but right now her warm blankets were too wonderful to leave.

A thump in the hallways put her on alert, but the alarms didn't sound and no one called for her. Reaching over to her nightstand, Alex picked up her phone and checked her messages. There weren't any. Her brothers didn't remember her, and at this point, her old high school friends and she didn't keep in touch anymore. Another thump made her smile when she heard Lance muffle a curse. She had a feeling that he hadn't gotten his morning coffee yet.

Putting her phone down, Alex threw back the blankets and swung her feet out of bed. She started her morning routine, deciding to skip a shower this morning, while she listened to the soft sounds of her housemates. Once she had her shoes on, Alex stopped by her bed long enough to make it and hug her stuffed dog Galahad. She glanced at Cathanáil and Mjǫllnir but dismissed them in favor of strapping her iron dagger to her belt.

The hallways had emptied by the time Alex left her room, and she headed downstairs. Timothy was in the kitchen with three pans on the stove, which held bacon, eggs, and sausages. Already the smells were filling the room, and Alex's stomach grumbled in response. The Brownie spotted her, set down the spatula that was larger than himself and waved at her. Alex detoured through the kitchen to find that there was still half a pot of coffee and she was quick to pour herself a cup and fix it to her liking. Then she headed into the dining room with her prize.

"Morning," Avani greeted. She was seated at the dining room table, but there was no sign of Jenny. "How'd you sleep?"

"No dreams," Alex answered. "So, I'm not going to complain."

Sitting down, Alex took a long sip of her coffee and smiled. Maybe it was cliché, but some mornings she needed the help to get moving and turn her brain on. Avani smiled sweetly at her and didn't push for conversation. This was a lazy morning, even if it wasn't going to be a lazy day.

Then Nicki stalked in, her braided hair already in disarray and carrying something with a determined raise of her chin. Alex didn't even have time to ask before the other mage was next to the table.

"Well, I got it working." Nicki slapped the familiar looking enchanted book down on the table. "Managed to finish one project before starting another."

"I hope you got some sleep," Avani said. There were small worry lines around her eyes.

"I did," Nicki assured her quickly. Thankfully, there were no bags under her eyes. "Honestly, the biggest issue was just figuring out how to make the best use of the blood."

Alex grimaced a little at the reminder. It was too much like how Arthur had stolen her donated blood and used it to make his magic seem like that of the Iron Soul. That had been part of his plan from the start, and it was one of the things that haunted her the most when she looked back — one of many little details that she should have noticed.

Alex was saved from commenting by Aiden sweeping in with bright, alert eyes and a wide smile. She smiled a little in greeting and then took another sip of her coffee. Going back to bed was far too tempting.

"Morning all," Aiden called. His eyes dropped to the book, and Nicki preened. "Got it working?"

"I did. And just in time, too. I want to know what the Light is up to when we're working with the poison. The last thing we need is a surprise visit."

"Fair point," Alex agreed. The Light was intense and wasn't making its views a secret. "Nicely done, Nicki."

"I suppose so," Nicki said. Something passed over her face, making Alex frown.

"I'm still impressed you got that thing working," Aiden added. He smiled at Nicki, but she kept scowling. "Oh, come on, Nicki. I know you haven't figured out how to make a bag of holding yet, but you should be more than a little pleased with yourself."

"I don't know," Nicki said. She looked at the book almost distrustfully. "Yeah, it's working, and I'm getting some reports of what the Light is doing, but it just..." She trailed off and shook her head. "I'm not sure how long it will work. The blood came from Arthur's body. If the Light leaves that body, then there's no connection. I just don't want to get too excited. It works, but I keep thinking that we can't depend on it."

"It's still good work." Alex picked up the book and opened it. She blinked in surprise as she found that the book was giving them fairly frequent updates on what the Light was doing. There were no dates or time, but Alex was given a series of events such as eating, researching, and then sleeping from the night before. "Uh..."

"Yeah," Nicki sighed. "It's... it was good in theory. So far, the only thing I've learned is that the Light is eating and sleeping, which makes me wonder how that body possession thing works."

"I don't know." Alex set the book back down and shook her head. "Honestly, I'm not sure I want to understand." Leaning against the table, she inhaled slowly and then turned her attention to the wooden box in the middle of the table. "Speaking of understanding, you sure you're ready for this, Nicki?"

"No." The redhead shrugged, but moved down the table and gently took the lid off the box. Alex could see thick blankets and foam from her position, but she already knew what was in the box. "We need to learn more. We're heading to Wyoming soon, and I don't want to go in without having a better idea of what to expect."

"I get that."

"Breakfast!" Timothy called from the kitchen.

Nicki slumped into a chair beside Avani, and Alex hoped that Avani could cheer Nicki up. The book had been a good idea, even if her own discomfort with using blood and Nicki's doubts dampened her enthusiasm. She figured that sheer stubbornness and maybe a touch of petty anger had powered Nicki through finishing the changes to the book. Aiden stood up and headed into the kitchen. Alex put down her coffee and followed a moment later to help.

Breakfast brought everyone together at the dining room table. They ate around the box with the poison in it, everyone giving it plenty of space. No one talked about the experiments, allowing them to stay in a warm cocoon of safety and sanity for a little longer. But they were barely done eating and cleaning up the kitchen when the sound of cars on the drive alerted Alex to the arrival of Merlin and Morgana.

Greetings were exchanged quickly and with muted emotion. Morgana gave Alex a soft smile and kissed her cheek, but her behavior was cautious. Alex wondered what Merlin might have told her about the poison that he hadn't told them. Merlin laid his hand on the top of her head and smiled warmly, but it didn't dispel the worry in his eyes as they all headed out the back.

They were having a mild weather day, and the brittle, dead grass of the backyard was clear of snow. A Ravenslake sweatshirt and gloves were all Alex needed to keep warm, thanks to the sunshine. Bran and Aiden carefully carried the box to a plastic camping table that Nicki had brought home the day before. Spread out across the table were stacks of towels, small jars, and an assortment of tools.

The trees around the property shielded them from view of the nearest neighbors, but Alex still went over to the tall wooden fence to make sure. Nervousness hung in the air, and she glanced towards the house to find Avani, Lance, and Jenny all watching out the back window. At least they'd agreed to let the mages handle the poison. Alex had no idea if that would actually help if something went wrong, but it made her feel better.

Merlin and Morgana stood off to the side, still and solemn as statues. Alex wasn't sure if she was grateful that they were letting them take the lead on this or not. Maybe a little, since it showed trust. Then again, this wasn't the sort of thing that a person in their early twenties wanted to be responsible for.

"Are we ready?" Nicki asked. She looked towards the camera on the tripod that she'd insisted on setting up. "Are we recording?"

"Yes, Nicki," Aiden said. He was beside the camera and gave her a thumbs up.

Bran was a few feet away, holding his phone and a stopwatch, and he nodded to Nicki when she looked his way. Alex flexed her fingers. They'd agreed that with her power, she should be on standby without another task, but Alex wasn't sure what they thought she could do. Or maybe it had been the result of a conversation she'd missed about protecting the Iron Soul. That idea made her frown. That sounded like something Merlin and Morgana might do.

Nicki pulled on thick leather gloves, took a deep breath, and reached into the box. She pulled out one of the ancient jars which were made of earthen clay. Honestly, Alex was amazed that it was still intact. Merlin tensed, and even from a few feet away, Alex thought she heard him inhale sharply. The top of the jar had been sealed with more dried clay, and Nicki carefully examined it, trying to figure out the best way to open it. She set it on the table and clamped it in place.

"Nicole, perhaps-" Merlin started to say.

A blade of ice sliced through the top in a thin blade. Everyone held their breath while Nicki smiled. There was no splash of poison. Alex blinked and slowly relaxed a little more. She glanced at Aiden to find that he'd paled and was staring at his friend in alarm.

"It's fine," Nicki said. "I could sort of feel the level of the liquid."

"Tell us in advance when you do things," Morgana ordered. Her voice left no room for argument.

"Right, sorry." Nicki nodded. "Didn't mean to scare you. I'll be careful."

Then, still holding the jar in place with the tongs, Nicki picked up a glass stirring rod and slowly brought it towards the open jar. Leaning forward, Alex tried to see the dark liquid in the jar, but the angle was wrong.

"I'm going to put the stirring rod in," Nicki announced. "Bran, start the stopwatch in three, two, one."

Alex watched silently as Nicki lifted the glass rod and turned so that the camera could zoom in. Bran held his phone up and kept glancing at the stopwatch in his left hand. There wasn't much to see. Alex could see a thin dark layer of something on the stirring rod, but nothing seemed to be happening.

"What's happening?" Merlin demanded.

"Nothing," Nicki said. "Bran? Is the stopwatch going?"

"Yes."

Nicki leaned closer to the stirring rod which made Alex hiss in alarm. Thankfully, she pulled back a moment later.

"It is dissolving," Nicki announced. "But it's slow."

"What?" The shock in Merlin's voice sank into Alex's bones. "How is that- it ate at the earth so quickly."

"I don't know," Nicki said. She turned and dropped the disappearing stirring rod into a beaker. "Let's see how long it takes."

It took almost three minutes for the stirring rod to vanish, and only a small hole was eaten into the bottom of the beaker. Aiden dutifully wrote it down while exchanging a look with Bran. Curiosity burned through Alex, and she frowned but stayed silent. That was the first test; she knew better than to start trying to theorize just yet.

Merlin was all but vibrating at the side of the yard. Morgana put a hand on his shoulder to still him, and Alex watched his face carefully. Emotions swept over his features, running a gauntlet of confusion, worry, curiosity, fear, and anger before returning to a neutral and thoughtful look.

Then Nicki took another stirring rod and used it to collect a couple of the thick dark droplets. She held out her hand and shook it just enough to send them falling to the ground. As Nicki backed up, a small hole began to be eaten in the frozen ground. It stopped after mere seconds, leaving a small divot that exposed a rock which the poison had completely smoothed out. Bran walked closer with his phone to take a picture and record it.

"That was much faster," he observed, "it only took a few seconds."

"Yes," Nicki said. There was a small, cautious smile on her face. "Maybe the material matters more than we thought."

"There was still matter left in Sídhean," Alex heard herself say. Everyone looked at her. "I didn't think of it before, but that world is still there in some form. It's dead, but it's there."

"Which doesn't match what the Light told us," Nicki finished.

"The Light's world was mostly energy," Bran pointed out. "It wasn't based on matter." He shook his head. "It was stupid to assume that the results would be the same."

"Let's not jump to conclusions," Aiden said. "We need to keep testing."

Nicki and Bran nodded, both blushing a little at getting carried away. Next, Nicki picked up a rock that she'd found down by the lake that was about the size of her hand. She set it on the ground away from everyone and using the glass rod, released a few droplets of the poison onto it before backing up. There was no sound as the poison quickly ate through the rock, with no hissing or bubbling or any kind of visible reaction beyond the rock itself vanishing.

"Two seconds," Bran announced.

It was recorded, and Alex licked her lower lip. They tried again, this time using a large broken off piece of concrete. The poison ate it a bit more slowly, but still worked its way through in five seconds. A crushed plastic jug took almost a full minute, and it wasn't even gone when the poison stopped working. They tried it on the damaged beaker, which took several droplets and over a minute to be totally destroyed. A stray droplet burned another hole in the soil of the yard, reminding them to be careful.

Nicki sent Aiden to her room to retrieve an old pair of sneakers. When the poison hit the rubber sole which was turned up, there was a split second that Alex thought it might not even work. It burrowed a tiny hole in the sole over the span of thirty seconds, leaving the sole mostly intact. A few more droplets allowed them to observe how it interacted with the fabric. Something like hope was building in Alex's chest, but she did her best to contain it. There was no good becoming too excited. Nothing was immune to the poison yet.

"I don't know," Bran said. "It's clear that the more manufactured something is, the slower that the poison eats it, but we can't be sure of the exact rate."

"We can't be exact about anything," Aiden huffed. "The stirring rod was a nice surprise, but droplet sizes vary slightly." He nodded towards the small hole in the yard. "It does burn through itself fast in nature. That much we can be sure of. Small amounts aren't bad, but there's still the question of larger amounts."

"That doesn't explain the earthen pot," Merlin said. He gestured at the molded clay jar that was still holding about an inch worth of poison. "The clay was dug from the earth and didn't have any special processing."

"But it might carry some magic." Nicki leaned forward to examine the jar more closely, but Aiden pulled her back. "Yeah, okay," she agreed "I'll leave it alone."

"We should try it with magical iron," Bran said. He pulled out his dagger and studied it for a moment. "That might give us a clue about the Iron Jar."

"Use mine." Alex reached down and pulled out her knife. "I have Cathanáil."

"You sure?" Nicki asked.

"I'll make another one." Alex shrugged and tried not to look too eager. "But Bran's right. Trying it on magical iron seems like the next step."

"I'd also like to look at how larger amounts work," Nicki said. "So far, the plastic and rubber seem to have the greatest resistance."

"What? You want to dunk it in?"

"Not today," Nicki said. She eyed the jar. "There isn't enough for that. But since we know that plastic and rubber are more resistant, we can try to build an actual testing base." She gestured at the two holes that were now in the yard. "They aren't deep, but I don't love putting this stuff out into the world."

"Right," Bran said. He paused and then stepped towards the house. "I'll be right back. Wait on the dagger."

"Of course," Morgana said. She looked curious as he vanished inside. "As interesting as all of this is, it still doesn't give us anything to use against the Darkness."

"Well," Nicki began, "the Darkness probably doesn't just rush in all at once. There are defenses, so if we can figure out how to slow it down, that might buy us time to figure out how to seal it out."

Alex reached once more for the memories that she knew intellectually she wouldn't find. That didn't stop her from hoping. There was only a fog, and her heart thumped painfully as a warning. Whatever had happened to him still lingered in her.

While they were waiting, Nicki walked around the table and picked up the book she'd crafted for tracking Arthur. Alex blinked in surprise. She hadn't realized that Nicki had brought it outside. The redhead checked a few pages in and nodded to herself before putting it back down on the seat. Alex noted that it was far from the poison. When Bran came back, he was carrying a plastic tray and smiling.

"This might help," he said. It's heavy plastic. There's two." He twisted it enough that Alex could see the two lips of the trays that were pressed tightly together. "This should slow down the poison enough to keep the ground safe."

"Good idea." Nicki grinned and motioned for him to put it on the ground.

Bran walked it out to the middle of the yard and set it down. Alex followed and gently laid her dagger in the middle of the plastic tray. There was a hint of regret in her chest, which was silly. She could make another dagger soon, and this was an important test. Nicki waited until they'd backed away. Then she pulled her leather gloves back on, picked up a pair of metal tongs and lifted the small jar.

"I'm going to put more in this time," Nicki said. "Not just a few drops. We don't know if we can safely reseal this."

"Not with the way you opened it," Merlin muttered.

"Speaking of that," Aiden pointed out, "we should also note that it didn't interact with the air. At least not in a way that we could see."

Then Nicki knelt and poured out the rest of the poison. As it spilled out, the poison started to eat the earthen jar that had held it safely for so long. Nicki squeaked, dropped the tongs into the plastic tray and scrambled back. Aiden adjusted the camera as Alex stared at the tray, trying to understand what she was seeing as the poison swarmed over the dagger and the tongs.

Alex shivered. She could see wisps of something like dark smoke rising out of the plastic tray. Her magic stirred in her chest as if distressed, and her vision threatened to blur. Closing her eyes, she gave up on normal vision and carefully released a pulse of magic out across the yard. Her fellow mages appeared as brightly colored outlines, but she focused her attention on the tray. Inside was a blackness that was too deep and unnatural. It pulled light and color into it, but as it did, Alex couldn't help but notice that the blackness was being lost.

There were flickers of green and gray magic from the dagger, and Alex could see them being pulled into the blackness. Other, smaller specks of color and light faded. After what seemed like an hour, all that was left was a monotone mass of gray. Only... Alex noticed that more color was slowly seeping into the gray mass. It was like the world was trying to balance it out. Something tugged at her mind, an idea trying to form itself into an easily understood and communicated structure.

"Well, that happened," Aiden said. "Whatever that was."

Opening her eyes, Alex shook her head and moved forward to look at the tray. There was something in the air as she moved, a slight vibration that she couldn't put her finger on. Nicki reached the tray first and grinned. Alex joined her and exhaled. The tongs were gone, but the plastic was mostly intact. The handle of her dagger was gone, but sitting there amongst tiny droplets of poison that were still seeping into the plastic, was the blade of her iron dagger.

26

Tip of the Tongue

M organa's living room was so quiet that Merlin could hear the soft ticking of an old clock on the wall. He looked over at it, admiring the gold and varnished wood. It wasn't as old as someone might assume, based on their ages. She'd gotten it less than one hundred years ago. He knew it was far from the most valuable thing in her home. Morgana had boxes of antiques up in the attic, and she had much better taste than he'd ever had.

He tapped his fingers on the armrest of the armchair and listened to the sound of Morgana in the kitchen. Flexing his fingers, he tried to dispel the last lingering cold in them. Proper central heating was an amazing invention, and he wasn't one for spending time outside anymore. He'd done more than enough of that over the millennium.

"Stop brooding," Morgana said. She walked over carrying a silver tray with two teacups and a pot. "You're too old for that."

"I'm fairly certain that the brooding immortal is a staple of fiction."

"That's your department, not mine, but it isn't productive, Merlin." She sat down on the sofa and took her tea, giving him an expectant look. "How did you feel about the tests today?"

"I don't know what to make of it," Merlin admitted. He shook his head instead of taking a drink. "I'm grateful that they finished when they did. Watching Nicki handle the jar, even with protective gloves and tongs, put me on edge." Merlin swallowed, trying to understand the storm of emotions in his chest. "It's so dangerous, Morgana. When the jar broke in the tunnels, I watched it destroy the Fae attacking me and the wall!"

"But it did stop."

"Yes, but it took some time. It's a question of volume. If Alex is right about the poison being like the Darkness, then I can't help but worry. How could a jar stop that? All I can think is that it caught the Darkness falling into our world and then that Iron Soul sealed up the hole. How they did it, I don't know! But here we are, about to head to the only place that Alex has a clue about to try and find something."

"I'd feel better about this trip if we knew more," Morgana confessed. "While I don't doubt Alex's visions, the lack of memory when she knows so much about her other lives disturbs me. I understand your worry. I really do."

A sigh escaped Merlin. That didn't make him feel better. If he couldn't be the calm one with the answers then he at least wanted Morgana to be in control. He shoved down the panic trying to overtake him. It didn't hold and came rushing back up. Gulping down his hot tea, Merlin grimaced and stood up. He started to pace. At least Morgana didn't try to stop him.

"I just don't understand how something like this could have happened without us ever finding out." Merlin paced across the room, his mind whirling and trying to make sense of everything they knew so far. "We are always vigilant!"

"True," Morgana said. She sounded calm and rational. What was happening that she was the collected one? "But this life lived in North America, and let's be honest, even with our magic, we didn't know about it much before most humans."

Merlin made a noise of agreement and Morgana sighed. "And if this life was facing the Darkness, then it's possible that it blocks magical attempts to view it." Morgana made a small, thoughtful sound, and Merlin stopped pacing to look at her. "In fact... it occurs to me that only Alex has had any luck even perceiving anything to do with the Darkness. Arthur tried, but he was created using the Iron Chain, which may have helped him. You and I have had no luck."

"You think the Darkness is tied to why the Iron Soul exists?" Merlin couldn't keep the disbelief out of his voice.

"I'm saying nothing of the sort," Morgana replied. "But to be honest, I've attempted to see Sídhean for myself without any luck. Alex was shown it without any effort on her part. And the Sídhe were a threat long before your birth, and before the Iron Soul was created. It's possible that it was made to face the Darkness, and everything else has been extra."

"No." Merlin shook his head. "We would have known. Surely we would have known."

"Our scope, while beyond that of most humans, is still limited." Morgana took a sip of her tea. Merlin felt a bit better that she didn't look happy with the suggestion either. "Alex is different. Her ability to take in energy and transform it is special. I don't understand physics, but even I can recognize that there is something there. She has the memories of her other selves, for the most part, and her biological sex is different. Everything seems to be hinting to us to pay attention."

"So, if you're right, then this is what everything has been building towards." Merlin resumed his pacing, flexing his fingers and struggling to keep his magic from reacting to his storming emotions. "Then all the battles in the past have been what? Training?"

"Our past experiences have kept the Iron Realm safe," Morgana stressed. "I'm not saying that none of it matters. I still stand by our actions in the past in keeping the Iron Realm safe, but perhaps it was not the true purpose of the Iron Soul. After all, there have been times when we took care of a threat without the Iron Soul."

"Not often. Almost every time, at least…" Merlin struggled for a moment. "At least 96% of the time there was an incarnation close by! They were almost always nearby, ready to protect the Iron Realm."

He walked to the window and looked out into the front yard. The world seemed peaceful enough, but the Light's words rattled in his mind. That fear had been so raw and potent that Merlin couldn't help but take note of it. He tapped his fingers on the windowsill and watched the snow gently falling. It was beautiful, but it brought him no comfort. He'd seen too many winters to be impressed.

"Ambrose, we cannot break the connections between worlds," Morgana said gently. "We have so many questions right now. It only proves that we don't know everything. I'd hate for us to spend three thousand years protecting the Iron Realm only to doom it."

"I understand," Merlin agreed. He sighed and fogged up the glass. "I've tried scrying, Morgana, with no luck. I've even tried looking into a bowl of my blood, but I only see the Medicine Wheel. Nothing more, no clues as to what happened there or will happen."

"It is the same for me." He heard Morgana move, but she did not join him at the window. "That place is… there is something strange there. It is as if a veil surrounds it and blocks it from our sight."

"Do you think that is intentional?"

"It could be. Some frantic wish made by that unknown Iron Soul to keep others from investigating. Maybe he feared someone unleashing the Darkness and wanted to hide it."

"That could explain Alex's memories." Merlin nodded to himself. Such a thing was possible, even if the magic to manage it would be immense. Then again, depending on what happened, perhaps there had been enough magic in that place. "That veil hides what happened even from her."

"Once again, we are speculating without any proof," Morgana reminded him. "I have faith that we will learn the truth once we are there. I've arranged a hotel nearby, and the rental SUVs. They won't get us far up the mountain, but it'll be a start."

"I haven't hiked in deep snow in years," Merlin grumbled. He wasn't looking forward to it. Not at all. "But what if it doesn't work? What if this Iron Jar isn't enough?"

"The other Iron Artifacts have always been remarkably powerful."

"That we know of." Merlin dropped the curtain back into place and started pacing. "I don't like it, Morgana. We are walking on a knife's edge."

"We have to do something. As interesting as these experiments with the poison are, they are going to take time. There are only two solstices a year. We cannot waste this opportunity."

"I know." The words came out sharper than he meant them to. "I apologize, Morgana."

"We're both stressed, but today was productive. I assumed from how you talked about the poison that it just destroyed until it ran out of power, but it's clear that there's more to it than that. It seems more like acid. As if it can only react until it reaches a certain threshold. I don't know what the numbers are, but if that's true then-"

"Then that is the poison," Merlin interrupted. He turned to face her. "But the Darkness keeps sweeping across worlds. It isn't running out."

"No, it isn't." Morgana nodded. "At least, that's what the Light said." She tapped her teacup and hummed thoughtfully. "There's something that we're missing. Something just out of reach. It's a simple thing, and I know it, but as for what it is...." Sighing, she shook her head and looked up at Merlin. A soft smile appeared on her face. "But try to stay positive, Ambrose. After all, we have four clever young mages, and even a magician helping us. Alex has proven herself better than all of our expectations."

"You have so much faith in the girl." Merlin smiled warmly, his tension easing for a few moments. It was pleasant to see Morgana so attached, even if it would only make Alex's eventual death more difficult. "It's a nice change."

"Arthur may have been right to be so interested in Alex," Morgana said. "Some differences shouldn't be ignored. I don't know what it all means, but she is still the Iron Soul. The Iron Realm created that soul for a reason. I don't believe in much, but I can believe in her."

Merlin slumped back into his seat. Morgana's words pushed back against the doubts that the Light had sought to sow in his mind. He wasn't sure what to think. Even the poison that he'd assumed he understood on a basic level was different than he had thought. He hummed softly, trying to organize the thoughts and emotions tugging him in different directions.

"You're right that there is something we're missing," Merlin agreed. "It feels like there is a question on the tip of my tongue, but I keep forgetting. I hope that you're wrong about that magical veil. It sounds more like danger than help."

"I suppose it depends on what happened at the Medicine Wheel." Morgana reached into a side table drawer and pulled out a polished bronze disk. She shifted it gently, letting it catch the light, and sighed. "I want to know just as badly as you, Ambrose."

"You're right," he sighed. "We can't allow fear to make us act foolishly." He stretched out his legs and looked up at the ceiling. "I must say, Nicki is proving herself very impressive, making the book work again."

"It works even better than before. It was never able to record Arthur's actions with such precision. So far, there aren't any signs that he gave the amulets to the Fae. Let's hope that there are only a few left and they will be eroded by the magic of the Iron Realm soon."

"Yes." Merlin nodded and let his eyes trace a faint crack in the ceiling. "When I stop to think of it, I must admit that we've come a long way."

"I'm very aware of that."

"No, I mean recently." He straightened up and smiled at his partner. "In the last few years, the Iron Gates have been rebuilt, several ancient artifacts have been recovered, Alex has renewed old alliances, and even the Demons have been brought to heel."

"Not completely. Shiva is still working on that in India, and according to Sun Wukong, he's been fighting some that crossed into China."

"Yes, yes, but you get my meaning." Merlin nodded to himself. "If I start brooding again, remind me of that."

"You have been very unsettled lately," Morgana observed. "Try to get some rest, and ignore what the Light tells you. We'll find the way forward, the correct way forward."

A soft chuckle escaped Merlin. Looking at Morgana, he nodded in agreement. She was right, but it didn't stop the aching sensation that he was missing something. There was more that they needed to know. He desperately hoped that they figured out the answers soon. Otherwise, he really was going to go crazy. Then the phone in his pocket rang. Mouthing an apology to Morgana, Merlin wrestled out the phone and frowned at the unfamiliar number.

"Hello?" He waited to see if it was one of his graduate students calling.

"Hello, Merlin." The familiar voice of Arthur spoke through the phone with the Light's syntax. "How are you?"

"I'm well." Merlin motioned Morgana to stay quiet and turned on the speaker. Carefully, he set the phone on the coffee table between them. "And yourself?"

"I am well, but I fear my attempts to learn more about the Darkness are proving for naught. I don't have enough power in your world to make a significant push." Merlin wasn't sure what that meant. Morgana narrowed her eyes at the phone. "Have you discovered anything more?"

Morgana shook her head at him, and Merlin hesitated. "We've had some luck with a few attempts," he answered carefully. "But we don't know how everything fits together just yet."

"Has Alex changed her mind?"

"No. We all agree that breaking the connections at this time is too dangerous." Saying that he agreed with Alex made Merlin feel stronger. "I will keep you informed."

"Merlin, I'm having trouble keeping this body intact."

"Oh?" Merlin swallowed. He'd been avoiding thinking too much of the mechanics of the Light using Arthur's body. "Can you make your own form like the Old Ones?"

"No, I'm too different. I need a host."

There was something in the tone that put Merlin on edge. "I see. That's unfortunate."

"Yes." The Light's reply was flat.

Morgana started to reach for the phone but pulled her hand back before she touched it. They were both silent. Merlin had a bad feeling about what the Light was angling for, given the comment about lacking power and the host issue. He'd already seen part of the Light's method when Alex had been taken over. The power that it had unleashed through Alex was no laughing matter.

"I will keep you updated as we learn more," Merlin said. The words stuck in his throat. "Maybe your experiences will be able to help piece together the information." Morgana nodded in approval. "In the meantime, focus on keeping yourself safe. The Fae are still on the move. A group recently attacked, using amulets that Arthur made. There may still be more out in the world."

"I see. I will be cautious. You do the same. When you're ready to break the connections, you know how to contact me."

Then the Light hung up, and Merlin exhaled loudly. Leaving his phone on the table, he slumped back and rubbed his temple with his right hand. Morgana shook her head slowly while holding his gaze. She didn't need to say anything. As worried as Merlin might be about the Darkness and waiting too long, it was sinking in that the Light's agenda might be a bit more dangerous than he was prepared for.

27

Medicine Circle

4 33 C.E. Bighorn Mountains

Akule didn't know where he was going. The memory of the way the surrounding mountains had looked during that strange vision of the yellow-haired woman was his only guide. Taking care to follow the safest paths possible, Akule was aware that he didn't have much time. The longest day was coming soon. It could be tomorrow for all he knew, and he wasn't ready.

On his back, the weight of the Jar sat heavily against his spine, and when he moved wrong, it threatened to slip out of the bag around his shoulder and tumble down the hill. Grabbing onto the trunk of a small but deeply rooted tree, Akule pulled himself up onto a shoulder of flatter land. He breathed deeply, urging his heart to calm and his lungs to take in the air they needed.

He looked down the hill and swallowed. Already, he was high up and could see the ravines and rocky sides of the mountain below with frightening clarity. It was a reminder; a sharp and brutal reminder of what could happen if he wasn't careful. He'd been lucky last time, but the ache in his chest had yet to heal. With each moment he could feel the spark growing stronger, but making the Jar had taken its toll.

Adjusting the bag on his back, Akule resisted the urge to check on the Jar. He could feel its weight bumping around. With a huff, he resumed the slow climb up a steep path that curved around the mountain. He needed to get higher and find the right place for the circle. That much was clear to him. There wasn't anything like that around here, so he'd have to build it. He could guess that it would make his power stronger and that it would help him stop the Darkness, based on what the woman had said. That much he understood.

What he didn't understand was why a jar? Surely, he needed to heal the wound in the sky. Akule took a few more steps, and the Jar shifted against his back once more. So, why did he need it? Presumably to hold some of it, but why? What was the point of that? Unless it was meant to capture and contain a sudden rush when he patched up the sky. Maybe that was the reason. He just wished that the strange spirit woman who had appeared to him had given him answers rather than asking questions.

He kept moving. The sun crossed the sky overhead, mocking him with the march of time when he had so little. What were the signs that the wise men tracked that told them when the longest day was? If they'd ever told him, he'd long since forgotten it. His memory of the stone circle was already hazy, which worried him, but he vaguely recalled the piles of stone along the outer edge. He thought they'd lined up with a few stars. That sounded odd, but maybe that was part of figuring out when the longest day was.

Something moved in the corner of his vision. Akule stopped and braced himself, mindful that it could be a mountain lion or a mountain goat. His magic was stretched thin, and he didn't have time to take a longer path. He turned to look, only to stop. It was a hazy human figure. He blinked, and the figure became a little clearer.

It was the same woman. At least, he thought so. They were mostly hidden by the strange puffy clothing they wore and walking strangely with forceful movements that didn't seem to get them very far. She shimmered and didn't notice him. More figures flickered into view, moving up the mountain with her. Akule stared at them as they kept climbing. He didn't understand.

"Hello?" he called. "Hello?"

There was no response. He didn't think they could hear him. There was nothing here except the figures which weren't fully there. Moving after them, he counted six in total, all hidden in the strange clothing. A faint buzzing sound surrounded him as he followed them up the mountain. He ran forward, trying to see them better, and saw their mouths moving, but he couldn't hear them this time. The voices were the cause of the soft buzzing, and he frowned, wondering why the spirits would appear but not speak with him. And why were they moving so slowly?

They never properly came into focus. He couldn't look straight at them for long without his eyes watering, but he was able to notice a few things. They all were paler than him, and one had red hair that he saw briefly when it fell out of her hood. Another woman, bent over at one point and a shining necklace fell out of her covering. It had three curling lines that joined together. Upon seeing it, something flared in Akule's chest. He knew that symbol. It was familiar.

A goat rushed across his path, running straight through the figures and higher onto the mountain. Akule looked up and spotted a few more nearby. They paid him no mind and thankfully didn't seem to object to his presence. He couldn't help but note that the goat hadn't seen these figures. Doubt tore at him even as he kept following them. Was he seeing phantoms of his own mind?

The people flickered, appearing and then disappearing time and time again. Akule kept climbing and checking to see if he could find them. Every time they appeared, he hurried to get close, but he was moving faster than they were. Even with the Jar rolling around on his back, he was going up the slope at a better pace.

Then the landscape evened out. Akule stumbled forward onto the flatter surface and leaned down to touch his toes and stretch his body. His legs throbbed and his feet hurt, despite the protection of his moccasins. He closed his eyes and caught his breath. When he opened them, he blinked and looked around. There was no sign of his ghostly guides, but as he turned, he could see the surrounding mountains and the view into the plains.

This was where the medicine circle was supposed to be built. There were a few small trees stubbornly growing in the rocky soil and some rough sections, but this was it. He finally set down the bag with the Jar and his supplies. A shaky laugh escaped him, and he offered a soft thank you to the spirits for their help. In his chest, the flare of power was dim, but he wasn't in pain yet. That was good, because Akule knew he had a lot of work to do.

Closing his eyes, he inhaled deeply and tried to pull the image of the circle from his vision to the front of his mind. It had been a circle, a slightly lopsided one, but a circle with lines in it. There had been twenty-eight rays spreading out from the center. One for each day of the lunar cycle; he remembered that detail. Had there been stone piles at the end of each line or not? Akule wasn't sure. He was pretty sure that the lines had been evenly spaced.

He'd been inside of it, so he had a decent idea of the size, but other small details eluded him. Akule frowned and worried once more if this was going to work. The spirit woman hadn't made much sense, but she and the other spirits had appeared again and led him here. That had to be a good sign.

But first, he needed to make the circle. It was a daunting task, but he could feel the spark of his power beginning to blaze to life. The first step was the base. He needed the ground for the circle to be clear. Flexing his fingers, he whispered his wish for the land to be laid bare for him. The power shuddered and rushed down his fingers, but it went no further, and he frowned.

Opening his eyes, he realized that he needed to guide it more carefully. It needed an explanation, so it did not run wild. Pressing his lips tightly together, Akule fought to gather his thoughts. The circle itself was the first step. If he could get the circle in place, then he could think things through with the lines. He wished that the magic could bring his band to him. He could have used their help and knowledge.

Still, Akule had no choice but to get working. The circle was first. That was where he needed to start. Walking slowly, he tried to mark out the diameter of the circle as best he could remember it from the vision. He stopped in what he thought was the center and closed his eyes. Rolling his shoulders, he focused on the beat of his heart and the soft pulse of the energy through his body.

Then he opened his eyes and took careful note of the rocky terrain around him. Noting the rocks and trees that needed clearing, he was aware of the magic in his chest shifting. It was moving down his arms and taking shape. Purple sparks swirled around his hand, and Akule gestured at the nearest tree.

The ground shuddered. Akule braced himself, flinching as the earth beneath his feet shifted, and the trees began to tumble. A tangle of roots was suddenly exposed as the ground pushed the tree up and away from itself. Rocks were breaking open the earth as they were torn free by unseen hands. Akule's hands trembled. Already, his chest was beginning to burn with the effort of the command. Too much, too fast. He pulled it back and sighed in relief when the magic obeyed. The rumbling eased.

He exhaled and focused his eyes on a nearby tree. The upturned trees were mostly roots that still had clumps of dirt crumbling off of them. Akule laughed at the ridiculous sight before it occurred to him that they were now in his way. Waving his hand, he pointed to the nearest one and narrowed his eyes. He ordered it moved like the mountain goat had been. The purple sparks swarmed around it and gently picked it off the ground. It floated a few feet away, and he dropped it amongst some other small trees. He'd deal with it later.

Akule repeated the process on the other upturned trees, which left him with an open area and lots of pale stones. He'd need them anyway, though some were larger than he wanted. Unsure of the limitations of his power, Akule made a sharp gesture with his right hand and imagined the largest of the rocks being cracked open. A moment later, a strange grinding noise filled his ears as a purple bolt smashed against the rock. It fragmented into pale pieces that were much closer to the size that Akule had seen making up the circle in his vision.

Stretching out his arms, Akule exhaled slowly and felt the power gather in his chest. His head swam as a dizzy sensation crawled up his spine, but he focused on the solid ground beneath his feet. The ground rumbled again. He braced himself and held his breath. More rocks were pulled out of the ground even as those already scattered around him rose into the air. Rocks floated through the space around him, occasionally bumping into each other with soft clicks. Akule didn't let himself watch the amazing sight, but instead kept his eyes moving around him to outline the circle. He suddenly wished that he'd drawn it out somehow

But it was enough. The rocks moved through the air, carried by shimmering waves of purple to fall to the ground with soft thumps. Sweat trickled down the back of his neck and a few hairs that had escaped his braid stuck to the skin. The flare was struggling to keep up with his demands. Beneath his feet, the ground pulsed in support, but fear was creeping over Akule.

The stones rolled across the ground until falling into place, forming the first curve of the medicine circle. It wasn't perfect; the ring sloped inward a little too much, but he thought it had been like that in the vision. He wasn't sure. Sweat fell into his eyes, making them sting and Akule hiss in pain. Still, he didn't stop. More stones floated to their places. Roughly half of the outer ring was done, and the first wave of rocks had been used up. He dropped his arms to his side and swayed. A faint breeze brushed over his skin, and Akule's eyes fluttered closed.

He stayed still and locked his knees, unwilling to fall over. If he sat down now, Akule knew he'd struggle to get back to work. When he'd caught his breath, he opened his eyes and smiled as he took in the circle. It wasn't as defined as it had been in the vision, but it was clearly marked out. It was good enough. The issue now was the lines. He frowned and tried to remember the vision.

The sunrise had been aligned with a ray of the circle, that much he was sure of. Turning to the horizon, he searched it and tried in vain to find the right spot. He didn't know. He didn't know the movements of the world that accurately. Fear stormed through him, but Akule refused to give into it. He'd made it this far, and with his magic had achieved hours of work in mere moments.

Maybe he didn't know the point of the sunrise, but surely the magic would. He sat down on the ground and crossed his legs. Closing his eyes, Akule breathed slowly and waited for the flare to settle. He needed to be calm. Listening to the wind, he began to hum a song softly and thought of his family. The ache of missing them sat uncomfortably in his chest, and he'd been doing his best to ignore it, but now he reached for it.

The grief and loneliness filled his throat, choking him like disease and bringing forth tears. Instinct screamed to pull away, but he embraced it and held the grief tightly, as he would have held his children if they were here. It was for them that this had to be done. He lacked the knowledge of an elder, he wasn't as strong as their uncle, but he had some power to command. The flare grew brighter, regaining strength at his conviction. A tear slipped down his cheek.

"Spirits," he called, his voice rough from going unused, "hear me. Guide my hand. Guide my power." He opened his eyes and looked towards the east where the sun would rise. "I have little time. I cannot risk waiting a year."

Pulling the magic forth, Akule opened his eyes and cupped his hands side by side to watch the purple glow gather. It pulsed and flickered, growing brighter and brighter. The sun was beginning to sink in the west. He didn't have much time.

"Show me where to align with the rising sun."

The glow solidified into an orb and left his hands. It shot forward like an arrow only to stop a few feet away, hanging over the edge of the circle. Scrambling to his feet, Akule looked around to find a rock to mark the spot. He found a few small ones and rushed over to lay them down. The orb continued to hang at the spot, and Akule slowly gathered more rocks to build the first line across the circle. When he reached the far edge of the circle, he turned and checked his work. It was straight and marked the path that the sun would take. A sigh of relief escaped him. The orb vanished.

Akule stumbled as a wave of exhaustion hit him, but he wasn't done. Retreating out of the circle, he found a stick and slowly drew out the other lines, doing his best to space them all evenly. A pattern emerged out of his lopsided circle with its single line. He could see it now: the circle from his vision. The cairns wouldn't be finished, but maybe they would come later. Akule decided that he liked that idea. He dug the stick further into the ground to be sure that the markings were clear.

The problem was the stones. He'd used much of what had come from leveling the area already. He cast his gaze around, searching for more of the pale stone without much luck. There was some visible on the slope below the circle, but Akule knew he wouldn't manage to carry up enough in one night. The spark of power in his chest hummed, and despite the lingering fatigue, he decided that it was the best option.

Walking to the center of the circle, Akule sat down and crossed his legs once again. He rolled his shoulders and exhaled slowly. Closing his eyes, he listened to the wind rushing past him and the distant sounds of birds. Then he pulled on the power and let it wash through him. Opening his eyes, he pushed the magic out around him.

The waves of purples spread across the circle, settling above the ground like a thick fog and bathing the area in a strange light. It reached out of the circle in small streams, grabbing rocks from the hillside and bringing them back, cradling them in purple sparks. Akule's breathing grew shallow, and he swayed. Putting out his right hand, Akule caught himself and leaned to the side. The rocks kept moving, being pulled from the side of the mountain and up from slopes below him. They swirled and spun before lowering into their places along the lines. Then, when the lines were covered, and the medicine circle lay spread out around him, the remaining rocks came towards him. Akule smiled as they settled to the ground around him to form one last small ring at the heart of the

Medicine Circle. He had the Jar, and now he had the Circle. He was ready.

28

Road Trip

Alex hadn't spent much time in the backseat of a car for many years. Ever since she got her license and her car at the age of sixteen, she'd driven herself most of the time. When she'd been growing up, however, she and her brothers had spent many days sitting far too close to each other for hours on end on family road trips. Her parents had decided when they were young that road trips were an ideal way to broaden their children's horizons. Alex, Matt, and Ed had all become experts in the most comfortable positions to sleep in the backseat of a car and entertain themselves when the scenery stopped being new and interesting.

Even with that background and years of building up a tolerance, Alex wasn't thrilled to be in the back seat of Merlin's SUV as they rolled down the highway to the east. Merlin was driving, humming along with a classic rock song at low volume with Morgana next to him in the passenger seat. The silence in the vehicle had been easy going most of the day, but Alex's stomach was becoming queasy.

"Should we go over the plan again?" Alex asked.

"I don't think that's necessary." Morgana turned in her chair to look at Alex and gave her a soft smile. "We'll leave town early in the morning and use magic to guide our way up to the mountaintop. That will give us time to get up there with the equipment. We may need to use magic to hide ourselves during the night. I had trouble nailing down how much the area is patrolled."

"We might be able to get away with taking up the vehicles," Merlin offered.

"There's too much chance of being noticed," Morgana stated. She shook her head. "Hiking in the snow doesn't sound fun, but nature will help cover our tracks. Clearing enough snow, even with magic, for the cars to get through would be difficult."

Alex wasn't sure about that, but they couldn't risk getting caught. The odds of the sides of the mountain being watched seemed very small compared to the roads. Still, she wasn't looking forward to a hike up the mountain in late December. Even if they weren't into the worst of winter, she doubted that it would make for a fun day.

"I hope this is worth it," Merlin said. He flexed his fingers around the steering wheel. "I'll be honest: I'm still not sure what to make of all of this."

"The only thing that any of us are able to see is the Medicine Wheel," Morgana said. "We can only work with what we have."

"I know." Merlin tapped his fingers against the wheel. "I'm afraid that I don't know much about Plains Indian culture and history. I don't know what to expect."

Morgana touched his arm. "I know, Ambrose. But we need to find out about this Jar Alex keeps seeing." She looked back at Alex as if to check on her. "We lack clues."

"The poison has been a good clue," Alex offered. She thumped her head against the back seat. "I keep thinking about it."

"Oh?" Morgana asked. "Any insights?"

"I'm not sure. I feel like there's something I'm still missing."

"We understand that," Morgana said gently. A hint of frustration seeped into her voice. "We feel much the same way." Merlin grumbled, and Morgana chuckled. "Still, I must say that the experiments have been interesting, even if they haven't answered some key questions."

"Yeah." Alex licked her lower lip as they all fell silent again. Her mind spun, and an idea tried to form. "What if... what if even in a vessel, the poison is being held in check by large amounts of magic?" Alex asked.

"The jars weren't magical," Merlin said. "Neither the clay ones nor the glass ones."

"I get that," Alex insisted. She struggled for the words, and once more wished that she had been a science major. "It's like pressure," she finally said. "What if the Iron Realm... recognizes the danger and is able to put the poison into, sort of a state of grace? Like, it won't let it hurt anything? The Iron Realm's magic puts enough magical pressure against the container to keep the poison from working. It keeps it at an equal pressure, so it's frozen. It naturally counteracts it when the poison is closed up."

"That doesn't seem possible."

"But the poison was made here," Alex said. "I think it is a lot like the Darkness, but they probably aren't exactly the same."

"If magic knows it's dangerous, then why not just destroy it?" Merlin pressed. He shook his head, and Alex couldn't help but think he had a point. "Why allow it to remain in the Iron Realm?"

"Maybe it still has a purpose," Alex said. She tapped the window thoughtfully and watched them sweep past the snowy landscape. "I mean by that logic, why have a potion that created the poison in the first place?"

"The potion opened-"

"I know," Alex interrupted, "but really, was that necessary? I mean, Bran and I have had visions of the creation of the Iron Soul. Nicki and Aiden have had dreams of the future. Surely there were other methods."

"She has a point," Morgana said. She almost sounded amused, though Alex couldn't see her face. "But I'm not sure that I want to think that this was all planned, Alex."

"I get that." Alex suppressed a shiver at the very idea. She hated to think that all of her lives had been planned out. Hated to imagine that they might all just be pawns on a chessboard. "But I think that the poison was created and allowed to exist because it's a clue."

"Maybe," Merlin conceded. His fingers tightened around the steering wheel. "I'm not sure we'll ever know, but I will agree that you children have learned a great deal about it."

"I'm not sure how useful that is," Alex said. "Though, it is nice to know that it has certain set properties. Makes it less scary in a way."

"That's understandable," Morgana said. "After all, humans used to create gods to help them understand the world and make it less frightening. We've lived through whole pantheons."

Merlin chuckled in response to the remark, and the pair shared a look. A few flickers of memory pushed at Alex's mind, but she didn't do anything more than glance at them. There were lots of familiar faces and various symbols, but none of it carried any real emotional impact. Alex wasn't interested in exploring that too deeply. They had to focus on what was up ahead.

"I think one of our issues here might be old assumptions," Alex said suddenly. "Things that we believe because you taught them to us. Things that you believe because, as you just said, you've lived through whole pantheons."

"How so?" Merlin asked.

"Manufactured materials aren't magical," Alex pointed out. "The poison seems to eat magic because it's devoid of magic, but that might not be correct. That might just be how Cyrridven understood it from the warning she got."

"So, what do you think?" Merlin inquired.

"I don't know." Alex shook her head. "It's on the tip of my tongue. I can almost see it, almost explain it, but I don't have the words. The poison does seem to affect energy more than matter; we know that from the other worlds, but maybe there is something metaphysical about manufactured goods that plays into this. They aren't magical, but there is intent in them. Someone has to make them deliberately."

Merlin made a disbelieving sound, and Alex had to confess that it sounded silly. Nothing was immune to the Darkness, but there was something about how it impacted things. At least, magical iron did seem to stand up against it better than other materials. However, Alex wasn't going to assume that iron was immune. That seemed like a dangerous idea to have. No, it just fought back long enough for the poison to be equalized and neutralized by the magic it pulled in from the rest of the world. Even if they didn't see it interacting with the air, it probably was.

She still didn't have it, but she was on track to figuring something out. Alex knew that much. The poison ate up matter in its path, and it wasn't that it stopped working at some point, but that it was neutralized. It got full, or its electrons balanced, or something like that. The issue wasn't how to stop it; the issue was the volume.

But it also didn't destroy everything. Sídhean was still there, even if it couldn't seemingly support life anymore. Or maybe with effort, it could, but the Sídhe had never looked back. Maybe the Darkness blocked the path as it kept washing forward.

"It is something to think about," Merlin begrudgingly conceded. He didn't sound convinced, but Alex wasn't convinced herself. "We have much to think about, and a very long drive in which to do it."

That was the truth. Alex swallowed and looked at a sign as they swept past it. They were approaching Spokane on 1-90 which they'd taken from Oregon and would follow across Montana over today and most of tomorrow. The drive was almost 1,000 miles, with very little to distract them from their thoughts.

Alex swallowed as a familiar billboard for a place her family had liked came into view. It made her stomach turn, and she was glad that they'd only be swinging through her hometown. Alex didn't think she could handle seeing more than just the highway.

"Too bad we couldn't use a water tunnel," Alex grumbled.

"That would have been easier," Morgana agreed, "but given how much trouble we're having even scrying in the area, I'm not sure that I'd want to try using a water tunnel to get close."

"Besides," Merlin reminded them, "it is winter. I imagine that Bighorn Lake is rather cold." He chuckled at his joke, and Alex rolled her eyes. "This may take longer, but it is safer, given we don't know what to expect."

"People live there," Alex reminded them. "They've lived there for centuries and tribes are still using the Medicine Wheel. I don't know what you're so worried about." They exchanged looks and said nothing. Alex frowned and then sighed. "Oh, you're worried about what will happen when I get close to it."

"A little," Morgana admitted. "Can you blame us?"

"No," Alex said. She thought back to the horrible pain in her chest when she'd tried digging for memories. It hadn't occurred to her that something might happen when they got close to the Medicine Wheel. "I guess I can't."

"We'll deal with it," Merlin said. At least one of them seemed confident. "We just want to approach slowly rather than drop in."

"Still, couldn't we have used a water tunnel and gone to a nearby town?"

"Water travel can be dangerous." Morgana turned in her seat once again, giving Alex a firm, but still slightly amused look. "Why risk it when there's lovely winter scenery to take in?"

Alex snorted and rolled her eyes with a glance out the window. They had a long way to go still, and she expected that Morgana would become bored with the scenery once they were through the Rockies. She looked over her shoulder into the back of the SUV. Their gear was all packed up and ready to go. They had supplies for staying overnight up at the circle, but Alex desperately hoped that they wouldn't need to stay beyond the one night. That one night would be bad enough.

Behind them, she saw Lance's truck following and smiled. It had been nice of Lance to insist that they take his truck rather than Aiden's. He wasn't wrong about it being higher and better able to handle snow. Still, the absence of Lance, Jenny, and Avani put her on edge. They'd promised to be careful in case of an attack. If anything really bad happened, they had a little bit of magic they could call on, and Robin was in town. The Old One had already proven herself capable in a fight.

"They're fine," Morgana said. "I'm sure that Nicki is talking Aiden and Bran's ears off."

"Probably." Alex turned forward again and reached for her phone. "I hope the others are alright."

"They have the book to keep an eye on the Light," Merlin reminded her. "And the house has defenses. They'll look after each other."

"I hope so," Alex said. She checked for any messages from Jenny. "Lance and Jenny are waiting to leave for Christmas until they get news."

"I'm not sure why," Morgana replied. "Their homes are protected. They can't really help us if something does go wrong."

"Ah, but them being in one place does make it easier for Alex to check on them," Merlin pointed out. He sounded amused. "And I'm sure they know that."

"The Light knows them," Alex insisted. "Even Avani, despite Arthur never meeting her. Given what you said about it needing a new host..." She trailed off and shivered. "They aren't mages, and Lance and Jenny can't use much magic yet, but Avani is a fully trained magician."

"I don't think it will come to that," Morgana said gently.

Alex didn't believe her. She didn't know if Morgana really believed that. While she'd been grateful that the pair had told her about the latest call and the Light's continued pressing for her to break the connections between worlds, she somewhat wished they hadn't. Suddenly uneasy, Alex leaned over to look into her backpack. Cathanáil was sitting in its sheath next to the bag with Mjǫllnir, and the Chalice was tucked away safely.

"Try not to worry," Morgana said. "We'll be there soon enough. There really isn't anything that you can do right now, Alex. Try to relax and maybe take a nap. We'll have to stop tonight, but we're making decent time."

Alex wanted to argue, but Morgana was right. Until they knew what they were dealing with, there wasn't much they could do. But she couldn't help but worry. The Medicine Wheel was built in alignment with the summer solstice and was inaccessible in the winter. They'd be relying on magic to get to and find it. She had no idea if it aligned with the winter solstice at all. Maybe they'd get up there, and there'd be nothing they could do.

As Spokane drew closer and she saw more and more familiar images and sights, she really wanted something to distract her. There were too many worries about the mission and too many things calling up old memories. Slumping in her seat, she grumbled and started to text Jenny. If there was one person she could count on to be ready for a text conversation, it was Jenny. Checking on them would at least take one of her worries off of her chest. Right now, if that was the only break she could get, Alex would take it.

29

Up the Mountain

Merlin's magic plowed through the snow, pushing it up to the sides around them, and clearing a narrow path for them. The couple of inches still on the ground made the path slippery and obscured rocks and roots. They moved slowly, and Alex looked up into the mountains. Doubt nagged at her: this was a horrible idea. They should have focused on the poison and waited for better weather. If they used magic, then they would have been able to take control of the Medicine Wheel on the summer solstice, as much as she disliked the idea of displacing any of the tribes that used it.

She pushed those doubts aside. It was too late now. They were moving. They were using magic. It was too late to turn back. And while summer would have been nice, Alex wasn't sure if they had that long to sit around; not with the Light hounding Merlin and potentially starting trouble. A strong wind sent snow from the drifts and walls that Merlin was making over the top of them. Alex shivered despite the layers of clothing she was wearing. At least, so far, her feet were staying dry in the double layers of socks and the boots.

"This is fun!" Nicki shouted over the wind.

Alex huffed but stayed silent. She wasn't going to waste energy by shouting. Merlin kept using his magic to throw the snow away from them. The pack on her back weighed her down, and she wasn't even carrying all the artifacts. Cathanáil was strapped to her right side awkwardly to make room for the backpack while Mjǫllnir's weight on her left side threatened to unbalance her. The Chalice was partially sticking out of Bran's backpack, so it was in easy reach if needed.

Slowly, they kept moving, and Alex tilted slightly so she could look forward past Morgana. Merlin was using his tall walking stick and gesturing with his right hand to move the snow. He didn't look back at them, and Alex hoped that he'd tell them when he needed to switch off. Ahead of him, the light from their guidance spell floated along and cast soft, warm light across the snow.

Everything looked the same under all the snow. It was no wonder to Alex that the area was closed in the winter. There was no way that they could keep the roads clear. At least, that ensured privacy. She took another careful step through the snow. She found a rock and leveraged herself a little more up the hill. Another wave of snow was pushed out of the way and piled up overhead. Eyeing it nervously, Alex shivered as a strange feeling rolled down her back. She looked around with a frown, certain that someone was here.

"Alex?" Bran asked. He was right behind her. "Everything alright?"

"I- uh, yeah."

She shook her head and kept moving, but she thought she saw someone out of the corner of her eye. It was hard to say for sure. The wind was blowing snow all around them, and there was a bit of light reflecting off of it despite the overcast weather. Turning her head, she studied the spot where something had been and frowned. There were no tracks. Maybe it was just her imagination.

But she saw it, again and again — a faint flicker of a shape near them. At one point, she stopped and looked back, but there was no one there. Panic should have been building in her chest, but instead, she was calm. It didn't frighten her, and that worried her far more. Alex kept moving and finally noticed a slight drain on her magic. The spark was glowing softly, and something was happening.

She pressed her lips tightly together and debated if she should say something. On the one hand, it could be a trap; on the other, it could be her magic reacting to something on the mountain that needed to happen. They'd encountered strange things before, like the bell sound she'd heard in Wales that guided them to the hidden cave with the Iron Chalice.

The hike dragged on. Merlin switched with Morgana once and then Aiden took over for a little while. They paused to eat energy bars and drink every so often. Alex could see the valley below them and wondered how much further they had to go. Then they were walking again with Merlin at the lead. The cycle continued all day, and all the while, she thought that she saw something out of the corner of her eye.

Then the ground suddenly evened out. Mounds of snow were all around them, but they were on some kind of cliff or bluff. The guide orb rushed forward and hung in the air a few feet away. Alex sighed in relief. They had finally reached the circle. If they hadn't had magic to help them, she did not doubt that they would never have made it this far. Snow drifts were piled over seven feet high in spots, while in other sections it wasn't very deep at all. They'd made it without anything strange happening. Morgana turned to look at her and Alex just shrugged, unsure of what to say.

"Thank goodness," Merlin groaned. He started to sway, panting for air and drawing sounds of alarm from everyone else.

"I've got you." Morgana caught Merlin's arm and kept a tight hold of him. "Well done, old man."

"I'm not that much older than you."

"You were old when I was a child," Morgana countered.

"That is hardly a valid comparison after three thousand years."

Morgana stayed next to Merlin, helping to hold the old man up as Alex and the others started to spread out. He leaned forward on his walking stick, his body visibly shaking and exhausted. Alex hesitated, but Morgana nodded to her.

"I'll watch over him," she promised. "Go on." Morgana smiled and nodded towards the backpacks. "Start setting up camp."

"First we'll need some cleared ground," Aiden said. He grinned and pulled off his right glove dramatically. "I can help with that!"

"Clear out the circle too," Nicki ordered. "We might as well get as much done tonight as we can."

Aiden's magic spread across the ground and sank into the snow. A soft hissing sound filled the air, and wisps of steam rose from the landscape. Snow melted at a rapid pace ahead of them. Alex smiled as the first of the cairns appeared. The small pile of stone marked the outer edge of a stone ring. Another drift of snow shrank down, and another stone cairn appeared.

"Great," Alex called. She minded her volume and eyed the peaks still covered with snow around them. "Keep going."

Aiden grumbled something under his breath, but the red sparks kept coming, and the bright glow around his hands flared. Nicki was keeping a close eye on him while Bran watched them both with a soft smile. Alex stepped away from the others as the lines of rock appeared and the snow retreated. Overhead, the sun was beginning to peek out from the clouds, and she smiled. It was close to the horizon, but they'd have natural light a little longer before night fell.

"I can't believe that took all day," Nicki said. She pushed her hood back a little and tilted her face towards the sun. "That's insane."

"Tomorrow is the shortest day of the year in the northern hemisphere," Aiden reminded her. "So, yeah, hiking up a snow-covered mountain is going to take some time."

Alex smiled at the familiar banter. The hike had been far too quiet with everyone keeping their heads down and focusing on staying upright while they couldn't see the ground. It was nice to see where her feet were now and not having to worry about a leg falling through into a hole in the snow.

She looked around critically, trying to determine the best spots to set up their little camp. A paved road went all around the circle, which would make it a bad place to pitch tents. There wasn't anywhere with good wind cover. The area around the Medicine Wheel was largely cleared of any trees. There was a hut down the hillside according to the books they'd read, but at the moment it was almost impossible to even see under the snow. Still, camping next to the visitor center might be their best option.

Alex was about to suggest it to Aiden when something flickered out of the corner of her eye again. It was that same shape that had been following them. Still, she didn't panic. Some instinct kept telling her that it was alright. Alex swallowed and headed towards it. Pulling on her magic, Alex let it fill her chest and raised her glowing gloved hands.

"Alex?" Nicki called.

"Something is here," Alex said. "There was something on the hillside earlier."

"What?" Aiden demanded. "Why didn't you say anything?"

"I don't..." Alex trailed off and shook her head. "It's okay."

"Alex?" Morgana called. "What is happening? Are there defenses?"

"I don't know." Alex hated to admit it, but she had to. A faint buzzing filled her head, drowning out the others. It was like something was trying to reach her, to talk to her, but was being muffled out.

With her hands still glowing, Alex extended her fingers towards the circle and pushed out a few wisps of magic. Closing her eyes, she inhaled slowly and urged the magic to show her the life she couldn't remember. That strange shape began to glow against the dimming light of the sun. The others stayed behind her, waiting for Alex to finish with whatever was going to happen. She didn't know what to expect as she stepped inside the wheel they'd cleared of snow. As soon as her foot touched the ground, Alex was aware of the magic building in her chest and all around her. It was like a pressure wave that threatened to pop your ears when a plane climbed in the atmosphere.

Excitement pounded through her along with nerves. Something was going to happen. A fog was rolling in around her, surrounding Alex and the Medicine Wheel, and it was thick with magic. Her magic flared in her chest, and Alex realized that it was being pulled from her. Alex stayed still and didn't panic. The air around her warmed slightly. A man appeared in front of her. His long black hair was tied back in a braid, and he was wearing leather clothing. Even though he was turned away from her, looking towards the east, Alex knew him at once.

"Who are you?" Alex called. Hope bubbled up in her chest that maybe she would finally have some answers.

The man spun around, his eyes wide with shock. His gaze jumped behind her, and he glanced around the Medicine Wheel in surprise. The air kept growing warmer around Alex, almost as if it wasn't winter any longer. She took a step towards him.

"Who are you?" she asked again. He didn't answer her. "Please," she whispered. "What did you do? How did you stop it?"

"I am Akule," he answered. The name rang through Alex's mind without recognition, but burned itself into her memory. The voices chattered excitedly, but this man's voice was still absent. "Stop what?"

The question surprised Alex. Surely he had to know what she was facing, or maybe he assumed that whatever he had done had fixed the problem forever. Her heart ached at taking that from him as she did not doubt that this man had suffered, but she had no choice.

"The Darkness." She took another step towards him. "Where is the Jar?"

"The Jar?" His brow furrowed at the words and he seemed truly confused.

"The one made of iron," she explained. Desperation began to claw at Alex's chest. What was wrong with him? Was his memory already gone? "The Darkness is coming back. I need help."

"Jar," Akule said slowly. The word almost seemed to confuse him. "What is iron?" His frown deepened, and he looked around them. "What is this place?"

Alex shook her head, trying to stay focused. A hundred questions rattled inside her skull, some her own and some belonging to her other selves, but she pressed on. Gesturing weakly with her right hand, Alex looked around at the circle.

"You built this," Alex said. "I'm sure you did. You built this to help you stop the Darkness on the Summer Solstice."

"Summer Solstice?"

"The longest day of the year," Alex explained. If the Medicine Wheel aligned with that day, then he had to know what it meant. "I came here, trying to learn what you did. To find the vessel you used to contain the Darkness."

For a moment, Alex thought that he might finally give her some information, but then he stumbled back and clutched at his chest. Alex reached for him, moving forward across the circle of stone. The fog was growing thicker, and magic tingled across her skin. He reached for her, and hope flared in Alex's chest. Their hands passed through each other as if they were ghosts. Then he was gone, and Alex was alone in the stone circle once again.

"Alex?" Bran called from behind her. "What happened? Are you okay?"

Searching the circle for any sign of the man, Alex shivered as the cold rolled over her once again. Summer Solstice. The wheel aligned with the Summer Solstice. Maybe he had been there on that day... no, probably not that day, she decided. The Wheel hadn't been made yet. Things were trying to come together in her head. Something was at the tip of her tongue.

"Alex?" Nicki called. "Are you okay? Answer now or we're coming over!"

Swallowing, Alex shook herself and turned around. The fog was already gone. She hadn't even noticed that. Her friends were standing in the snow, shivering slightly and waiting somewhat patiently for her. She exhaled and nodded.

"I'm okay," she said. "But I saw him. I saw Akule."

"You did?" Bran asked. Excitement filled his eyes. "Like a memory, or-"

"No," Alex said. She shook her head. "He was here. It was like we were in the same place, just at different times."

"That's a bit like what happened to me in Wales," Bran reminded her. "Was he helpful?"

"No." Alex frowned and dropped her gaze to the inner circle of the Medicine Wheel. "He didn't know what this place was. It was before he built it." She paused, and the thoughts finally came together. "I think... I think I accidentally told him what to do."

"What?" Nicki asked.

"He didn't know about the wheel." Alex gestured around her. "Or the Jar. Or what iron was! I think I gave him the idea." A nervous giggle escaped her. "He got the idea from the future because I wanted information about the past." Throwing up her arms, Alex's heart raced, and it became difficult to breathe. "And I've got nothing! I have no idea if that was what worked or not, or the details of what he did or where the Jar is!"

"Hey," Bran called. He was stepping into the Medicine Wheel with a guilty expression. The others hung back. "Hey, that's a good sign in its own way."

"How?!"

Bran reached her and put a hand on her shoulder, holding her steady before he took her left elbow in hand. He was right in front of her and met her gaze sternly.

"Breathe, Alex," he ordered. She obeyed and inhaled slowly, keeping it in for a few beats and then releasing it. "This was magical," Bran continued. "Magic clearly thought that he needed information from you rather than you needing it from him. That means you're on the right track."

"Okay," Alex said. "That's great, but uh..." She looked around uncertainly. "Do we need to stay here tonight or not? I mean, it wasn't sunrise, but something definitely happened."

The others looked at each other, and Bran shrugged. "Couldn't hurt," he said. "And I don't feel like going down a mountain when sunset is in only an hour, and Merlin is off his feet. Besides, that didn't tell you anything about the Jar."

"Right," Alex sighed. "Right." She cast her eyes at the surrounding slopes and mountains. "Maybe tomorrow will be helpful." Nervous excitement built in her chest. "I'll cast a locator spell for the Jar itself in the circle. That'll probably be enough to find it."

"I'm sure it will be," Bran agreed. "But, in the meantime, shelter and firewood." He nodded towards their bags. "Come on."

"I liked playing with the magic more." Nicki pouted but headed for the bags.

Alex didn't follow them. Her eyes remained on the center of the Medicine Wheel as she tried to figure out what to do next, as well as what it meant that she'd seen Akule like this. If her magic was connecting them, did that mean that his memories were truly lost to her? What had caused that? There were too many questions. Her magic was calming down now; the moment of connection had passed, but Alex still wasn't sure what to make of it. All she could do was hope that tomorrow went according to plan.

30

Lock Away the Dark

33 C.E. Bighorn Mountains

Akule hadn't slept at all that night. He'd stayed stretched out by his fire with his back pressed to the ground. Aware of the soft flutter in his limbs, he willed as much of his power to return as possible. It was slow, but he felt a bit stronger with each passing moment, despite fighting off the urge to sleep. The Wheel was ready, as ready as it could be with him, and the Jar was waiting. But the Wheel wasn't a perfect match for what he had seen in the vision, and it taunted him. The position of the cairns eluded him, and he wondered if that would be a mistake. All Akule could do now was pray that it was enough.

Maybe another would finish it. The thought made him smile. This was an achievement, and he hoped that he'd make it home to his family to tell them of it — a giant Medicine Circle close to the sky, but connected to the world. Whenever sleep had tried to creep over him, Akule had sat up and paced around the perimeter of the circle, letting the cold mountain air sting his skin. The silence around him was deafening, and he found himself wishing once more that it had been safe to bring the dog up here. Maybe he could have managed it if he'd found a better route, but there hadn't been time to worry about that.

Now the sky was beginning to lighten, and Akule tried to shake off his sleepiness. The first rays of the sun would soon be pouring over the horizon. Akule swallowed; nervous energy was building in his chest, and it was a struggle to stay still. He took a long drink from his waterskin and stretched out his legs. Then he climbed slowly to his feet, not letting the weariness weigh him down. He scooped up the Jar he'd labored over and stepped into the circle, carefully stepping over the lines.

Around him, the lines of pale stone marked out the circle he'd created. His circle of creation and protection to fight against the dark one far below. Something was happening. He hadn't been sure at first that today was the longest day, but as the stars began to fade except for the brightest ones, Akule felt it in his gut that this was the day.

Excitement and relief that he'd been in time overwhelmed him, but only for a moment. Fear and worry followed, and he swallowed back a sudden rush of bile. His stomach churned dangerously and an itch to run rattled at the back of his brain. His right hand twitched, and Akule wished again that the dog was here. Right now, it would have been nice to have some company, to have some other living thing here with him.

Akule reached the center and rubbed the sides of the Jar nervously. The surface was cool to the touch, still holding onto the cold of the night, and smoother than it had any right to be. While the shape was similar to the earthen jars he'd used his whole life, the weight and texture of this was something new. He stood on his toes and tried to look down into the valley below, but it was still too dark to see the dead patch. His eyes dropped to the Jar nervously. He still wasn't sure why he needed it. The spirits had yet to show themselves again, and his stomach turned painfully. Akule wished that he'd been able to eat something earlier, but food held no appeal. Now, he realized that might have been a mistake.

Should he stay in the center of the circle, or go to the edge? If he went, then which edge? Maybe the one closest to the dark patch. Akule nibbled on his lip as the sky slowly continued to lighten. In his chest, his heart began to beat faster and faster. The spark was growing. Beneath his feet, the ground pulsed with power. Akule didn't understand; he was exhausted and hungry, and yet power was building inside of him.

Akule shifted the Jar to his left hand, tucked it against his body and raised his right hand. The pressure of the power was growing. He opened his hand and pushed the magic out. There was no distinct wish that he could give it beyond to help him against the Darkness. Magic rolled across the ground. Beneath his feet, the pulse of the earth beat and pushed power up into him. The rays of the sun broke across the horizon, bathing the hills below in a golden glow. In his chest, the flare burst with new life. Today, on the longest day of the year, the light granted him yet more strength and yet more power.

Akule bent over and placed the Jar on the ground, suddenly fearful of holding it. Before he let go, he saw a strange glow blooming deep in its surface and spreading across it. Akule shifted his hand, watching as the glow chased his fingertips. He didn't know what it meant, but it made him smile. The Jar did have a purpose here. The power in it and all around him was reacting to something. Looking back at the rip in the sky, Akule thought he saw a droplet forming. He was too far away for that to be true, but he was somehow certain that it was there.

At his feet, the jar began to vibrate. The world quaked. He kept pulling on the power, demanding more and more magic from the world around him. This was it. This was the moment. He could feel it in his gut, hear it in how the wind sang through the mountains, and see it in the rays of the rising sun. His eyes found the spot in the sky, that strange rip through which the black droplets came. He stared at the dead patch and felt something inside him shift and settle.

Purple sparks exploded around his hand, swirling in a mass of power that made his body tremble, but he held it tight. The sparks gathered in his palm as more and more appeared. He let everything go, let it flow out. Rocks shook on the ground, and the pale stones that outlined the Medicine Circle began to glow a faint purple color.

"Close the wound," he said. "We have to close the wound."

The purple sparks blasted forward in a beam of light unlike anything he'd seen before. Golden sunlight warmed his skin and the sky around the rip shifted to a rich, deep purple shade. His magic washed over it and swirled around the wound, almost blending in with the sky and the fading stars.

"Close the wound!" He slammed his eyes shut and tried to see it; tried to imagine the sky sewing itself back together like pieces of leather bound together with animal sinew. "Heal the sky and stop the flow of death!"

A strange sound made him open his eyes. It was a hiss that filled the mountains and echoed off the stone. Out of the corner of his eye Akule saw a mass of birds take flight into the sky. There was a shift in the atmosphere of the mountains, but he had to focus on the wound. His magic was pushing against the rip in the sky, but the Darkness was fighting back. It was just like when he'd thrown his magic into the dead circle. It was being consumed in rippling waves. The beam kept shooting forward though as more and more power spilled forth to fulfill his wish.

The sky shook. The wound shifted as if being pushed and pulled into a new position, but it did not tear open. His magic glowed brilliant purple as it rushed forward. It matched the darkest edges of the morning sky, but Akule had only a moment to appreciate it. The Darkness started to swallow the magic, twisting around it, but Akule didn't falter. It churned together, the magic and Darkness pushing and pulling at each other. Like storm clouds, they swirled and shifted ominously.

Swallowing, he pushed that thought aside and released more magic. The beam brightened. An aura of light surrounded the rip, making the open wound all the more apparent. Akule gasped at the sight. It was wrong. Dread clawed at his chest. Animal instinct screamed at him to run.

His magic was decaying. Even now, it was being swallowed up by the Darkness, by the pitch blackness that consumed everything. He didn't know if this would work. Maybe the visions had been wrong, but it was too late now. Black lines swept towards him, barely held in check by his power. The burning in his chest was becoming too much. Every breath hurt. The rocks were quivering around him. His circle was trying to falter, but he only pulled harder on the power that rose from it.

Beneath him the earth shifted in response, but Akule dared not look down. The air was thick, and clouds were forming. A roll of thunder echoed in his ears. His chest was burning. The muscles were tight and quivering, locking into the wrong positions all across his body. Akule almost fell from the rush of pain, but he locked his knees and stayed upright. Around him, the circle was shaking. Rocks were clanking together as the ground rumbled. Purple magic rose off the rocks, rose from the circle, like colored smoke, twisting into the air and towards the battle.

Then the Darkness began to recede. Before Akule's wide eyes, the gap in the sky began to knit together. More and more magic battered against the breach, holding it back and stopping the Darkness from spilling forth. Akule's heart pounded. He couldn't move. His mouth was dry, his hands shaking. But hanging at the edge of the healing wound was a mass of pure black. It shimmered with the glow of his power and started to fall towards the ground.

Akule moved before any thought or realization formed. His body ached but obeyed him as he threw out both of his hands. Between his feet, the Jar rocked but stayed upright as magic erupted from his fingertips. Dual streams of purple rushed forward and surrounded the mass of blackness before it could hit the ground. Instantly, the two forces clashed, and even more magic was pulled from his body to restore that which was being destroyed.

He beckoned to the magic, imagining it bringing the mass of Darkness closer. It obeyed, and the spinning bundle of purple and black swept towards him. Akule's eyes widened as he realized what was happening. He didn't understand why the spirits wanted some of the foul liquid, but he would deliver it to them.

The Darkness was bound over the Jar. Akule fearfully grit his teeth and released his hold. Thick droplets fell the last foot into the object he'd spent so much energy creating. Bright color flashed across the surface of the Jar, but it held as the Darkness flowed inside. Shaking, the Jar threatened to tip over, but Akule shifted his feet to brace it. The Darkness poured inside. His body burned as his power drained away, but he didn't move. He didn't run. He couldn't: he had to stay.

Then it was all out of the air. The Jar shook even more. Akule didn't know what was happening or how much was truly inside, but if this kept up, then the Jar would fall. He dropped to his knees and reached for the lid. The Jar began to tip over, and Akule gasped in alarm.

Throwing his left hand over the top of the Jar, Akule screamed in agony as a droplet of the Darkness struck his hand. His skin burned as an impossible cold took over his mind. He fumbled for the lid with his right hand. His fingers found the chunk of stone and clutched it tightly. He turned his attention back to the Jar only to freeze in horror. His flesh was peeling away, dripping like melting fat off of roasting meat. With a scream, he brought the lid to the top of the Jar and slipped it under his burning hand. It slid into place, and Akule leaned his full weight on it.

Akule brought his left hand to his chest. Sobs wracked his body as he curled himself up on the ground. Still screaming, he turned the agony against the Jar, commanding it to stay closed. Beneath his hands, it warmed, and he let his useless left-hand fall to the ground. Looking into the sky, he focused desperately on the spot that had been torn. It was still rippling and mending. His magic was still working. Purple flashes illuminated his blurry vision as more magic burst forth.

He wanted it gone. He wanted things to go back to normal. The agony crashed down on him between the beats of his heart. Violent and fragmented thoughts whirled in his mind. Tears rolled down his cheeks. His heartbeat pounded in his ears. The Jar trembled for another moment, but he could see the last wisps of his purple magic sinking into the metal. To the east, the sun was climbing higher and higher, casting warm, comforting rays down on him. Then he could smell the earth and feel the sharpness of the small rocks against his face. He trembled but exhaled in relief.

He was dying. Akule's throat closed up, and a sob escaped him. Now the tears in his eyes obscured the world. Quivering, he slowly removed his hands from the Jar. The lid had melted into the rest of it, with only a thin seam still visible. It would not be freed. Akule cradled his left hand as whimpers tore from his throat. Everything hurt. Every muscle and joint ached. The power in his chest was all but gone, leaving a burning sensation in its wake. Akule groaned in agony but crawled slowly to his fire and bag.

With slow movements, he did what he could to clean his hand. The flesh appeared burned, but there had been no fire. Too weak to walk into the trees and seek remedies for the pain, Akule wrapped the wounded hand as best he could in a strip of leather cut from the top of his bag. Then, with the pain throbbing throughout his body, he collapsed by the nearly burned-out fire and fell into a deep slumber full of dreams.

31

Awaiting Dawn

Alex woke with a phantom pain in her left hand that made her swallow and shiver as she tried to grab the fragments of the dream. She could remember a burning in her left hand and a strange rip in the sky being mended. Other details were slipping away too quickly for her to catch. There'd been something between her feet and wild magic zinging through the air.

Then she tried to look around. It was dark, far darker than it should have been, and she began to roll over to turn on her cellphone. But she was wrapped up in thick, confining fabric. There was a flash of panic before she recognized it as a sleeping bag and remembered the last day. Closing her eyes, Alex exhaled slowly. She was safe. Her fellow mages were nearby, and the dream was over. Swallowing, she nodded to herself and opened her eyes to take stock of the situation.

They were in a small igloo made by Nicki's magic. She was safe. Alex's eyes started to adjust, and she slowly rolled onto her side, staying in her sleeping bag. The shapes of Nicki and Morgana were nearby; both of them sound asleep in their bags. It was quiet save for the soft snores coming from Morgana.

Slowly, Alex shimmied out of her bag and was pleasantly surprised by how warm the igloo was. There was a faint light visible through the opening, and she panicked for a moment, fearing that they'd missed the sunrise, but quickly calmed when she realized that it was firelight. Shifting again, she pulled her left hand out of the sleeping bag and carefully flexed her fingers.

They still hurt, but the pain was fading. Alex frowned and once more tried to remember the dream. There'd been so many images, and a few were burned in her mind, but they were disorganized. Arto whispered gently to her that she was alright and that it had been a dream. She almost snorted at his need to comfort. Then again, he was probably one of the more gentle lives she'd ever been.

Knowing that she wasn't going to fall back asleep, Alex dressed as quietly as she could and crawled out of the igloo and dragged out her sleeping bag. The firelight was coming from a few feet away in a cleared section. A small fire had been set, and someone was sitting beside it. They didn't turn towards her.

She blinked up at the sky, already overwhelmed by the impossible number of stars that could be seen. The moon had gone from the sky, and Alex hoped that dawn wasn't too far off. Shivering, she threw the sleeping bag around her shoulders like a cloak and headed for the fire. She was unsurprised to find that it was Bran sitting there, still wrapped up in his sleeping bag.

"Hey," Alex greeted.

"Morning."

"Is it morning?"

"About two hours to dawn, but it is past midnight."

"Oh."

"You okay?" Bran's tone was casual, but Alex knew he wouldn't have asked if he wasn't worried.

"Mostly." She shrugged and didn't look at him. He knew better than to believe her. Alex shuffled to the fire and sat down on the ground. Her nose wrinkled at the lack of chairs, but there was nothing for it. "Dreams," she admitted.

"Nightmare or memory?" Alex flexed her left hand and slowly brought it out into the light. Her hand was fine, her skin was intact, and there was no sign of damage. Memories of the dream came rushing back, and her chest tightened. "Alex?"

"Memory," Alex replied. "Of Akule. I saw… I think I saw what he did." Tilting her head back, she tried to find the spot in the sky that had been torn so long, but it was impossible. "His magic at the end was wild, there was so much of it, and he was in pain. Maybe that caused the memory issue." She tightened her hand into a fist. "But he also…"

"What?"

"He got splashed with Darkness." Alex shivered at the words. "I don't know. I think it was a memory. It's hard to say." Her hand was aching again, and Alex studied it once more.

"So the Darkness damaged him." Bran's voice was soft and gentle, as if he was afraid to spook her.

"I'm not sure." Alex shrugged and kept studying the night sky. "One of those things caused the memory issue. Since I had the dream here, maybe it really was a spell of some kind to protect this place." She dropped her gaze to the nearby hill. While she couldn't see the circle from here, she knew it was there. "He was very proud of the Medicine Circle."

Bran sighed, and she heard him shift. For a long time, he didn't speak, and Alex watched the fire. Something was soothing about it, and the cold slowly left her body. She kept shifting her left hand, trying to dispel the last of the pain while not thinking about how much it had hurt.

"Every time that I think you're going to be okay, something happens that makes me worry all over again."

"Sorry," Alex said dryly.

"I remember… At the start of all this, I was so excited. I was hoping that it would let me fix my leg. That the vision I'd had in the car would finally make sense. Now, I sort of wish it hadn't happened. Using the brace wasn't bad. The worst part was Mom's guilt, but now I have to worry about her all the time." Alex didn't say anything in response, but nodded to show she was listening. "And I know it's got to be worse for you."

"It's not too bad." Alex finally looked back at Bran. "I miss my family, but…" Trailing off, she licked her lips and debated what to say.

"But?"

"But sometimes it's muted," Alex finished. "Whenever something big happens, all the voices talk, and I get echoes of their emotions." Gesturing to her head, she almost giggled at how crazy she sounded. "It all kind of washes together, like paints turning to black. As a result, not much stands out. I can feel fear for my life and worry, but most of the time everything else just sort of… takes a back seat."

"Is that good or bad?"

"Probably good. Probably some kind of survival system. I'm sure a psychiatrist would argue, but it works."

"So far." Alex finally looked at Bran. He was sitting up with his sleeping bag still wrapped around him, making him look like a caterpillar. Only the frown marring his face kept her from giggling. "Doesn't sound good."

"It comes and goes," Alex said. "As I said, sometimes it's muted. I still feel things for myself. I can miss my brothers, feel affection for all of you and laugh at a joke. It's not like I can't feel anything. It's more that it's all too much with all the different reactions in my head." Chuckling, Alex looked up into the dark sky. "God, I sound crazy, don't I?"

"A little, but I suppose that it's just one more thing that we don't understand. Sometimes... sometimes I wish that I could remember the other Bran's life. I wish I could understand him and what happened."

One of the whispers grew louder. Shivering, Alex sucked in a breath as the others quieted for a moment. There was sadness, grief, and pride rolling through her. She could recognize that it wasn't her own. Gofiben. She was sure it was him.

"Remembering isn't all it's cut out to be. It can get confusing" Alex swallowed, her mouth and throat too dry. She wondered how much work it would be to try and make some tea. "Trust me on that. But I know that Gofiben cared a great deal about his friend. I felt pride when you mentioned him. And grief."

"Thank you, but I still wonder."

"One more thing we'll probably never have an answer to," Alex said. "For instance, I wonder about Jenny and Lance's reincarnation drama. Was that some sort of magic from another lifetime cast on them? Are there other people not connected with us stuck in cycles of reincarnation, or was it only because of their connection to the Iron Soul?"

"I figure it's because of the Iron Soul."

"Me too, but I'm not sure. I'm confident that Arto didn't want them punished, so what caused it?"

"Maybe Merlin and Morgana without realizing it. They loved Arto," Bran offered. "That's always been clear."

Despite herself, Alex smiled. That affection remained. She felt it often and even now, she was aware of a gentle fondness coming from the part of her that was Arto. It overpowered the lingering resentment that some of the other lives carried. Merlin and Morgana were complicated in some ways and impossibly simple in others. They were each only half human, but the array of emotions they inspired in Alex's various memory selves was the full gamut of human experience. Even those like Cuthbert, Temur, and Gottfried had plenty to say about them.

"Alex?"

"Everything is fine," she promised. "Just thinking. And listening."

"Do you miss who you were before the voices started?"

Alex wasn't sure that she liked that question, but it was a valid one. Thinking it over, she pressed her lips tightly together and stared into the fire. She wasn't sure if Bran understood what he was asking. Then again, it was Bran, so he probably understood the ramifications of that question even more than she did.

"Miss who I used to be?" she repeated. "I'm not sure. I don't really remember in detail what I used to be like. I know that I used to read more than I do now. There never seems to be time. I worried about things like dating and a social life. I suppose I've changed, but I'm not... I don't know. Everyone changes. That's part of life. I'm still Alex. Don't worry about that." Shaking her head, she closed her eyes for a moment. "Before I touched Arto's skull and unlocked whatever magical memory block was in place, I was confused. Aiden was in a coma, and I had to be the Iron Soul. I was determined to do a good job."

"And you have."

"Maybe, but it doesn't feel like it most days."

"Other Iron Souls didn't have to deal with as much as you've had to."

"Maybe. Merlin and Morgana don't share enough information for me to be certain of that." Alex now wished that she had something strong to drink. "And the memories are fuzzy on the best of days. They only clear up when I dream, and then they tend to jumble. Though now that I've been able to direct the dreams using magic, I might be able to start sorting them out."

"And tonight?"

"We're in an important place," Alex replied. She shrugged, but under the sleeping bag's material, she doubted that Bran could see it. "I'm sure that helped." She moved her left hand carefully. It was fine. It was fine, she told herself. "Maybe when I try to find the Iron Jar, that will trigger more memories and fill in some gaps."

"Do you think that's a good idea? Sorting them out and paying that much attention to them? I mean... I worry about you losing yourself to the other lives. A person is the sum of their memories and-"

"I think having some control over them would be better than this mess. I don't mind them anymore, but not understanding or worrying that I'm missing information is annoying. Imagine living with the sense that you've forgotten something all the time. It gets annoying."

She doubted that Bran understood and closed her eyes. Despite the cold winter air, she was finding it easy to relax. Maybe it was the smell of the small fire or the soft noises of the wind and nocturnal animals, or maybe it was this place and finally having some answers that put her more at ease. Closing her eyes, Alex listened intently to the soft crackling of the wood in the heat and let the warmth roll over her. The pain in her hand was finally gone.

Alex sighed again and looked up into the sky. Even with the light of the fire, there were far too many stars for her to be able to pick out any constellations. A stray memory of staring up at them at another time hit her. She wasn't sure if it was another memory from Akule or someone else. Either was possible. The stars were one constant in her many lives. They may move, the constellations may be different based on where she'd been and her culture, but the stars had always been overhead.

Then there was a beep from inside one of the igloos. Bran looked around and frowned. "It's not morning yet. Did you set an alarm?"

"No," Alex said. "And my battery died."

"Ah, the cold," Bran said. "Mine's plugged into a power bar. I'm not sure how much it will help."

Someone was moving inside the igloo. Alex thought it was the one she'd been in.

"Shit!"

The shout was loud, ringing through the night. Immediately there was movement in both igloos, and Bran started climbing out of his sleeping bag. Alex tossed hers off, ignoring the cold, and started towards the igloo. She was grateful that the ground had been cleared off with magic.

"Nicki?" she called. "Nicki, what's wrong?"

"Nicki?" Merlin called from the second igloo.

Aiden was crawling out, his hair a mess and his eyes wild as he looked around. "Nicki, you okay?"

A hand came out of the igloo and waved around a moment before retreating. Alex stared and waited impatiently as the chill of the cold began to sink into her body. A short time later, Nicki started fumbling her way out, pulling on boots.

"Call from Avani." Nicki gestured to them all to be silent as she struggled to climb to her feet on the uneven terrain and keep her cellphone at her ear. "Shit, Avani, you're breaking up." She shook her head. "What about the Light?"

Everyone tensed at that, and Nicki moved away from the igloo to let Morgana crawl out. Merlin was already coming out behind Aiden, not even wearing his coat, and watching Nicki with wide eyes. Nicki paced around and kept furrowing her brow. Then she pulled the phone away and scowled.

"Bad signal. And my battery is almost dead."

The phone chirped, and Nicki hurriedly tapped the screen. Even in the low light of the fire and amongst the shadows their bodies cast, Alex could see Nicki's face pale. Morgana hurried to her, putting a hand on her shoulder as Alex was suddenly frozen in place.

"Nicole?" Merlin called. "What is it?"

"The Light is coming," Nicki said. "I asked Avani to keep an eye on the book before we left. She says that the book recorded him driving through Lovell. No mention of the time."

"It's like 4 in the morning," Aiden protested. "How often is she checking it?"

No one answered him. Nicki shook her head and watched the phone. "No reply. I'm not sure my request for more information got through."

"So, the Light is coming," Morgana said. She looked around at everyone. "Get dressed and ready for sunrise. I'll prepare some breakfast. Meditate and prepare yourselves for the day." Her green eyes settled on Alex. "We need to be ready for anything. I doubt that the Light followed us here for a chat."

"He'll have to take the old highway as we did," Merlin said. His gaze was stern. "And climb the mountain to reach us. He might not reach us for hours, but be on your guard. The Light could have powers we know nothing about." Merlin paused and exchanged a look with Morgana. "The Light revealed recently that Arthur's body is failing. He wants a new host. That might be why he tracked us; he may be seeking a mage. I know that we came here for information and to find the Jar, but be extremely careful. We don't know if the Light can transfer to an unwilling host or what that process looks like."

Something about hearing the words here on a lonely mountain in the depths of winter made that statement terrifying. Alex's eyes jumped to the east. There was still no sign of the sun, and she had a bad feeling that if the Light truly was that desperate, it wouldn't wait until dawn to follow them here.

32

The Hidden Jar

There was no peace in camp as dawn approached. While it was possible that the Light was coming merely out of curiosity, Alex doubted it. She was dressed for the weather and had Mjǫllnir on her hip, with Cathanáil once more strapped to her back. Both hummed in response to her worry and perhaps to this place.

Breakfast had been nothing too special. The ready to eat backpacking meals that they'd brought were filling, but the taste left something to be desired. No one had complained; they were all too much on alert. Overhead, the sky remained clear and the stars started to fade as the earth turned towards the sun. She called on her magic to create a small, floating orb of light as she moved further from the fire.

Alex's magic was thrumming. The strange memory of her dream kept trying to replay itself. It was a memory from Akule, she was sure of it, but still lacked a clear reason for the problem with her memory. She sniffed the air, taking in the sharp smells of the campfire smoke and the snow. This point on Medicine Mountain let her see into the valley below, and she searched the darkness for any sign of headlights or movement. It was still too dark for her to see anything clearly. To the east, the sky began to turn a soft shade of purple.

She walked towards the Medicine Wheel without thinking about it. Behind her, Alex heard the others talking. Merlin ordered Nicki, Bran, and Aiden to follow her before promising that he and Morgana would stand guard against the Light. Tension and worry filled the air. No one knew what to expect. They all had their hopes, Alex was sure of that, but she wasn't sure what would happen. Would she see Akule once again? Would she suddenly gain his memories?

Alex's feet sunk into the snow in places they hadn't cleared. There was no point in wasting their magic. They were going to need it if the Light came with ill intentions in mind. Her hand dropped to Mjǫllnir, and she gently traced the triskelion symbol in the metal. She couldn't help but wonder if the Jar had that symbol on it as well.

Upon reaching the edge of the stone circle, Alex paused and inhaled slowly. It still felt wrong to be walking through a fragile monument like this, especially since their research had indicated how important it was to local tribes, but there was nothing for it. She stepped inside the outer line of stone, taking care not to step on the lines themselves or disturb the stone cairns. Respect was the best she could do, and hopefully, unlike Stonehenge, they wouldn't end up needing to dig into someone's tomb.

Alex summoned her magic to her right hand and smiled as a strange, dark gray flame formed in her hand. It danced across her skin, not burning the flesh, and immune to the icy wind that would have snuffed it out. The center pile of rocks was shorter than she remembered from her dream. Things were just a tiny bit off. But then again, she was aware that tribes had been using the Medicine Wheel for centuries — people who were removed from Akule's tribe and wouldn't have known his story.

The voices were quiet for once, leaving her to think. There was a soft hum at the back of her mind that reassured her that they were there. On her hip, Mjolnir's magic seeped into her body even as the Hammer pulled some magic from her. A cycle of strength and renewal.

"Alex?"

"I'm not sure," she said. Alex flexed her fingers and studied her magic. "I'm not sure what I'm supposed to do. There is... something here."

"Try to see it," Nicki suggested softly. "Like you see the blood spells."

Alex nodded; it was a good suggestion. It also had the added benefit of potentially letting her see the Light when it came. Looking towards the others, she noted that they all had their orbs of light as well. She checked the horizon. Sunrise would be soon. The Wheel had no alignment point for winter solstice, at least not to Alex's knowledge, so she wasn't sure where to stand. Moving to the center of the wheel, Alex minded her footing and then released the orb of light, letting its power dissipate out around her.

Exhaling, Alex pushed her magic out across the terrain. It shimmered along the ground, and the Medicine Wheel on the hill lit up brightly with brilliant purple lines. But they were strange. Alex frowned and studied them, ignoring the colorful outlines of her friends. The magic of the Medicine Wheel was sunk into the ground, going several feet down and creating a strange, almost 3-D shape. It pulsed softly and the magic rippled outward.

Alex turned to look around them. There was a bubble. She had no other word for it. Unlike the blood spells which covered the ground, this spell dug into the ground only to emerge a few miles down the hill. It formed a dome over her head of softly shimmering purple and surrounded the area around the Medicine Wheel. All the while, the Wheel hummed softly.

She didn't understand. What had Akule done? Was this part of her memory issue? This dome had a purpose. It shielded the area. Was he trying to block the Darkness, or something else? She started to reach for the soft ripples of magic but pulled her hand back. Alex dared not disturb it until she understood it. If she could. The rays of sunlight hit her face, instantly pushing back the cold clinging to her skin. Alex didn't open her eyes but kept her attention on the magic around her. It rushed through her body, suddenly renewing it, and Alex smiled. The alignment day was not letting her down.

Then the voices began chattering, filling her head with their worries and doubts. Her chest ached, and something was shifting in the back of her head. It hurt, and Alex wanted to pull away. Around her, the magic's hum changed, and she frowned. She turned her attention outward only to find the strange dome shimmering and shuddering. Alex tightened her hands into fists, worried that she'd done something. The magic was slipping away from the dome in a wave that Alex had no control over. A sharp pain radiated out of her heart. Alex gasped and grasped at her chest with her right hand. Her magic tingled across her skin, but the pain didn't ease. She kept her eyes shut, aware of the purple magic crashing towards her. She couldn't move. Distantly, Alex heard Nicki asking if she was alright.

"Stay back!" Alex ordered. "Something is happening! Stay back!"

Sunlight spilled into the Medicine Wheel. Alex could feel it against her closed eyelids, and in her magical view of the world, it appeared as a soft glow that made the lines of magical power even brighter. The purple magic flooded around her and Alex pushed it forward. It spun together at her command into a column of shimmering power and slowly turned gray.

Struggling to catch her breath, Alex watched as more and more of the power gathered together. Then before she could second guess herself, she reached forward and touched the surface of the pillar. It hummed at her touch. The voices grew louder, and flashes of images and faces marched across her vision. Her knees quaked, and Alex almost fell over.

'He hid the area from magic,' Arto whispered. 'That was the spell.'

'Can't be,' Thor argued 'too large. There was too much power.'

Alex ignored them both. It was a potential theory, but she was going to be sick. Pushing down her unease and dismissing the clamor in her head, Alex left the magic alone for the time being. Maybe Arto was right, but maybe it had built up slowly over the years after Akule was gone. Not enough to hide the circle itself, but enough to keep anyone magical from detecting anything odd about it. Shaking her head, she gestured to the others to come back.

"I'm fine," Alex said. "Surge of magic."

"Alex, we need to find the Jar," Aiden said.

"Yeah, I know."

Alex swallowed a rush of bile and returned her attention to the glittering lines of magic around her. The Medicine Wheel was the brightest thing for miles around, eclipsing even her fellow mages. In the distance, Alex saw a solid glow moving towards them and frowned. The Light was coming towards them, and fast. She tried to find the Jar, searched for a sign of it near the Wheel.

It wasn't there. Alex was sure that Akule didn't put the Jar so close to the Medicine Wheel. She remembered... She remembered his pride. Maybe it was the dream, or something else happening because of that purple dome. Alex swayed again, feeling off center, but she couldn't sit down.

"Alex?" Nicki called. "What is happening?"

"I'm working on it, just shush!"

At another time, Alex might have felt bad for being so abrupt, but she needed to find the Jar. It pounded in her head, the need to find the Jar and try and figure out what had happened here. Flinching as another series of images flashed in front of her, Alex summoned the magic in the pillar and ordered it to find the Jar. It condensed into an orb, and Alex opened her eyes.

Her chest was hot and tight. Reaching out, she touched the orb and let some of the magic seep into her. The purple color was gone now, replaced with her dark gray. Alex didn't want to think too much about that. When the orb started to move down the slope of the hill, Alex didn't hesitate to follow it. Another orb swung up next to her to provide more light around her, and she smiled at the knowledge that the others were with her.

No one spoke, and Alex didn't look back. The orb was taking them into the drifts of snow, and Alex inhaled sharply before releasing a wave of magic to start clearing a path. Pulling wisps of magic still lingering in the air from the dome, Alex drilled through the ice and snow as the sun rose higher and higher behind them.

There wasn't much to see. The ground she cleared was rocky and covered with brown vegetation and rocks. Snow piled up around them, and Alex briefly chuckled at the idea of what the park service might think if they ever found evidence that they were here. Of course, that made her think of the Light, and she moved faster. Then the orb stopped alongside a rocky slope. It didn't burst or sink into the ground, it stopped, and Alex frowned.

"Alex?" Nicki called softly.

She didn't answer. Alex's hands trembled. Magic pulsed up her legs and through her arms. The smell of ozone danced on the air, radiating out of the orb she'd commanded to guide her as more and more of the magic dissipated into the air. The pounding in her head was even worse now. Alex pushed another wave of magic across the surface of the ground. It pushed the snow away like a sweeping hand to reveal more dead plants, packed down dirt, and stones. Nothing interesting. Nothing that looked like a marker.

Her magic flared in her chest, but Alex didn't even bother with it. Lunging forward, she pulled at the rocks and weeds, tearing them out of the earth frantically. Icy soil met her hands, reminding her that it was winter in the mountains. Still, she dug her nails in and tried to dislodge the next stone.

"Alex!" Nicki called sharply. "Wait. Stop!"

Someone grabbed her and physically pulled her back. Shivering, Alex fought against them, trying to keep digging, but the warm arms held her tight. A familiar smell reached her nose, and she relaxed without wanting t o.

"Easy," Bran whispered. "Easy. We'll find it."

"Are you sure it's here?" Nicki asked. She stepped in front of Alex and gestured to the hillside. "This doesn't... it doesn't look like anything special."

Alex didn't answer. Something tugged at her, not a memory, but an awareness. Closing her eyes, she focused on the strands of magic that she could see outlining the world. There were so many, and her head was spinning. She was close. Her fingers twinged, and she almost started digging again, but instead, she slowly stood and opened her eyes.

The snow glittered in the light. It was pure white with no sign of dust or pollution. Not here. Still, she didn't linger on the beauty, but focused on the spot that she'd already started to tear up. Her fingers ached, and she was aware of how cold they were even through her gloves. Bran gently pulled her further back and turned her so that he could grip her hands. Magic seeped through the material and warmed her skin.

"Is it here?" Aiden asked gently.

"Yes." Her voice was hoarse, and Alex swallowed. "Yes. Akule buried it nearby, but not too close."

The others exchanged glances, but no one argued with her. More sunlight was reflecting off the snow and into Alex's eyes, making them water. Aiden stepped forward and summoned an orb of magic in his right hand.

"I'm thinking a slow digging spell." Aiden looked at Nicki who nodded her agreement.

"Don't hurt it," Alex said. "There's Darkness inside."

They both turned to look at her sharply with barely hidden horror. Alex wasn't sure why Akule had caught the Darkness. Once the rift was sealed, it couldn't have done much more damage, but she had the nagging sense that he'd done it for her because she needed it. Furrowing her brow, Alex shook her head as if that would knock things into alignment. Akule's thoughts were trying to push forward. They were there after all, just hidden like the magic in this place.

Dirt was thrown into the air. Alex stared at the spot they were digging. Aiden and Nicki had to push the magic forward slowly to break apart the frozen ground without causing the whole hillside to give out. A sudden pressure in Alex's chest made her gasp, but she was quick to catch her breath.

"Stop!"

Both Aiden and Nicki instantly halted. The streams of blue and red vanished. Alex dropped to her knees and clawed away the last few small stones that had fallen in her way. Reaching into the hole, Alex exhaled in relief as her fingers found metal. It was mostly smooth, though there were a few strange lines under her searching fingertips. Without any handles, Alex wasn't sure how to grab it and scooted forward on her knees. She couldn't see far into the hole thanks to the low sun and shadows, but she found the sides of the Jar and drew it out.

The first thing she noticed was that the lid was almost melted closed. It was rough, and Alex did not doubt that Akule had done the whole thing using magic. A memory of a shooting star suddenly pushed forward, and she hissed in pain at the intrusion. That probably explained the source of the iron. She didn't bring it too close to her chest and set it on her lap. As her hands moved over it, Alex noted with a flare of satisfaction that it was exactly the size she'd imagined it to be in her strange visions.

Her fingers moved across its surface as flickers of memory asserted themselves. It was a lot all at once. Akule hadn't known what he was doing, but he'd tried to do what needed to be done and had hidden the Jar. Alex understood that. The image of that dark scar on the landscape was already becoming familiar. Of course, he'd feared someone finding the Jar.

"Alex?" Bran was kneeling next to her. "You okay? You're acting a bit... off."

"Loopy," Nicki said. Her phone was out, and Alex had the feeling that the camera was going. "So... that's the Jar?"

"This is it." Alex swallowed and nodded. "I'm okay." She shook her head and stood up, keeping the Jar carefully cradled against her chest. "I'm okay."

"Are you sure it's safe to carry that?" Aiden asked. "We could use magic."

"I'm okay." She repeated. She didn't want to let go of the Jar just yet. That was dangerous.

"It doesn't look dangerous," Bran said thoughtfully. "And yet, there's Darkness inside. Why did he do that?"

"Maybe so we could experiment with it," Nicki said. Alex didn't turn around, but she knew there'd be a thoughtful look on Nicki's face. "I mean, we've already had the time crossing magic happening, so maybe he stored it for Alex."

"He did," Alex agreed. Her left hand ached and reminded her of the cost Akule had paid to store the Darkness. "But he stopped it. Using the Wheel to channel his power, he used it on the dawn of the summer solstice and healed a rip in our world that the Darkness was coming through."

"So, you remember now?" Bran asked. "Was that part of what he did?"

"He protected this whole area," Alex said. They were almost back to the Wheel now. "He wanted to keep it hidden, but it hid the memories too."

"That's..." Bran didn't finish. Alex could hear the frustration and doubt in his voice.

"Not now," Alex grumbled. Her head was pounding and the voices were a mess of noise. Small flashes of light zoomed through her vision, but she wasn't sure if it was a migraine or magic. "Later."

Thankfully the others picked up on Alex's hints not to talk. Each breath helped to dispel the pain in her head. Magic was still flowing around them, and Alex could see the thin strands of purple in the air that still lingered. Her eyes moved to the orb of gray magic that was following along beside her. She didn't remember telling it to do that.

"Alex!" Merlin rushed over to them once they reached the small camp. "Are you alright?"

"I'm fine." Alex tucked a strand of blonde hair behind her ear. "Just a little tired."

The old mage smiled softly at her and reached up. He pushed back the hood of her coat and laid his hand on her head. Alex's throat tightened. Tears sprang to her eyes that she didn't understand. Merlin's eyes dropped to the Jar, and she could see the questions gathering.

"Merlin," Morgana called. "The Light is here."

Merlin turned away from them and quickly walked towards Morgana. A figure in a heavy winter coat walked into Alex's view, and the others tightened around her. A ski mask covered its face, but Alex recognized the Light at once. Her vision blurred and she swayed. The bright outlines of magic appeared around her, and she shifted her fingers just enough to start calling all the stray sparks of power to her.

"Why are you here?" Merlin asked. He leaned forward on his staff and gave the Light a cold smile. "A strange place to take a vacation."

"I was curious as to why the mages left Ravenslake."

"You've been spying on us?" Morgana asked. Her tone was dangerous, and Alex knew that her green eyes would be icy.

"Spying is a harsh word." The Light held up its gloved hands as the wind ruffled its short blond hair. "Keeping tabs on you, but not to threaten. I just need to know what is happening. I'm sorry, but I lost everything. You can't expect me to simply ignore your stubbornness."

The Light's eyes moved to Alex, and she tightened her hold on the Jar. Around them, the wind picked up as the sun rose higher above them and magic thrummed in the air. The voices in her head cautioned Alex to be careful, but she didn't need their warnings as the Light's eyes moved to Mjolnir on her hip, and it smiled.

33

Departing the Mountain

33 C.E. Bighorn Mountains

Akule woke slowly. The world was bright and hot, with the sun beating down on him. He could see the glow through his eyelids and turned his head to the side. Everything hurt and he groaned, trying to shift into a more comfortable position. His back dragged across rocks and he frowned, trying to remember where he was and what had been going on. Then he moved the wrong way and knocked his left hand against the ground. Brutal, sharp pain that stole the air from his lungs and left him trembling overtook his body.

His eyes flew open as Akule gasped for breath. He was in the middle of the stone circle. The memories trickled back to him slowly, and he shivered. The sealed Jar was right beside him, sitting innocently almost at the very center of the circle. As the pain slowly receded, Akule glared at the Jar and avoided looking at his hand.

The smell of blood hit his nose, and he swallowed. He was alive, so surely the damage couldn't be that bad. Repeating that thought as he tried to calm down, Akule slowly moved his body to check for damage. While he was sore, nothing but his left hand truly felt injured. He was exhausted, and it was tempting to shut his eyes again and go back to sleep, but the rocks were uncomfortable.

Slowly, very slowly and gingerly, Akule leveraged himself up on his right hand. He tucked his left arm protectively against his body and controlled his breathing. It was difficult to think through the throbbing pain. It was worse than when he had damaged his arm as a child. It had been carefully realigned and bound against his body for over a month. As unpleasant as that memory was, Akule was certain that the injury from the Darkness was far worse.

Blood was splattered around him and seeping into the ground. It shimmered with a strange purple tint, and Akule's stomach tightened at the sight. In his chest, the spark of power flared as if to confirm that the blood carried his power, but to what end he wasn't sure. At the end of his task of sealing the sky, the pain had robbed him of most of his awareness. He shifted his body and winced when he put too much pressure on his left arm, but he managed to get to his knees.

Standing up was difficult with only one hand. He felt off balance and nearly used his left arm to help him move. Every muscle protested, but he knew that he couldn't just stay in the circle in pain. It took some doing, but he bent down and picked up the Jar with his good hand.

Walking carefully, Akule made certain with each step that his footing was secure. The fog was retreating from his mind, but what had happened was still unclear. The scent of the air was off, and he didn't know what to make of it. Yet, despite his confusion, there was a weight gone from his shoulders, and he was grateful for it.

Stumbling out of the circle, Akule paid no notice to the stones that he accidentally kicked out of place. He lifted his face towards the sun and let it warm his sore body. Hair was sticking to the back of his neck, and Akule imagined that he was a complete mess. But he stayed still and inhaled and exhaled air slowly, waiting for his heart to calm. Bending over, he gently placed the Jar on the ground and braced himself. It was time to inspect the damage even if he was terrified of what he was going to find.

Akule was frightened of what he would find when he looked at his aching limb. He knew that he needed to look, but didn't want to. Nonetheless, he slowly shifted the limb into the light for inspection. His left hand appeared badly burned, with only small stubs of his fingers remaining. The skin between them had melted together, leaving them as a fused mess with only the barest trace of knuckles. Black scraps of skin were already scraping off the end of the stumps, warning him that they would likely fall off soon. His thumb was now a mere stump and a burn to the bone was visible between his thumb and fingers.

Akule could only stare in horror. It took time for his mind to process the damage. His hand was unusable. There were no fingers and no thumb. It was all gone, with only an aching black palm remaining. He swallowed and looked at his wrist. The burn extended across it and up his forearm, stopping before the elbow. He didn't dare touch the flesh. It appeared too much like a burned-out piece of wood, and Akule feared it would crumble. A hysterical, pained laugh escaped him, and tears rolled down his cheeks.

It took some time for him to recover his wits and focus his senses on anything else. The rip in the sky was gone, but he needed to see the land below. Leaving the Jar on the ground, he walked around the Medicine Circle in search of a good viewpoint. He hesitated to go too close to the Circle, well aware of the power he could sense radiating off the rocks. It would dissipate quickly, at least he believed so, but he looked towards the patch of his blood on the ground suspiciously. It nagged at him, like a memory from a dream, and he couldn't help but believe that he was missing something important.

He looked below to the dead circle. The wound above it was gone and the black fog that had surrounded it was finally absent. Sunlight was pouring down on it, and for the first time, Akule was sure that it was touching the soil; that the land wasn't bathed in shadow. It was a scar, but it would heal over. Birds would drop seeds. Worms would crawl beneath it, and life would return. Akule knew it with a certainty that astounded him. It was a comfort.

And he was alive. Akule closed his eyes and welcomed the sunlight on his face. It was hot, and already sweat was building upon his skin. He was alive. The pain was great in his hand, and he knew that the limb would never work properly again, but he was alive. In his chest, the purple flare was weak, but he could still sense it.

Akule stayed there, staring down at the landscape below and letting the mountain winds cool him. He kept his hand protectively against his body. The pain lingered. He wondered if it would ever leave him or if he'd carry it always. He could live with that. He wouldn't be the first warrior to lose a limb in the tribe, and this had been a battle. Then Akule inhaled deeply and turned away from the dark circle. His gaze fell on the Jar. It was shining in the sun, bright as a flame which he knew only hid the true nature of what was inside.

He didn't know why the spirits wanted the Darkness, but he'd made a Jar, and Jars contained something. This had surely been its purpose. Given that it had cost him his hand, he hoped so. Exhaustion crashed over Akule, and a loud sigh escaped him. He longed to see his family again, and tears pricked at his eyes at the very thought. Akule shook his head. It was almost over now; he just had to take care of the Jar, and then he could start working on finding his family. Bending over, he carefully picked it up with his right hand, keeping a close eye on the lid. It looked sealed, but he didn't trust it.

He had to hide the Jar. His grip on the foul thing tightened. For an instant, he thought he felt it wobble in his grasp as if the Darkness still wanted to escape. It was still in there. His magic had caught it, but he doubted it could hold it forever. Pain flashed through his left side, and Akule had to swallow a whimper.

But it was over. He calmed himself and closed his eyes for a moment to settle his nerves. It was over. He just needed to hide the Jar. Akule considered taking it with him down the mountain very briefly before dismissing it. With only one hand, it wasn't possible. He couldn't carry it all the way in his right arm, and he didn't trust having it in a pack on his back. It would have to stay here. He glanced at the medicine circle but dismissed it quickly. That was a sign of healing. He would not put something so dangerous beneath it.

Akule moved down the sloping hillside. His feet kept trying to slip, and he couldn't rely on his left hand to catch him if he fell. When he stopped walking, he noted with displeasure that he was still closer to the circle than he would have liked. The hillside was rocky and covered with lush growing plants soaking up the sunlight. Indecision gripped him. This didn't seem like enough, but he was at a loss of what else he could do. Looking around, he searched for any sign of the female spirit he had seen, but there was nothing. He was alone and holding a Jar full of Darkness. Every moment he held onto it in his weakened state was a gamble.

Finally, he shook his head and knelt. His body still ached, but he could at least move. He found a flat rock that would serve in a pinch and started clearing away the outer layer of fallen rocks. He hurt too much to try and use his power. It was slow work, but he dug deeper and deeper into the hillside, shifting away rocks as he had to. Cool damp soil hit his fingers, and he tossed away a handful of earthworms. This wasn't ideal, but he had to hide it, and he was in no condition to carry it down the mountain.

With a final burst of energy, Akule pulled on his magic and felt the spark stir to life. It was weak, and while its power washed down his arms, it was a trickle rather than the crashing wave he'd come to know. Purple sparks appeared and drove further into the ground, widening the space and reaching further into the earth. The final result wasn't perfect, but it satisfied Akule. It was unlikely that anyone would ever have reason to dig so deeply into the hill.

He carefully shifted the Jar into the hillside, being mindful of the lid. While he was fairly confident that his power had sealed it for good, the pain in what remained of his left hand ensured that he wouldn't take risks with the Darkness. As he pushed the Jar into place using only his right hand, he thought that he could hear the liquid sloshing around. Thankfully, the strange stone of the Jar held it. He didn't understand how, but at this point, he no longer cared.

Akule mounded the dirt around the Jar to carefully pack it in place. Already the heat was fading from the shining stone, and he took that as a good sign. Once he was done, he filled the remaining indent in the ground with a layer of rocks. He frowned. It was obvious that someone had been digging, but he could only hope that the slope would discourage animals from trying to dig it up.

It wasn't ideal, but it was what he could manage. Standing up slowly, Akule slipped in the dirt and nearly crashed to his knees. He caught himself against the ground of the slope with his right hand. Akule groaned and struggled for air. His right shoulder now hurt, but he'd managed not to damage his left hand further. Once he was stable, he looked around the slope for anything to help him make his way back up the hill. Akule quickly spotted a solid looking branch a little shorter than himself. The wood was bleached from the sun, and he could only guess that it had been blown down here in a storm. Making his way over to it, Akule almost slipped twice more before he wrapped his right hand around the thick piece of wood.

It was solid in his hands, and Akule used it to leverage himself up the hill. The old branch took his weight and allowed him to move faster. He wasted no time once he was back at his small camp. Akule picked up his bag and looked around one more time. The stones of his medicine circle almost gleamed in the sun. Rainwater would smooth them out even more in the coming years, depending on how long it lasted. He allowed himself a moment of pride.

Somehow, he was certain that it would be safe for the time being. Maybe someday he'd bring his children to see it and tell them of the spirits he saw and the visions they had granted him. Even now, without him trying, there was power here. Akule couldn't see it, but he could feel it in the air. A soft hint of power surrounded the circle. It would keep it safe and hide the Jar. He wasn't sure when it had formed or if it had even been him that created it. Maybe the spirits had erected it to keep the land safe. A faint purple hue tinted the sky, and he slowly moved away.

Leaning on the stick for support, Akule slowly made his way down the slope of the mountain and started to smile. The pain in his hand was still there, but a sense of accomplishment had settled on his shoulders like a bison robe, warm and comforting. He took strength from it and leveraged himself carefully around a large stone.

As he followed the slope of the hillside, Akule was slowly brought around to face the east once more. Below him lay the dark dead circle, but already he could see slight changes. The once stark edge already seemed a bit fuzzy. It was foolish to think that already the grass was trying to regrow, but Akule thought that maybe, just maybe, it was possible.

It took all day to descend. He had to stop for drinks of water frequently and was sure to gather berries whenever he spotted them. Had he not been so exhausted, he might have even been tempted to use his powers on a mountain goat that ran up the mountainside near him. But the weakness had not faded. There was still power pulsing into his body, but it was soft and weaker than before. Akule was left to wonder if his powers would fade now that his work was done. Strangely, the idea saddened him, but if his work was truly done, he would be grateful.

As his hut came into view, Akule's knees quivered and threatened to give out. The sun was sinking towards the horizon, but there was still some time left in the day. The dog sprang up and rushed towards him with a happy bark. It came to a stop a short distance away, cocking its head and sniffing the air. Then it joined him at a slower, more cautious pace. Akule sighed in relief, easing his protective stance as his fear of the dog jumping on his arm faded. When the dog was beside him, Akule smiled and leaned his walking stick against his chest so he could rub the dog's head with his right hand.

"Hello, boy. I'm glad to see you."

The dog rubbed itself against his leg, and a soft laugh escaped Akule. He looked around the camp and was happy to note that the dog hadn't destroyed anything. The drying rack had been knocked over, and the last strips of meat were gone, but that wasn't a surprise. Sighing, Akule shook his head and looked down at the dog.

"Well, we'd better gather some food. Tomorrow, we're going to find the others."

As if the dog knew what he was saying, it started wagging his tail. Akule looked up into the sky once again and took comfort in the smooth patch of blue. The world was as it was supposed to be once again.

34

Light and Dark

Placing her hand over Mjǫllnir, Alex did her best to ignore the cold closing in around them. Adrenaline thrummed through her veins and embraced the jolt of energy and alertness. The Light's expression hadn't changed, but a sense of urgency built in her chest. It was tight and uncomfortable. It was watching her with a calculating stare. Merlin shifted to stand in front of her, almost completely blocking Alex's view of the Light.

"Coming here after us is a worrying action," Merlin said. His tone was calm, but there was a hint of iron in it. "What was so important that it couldn't wait?"

"It is the winter solstice." The Light shrugged and tilted its head, the actions too human for Alex's nerves. "According to the Fae I've been in contact with, it is one of the most important days to you mages."

"Yes," Merlin answered. "The magic of the realm is naturally at a peak. We can achieve more than normal on such days."

"And yet, you didn't break the connections between worlds. We don't have time for this, Merlin." The Light shook its head. "What do I have to say to convince you?"

Alex spoke up, "You need proof that we won't kill Earth in doing so. Escaping one dying world only to doom another isn't productive." She moved out from behind Merlin so she could see the Light and it could see her. "How did you find us?" Alex asked. She tilted her head and considered the Light. The magic in the air thrummed around him, creating an outline that she could see even without closing her eyes and focusing on it.

"You left travel guides on the coffee table in the living room," the Light answered. "Then I saw that the Hammer and the Sword were gone. It was clear that you had plans."

"You broke into our home," Alex said. The wind stilled as she spoke, and the mountains seemed to fall silent.

"I did-" The Light must have seen something in her expression because it straightened up. "Yes, I did. I came looking for you." Then it held up its hands in a calming gesture that didn't work at all. "There isn't time. I can feel the Darkness coming!" He gestured into the distance. "It's close. There's something here. I don't know what; maybe you perceive it, but there is a scar here. You have to use the Hammer!" The Light stepped closer to her. "If you won't, then I will."

"Mind your tone," Morgana said. Merlin pushed Alex away from the Light gently, and silver sparks appeared around Morgana's hands. "That sounded like a threat."

"I've tried to be reasonable," the Light said. It glared at Morgana. "You won't listen."

"You're not wrong," Alex said urgently. "Long ago, some Darkness did break through to Earth, but another life of mine sealed the opening. It is possible to keep Earth safe." She shook her head. "Besides, knowing that, there is no reason to assume that breaking Earth away from the rest of the Tree of Reality would even help."

"There was Darkness here?" The Light flinched and looked around nervously. Then his eyes landed on the Jar suspiciously. "Is that why you came here? To learn about what happened?"

"Yes, to get information. I want to stop the Darkness, but we can't be rash."

For a moment, Alex hoped that maybe the Light was finally hearing her. Merlin relaxed a little in front of her and Morgana's silver sparks softened in intensity. The Light looked at the ground and then shook its head.

"I'm afraid I don't have time to wait." It raised its head. "I'm sorry," the Light said to Merlin. "I'm so sorry, but I need more power. I need a new host-"

A blast of silver hit the Light in the side, sending it falling into the snow bank piled up beside camp. Morgana's hands were extended towards it. Everything erupted into chaos. Waves of energy exploded off of the Light. Alex's vision blurred as she stumbled back and she closed her eyes and reached for the ambient magic lingering in the air.

Arthur's skin was melting off of his dead body. Cracks covered the surface of his face with beams of Light escaping. A sudden smell of decay hit Alex's nose. Bile filled her mouth as her stomach turned. Arthur had been dead for months, and now the Light wasn't disguising that fact. His body was lit up. Beams of pale-yellow light were bursting out of the corpse, and there were brighter sections that looked ready to crack open. It was moving towards them, reaching for Merlin. Raising her hand, she sent a bolt of dark gray magic right at the Light. Twisting to the side, it dodged the attack and the brightness only increased.

"Get back!" Merlin shouted. "Get back!"

"What's going on?" Nicki shouted. "Why is it glowing?"

"It needs another host!" Merlin warned. "Don't let it get near you!"

Alex kept her eyes closed. She could see more this way. The rising sun reflecting off the snow couldn't blind her and the Light's form escaping Arthur couldn't make her look away. The jar in her arms was heavy, and for an instant, she thought she heard liquid sloshing inside as she moved. Awkwardly, Alex reached across her body and pulled Mjǫllnir free from the loop on her belt. She was used to its weight in her left hand, but today she held it up with her right. The metal thrummed with magic through the leather wrap covering the handle, making Alex's skin tingle.

Whatever had been holding the Light back was gone. More of its true form spilled out of Arthur's body. The scent of barbeque reached Alex's nose, temporarily replacing the rotten smell. This was almost worse, as she realized that the Light's energy was cooking what remained of the body. Nausea crashed over Alex. She swayed. Despite the magic around her, weakness from this morning lingered.

'Stay back,' Arto ordered.

'Get Mjǫllnir away from it,' Thor added. Anger made his voice rumble like thunder. 'That's what it wants. Keep the Hammer from it.'

Alex struggled to think. She could see the outlines of the others through their magic, but it was becoming more and more difficult. The Light's power was spreading out like a fog, obscuring the others, and their frantic attacks left lines of colors in the air that further confused her. There was too much. Her mind was still raw from whatever Akule had done. His voice was still absent, but flashes of memory were pushing through, trying to give her information that right now she didn't need.

The Light was more than a spark now. Maybe it was losing strength, but right now it isn't weak at all. Alex couldn't see. There was just a mass of energy. Her hands tightened around Mjǫllnir and the Jar. Overhead, the sky began to rumble. A stray thought warned Alex to be careful.

They were in the mountains and surrounded by snow. The last thing they needed was a storm.

'It's trying to get Merlin,' Arto shouted. 'Don't let it!'

The words were unnecessary. The Light was moving towards Merlin, and the old man wasn't backing down. A beam of green was striking the Light, but Alex wasn't sure if it was having any effect. Suddenly aware of someone at her back, Alex almost pulled away.

"It's me!" Nicki called. "I'm getting the Sword!"

The angle was all wrong, but Alex bent her knees to allow Nicki to pull the scabbard off of her back. Alex wasn't sure if Nicki was right to use the Sword. The defeat of the Light that had taken her was fuzzy to Alex, and stabbing Arthur hadn't been enough to destroy the Light. The sparks had joined and created something even more powerful. Once the Sword was free, Alex shifted the Jar and transferred Mjǫllnir to her left hand. She kept her arm wrapped around the Jar, keeping it tight against her body.

Extending her hand, Alex focused her attention on the brightest spot. The Light was spread too far out as Arthur's body continued to collapse. She nearly screamed when the torso fell apart in an avalanche of meat and bone, exposing a central, swirling mass of blinding gold. Nicki screamed behind her in pain, and her presence withdrew. Alex flexed her fingers and watched the streams of energy begin to shift. Confidence rose in her chest, and she pulled.

The Light screamed. Alex didn't care. Keeping her hand extended, she pulled at the energy. Pulled at the mass of power that was the Light. Its screams echoed around her, but she didn't stop. Strands of energy ripped out of the body, spinning towards her and gathering in her hand. She kept pulling on the energy. The Light lashed out. Long lines of gold gathered together into tight coils and thrashed around like tentacles. Heat filled the air, and Alex hissed in pain as her skin began to burn.

"STOP!" The voice was not Arthur's. It was vibrating the air, causing a wave of pressure that hit Alex in the chest. She heard the Darkness slosh once more in the jar.

"That's it!" Merlin shouted. Glee filled his voice. "Keep it up, Alex! Everyone, put all you have into keeping the Light back!"

"MERLIN!" The Light shouted. "STOP THIS!"

A long limb of light lashed out at Merlin. It hit the bright green outline and into it, lancing through Merlin's chest. The Light's energy rippled across the limb, traveling towards Merlin, trying to take him. Alex kept pulling on the energy, ordering it to come to her, to leave the shape it was in. Her eyes were still closed, and she could see the streams of light fighting her control. It unraveled. The sound stopped, and the features vanished into a stream of power that rushed towards her. Alex turned her attention to the wisps of color that hung in the air. Green, silver, blue, red, and yellow that pulsed with power even as they began to fade into the air. She didn't let them. Alex summoned all the lingering magic of her fellow mages to her.

The energy grew beyond her hand. She dropped her palm, letting it gather into a column beside her. The bright colors dimmed to a solid gray. It pulsed in time with Alex's heart as she looked into the sky. Everything was muted, now; all the colors of the others' magic were dim except for the bright outlines that were her fellow mages. The Light was growing dimmer, but it was slow. It seemed to be trying to pull the energy back in a tug of war that Alex wasn't sure she could win.

The beam of Light was still focused on Merlin. It was trying to take Merlin. The bright green of Merlin was fading. The Light was winning that fight. The thought echoed in Alex's head. She pulled more of the energy. It gave way to her, but there was a center, a small spark of some-thing at the center of the swirling glow that she couldn't touch. It kept drawing energy towards it. That was the center of the Light.

Alex screamed, taking the energy from the others and hurling it at the Light. The center flashed and drew the power in. The Light's brightness grew. Something like a laugh echoed. She reached for the center, trying to unravel it, but was pushed back. A burning in her chest warned her to be careful. Maybe, maybe on another day when she wasn't already tired, she could...

She dropped Mjǫllnir on the ground, listening to it hit the snow with a sharp crackle. Thunder rolled above them, but she was shifting the jar. Her hand touched the metal, which turned hot beneath her palm. All the magic inside of the iron flickered in response to her touch. It was almost exhausted, she realized. Akule had held it back. He'd kept this bit of Darkness for her, but even his will couldn't hold it forever.

Her right fingertips glowed dark gray as she dug them into the metal of the lid. Magic flashed down her arm, and the metal glowed along the faintly visible seam. Another wave of magic hit the Light, trying to force it back. It wouldn't be enough. Even killing Arthur hadn't been enough to extinguish the Light in him, and her own battle with the one possessing her hadn't destroyed the second one. She wasn't going to risk even a flicker escaping and rebuilding itself — not this time.

The lid came free with a soft hiss. She dropped it on the ground and pulled on the magic around her. It rushed towards her in dozens of thin strands of power, swallowing the lingering power from Akule and all the magic left from her fellow mages, and gathered around her like a thick gray fog. Pouring the magic into the jar, Alex watched the Darkness fight back. Black met dark gray. It sparked around the edges. Even after all this time contained, the Darkness remained dangerous. She pulled on the magic, drawing the Darkness out. Around her, she heard horrified worried shouts from the others, except for a triumphant laugh from Nicki. The redhead understood. Merlin's green was fading fast.

Alex pushed the energy she'd collected forward, coiling it around the Darkness. The mass of black in her vision made her shiver. There was nothing. It swallowed the magic, consuming it even as it began to fade. Not yet; she couldn't destroy it yet. One of the tentacles of pure light shifted towards her. Alex moved.

The Darkness splashed against the Light radiating out of Arthur's broken body. A howl shook the hillside, high pitched and inhuman. Vibrations echoed against the mountains, shaking Alex's bones and filling her ears. It hurt. She opened her eyes, releasing the vision through the lines of magic. Alex dropped the empty jar. Extending her hands, she pulled on the energy. The tentacles of light were falling apart as the Darkness burrowed into the center. The Light thrashed. Screams filled the air.

"STOP! STOP! I AM THE LAST!" Alex glanced at Merlin. He was on the ground, on his back, and unmoving. "I HAVE TO LIVE!"

The last of the Light's tentacles was reaching for Merlin. Alex ripped the power away, watching with satisfaction as it vanished in a flicker. The sparks rushed to her, and she gathered them in her hand. The Light's form twisted inward, turning from a sprawling creature to a small glow. A mutilated cooking corpse was sprawled beneath it.

"DON'T, PLEASE. SAVE ME. I AM ALL THAT SURVIVED."

Alex looked at the Light. She could see the Darkness eating at the center. The Light hadn't been exaggerating when it had said that its kind died quickly. Merlin still didn't stand up.

"I don't care."

Then the Darkness consumed the last of the spark while Alex watched. She didn't smile. She didn't cheer. She just watched. Two droplets of Darkness remained. They hung in the air for a split second before falling to the ground. Alex waved her hand and released a wave of magic that swirled around them. The droplets barely burned into the ground before the energy of the magic canceled them out.

Everything was silent on the mountain. The rapid, fearful breathing of the others had stopped. Alex reached down and picked up Mjǫllnir. Beside the Hammer was the Jar, laying open and empty to the wind and snow. Then she turned back towards Merlin.

He was still. Too still. Alex was frozen in place. Hundreds of memories surged forth at once as if the dam had shattered. Merlin never moved when asleep. He was a quiet man, never speaking or rolling around, but he always breathed. There was always some sign of life. Now... she didn't see it.

'No,' Arto chanted. 'No. No. No.'

'He can't be,' Michel whispered.

The voices kept shouting. Varying degrees of pain and horror were resonating through Alex's skull. Morgana cried out and rushed forward. Alex barely saw her move, barely saw her use any of her magic. Silver hands were placed on Merlin's chest after Morgana tenderly rolled him over. His eyes were open. They were vacant, already turning glassy. Morgana's hands trembled, but she scrambled for the Iron Chalice. Snow was scooped into it with one fast movement. It glowed in her grasp, and she poured the liquid down his throat.

Some spilled out. There was no sputtering — no pushing her away. There was nothing. He didn't move. He stayed still. Morgana grasped the side of his face, hands still glowing. A soft sound escaped her, a wounded sound, a desperate cry that tore at Alex and much deeper. The voices all recoiled at the sound.

The Iron Chalice fell from Morgana's hand. Merlin didn't stir. Silence surrounded them, pressing down on Alex's shoulders as Morgana's body quivered. Then her soft cries could be heard and began to echo around them. Shock kept Alex pinned in place. This wasn't real. Arto joined Morgana in wailing, and even Thor and Gofiben couldn't silence him.

35

Ashes

Merlin was dead. The thought settled uneasily in Alex's mind, but it was there nonetheless. The Chalice had failed to save him because he was already gone. He'd probably been dying as soon as the first attack of the Light had hit him. It hadn't needed a living body. The cooked remains of Arthur a few feet from her were proof of that.

At least it was dead. That should have been some kind of comfort, but it wasn't. The last of its species was dead by her hand, and she didn't even feel guilty. But even that action hadn't been enough to... Alex swallowed and took a few steps forward. The voices were loud now, almost deafening with their various reactions. Some had known Merlin well, some had known him only in passing, and many had never met him at all.

Morgana had stopped sobbing. Her eyes were red, and a soft hiccup escaped her. Haunted green eyes stared down at Merlin's corpse. Part of his chest had been torn open, exposing his ribs and spraying blood everywhere. Alex had been too caught up in the magic around them to notice the wound.

"Morgana-"

"Don't!" Morgana's voice was sharp. Broken. "Do not, Alex. As much as I care about you, say nothing. Three thousand years of companionship when there was no one else. Three thousand years of battles, trials, and grief. Three thousand years of goodbyes. This was the one I wasn't supposed to have to say."

Alex knelt beside Merlin. She didn't touch Morgana and avoided looking at the wound. He was too still. That kept repeating. Something slipped off her cheek; a tear. She was crying. She hadn't realized that. A trembling hand came up and wiped at her cheek. It was damp. She was crying a lot. Her chest shook as a sob escaped.

Merlin's eyes were all wrong. The soft brown color was growing pale. They were empty. There was no humor, no sharp intelligence, and no affection. She'd never seen his eyes like that. It wasn't right that they could be so empty. Somehow, she reached out and gently moved her hand over his eyes. At first, it was just to cover them, hide them from view, but then she felt his eyelashes. Another sob rattled her bones. Grief. So much grief, and somehow both all and only some of it was truly hers.

Michel was crying. Lokpal was whispering prayers for the old mage's soul. Gofiben was sniffling, trying to be brave, but Arto had fallen silent. His grief weighed them all down. Too complete and too deep to even voice. The top of her head was cold, bare and chilled without Merlin's hand resting on top of it.

She closed his eyes and slowly retracted her hand. A lump filled her throat, and her nose was clogged up, leaving her bereft of air. Awareness of the others seeped in, but Alex didn't turn to look at them. The weight of... everything that the others were feeling left her weak. She couldn't move. Standing up under the pressure was unthinkable.

The wind blew, messing up her already chaotic hair. She hadn't even bothered with a brush this morning. She hadn't thought to bring one on this journey at all. Alex was aware of the others and that they should move, but she had no strength to do so. Her, Arto and Michel's grief filled her mind and left little for anything else. Even those who had never known Merlin, even Cuthbert, were being respectfully silent.

"What do you want to do?" Nicki asked Morgana softly. "We should burn what is left of Arthur's, but what about Merlin?"

"Leave the traitor for the animals," Morgana snarled. "They'll be grateful for the food."

"Morgana, we're pretty high up for large animals in winter," Aiden said. His voice was soft and betrayed his nervousness. "And we don't want questions when they find the bones."

"Fine." Morgana closed her eyes. Waving her hand towards the corpse, she hissed something under her breath that sounded like a curse to Alex. Bright silver flames licked across Arthur's body, quickly consuming it in a rush of thick foul-smelling smoke. "There."

Alex flinched at Morgana's tone. It was angry without a target for her rage. The Light was dead, and Arthur's corpse held nothing. Yet the underlying sorrow broke Alex's heart. Somehow, she moved closer to Morgana. She didn't dare touch the older mage. Bran returned a moment later with a sleeping bag and gently draped it over Merlin's body, hiding the terrible wound.

"He was older than I," Morgana said softly. "But at this point, it hardly mattered. There were times that we lived separate lives when the world had no need of us, but he was still out there in the world. I knew that if I needed him, he would come to my aid." A sob ripped itself from Morgana's chest. "I- I can't believe this." She shook her head. "We joked... sometimes jested that we might truly be immortal, but we never tested i t."

"I'm sorry," Alex whispered. "I grieve with you."

Morgana turned to look at her. Green eyes bored into Alex's, and then the older mage nodded. "Yes," she croaked. "I suppose you do." Then she dropped her gaze back to Merlin. "I will take him to Stonehenge. I will not make it in time for this Solstice, but he should be there. If any warrior and leader ever deserved to be honored at that circle, it was Merlin."

"So..." Aiden flinched when Morgana looked at him with a sharp glare. "What do you want to do with Merlin?" His voice cracked at the end of the question. "Should we cremate him here?"

Morgana inhaled slowly, the sound labored. Alex finally risked touching her and gently supported her arm. The older mage stood slowly, very slowly, and her right hand remained stretched towards Merlin. Another shudder shook Morgana's body, and Alex heard a tiny, muffled sob escape the woman. She hated that they had to ask, but they couldn't stay up here. It wasn't safe. She shifted closer to Morgana, pressing her arm against Morgana's shoulder.

"Yes," Morgana finally said. "Yes, we need a pyre. I'll not leave him on the ground like this." Her voice trailed off, catching at the end of the sentence.

Nicki, Aiden, and Bran nodded and then scattered. Looks were exchanged between the three of them. Alex wasn't sure what they were going to do, but they were headed through the snow towards a group of trees. She just hoped that they still had enough magic to pull off what they were after. Alex didn't move to help them. There was still magic swirling through the air. The last of the dome was gone, and its power radiated across the area. Something in her mind was stirring, trying to shift and settle, but it was impossible to focus on it around the grief.

She stayed next to Morgana, silent and still. No words came to mind. How could she even begin to comfort Morgana? Then, without a word, Morgana knelt and reached down, slowly moving her hand under the sleeping bag. Alex flinched, imagining the blood that Morgana was encountering, but she stayed silent. A moment later, Morgana withdrew her hand, and now clasped within it was Merlin's triskelion pin. She hadn't even noticed him wearing it under his coat. Standing up, Morgana stared at the small pin. She ran a gloved finger over the metal and sighed.

"There isn't much magic in this. Merlin claimed that he put magic in it to help control his temperature. Iron coated with silver."

"When was that?" Alex asked. Her voice was rough.

"Around World War I. It was newer. There was nothing we had that remained from our old lives." Morgana's hand closed around the pin. "We only had each other to help us remember. Even then... sometimes it threatened to slip away. I do not remember what Arto looked like, or Airril. They are wisps of memory." A strange, pained sound left Morgana. "And now so is Merlin."

Alex's eyes dropped to the Iron Chalice. The smooth metal glittered in the sun. It had failed them. She'd failed. The Light had- Alex shook her head. There was too much. Her eyes landed once more on the covered form of Merlin. A knot formed in her chest and tears burned her eyes. A soft sob escaped her. Morgana reached over and touched her back gently.

More tears came. She shook her head and turned to retrieve Mjǫllnir. As her fingers closed around the handle, Alex looked into the sky. There were a few dark clouds, but they were already dispersing. They should be gathering. The sky should be dark, not growing brighter with the rising sun, and rain should be falling. Merlin was dead. Mjǫllnir thrummed in her hand and overhead, and the sky began to rumble. Taking a deep breath, Alex shook her head. A storm wouldn't change anything. While the rain would be appropriate, at this altitude it would be snow and threaten them all. Merlin wouldn't want that. The thought brought new tears to her eyes.

Alex returned the Iron Hammer to the loop on her belt. The familiar weight offered no comfort to her. Alex glanced around but did not find Cathanáil. Hopefully Nicki wasn't using it to chop wood. Merlin would have snorted at the idea. Her chest tightened in pain, and she sucked in a breath. It still- how could this be real?

Morgana was unmoving. She was a statue at Merlin's side, like an angel carved from stone and placed in a cemetery over a beloved gravestone. Alex's grief intensified and guilt tried to claw its way to the forefront. If she'd been faster, then maybe... She pushed the thought aside. This was the Light's fault, and it was dead.

Stepping closer to Morgana, Alex reached over and took the older mage's hand. Morgana didn't resist. Her gloved fingers tightened almost painfully around Alex's. Still, she did not move. She kept staring at the body. Its blank expression was all wrong – lacking Merlin's humor, wisdom and animation. His mouth was slightly ajar.

Trembling, Alex shook her head. She couldn't see him like this. Pulling her hand away from Morgana, Alex stumbled forward and gently pulled the sleeping bag over Merlin's head. The thick cotton fabric hid his features, and she gently tucked the bag around his body as if to keep him warm. She didn't understand it, but Alex completed her task as gently as she could even as the tears tried to blind her.

When she was done, Alex returned to Morgana. This time, Morgana grabbed Alex's hand on her own. Alex shivered as more tears rolled down her cheeks and blurred her vision until she couldn't see the body anymore. Reaching out with her magic, Alex saw nothing. Merlin's green outline was gone. There was no vibrant shape, no green to compliment Morgana's silver, and Alex pulled her magic back sharply, but not before noticing that Morgana's own outline was duller than usual.

She refused to leave Morgana's side. The Chalice and the Jar sat in the snow. The last of the dawn was washed away by warm rays of sunlight beaming down on them. Every so often, the others came back with long crooked branches and started to lay them out. None of them spoke. Nicki's eyes were red, and the boys were avoiding looking at Merlin's body. Alex wanted to comfort them, but she couldn't stop her own tears. She didn't sob, she didn't shake or tremble, but the tears kept flowing as the voices grieved with her. Their shared sorrow multiplied to a form beyond words, and soon even the tears weren't enough.

The pyre took shape quickly. Multiple logs with clean, unnaturally precise cuts were dragged or levitated over. Aiden took over arranging them and laid them out first as a sort of platform with small pieces leaning on it. No one spoke as Bran's yellow magic lifted Merlin off the ground and to the narrow platform. It was just large enough to hold him. Nicki glanced at Morgana before she and the others gently laid thinner branches around his body. Even with the aid of their magic, they had gathered barely enough to create the rough pyre. Merlin deserved better, and Arto pushed a memory of another pyre to the forefront of her mind.

Still, it was all they had. They were too weak and too far from water to carry his body across the sea to Stonehenge in a water tunnel. The Medicine Wheel wasn't the same, but Alex was at least grateful that it was the winter solstice and they were at a place of power. She was sure that Merlin would have understood. Aiden snapped his fingers and lit the end of a small branch on fire. With reverence, he offered it to Morgana, and waited as she gazed uncertainly at it.

For a moment, Alex thought that Morgana would break down. The ancient woman swallowed, and her breath shook, but then she took the branch in her free hand and nodded. Aiden, Bran, and Nicki all drew back, and Morgana released Alex's hand. Even the wind stilled as

Morgana gently lit the edges of the sleeping bag and the wood on fire. It caught quickly. Alex wondered for an instant how much magic the others had used to dry the wood out. The flames grew quickly, and heat rolled off the pyre.

The smell of the smoke overwhelmed Alex, and she focused on the scent. That was what she wanted to smell, not the burning fabric or the worse smell that was to come. Flames crackled, and the wood shifted. No one spoke. Alex felt that she should say something, talk about what kind of a man Merlin was and how grateful she was that he'd been there. But no words would form. Nothing that came to mind was enough.

Then she smelled burning hair and braced herself for what would come next. Alex started to gag, her eyes filling with tears, but this time not due to sorrow. Morgana waved her hand and the air cleared with scattered flickers of silver glittering in the sunlight. The terrible smells faded, and Alex was left to once more focus on Merlin's still form as flames flicked up around him.

Closing her eyes, Alex stretched out with the flicker of magic she still had. It spread out around her like a mist, illuminating the colored sparks of magic still lingering in the air from the others. Alex's throat tightened as she noticed a swirl of bright green hanging in the air. The last of Merlin's magic. Tears pricked at her closed eyes. Her hands trembled. She gently called the sparks to her and watched with a heavy heart as the bright green color of Merlin's power darkened to the deep gray of her own. She opened her eyes and looked down at the orb of magic in her hand. It was warm. Another sob rose in her chest, threatening to choke her.

No one left the side of the pyre. It took time, but there was a sudden strange noise, and half of it collapsed. The sleeping bag was all but ash now, and Merlin's clothing and flesh were burning. Morgana raised her free hand over her mouth and closed her eyes, muffling her crying and trying to stem the tears. Nicki was leaning her face into Aiden's shoulder, crying so hard that her whole body was shaking. Bran was leaning on the walking stick that Merlin had been using the previous day, tears staining his cheeks while Aiden seemed to be in shock with glazed eyes.

The pyre fully collapsed as the logs broke and shifted. Red-hot coals spilled out across the ground which was too wet still to catch. Alex watched the coals flicker, preferring to keep her attention on them rather than watch the last of Merlin vanish. But soon it was over. Morgana's tears stopped, and numbness settled in. She finally looked at the large fire again. Morgana released her hand and released a wave of silver sparks. The fire was pulled inward and tightly packed around dark bones to finish the job. Alex's stomach turned as she thought of her parents. They'd been cremated at her insistence too.

Alex released the magic she'd been holding onto, closing her eyes and envisioning the ashes gathering in the Jar. She moved her lips and silently whispered what she wanted as she opened her eyes. The orb of magic in her hand shifted into a stream of dark gray magic and flowed into the smoldering remains of the pyre. It twisted around the still burning logs.

"Alex?" Nicki's voice was shockingly loud after the long silence.

Adjusting the Jar, Alex held it out as the first wave of small dark ashes rose out of the pyre. Morgana inhaled sharply. Alex expected her to say something, but the older mage remained quiet. More and more flickers of ash rose into the air. They swirled gently together before flying through the air towards Alex. Her hands trembled as the first of the ashes were deposited into the Jar. A second stream brought more ashes and small fragments of blackened bone. Another shudder shook Alex's body, but she kept the Jar still.

"I'll take them to Stonehenge soon," Morgana said. Her voice was a wreck, weak and shaky. Then she coughed and wiped at her cheeks. "We can't stay here forever. Gather up the supplies we still have, and we'll get moving."

The order was abrupt but punctuated by the last of the fire collapsing. Alex wondered if they'd really gotten all of the bones destroyed. If not, there could be terrible questions come spring when the Medicine Wheel reopened. Still, Morgana was right. They couldn't stay. Nicki, Bran, and Aiden slumped towards the igloos, all of them moving slowly with downcast eyes.

Alex stared down at the Iron Jar and frowned. No, it was now an Urn. The power that Akule had poured into it was exhausted, but small flickers of deeply woven magic lingered. They would draw power from the world around it and regain strength in time as the other artifacts did. She looked around for the lid of the Urn. Her fingers had burned marks into the metal. A memory of the trail of fire that it had left in the sky as a meteorite almost amused Alex. Merlin would have liked that.

The Urn was almost full as Alex slipped the lid back on. Pulling on her magic, she reverently sealed it once again. Morgana was watching her, a sad but relieved expression on her face. As she started to turn away, Alex caught a glint of sunlight off of Merlin's pin that Morgana was still holding.

"Morgana?" Alex asked softly. "His pin... do you want to hold onto it?"

Blinking at the question, Morgana looked down at it with a strange expression. Then, she slowly shook her head and held it out towards Alex. "No," she said. "It was a trinket. There are things... things at his home with more meaning to me."

Alex didn't believe that, but she took the pin. Maybe Morgana knew what she was thinking, but maybe she didn't. The pin was warm in Alex's hand, and there was a soft hint of green magic just below the surface. A new wave of tears sprang to Alex's eyes, driving away the numbness that she'd wanted to embrace.

Holding the pin against the side of the Urn, Alex pulled up the memory of the urns that had held her parents' ashes. They'd had small designs and her parents' names engraved into them. They were with Matt and Eddy now, wherever they were. Her magic sank into the two pieces of iron. A spark of Merlin's magic brushed against her skin like one final caress. Somehow she held back the tears, and when she removed her hand and looked down, she saw the triskelion pin proudly set into iron.

It was a poor ending for one such as Merlin, but at least that last part of him could be protected by the power of the Iron Soul and the Iron Realm. She owed him that, many times over. Many parts of her owed him that. Morgana nodded to her before joining the others. Their gear had been packed up, and Nicki was holding Cathanáil awkwardly in her hands. It was time to go.

Her Sword was put back into its sheath. Alex took her now-lighter bag, thanks to her sleeping bag being gone. She didn't pack up the Urn. Casting one last look towards the stone circle, Alex shivered at the cold and started to walk. There was nothing more for her here. The hidden danger had been removed, and the power of nature would remove the last stains of the Light's demise and the final end to the abomination of Arthur. Akule's Medicine Wheel would heal what remained and be a guide to those who followed him.

'That is enough,' Akule whispered. 'That is all I could have asked for.'

His voice surprised her. It shouldn't have, but Alex was startled nonetheless. Looking into the sky, she admired the clear morning.

Akule's protection spell was gone. The need for secrecy had passed. She tightened her grip on the Iron Urn and ran her fingers gently over the triskelion symbol that now guarded Merlin's ashes.

www.ingramcontent.com/pod-product-compliance
Lightning Source LLC
Chambersburg PA
CBHW060229100726
47907CB00003B/560